"The door's a gateway. Leads to different times."

Jeff set the mug of steaming coffee on the table and reached out to touch the curtain.

The curtain felt just like . . . well, just like curtain. Like any other kind of material he had ever felt. Like, maybe, his mother's skirt fabric or the cotton weave of his father's work overalls; the thick grain of his first baseball uniform or the cool blackness of his Batman cape from childhood. He tried to think of other things-contemporary things—but couldn't. All of the things the curtain reminded him of were in the past.

"Jeff—"

Jeff glanced across at Lorraine and gave her a very slight shake of the head. He had no idea why. He had no idea as to why he might need to be quiet, but, deep down, he realized that it wasn't because of danger or the fear of being discovered . . . but rather of reverence.

He pulled the curtain aside to expose a door.

—From *The Door in Stephensons Store*
by Peter Crowtller

GATEWAYS

Edited by

Martin H. Greenberg

DAW BOOKS, INC.

DONALD A. WOLLHEIM, FOUNDER

375 Hudson Street, New York, NY 10014

**ELIZABETH R. WOLLHEIM
SHEILA E. GILBERT
PUBLISHERS**

http://www.dawbooks.com

First Printing, June 2005

1   2   3   4   5   6   7   8   9

ACKNOWLEDGMENTS

Introduction copyright © 2005 by John Helfers

"On the Brane," copyright © 2005 by Abbenford Associates

"The Two Sheckleys," copyright © 2005 by Robert Sheckley

"Midnight at the Half-Life Café," copyright © 2005 by Russell Davis

"Postcards," copyright © 2005 by Rebecca Moesta

"Shift Out of Control," copyright © 2005 by Daniel M. Hoyt

"The Trigger," copyright © 2005 by Janet Deaver-Pack

"Spring Break," copyright © 2005 by Rebecca Lickiss

"Welcome to the Crystal Arches," copyright © 2005 by Phyllis Irene Radford

"Double Trouble," copyright © 2005 by John Zakour

"By the Rules," copyright © 2005 by Phaedra M. Weldon

"Manifesting Destiny," copyright © 2005 by Patricia Lee Macomber

"At Best An Echo," copyright © 2005 by Bradley H. Sinor

"Opening Doors," copyright © 2005 by Josepha Sherman

"Circle of Compassion," copyright © 2005 by David D. Levine

"Iron Flames and Neon Skies," copyright © 2005 by Jim C. Hines

"Carded," copyright © 2005 by James W. Fiscus

"Wait Until the War Is Over," copyright © 2005 by Sarah A. Hoyt

CONTENTS

Contents

INTRODUCTION

John Helfers

MANKIND has always been a race of explorers, possessed with a burning curiosity to see what might possibly lie over the next hill, across the ocean and, hopefully soon, beyond the stars. It is in our nature to learn, to discover, to seek out new worlds, from planets outside our galaxy to the smallest microscopic universes contained within each atom. If there is a means to get there, we'll find it, one way or another.

And that, in a nutshell, is the heart of this anthology: the means to access another time, another place, another world. A gateway that takes its discovers to fantastic new places in the blink of an eye, to lands that they sometimes could hardly conceive of existing, or perhaps even bringing someone from that other world back with them into this one.

Of course, gateways have been transporting intrepid adventurers to other worlds in media for centuries, from Lewis Carroll's *Alice's Adventures in Wonderland* to

H.G. Wells' *The Time Machine* to more recent realizations like *The Matrix* (in which the gateway takes a person from virtual reality into the real world) and the *Stargate SG-1* television series, which posits a whole other universe somewhere. Whether it be through magic or science, wormholes or spellcasting, the idea of a gateway to another dimension or world is a powerful concept that has drawn authors to it time and time again.

And in its own way, this book is another gateway, a portal of pages that will take you to nineteen different versions of various doorways both to and from other worlds, as written by some of today's finest authors. Greg Benford, the master of hard science fiction, tells of the first manned trip through a space gateway and of the wonders the crew encounters on the other side. Rebecca Moesta stays on the ground with her story of a very unusual correspondence between two girls in two very different worlds and how they team up to help each other. From David Levine comes a tale of a magical land besieged by ruthless invaders and how one woman possesses the means to save her people. And Peter Crowther brings to life a special doorway in a rundown old store in the middle of nowhere—that can make your fondest wish come true.

Nineteen stories by some of today's finest science fiction and fantasy authors await to take you to other lands—through the gateway.

ON THE BRANE

Gregory Benford

Gregory Benford is a working scientist who has written some 23 critically acclaimed novels. He has received two Nebula Awards, principally in 1981 for Timescape, *a novel that sold over a million copies and won the John W. Campbell Memorial Award, the Australian Ditmar Award, and the British Science Fiction Award. In 1992, Dr. Benford received the United Nations Medal in Literature. He is also a professor of physics at the University of California, Irvine, since 1971. He specializes in astrophysics and plasma physics theory and was presented with the Lord Prize in 1995 for achievements in the sciences. He is a Woodrow Wilson Fellow and Phi Beta Kappa. He has been an advisor to the National Aeronautics and Space Administration, the United Sates Department of Energy, and the White House Council on Space Policy, and has served as a visiting fellow at Cambridge University.*

His first book-length work of nonfiction, Deep Time
*(1999), examines his work in long-duration mes-
sages from a broad humanistic and scientific perspective.*

MINA peered out at a universe cooling into extinction.
Below their orbit hung the curve of Counter-Earth,
its night side lit by the pale Counter-Moon. Both these
were lesser echoes of the "real" Earth-Moon system, a
universe away—or twenty centimeters, whichever came
first.

Counter was dim but grayly grand—lightly banded in
pale pewter and salmon red, save where the shrunken
Moon cast its huge gloomy shadow. Here the Moon clung
close to the Counter-Earth, in a universe chilling toward
absolute zero.

Massive ice sheets spread like pearly blankets from
both poles. Ridges ribbed the frozen methane ranges. The
equatorial land was a flinty, scarred ribbon of ribbed
black rock, hemmed in by the oppressive ice. The planet
turned slowly, gravely, a major ridge just coming into
view at the dawn line.

Mina sighed and brought their craft lower. Ben sat
silent beside her. Yet they both knew that all of Earthside—the real Earth, she still thought—listened and
watched through their minicams.

"The focal point is coming into sunlight 'bout now,"
Ben reported.

"Let's go get it," she whispered. This gloomy universe
felt somber, awesome.

They curved toward the dawn line. Data hummed in
their board displays, spatters of light reporting on the
gravitational pulses that twisted space here.

They had already found the four orbiting gravitational wave radiators, just as predicted by the science guys. Now for the nexus of those four, down on the surface— the focal point, the coordinator of the grav wave transmissions that had summoned them here.

And, just maybe, to find whatever made the focal point. Somewhere near the dawn line.

They came arcing over the Counter night. A darkness deeper than she had ever seen crept across Counter. Night here, without the shrunken Moon's glow, had no planets dotting the sky, only the distant sharp stars. Apparently the rest of the solar system had not formed, due to less mass in the Counter-Universe.

At the terminator shadows stretched, jagged black profiles of the ridgelines torn by pressure from the ice. The warming had somehow shoved fresh peaks into the gathering atmosphere, ragged and sharp. Since there was atmosphere thicker and denser than anybody had expected, the stars were not unwinking points; they flickered and glittered as on crisp nights at high altitudes on Earth. Near the magnetic poles, she watched swirling blue auroral glows cloak the plains where fogs rose even at night.

A cold dark world a universe away from sunny Earth, through a higher dimension . . .

She did not really follow the theory; she was an astronaut. It was hard enough to comprehend the mathematical guys when they spoke English. For them, the whole universe was a sheet of space-time, called "brane" for membrane. And there were other branes, spaced out along an unseen dimension. Only gravity penetrated between these sheets. All other fields, which meant all mass and light, were stuck to the branes.

Okay, but what of it? had been her first response.

Just mathematics, until the physics guys—it was nearly always guys—found that another brane was only twenty centimeters away. Not in any direction you could see, but along a new dimension. The other brane had been there all along, with its own mass and light, but in a dimension nobody could see. Okay, maybe the mystics, but that was it.

And between the two branes only gravity acted. So the Counter-Earth followed Earth exactly, and the Counter-Moon likewise. They clumped together, hugging each other with gravity in their unending waltz. Only the Counter-brane had less matter in it, so gravity was weaker there.

Mina had only a cartoon-level understanding of how another universe could live on a brane only twenty centimeters away from the universe humans knew. The trick was that those twenty centimeters lay along a dimension termed the Q-coordinate. Ordinary forces couldn't leave the brane humans called the universe, or this brane. But gravity could. So when the first big gravitational wave detectors picked up coherent signals from "nearby"— twenty centimeters away!—it was just too tempting to the physics guys.

And once they opened the portal into the looking-glass-like Counter system—she had no idea how, except that it involved lots of magnets—somebody had to go and look. Mina and Ben.

It had been a split-second trip, just a few hours ago. In quick flash-images she had seen: purple-green limbs and folds, oozing into glassy struts—elongating, then splitting into red smoke. Leathery oblongs and polyhedrons folded over each other. Twinkling, jarring slices of hard actinic light poked through them. And it all moved as though blurred by slices of time into a jostling hurry—

Enough. Concentrate on your descent trajectory.

"Stuff moving down there," Ben said.

"Right where the focal point is?" At the dawn's ruby glow.

"Looks like." He closeupped the scene.

Below, a long ice ridge rose out of the sea like a great gray reef. Following its Earthly analogy, it teemed with life. Quilted patches of vivid blue green and carrot orange spattered its natural pallor. Out of those patches spindly trunks stretched toward the midmorning sun. At their tips crackled bright blue St. Elmos fire. Violet-tinged flying wings swooped lazily in and out among them to feed, Some, already filled, alighted at the shoreline and folded themselves, waiting with their flat heads cocked at angles.

The sky, even at Counter's midmorning, remained a dark backdrop for gauzy auroral curtains that bristled with energy. This world had an atmospheric blanket not dense enough to scatter the wan sunlight. For on this brane, the sun itself had less mass, too.

She peered down. She was a pilot, but a biologist as well. And they knew there was something waiting . . .

"Going in," she said.

Into this slow world they came with a high roar. Wings flapped away from the noise. A giant filled the sky.

Mina dropped the lander closer. Her legs were cramped from the small pilot chair, and she bounced with the rattling boom of atmospheric braking.

She blinked, suddenly alarmed. Beside her in his acceleration couch Ben peered forward at the swiftly looming landscape. "How's that spot?" He jabbed a finger tensely at the approaching horizon.

"Near the sea? Sure. Plenty of life forms there. Kind of like an African watering hole." Analogies were all she had to go on here, but there was a resemblance. Their recon scans had showed a ferment all along the shoreline.

Ben brought them down steady above a rocky plateau. Their drive ran red-hot.

Now here was a problem nobody on the mission team, for all their contingency planning, had foreseen. Their deceleration plume was bound to incinerate many of the life forms in this utterly cold ecosystem. Even after hours, the lander might be too hot for any life to approach, not to mention scalding them when nearby ices suddenly boiled away.

Well, nothing to do about it now.

"Fifty meters and holding." He glanced at her. "Ok?"

"Touchdown," she said, and they settled onto the rock.

To land on ice would have sunk them hip-deep in fluid, only to then be refrozen rigidly into place. They eagerly watched the plain. Something hurried away at the horizon, which did not look more than a kilometer away.

"Look at those lichen," she said eagerly. "In so skimpy an energy environment, how can there be so *many* of them?"

"We're going to be hot for an hour, easy," Ben said, his calm, careful gaze sweeping the view systematically. The ship's computers were taking digital photographs automatically, getting a good map. "I say we take a walk."

She tapped a key, giving herself a voice channel, reciting her ID opening without thinking. "Okay, now the good stuff. As we agreed, I am adding my own comments to the data I just sent you."

They had not agreed, not at all. But who could stop her? Many of the Counter Mission Control engineers, wedded to their mathematical slang and NASA's jawbone acronyms, felt that commentary was subjective and useless. Let the expert teams back home interpret the data; the PR people liked anything they could use.

"Counter is a much livelier place than we ever imagined. There's weather, for one thing, a product of the planet's six-day rotation and the mysterious heating. Turns out the melting and freezing point of methane is crucial. With the heating-up, the mean temperature is well high enough that nitrogen and argon stay gaseous, giving Counter its thin atmosphere. Of course, the ammonia and carbon dioxide are solid as rock. Counter's warmer, but still incredibly cold by our standards. Methane, though, can go either way. It thaws, every morning. Even better, the methane doesn't just sublime—nope, it melts. Then it freezes at night."

Now the dawn line was creeping at its achingly slow pace over a ridgeline, casting long shadows that pointed like arrows across a great rock plain. There was something there she could scarcely believe, hard to make out even from their thousand-kilometer high orbit under the best magnification. Something they weren't going to believe back Earthside. So keep up the patter and lead them to it. *Just do it.*

"Meanwhile, on the dark side there's a great 'heat sink,' like the one over Antarctica on Earth. It moves slowly across the planet as it turns, radiating heat into space and pressing down a column of cold air—I mean, of even *colder* air. From its lowest, coldest point winds flow out toward the day side. At the sunset line they meet sun-warmed air—and it snows. Snow! Maybe I should take up skiing, huh?"

At least Ben laughed. It was hard, talking into a mute audience. And she was getting jittery. She took a hit of the thick, jolting Colombian coffee in her mug. On-ward—

"On the sunrise side they meet sunlight and melting methane ice, and it rains. Gloomy dawn. Permanent, moving around the planet like a veil."

She close-upped the dawn line and there it was, a great gray curtain descending, marching ever-westward at about the speed of a fast car.

"So we've got a perpetual storm front moving at the edge of the night side, and another that travels with the sunrise."

As she warmed to her subject, all pretense at imper-sonal scientific discourse faded from Mina's voice; she could not filter out her excitement that verged on a kind of love. She paused, watching the swirling alabaster bliz-zards at twilight's sharp edge and, on the dawn side, the great solemn racks of cloud. Although admittedly no Jupiter, this planet—her planet, for the moment—could put on quite a show.

"The result is a shallow sea of methane that moves slowly around the world, following the sun. Who'd a thought, eh, you astro guys? Since methane doesn't ex-pand as it freezes, the way water does"—okay, the astro guys know that, she thought, but the public needs re-minders, and this damn well was going out to the whole wide bloomin' world, right?—"I'm sure it's all slush a short way below the surface, and solid ice from there down. But so what? The sea isn't stagnant, because of what the smaller Counter-Moon is doing. It's close to the planet, so it makes a permanent tidal bulge directly underneath it. And the two worlds are trapped, like two dancers forever in each others' arms. So that bulge travels around from daylight to darkness, too. So sea currents form, and *flow*, and freeze. On the night side, the tidal pull puts stress on the various ices, and they hump up and buckle into pressure ridges. Like the ones in Antarctica, but *much* bigger."

Miles high, in fact, in Counter's weak gravity. Massive peaks, worthy of the best climbers . . .

But her enthusiasm drained away, and she bit her lip. Now for the hard part.

She'd rehearsed this a dozen times, and still the words stuck in her throat. After all, she hadn't come here to do close-up planetology. An unmanned orbital mission could have done that nicely. Mina had come in search of life— of the beings who had sent the gravitational wave signals. And now she and Ben were about to walk the walk.

The cold here was unimaginable, hundreds of degrees below human experience. The suit heaters could cope— the atmosphere was too thin to steal heat quickly—but only if their boots alone actually touched the frigid ground. Sophisticated insulation could only do so much.

Mina did not like to think about this part. Her feet could freeze in her boots, then the rest of her. Even for the lander's heavily insulated shock-absorber legs, they had told her, it would be touch-and-go beyond a stay of a few hours. Their onboard nuclear thermal generator was already laboring hard to counter the cold she could see creeping in, from their external thermometers. Their craft already creaked and popped from thermal stresses.

And the thermal armor, from the viewpoint of the natives, must seem a hot, untouchable furnace. Yet already they could see things scurrying on the plain. Some seemed to be coming closer. Maybe curiosity was indeed a universal trait of living things.

Ben pointed silently. She picked out a patch of dark blue-gray down by the shore of the methane sea. On their console she brought up the visual magnification. In detail it looked like rough beach shingle. Tidal currents during the twenty-two hours since dawn had dropped some kind of gritty detritus—not just ices, apparently—at the sea's edge. Nothing seemed to grow on the flat, and—swiveling point of view—up on the ridge's knife-edge also seemed bare, relatively free of life. "It'll have to do," she said.

"Maybe a walk down to the beach?" Ben said. "Turn over a few rocks?"

They were both tip-toeing around the coming moment. With minimal talk they got into their suits.

Skillfully, gingerly—and by prior coin-flip—Mina clumped down the ladder. She almost envied those pioneer astronauts who had first touched the ground on Luna, backed up by a constant stream of advice, or at least comment, from Houston. The Mars landing crew had taken a mutual, four-person single step. Taking a breath, she let go of the ladder and thumped down on Counter. Startlingly, sparks spat between her feet and the ground, jolting her.

"There must be a *lot* of electricity running around out here," she said, fervently thanking the designers for all that redundant insulation.

Ben followed. She watched big blue sparks zap up from the ground to his boots. He jumped and twitched.

"Ow! That smarts," Ben said.

Only then did she realize that she had already had her shot at historical pronouncements, and had squandered it in her surprise. "*Wow*—what a profound thought," huh? she asked herself ruefully.

Ben said solemnly, "We stand at the ramparts of the solar system."

Well, she thought, fair enough. He had actually remembered his prepared line. He grinned at her and shrugged as well as he could in the bulky suit. Now on to business.

Against the gray ice and rock their lander stood like an H. G. Wells Martian walking-machine, splay-footed and ominous.

"Rocks, anyone?" They began gathering some, using long tweezers. Soil samples rattled into the storage bin.

"Let's take a stroll," Ben said.

"Hey, close-up that." She pointed out toward sea.

Things were swimming toward them. Just barely visible above the smooth surface, they made steady progress toward shore. Each had a small wake behind it.

"Looks like something's up," Ben said.

As they carefully walked down toward the beach, she tried her link to the lander's wide-band receiver. Happily, she found that the frequencies first logged by her lost, devoured probe were full of traffic. Confusing, though. Each of the beasts—for she was sure it was them—seemed to be broadcasting on all waves at once. Most of the signals were weak, swamped in background noise that sounded like an old AM radio picking up a nearby high-tension line. One, however, came roaring in like a pop music station. She made the lander's inductance tuner scan carefully.

That pattern—yes! It had to be. Quickly she compared it with the probe-log she'd had the wit to bring down with her. These were the odd cadences and sputters of the very beast whose breakfast snack had been her first evidence of life.

"Listen to this," she said. Ben looked startled through his faceplate.

The signal boomed louder, and she turned back the gain. She decided to try the radio direction-finder. Ben did, too, for a crosscheck. As they stepped apart, moving from some filmy ice onto a brooding brown rock, she felt sparks snapping at her feet. Little jolts managed to get through even the thermal vacuum-layer insulation, prickling her feet.

The vector reading, combined with Ben's, startled her. "Why, the thing's practically on top of us!"

If Counter's lords of creation were all swimming in toward this island ridge for lunch, this one might get here first. Fired up by all those vitamins from the lost probe? she wondered.

Suddenly excited, Mina peered out to sea—and there it was. Only a roiling, frothing ripple, like a ship's bow wave, but arrowing for shore. And others, farther out.

Then it bucked up into view and she saw its great, segmented tube of a body, with a sheen somewhere between mother-of-pearl and burnished brass. Why, it was *huge*. For the first time it hit her that when they all converged on this spot, it was going to be like sitting smack in a middling-sized dinosaur convention.

Too late to back out now. She powered up the small lander transmitter and tuned it to the signal she was receiving from seaward.

With her equipment she could not duplicate the creature's creative chaos of wavelengths. For its personal identification sign the beast seemed to use a simple continuous pulse pattern, like Morse code. Easy enough to simulate. After a couple of dry-run hand exercises to get with the rhythm of it, Mina sent the creature a roughly approximate duplicate of its own ID.

She had expected a call-back, maybe a more complex message. The result was astonishing. Its internal rocket engine fired a bright orange plume against the sky's black. It shot straight up in the air, paused, and plunged back. Its splash sent waves rolling up the beach. The farthest tongue of sluggish fluid broke against the lander's most seaward leg. The beast thrashed toward shore, rode a wave in—and stopped. The living cylinder lay there, half in, half out, as if exhausted.

Had she terrified it? Made it panic?

Cautiously, Mina tried the signal again, thinking furiously. It *would* give you quite a turn, she realized, if you'd just gotten as far in your philosophizing as I think, therefore I am, and then heard a thin, toneless duplicate of your own voice give back an echo.

She braced herself—and her second signal prompted a long, suspenseful silence. Then, hesitantly—shyly?— the being repeated the call after her.

Mina let out her breath in a long, shuddering sigh.

She hadn't realized she was holding it. Then she instructed DIS, the primary computer aboard *Venture*, to run the one powerful program Counter Mission Control had never expected her to have to use: the translator, Wiseguy. The creation of that program climaxed an argument that had raged for a century, ever since Whitehead and Russell had scrapped the old syllogistic logic of Aristotle in favor of a far more powerful method—sufficient, they believed, to subsume the whole of science, perhaps the whole of human cognition. All to talk to Counter's gravitational signals.

She waited for the program to come up and kept her eyes on the creature. It washed gently in and out with the lapping waves but seemed to pay her no attention. Ben was busily snapping digitals. He pointed offshore. "Looks like we put a stop to the rest of them."

Heads bobbed in the sea. Waiting? For what?

In a few moments they might have an answer to questions that had been tossed around endlessly. Could all language be translated into logically rigorous sentences, relating to one another in a linear configuration, structures, a system? If so, one could easily program a computer loaded with one language to search for another language's equivalent structures. Or, as many linguists and anthropologists insisted, does a truly unknown language forever resist such transformations?

This was such a strange place, after all. Forbidding, weird chemistry. Alien tongues could be strange not merely in vocabulary and grammatical rules, but in their semantic swamps and mute cultural or even biological premises. What would life forms get out of this place? Could even the most inspired programmers, just by symbol manipulation and number-crunching, have cracked ancient Egyptian with no Rosetta Stone?

With the Counter Project already far over budget, the decision to send along Wiseguy—which took many terabytes of computational space—had been hotly contested. The deciding vote was cast by an eccentric but politically astute old skeptic, who hoped to disprove the "bug-eyed monster Rosetta Stone theory," should life unaccountably turn up on Counter. Mina had heard through the gossip tree that the geezer was gambling that his support would bring along the rest of the DIS package. That program he passionately believed in.

Wiseguy had learned Japanese in five hours, Hopi in seven, and what smatterings they knew of Dolphin in two days. It also mastered some of the fiendishly complex, multilogic artificial grammars generated from an Earth-based mainframe.

The unexpected outcome of six billion dollars and a generation of cyberfolk was simply put: A good translator had all the qualities of a true artificial intelligence. Wiseguy *was* a guy, of sorts. It—or she, or he; nobody had known quite how to ask—had to have cultural savvy *and* blinding mathematical skills. Mina had long since given up hope of beating Wiseguy at chess, even with one of its twin processors tied off.

She signaled again and waved, hoping to get the creature's attention. Ben leaped high in the one-tenth of a g gravity and churned both arms and legs in the ten seconds it took him to fall back down. Excited, the flying wings swooped silently over them. The scene was eerie in its silence; shouldn't birds make some sort of sound? The auroras danced, in Mina's feed from *Venture* she heard Wiseguy stumblingly, muttering . . . and beginning to talk.

She noted from the digital readout on her helmet interior display that Wiseguy had been eavesdropping on the radio crosstalk already. Now it was galloping along. In contrast to the simple radio signals she had first heard, the spoken, acoustic language turned out to be far more sophisticated. Wiseguy, however, dealt not in grammars and vocabularies but in underlying concepts. And it was *fast*.

Mina took a step toward the swarthy cylinder that

heaved and rippled. Then another. Ropy muscles surged in it beneath layers of crusted fat. The cluster of knobs and holes at its front moved. It lifted its "head"—the snubbed-off, blunt forward section of the tube—and a bright, fast chatter of microwaves chimed through her ears. Followed immediately by Wiseguy's whispery voice. Discourse.

Another step. More chimes. Wiseguy kept this up at increasing speed. She was now clearly out of the loop. Data sped by in her ears, as Wiseguy had neatly inserted itself into the conversation, assuming Mina's persona, using some electromagnetic dodge. The creature apparently still thought it was speaking to her; its head swiveled to follow her.

The streaming conversation verged now from locked harmonies into brooding, meandering strings of chords. Mina had played classical guitar as a teenager, imagining herself performing before concert audiences instead of bawling into a mike and hitting two chords in a rock band. So she automatically thought in terms of the musical moves of the data flow. Major keys gave way to dusky harmonies in a minor triad. To her mind this had an effect like a cloud passing across the sun.

Wiseguy reported to her and Ben in its whisper. It and Awk had only briefly had to go through the me-Tarzan-you-Jane stage. For a life form that had no clearly definable brain she could detect, it proved a quick study.

She got its proper name first, as distinguished from its identifying signal; *its* name, definitely, for the translator established early in the game that these organisms had no gender.

The Quand they called themselves. And this one—call it Ark, because that was all Wiseguy could make of the noise that came before—*Ark-Quand*. Maybe, Wiseguy whispered for Mina and Ben alone, Ark was just a place-note to show that this thing was the "presently here" *of* the Quand. It seemed that the name was generic, for all of them.

"Like Earth tribes," Ben said, "who name themselves the People. Individual distinctions get tacked on when necessary?"

Ben was like that—surprising erudition popping out when useful, otherwise a straight supernerd techtype. His idea might be an alternative to Earth's tiresome clash of selfish individualisms and stifling collectivisms, Mina thought; the political theorists back home would go wild.

Mina took another step toward the dark beach where the creature lolled, its head following her progress. It was no-kidding *cold*, she realized. Her boots were melting the ground under her, just enough to make it squishy. And she could hear the sucking as she lifted her boot, too. So she wasn't missing these creatures' calls—they didn't use the medium.

One more step. Chimes in her ears, and Wiseguy sent them a puzzled, "It seems a lot smarter than it should be."

"Look, they need to talk to each other over distance, out of sight of each other," Mina said. "Those waxy all-one-wing birds should flock and probably need calls for mating, right? So do we." Not that she really thought that was a deep explanation.

"How do we frame an expectation about intelligence?" Ben put in.

"Yeah, I'm reasoning from Earthly analogies," Mina admitted. "Birds and walruses that use microwaves—who woulda thought?"

"I see," Wiseguy said, and went back to speaking to the Awk in its ringing microwave tones.

Mina listened to the ringing interchange speed up into a blur of blips and jots. Wiseguy could run very fast, of course, but this huge tubular thing seemed able to keep up with it. Microwaves' higher frequencies had far greater carrying capacity than sound waves, and this Awk seemed able to use that. Well, evolution would prefer such a fast-talk capability, she supposed—but why hadn't it on Earth? Because sound was so easy to use, evolving out of breathing. Even here—Wiseguy told her in a sub-channel aside—individual notes didn't mean anything. Their sequence did, along with rhythm and intonation, just like sound speech. Nearly all human languages used either subject-object-verb order or else subject-verb-object, and the Quands did, too. But to Wiseguy's confusion, they used both, apparently not caring.

Basic values became clear, in the quick scattershot conversation. Something called "rendezvous" kept coming up, modified by comments about territory. "Self-merge," the ultimate, freely chosen—apparently with all the Quands working communally afterward to care for the young, should there luckily occur a birthing. Respect for age, because the elders had experienced so much more.

Ben stirred restlessly, watching the sea for signs that others might come ashore. "Hey, they're moving in," Ben said apprehensively.

Mina would scarcely have noticed the splashing and grinding on the beach as other Quands began to arrive—apparently for Rendezvous, their mating, and Wiseguy stressed that it deserved the capital letter—save that Awk stopped to count and greet the new arrivals. Her earlier worry about being crunched under a press of huge Quand bodies faded. They were social animals, and this barren patch of rock was now Awk's turf. Arrivals lumbering up onto the dark beach kept a respectful distance, spacing themselves. Like walruses, yes.

Mina felt a sharp cold ache in her lower back. Standing motionless for so long, the chill crept in. She was astounded to realize that nearly four hours had passed. She made herself pace, stretch, eat, and drink from suit supplies.

Ben did the same, saying, "We're eighty percent depleted on air."

"Damn it, I don't want to quit *now!* How 'bout you get extra from the Lander?"

Ben grimaced. He didn't want to leave either. They had all dedicated their lives to getting here, to this moment in this place. "Okay, Cap'n sir," he said sardonically as he trudged away.

She felt a kind of silent bliss here, just watching. Life, strange and wonderful, went on all around her. Her running digital coverage would be a huge hit Earthside. Unlike Axelrod's empire, the Counter Project gave their footage away.

As if answering a signal, the Quand hunched up the slope a short way to feed on some brown lichen-like growth that sprawled across the warming stones. She stepped aside. Awk came past her and another Quand slid up alongside. It rubbed against Awk, edged away, rubbed again. A courtship preliminary? Mina guessed.

They stopped and slid flat tongues over the lichen stuff, vacuuming it up with a slurp she could hear through her suit. Tentatively, the newcomer laid its body next to

Awk. Mina could hear the pace of microwave discourse Awk was broadcasting, and it took a lurch with the contact, slowing, slowing . . . And Awk abruptly—even curtly, it seemed to Mina—rolled away. The signal resumed its speed.

She laughed aloud. How many people had she known who would pass up a chance at sex to get on with their language lessons?

Or was Wiseguy into philosophy already? It seemed to be digging at how the Quand saw their place in this weird world.

Mina walked carefully, feeling the crunch of hard ice as she melted what would have been gases on Earth—nitrogen, carbon dioxide, oxygen itself. She had to keep up, and the low-g walking was an art. With so little weight, rocks and ices that looked rough were still slick enough to make her slip. She caught herself more than once from a full, face-down splat—but only because she had so much time to recover, in a slow fall. As the Quand worked their way across the stony field of lichen, they approached the lander. Ben wormed his way around them, careful to not get too close.

"Wiseguy! Interrupt." Mina explained what she wanted. It quickly got the idea and spoke in short bursts to Awk—who resent a chord-rich message to the Quand.

They all stopped short. "I don't want them burned on the lander," Mina said to Ben, who made the switch on her suit oxy bottles without a hitch.

"Burned? I don't want them eating it," Ben said.

Then the Quand began asking *her* questions, and the first one surprised her: *Do you come from Lightgiver? As heralds?*

In the next few minutes Mina and Ben realized from

their questions alone that in addition to a society, the Quand had a rough-and-ready view of the world, an epic oral literature (though recited in microwaves), and something that resembled a religion. Even Wiseguy was shaken; it paused in its replies, something she had never heard it do before, not even in speed trials.

Agnostic though she was, the discovery moved her profoundly. *Lightgiver.* After all, she thought with a rush of compassion and nostalgia, we started out as sun worshippers too.

There were dark patches on the Quands' upper sides, and as the sun rose these pulled back to reveal thick lenses. They looked like quartz—tough crystals for a rugged world. Their banquet of lichen done—she took a few samples for analysis, provoking a snort from a nearby Quand—they lolled lazily in their long day. She and Ben walked gingerly through them, peering into the quartz "eyes." Their retinas were a brilliant blue with red wire-like filaments curling through and under. Convergent evolution seemed to have found yet another solution to the eye problem.

"So what's our answer? Are we from Lightgiver?"

"Well . . . you're the Cap'n, remember." He grinned. "And the biologist."

She quickly sent *No. We are from a world like this, from near, uh, Lifegiver.*

Do not sad, it sent through Wiseguy. *Lightgiver gives and Lightgiver takes; but it gives more than any; it is the source of all life, here and from the Dark; bless Lightgiver.*

Quands did not use verb forms underlining existence itself—no words for *are, is, be*—so sad became a verb. She wondered what deeper philosophical chasm that linguistic detail revealed. Still, the phrasing was startlingly familiar, the same damned, comfortless comfort she had heard preached at her grandmother's rain-swept funeral.

Remembering that moment of loss with a deep inward hurt, she forced it away. What could she say . . .?

After an awkward silence, Awk said something renderable as, *I need leave you for now.*

Another Quand was peeling out Awk's personal identification signal, with a slight tag-end modification. Traffic between the two Quands became intense. Wiseguy did its best to interpret, humming with the effort in her ears.

Then she saw it. A pearly fog had lifted from the shoreline, and there stood a distant spire. Old, worn rocks peaked in a scooped-out dish.

"Ben, there's the focal point!"

He stopped halfway between her and the lander. "Damn! Yes!"

"The Quand built it!"

"But . . . where's their civilization?"

"Gone. They lost it when this brane-universe cooled." The idea had been percolating in her, and now she was sure of it.

Ben said, awed, "Once *these* creatures put those grav wave emitters in orbit? And built this focal point—all to signal to us, on our brane?"

"We know this universe is dying—and so do they."

The Counter-brane had less mass in it and somewhat different cosmology. Here space-time was much further along in its acceleration, heading for the Big Rip when the expansion of the Counter-universe would tear first galaxies, then stars and planets apart, pulverizing them down into atoms.

*   *   *

Mina turned the translator off. First things first, and even on Counter there was such a thing as privacy.

"They've been sending signals a long time, then," Ben said.

"Waiting for us to catch up to the science they once had—and now have lost." She wondered at the abyss of time this implied. "As if we could help them . . ."

Ben, ever the diplomat, began, "Y'know, it's been hours . . ." Even on this tenth-g world she was getting tired. The Quand lolled, Lifegiver stroking their skins— which now flushed with an induced chemical radiance, harvesting the light. She took more digitals, thinking about how to guess the reaction—

"Y'know . . ."

"Yeah, right, let's go."

Outside they prepped the lander for lift-off. Monotonously, as they had done Earthside a few thousand times, they went through the checklist. Tested the external cables. Rapped the valves to get them to open. Tried the mechanicals for freeze-up—and found two legs that would not retract. It took all of Ben's powerful heft to unjam them.

Mina lingered at the hatch and looked back, across the idyllic plain, the beach, the sea like a pink lake. She hoped the heat of launching, carried through this frigid air, would add to the suns thin rays and . . . and what? Maybe help these brave beings who had sent their grav-wave plea for help?

Too bad she could not transmit Wagner's grand *Liebestod* to them, something to lift spirits—but even Wiseguy could only do so much.

She lingered, gazing at the chilly wealth here, held both by scientific curiosity and by a newfound affection.

Then another miracle occurred, the way they do, matter-of-factly. Sections of carbon exoskeleton popped forth from the shiny skin of two nearby Quands. Jerkily, these carbon-black leaves articulated together, joined, swelled, puffed with visible effort into one great sphere.

Inside, she knew but could not say why, the two Quands were flowing together, coupling as one being. Self-merge.

For some reason, she blinked back tears. Then she made herself follow Ben inside the lander. Back to . . . what? Checked and rechecked, they waited for the orbital resonance time with *Venture* to roll around. Each lay silent, immersed in thought. The lander went *ping* and *pop* with thermal stress.

Ben punched the firing keys. The lander rose up on its roaring tail of fire. Her eyes were dry now, and their next move was clear: *Back through the portal, to Earth. Tell them of this vision, a place that tells us what is to come, eventually, in our own universe.*

"Goin' home!" Ben shouted.

"Yes!" she answered. *And with us and the Quand together, maybe we can find a way to save us both. To rescue life and meaning from a universe that, in the long run, would destroy itself. Cosmological suicide.*

She had come to explore, and now they were going back with a task that could shape the future of two species, two branes. Quite enough, for a mere one trip through the portal, through the looking-glass. Back to a reality that could never be the same.

THE TWO SHECKLEYS

Robert Sheckley

Robert Sheckley was born in Brooklyn, New York, and raised in New Jersey. He went into the U.S. army after high school and served in Korea. After discharge he attended NYU, graduating with a degree in English. He began to sell stories to all the science-fiction magazines soon after his graduation, producing several hundred stories over the next several years. His best-known books in the science-fiction field are Immortality, Inc., Mindswap, *and* Dimension of. *He has produced about 65 books to date, including twenty novels and nine collections of his short stories, as well as his five-volume* Collected Short Stories of Robert Sheckley, *published by Pulphouse. In 1991 he received the Daniel F. Gallun award for contributions to the genre of science fiction. Recently he was given an Author Emeritus award by the Science Fiction Writ-*

ers of America. He is married to the writer Gail Dana and lives in Portland, Oregon.

SHECKLEY got an invitation to create a story for an anthology about a Gateway leading to "strange and alien lands, alternate dimensions, pasts or futures, or who-knows-where." In brief, to worlds of heart's desire. The makeup of the Gateway, and of the worlds that lay beyond it, was entirely up to him. It was just the sort of assignment a science-fiction writer likes.

Sheckley was a fantasist not entirely unknown to the public. For fifty years he had pursued his calling, inventing worlds both characteristic of the genre and unique to himself. From his teeming brain had come planets of pleasure and worlds of pain. Nor had he neglected the multitudinous possibilities in between, the many worlds of possibility where tedium sometimes vies with expectation.

At the beginning of his career he had possessed a considerable Central Posterior Imago, a structure that develops in some individuals shortly after puberty and is most often located below and slightly to the right of the amygdala. Due to his possession of this, the making of imaginative worlds had become almost second nature for him. But in recent years, that subamygdalic organ had begun to shrink and atrophy, thus leaving him at a disadvantage in the making of his confections.

That was bad enough; but also, in recent years Chaos Theory had come to his attention, and its pernicious influence had come to infect his imaginative faculty. Especially difficult had been the idea of bifurcations, with the strong and unwelcome implication that deviation from a desired goal was in the very nature of things. But equally damaging was The Theory's insistence on sensitivity to initial conditions, which could not be planned out in advance. To start at the wrong point or the wrong moment was to doom yourself to failure; yet there was no avoiding the very strong likelihood of this, given the almost infinite number of points in time and space you could begin from, and the inevitable conclusion that most of them were wrong. Any and every moment could be a fruitful starting-point; or, more likely, a disastrous one, undertaken under the influence of unknown factors and mediated by invisible conditions. Awareness of all this was a detriment to output.

Sheckley's production dwindled in the knowledge that any beginning was more than likely a wrong one, which would follow the trail of bifurcations to an unwanted result. This was the fate that had been meted out to this impecunious weaver of yarns—to be in the position of Penelope of the ancient Odyssean legend, unweaving at night what he had wrought during the day—the marvelous figures of his yarn, which, upon reflection, never seemed good enough to him.

This time had to be different, however. Sheckley had bills to pay—bills that were in themselves memories of past indiscretions and bad decisions—alimony bills, rent bills, heating bills, water and power bills. These had come of late in the shocking red color of imminent action. The grim figure of Retribution was moving into his life, ready to wink him out of his apartment, cut off his cigarettes, turn off his water, and disconnect his power—in effect, cut off life itself.

But it didn't have to be that way! This assignment was his key to extricating himself from a fate long brooded upon. Successful completion would bring other assignments in their wake, and others beyond that. He simply had to tell a tale about the Gateway, and the worlds of desire that lay beyond it.

So, that evening, well supplied with cigarettes, he sat down at his computer and tapped out the words of an opening. He was sure it was the wrong opening, but you have to begin somewhere.

Glancing up from his endeavors, he saw that he was in an unfamiliar place. Instead of the smoky front room of his apartment, he was sitting in what looked like a large office lobby with a high ceiling. His laptop was on his lap. There were a lot of people coming in and out of the main doors, and above them was a large sign which read: WELCOME TO GATEWAY.

He blinked several times, perhaps unnecessarily. He suddenly realized what must have happened. He had somehow projected himself into his own story. He was in that Gateway that he had contracted to write about.

To be a character in a story one is composing is not the usual order of things. But it was one that Sheckley was not entirely unaccustomed to. Many years ago he had written himself into a novel entitled *Options*. This was not unheard of in the world of letters, but to Sheckley it had been uncomfortable, and he had soon written himself out again. Some perversity made him keep his appearance in that book. He had considered the act of self-insertion to be unallowable; but it had happened, and he refused to undo what had come to pass. His appearance in *Options* had gone unnoticed by the reading public, or at least uncommented upon, except for Mike Resnick, who said Sheckley should stay there until he came up with the twenty dollars he owed Resnick. So Sheckley thought, perhaps this lapse would be allowed, too.

He felt a little uncomfortable being in an invention he was supposed to be inventing, but he decided to make the best of it. Closing his laptop, he walked to the lobby doors and gazed outside. He saw that he was in a city, a European city from the look of it. In fact, it looked like what he imagined Prague might look like: a vertiginous collection of buildings leaning one against the other, crowds of people in drab gray and brown clothing, looking much like the people in the lobby.

So this was The Gateway! And beyond it lay the worlds of heart's desire. But how to get from here to there? He would have to ask someone. He picked out a middle-aged man with a small moustache (a Czech moustache, no doubt) and said to him, "Excuse me, sir, could you tell me how to get to the next world?"

The man pursed his lips. "You must be referring to the world of heart's desire that lies beyond Gateway, or so we are taught."

"That's it exactly," said Sheckley.

"You are referring, of course, to the Great Good Place that will satisfy our desires after our long confinement in the Vale of Tears which is the Earth."

"Precisely."

"Well then, you will have to ask one of the People on the Advisory Committee."

"Whom do the Advisory Committee advise?" Sheckley asked.

"No less an entity than the universe itself."

"Why would the universe call upon this committee for advice?"

"It is part of the universe's plan for self-organization."

"I don't get it."

"It's simple enough," the Czech-looking man said.

"This universe is self-organizing; but what will it self-organize itself into? That is the question that constantly perplexes it. And, of course, the universe has a great deal else to do apart from self-organization. So it created a Committee for Advice to the Self-Organizing Universe, which in turn created my committee, The Advisory Committee to the Committee for Advice to the Self-Organizing Universe, and it calls upon this committee for suggestions as to what to organize itself as next. It does not require itself to take these suggestions, of course, but a surprising amount of the time it does take them. In fact, it wouldn't be too much to say that the universe gets many of its best ideas from the committee."

"Really?" said Sheckley in demurring tones of deepest skepticism.

"Well you may demur," the Czechish man said. "It is no small thing to claim to be the inspiration of the universe, which is perhaps too vast and weighty, and to concerned with the quotidian, to concern itself with matters of the future. For that reason it relies on people such as ourselves, who, unimaginative though we may be, supply imagination for the committee for the universal purpose. But you must excuse me now; my fellow members are waiting for me."

And with that, the man hurried off down the corridor.

Sheckley stood for a moment perplexed, there in the long, tedious corridor with its almost infinite cross-corridors, all suffused with a gray light from ceiling fixtures. And he heard a voice which seemed to emanate from within his own head, saying, "Sheckley!"

Glancing around, and seeing that he was alone for the moment, he said, "Yes?"

"It is I, the alternate Sheckley."

"Why is there an alternate Sheckley?"

"Blame it on the universe, which for its own reasons, abhors a vacuum. I was created to fill the spot you vacated when you went to the Gateway, which, being a bridge between worlds, is neither of them."

"So you're on Earth and I'm in the Gateway?"

"You've got it, boychick."

"So how do we refer to ourselves and each other?" Sheckley asked, going to the nomenclatural heart of the problem.

"For the present, let's have you call yourself 'Sheckley,' while I will take the homelier and more familiar appellation of 'Bob.' It doesn't matter. Eventually we will coalesce back into the single being we started out as. You get the better deal. All you have to do is look for the world of heart's desire, while I stay here on Earth and try to take care of the bills."

"You are a writer, then?"

"A writer, and the inheritor of a writer's debts," said Bob.

"I admit to them," said Sheckley.

"Perhaps we can do something to rid ourselves of them," said Bob.

"What would you suggest?" asked Sheckley.

"That you live the story, up there in Gateway, and I write the story, down here on Earth," said Bob.

"How can I live the story?"

"Go find your world of heart's desire."

"Easy for you to say. But meanwhile, I'm sitting here in Gateway, and nothing has happened except for a nondescript conversation with a guy who looked like a Czech. I doubt you'll be able to sell that."

"You're right. What we need here is a little action. I suppose I could supply you with some characters and plot twists."

"That would be useful."

"Just hang on, then. I'll come up with something as soon as possible. This is Bob, signing off."

And so the connection was broken. Sheckley was left marveling at how much Bob sounded like him. They had so much in common: There was that same note of panic in Bob's utterances, the same grasping for words that didn't quite fit the case, the same air of hangdog defiance.

It was a quiet evening. Sheckley found a place to sleep in an unused office. He found an old TV set tuned to reruns of *Star Trek*, with occasional interpolations of *Mork and Mindy*. He fell asleep on the wall-to-wall carpet. Waking up in the morning, he found a box of Ralston's Purina in a desk drawer, and a container of Everlast milk. He brewed himself a cup, then showered and shaved in the adjoining bathroom, and, at last, ventured out again into the corridor.

In the distance, from the far end of the corridor, Sheckley heard a noise. It was a strange sort of sound, composed of women's sighs, a man's gruff barking voice, and the grating sound of metal being dragged across marble. Then the source of the sound appeared. It was a man, at least seven feet tall, a Hercules clad in a lion skin, a man with a heavy sullen face, little pig eyes, and a stomach that in fifty years or so would have a paunch but that now was rock-hard ribbed muscle. And did I mention that in one hand he carried a club made of some dense metal, and in the other hand he held a chain, and at the end of that chain were a dozen or so weeping women, some with babes in arms, being pulled along.

"What is this?" Sheckley asked.

"I am the Bleak Barbarian," the half naked figure responded. "These are my captives."

"What do you need captives for?"

"They will be my wives, as soon as I reach my world of heart's desire."

"How are you going to get in?"

The Bleak Barbarian smiled and twitched his club. "I'll bash my way in."

Sheckley noticed that the Barbarian had a small plastic box, hanging around his neck by a silver chain. "What's that?" he asked.

"It is one of a class of objects that may be termed an Orpheus Machine, a musical device that transmits sweet and pacifying sounds to the ear, music which, in the words of the poet Tennyson, 'gentlier on the spirit lies than tired eyelids upon tired eyes; music that calls sweet sleep down from the blissful skies.' This is necessary for me since, I am of such an irascible nature that I would be apt otherwise to tear myself to pieces, and utterly destroy these ladies entrusted to my care."

"Wait just a moment," Sheckley said. He went into an empty office and closed the door. "Bob! Are you there?"

"So where should I be if I'm not there?"

Sheckley ignored that. "You sent me a barbarian."

"I thought he'd help to spice up the plot, lend a little action."

"He's got women captives! He's enslaving them!"

"He did that on his own. I didn't plan it. Those damned bifurcations!"

"Why did you send this guy?"

"I was trying to do something for the story. You said it wasn't exciting enough. So I'm bringing you back to your pulp origins."

"But I need someone I can talk with. Reason with!"

"Follow the formula."

"What formula?"

"You know, the formula. You were raised on those old pulp magazines just like I was. You need the formula to get these people to do what you want them to do."

"What do I want this guy in the lionskin to do?"

"To use his strength to get you into the Next Place."

"Gateways don't work by bashing them," Sheckley said.

"How do they work?"

"I don't know, but not that way."

"Why not give it a chance?"

"Because this barbarian guy won't let me. He isn't smart enough for one thing."

"He's plenty smart for a barbarian."

"This is a more sophisticated setup."

"Look," Bob said, "I've got a lot on my mind these days. I didn't know it was a sophisticated setup. I'll come up with something else. Signing off, buddy."

Sheckley wanted to ask about the Orpheus Machine, but the connection had been cut before he could begin. When he came out of the office, the Bleak Barbarian was gone, though rust marks and several bobby pins on the corridor carpeting showed where he had passed with his entourage.

Sheckley spent the rest of the day wandering through corridors and from office to office, trying to find a way to the Next Place. That evening, he found a place to sleep in an abandoned office. He found an old TV set tuned to reruns of *Mork and Mindy*, and after that, *Star Trek*. There was a little kitchenette stocked with various popular cereals, and there were frozen hamburgers in the freezer. So he wasn't about to starve to death. He slept that night on an office couch, woke up in the morning and brewed himself a cup of Ralston. Then, after a shower and shave, he ventured out again.

He was beginning to wonder if Bob, his alter ego back on Earth, had much in the way of smarts. To pick a barbarian as a plot device . . . But there was really no sense thinking about it. Bob's smarts were his, Sheckley's smarts, and wondering about your smarts was a good way to lose what little you had. And anyhow, Bob on Earth had his own troubles—all of those debts, those bills. At least he, Sheckley, was spared that. There were no bills here in the Gateway, no debts . . . no home either, now that he came to think about it, no good food, no beautiful young woman to greet him in the evenings, loving arms outheld, perhaps holding a steaming casserole in her hands. None of that; and, as far as he could tell, no story. And no plots twist, either.

No debts . . . no woman. There seemed to be some sort of an equivalency in that thought, but he couldn't figure out if it was true or not. When he went to The Next Place—the Great, Good Place—would there be a woman there for him? Or was he supposed to capture his own, chain her up, and take her to The Next Place with him? No, that didn't seem right, what had Bob been thinking about?

These were uncomfortable thoughts, so he shook his head to rid himself of them and went to the Gateway lobby, where there were vending machines with sandwiches and chili and hot soup, and where somebody had laid out sleeping bags on folding cots for those who hadn't found their way to The Next Place yet.

He ate, drank, and lay down. Just before falling asleep he remembered that he hadn't found the plot twist he needed for his story, the plot twist that would make everything work. But he was too tired to worry about it. He fell asleep.

A hand on his arm awakened him, and he heard a voice saying to him in a whisper, "Sheckley . . . Are you awake?"

Sheckley opened his eyes. He felt in serious need of coffee.

As though the man had been reading his mind, a mug was pressed into his hand, and he sipped the hot brew gratefully.

"Thanks a lot. Got any sugar? No matter. Who are you?"

"A friend. Bob sent me."

"He's Sheckley, too," Sheckley said.

"He said you needed help," the man said, his whisper that made him sound like the old film star Peter Lorre.. "And I'm here to give it."

"Help? What sort of help did he mention?"

"Something about a plot twist. And that you needed to get into The Next Place."

The man sat down on the cot beside Sheckley, who saw that this man was lean and hard looking, perhaps in his midforties, his hair a platinum blond, which he wore in a brush cut. There was something about his face, and a slight foreign quality to his whispering voice, that made Sheckley think he was not an American native. The guy was dressed entirely in black leather, but Sheckley didn't think he was a rock star.

"What is your name?" Sheckley whispered.

"Erich von Turendeldt, at your orders," the man whispered in his Peter Lorre voice, extending a gloved hand.

"German?" Sheckley questioned.

"A once and future German," Erich said.

"What does that mean?"

"The present regime in my country has stripped me of my nationality. They don't want to know me, and have declared me non-German, to be arrested on sight. The fools!"

"What did you do wrong?"

"Espoused unpopular views," von Turendeldt said. "But let's not talk about that. It's a painful subject for me. I am a man without a country. But that changes when we have succeeded in our conquest of The Next Place . . ."

"Do we have to conquer it?" Sheckley asked. "I thought we just walked in and lived there."

"Things are rarely that simple, my friend. Throughout European history it has been known that if you want a good thing, you must seize it."

"Even if it's something as—esoteric—as The Land of Heart's Desire?"

"Especially then! You see, really desirable places—and especially The Next Place—are filled with undesirables."

"I thought anyone could go to The Next Place," Sheckley said.

"So far that has been true. Or was true until the nonAryan Kafka organization took charge of it. But I mean to change all of that. Undesirable elements will get what they deserve—a painful hell of endless punishment. And this punishment will be meted out at the hands of the Righteous."

Sheckley decided not to pursue the topic any further. This von Turendeldt was a frightening man, and Sheckley wanted nothing to do with him. He suspected that he, Sheckley, was one of the undesirables von Turendeldt was planning to wipe out, in this life and in the next.

"Do you have any ideas? Any plans?" Sheckley asked.

"Oh, I have arranged everything. As you Americans say, the fix is in. The right people have been bribed—or, if unbribable, disposed of in ways none will suspect until too late. We should be able to go through the Gate today and then, with a little luck, cross the bridge."

"That's how you get to The Next Place?"

"Of course. How else?"

"Then what's holding things up?

"Politics," said van Turendeldt. "And the ill will of certain persons who have entrenched themselves in high places and now to seek to keep everyone else out. Come. We must leave at once."

"Have you thought of a way to persuade them?"

"Oh, it's not quite as simple as that. They have the entrance to The Next Place well guarded. They are allowing none to pass through until they can show credentials satisfactory to the present regime. And since headquarters hasn't decided on what those credentials are, none are allowed through."

"It sounds hopeless."

"It would be, except for a certain expedient I happened upon while coming here."

"What sort of expedient?"

"This!" and von Turendeldt held up a small box that

Sheckley had last seen around the neck of the Bleak Barbarian.

"The Orpheus box!" Sheckley cried.

"I call it the Valhalla Box," said. "Oh, it plays music, to be sure, but that is to disguise its true use. What you see here, my friend, is a propaganda machine of the rarest quality. With this in hand, anyone can be persuaded to do anything."

"You mean the people guarding the gate will just let us through after hearing this?"

"Seems impossible. And yet, that's exactly what the machine will do."

"And the barbarian gave you this?"

"Let's say I persuaded him." He tapped the holster on his waist. Visible in it was a dark gray automatic pistol— a Luger, to judge by its ominous shape. "One in the knee cap ensures cooperation. Two more in the skull provide the convincer."

Von Turendeldt led Sheckley to an elevator that took them to an empty basement. The large, gloomy, ill-lit area was plastered with signs reading "Authorized Personnel only! No one may enter without a Class AAA pass! Attack guards and sniper dogs present, armed, and ready to shoot on sight!" And other words of a similar intimidating nature.

"Are you sure this is the right way?" Sheckley asked.

"Down is the way up," von Turendeldt, said in his whispery, frightening voice.

They came to a huge brass door. On it was a sign: "Eternal damnation beyond this point! You have been warned!"

"This doesn't sound so good," Sheckley said.

They opened the brass door and proceeded by staircases and then ladders through wide concrete spaces where flickering florescent lamps revealed parking spaces empty except for the occasional forlorn BMW sitting all alone by itself. The lighting became worse as they descended, the rooms shabbier and covered with mildew, verdigris, and other bad things. They heard occasional clangorous sounds from above, but Sheckley could not identify them. They passed through a region of prison cells, dank, noisome places empty except for the occasional skeleton, still in chains, grimacing skull pressed toward what little light came from flickering fluorescents in the ceiling. It was a region of lost hopes and broken promises.

"I believe they call this the Slough of Despond," von Turendeldt said.

"I don't think this is going to lead us to anywhere but further bad stuff," Sheckley said.

"Have faith! Don't let the window-dressing get you down."

"What is all this?"

"What we have here is the anticipation of a doom quite irrespective of outcome," von Turendeldt said.

"Is that a fact?" said Sheckley, with feeble but deeply felt sarcasm.

After a while they became aware that something heavy and deadly sounding was following them. Its footsteps became increasingly loud, and there was a scratching sound as of steel toenails digging into the concrete floor.

"Pay it no mind," von Turendeldt said. "As I mentioned, anticipation of horror to come is worse, in its own right, then the thing itself, whatever it is."

And then, suddenly, they turned a corner, and there was a creature standing in front of them. It was a gigantic reptile, standing upright on its sizable back legs. Its small front legs were raised in front of it. Its mouth gaped open in a hideous grin, in which large triangular teeth could be seen. Even the meanest intelligence could make out that this was a Tyrannosaurus, one of the most feared of the great dinosaurs, believed extinct until this moment.

"Sometimes," the Tyrannosaurus said, "the actual event turns out to be worse than the anticipation of it. This is what we call the fact of the fiction. The fiction is the imagining of it, and the fact is the embodiment of that imagining. But there are things to be learned from all this."

"What, for example?" von Turendeldt asked.

The Tyrannosaurus' left forelimb flicked out and with his extended foretalon he disemboweled von Turendeldt. The brush-haired fellow barely had time for an expression of astonishment before his guts tumbled out and he collapsed into them. The Tyrannosaurus picked the Orpheus Machine out of the mess.

"No one likes a wise guy," the Tyrannosaurus remarked. "But at least he served to provide something useful." He swung the Orpheus Machine gently from its silver chain.

"What am I supposed to learn from this?" Sheckley asked, too heartsick and footsore to evince much surprise.

"That the advantage of being a viewpoint character is that worse things are always happening to someone else."

"How can you be talking like this? You're a stupid reptile, if you'll excuse my saying so, and you're not supposed to philosophize."

" It is the work of your intelligence to figure out why I can speak like this."

Sheckley's mind took up the challenge. It was obviously a case of ancient heredity, he thought. The Tyrannosauruses had been the cleverest of the great reptiles. With their convoluted brains and opposable talons they invented consciousness, back at a time when man was but a cowering lemurlike creature, given little chance to survive. Who could have guessed that an asteroid was even then on its way to Yucatán, its destiny to wipe out the giant reptiles and encourage the development of Man? Yes, the great reptiles were all dead—except for this one that Bob had apparently conjured up for his own purposes.

Sheckley further surmised that this must be Bob's most recent attempt at a plot device to bring the story to its desired conclusion. But what conclusion was he reaching for?

Shortly after this conjecture, Sheckley heard a sound—a musical sound so beautiful that his horror at the turn of events was overmastered by his rapture at the music. He had never cared for von Turendeldt anyway. Sheckley's mind conformed to the new pattern imposed by the succulent sounds, and his mind became ordered, harmonious, at peace. Stray thoughts fell away like dandruff in the hands of a giant lotion.

He looked up. The Tyrannosaurus was playing the Orpheus Machine at him.

Sheckley asked the obligatory question, since the Tyrannosaurus seemed to be expecting it.

"How can such things be?"

"You must realize, Sheckley, that you are a part of the

plot as well as the writer of it. I am a part of the plot device Bob sent to expedite matters and to bring you to the Great Good Place. And now, we are at the setting off point."

The Tyrannosaurus led Sheckley through the final brass door of impossibility.

Suddenly Sheckley found himself out of doors, in a vast, brightly lit place. He was standing on a cliff. On the other side, he could see a rainbow bridge stretching from where he was, across a bottomless abyss into a beautiful new land.

But standing at the near entrance to that bridge were guards in black uniforms, carrying automatic weapons, which they raised threatingly when they saw the Tyrannosaurus and Sheckley

"Who goes there?" their captain barked.

"A Tyrannosaurus and a man," the Tyrannosaurus said.

"You have no passes. We have received no authorization. You cannot pass."

The Tyrannosaurus turned on the Orpheus Machine. It sang to the guards a song of homecoming and of man's inalienable right to it. It pointed out without words, in emotional, irrefutable language, that man didn't need no stinking passes, man had the right to go wherever his imagination took him.

And the guards were lulled by this music of peace and reason. They holstered their weapons and, saying to themselves, "I don't know why I'm doing this," let down the chain that barred the path across the rainbow bridge.

With the guards singing hosannahs behind them, Sheckley and the Tyrannosaurus crossed, and they stepped into the new land.

*   *   *

There was a forest to one side, and the Tyrannosaurus galloped toward it. As for Sheckley, in a green meadow on the forest's edge he had discerned a figure, and now, with mounting excitement, he made his way toward it.

It was a woman. A beautiful young woman, with more than a passing resemblance to Paulette Goddard, and to many other dreams who had walked the Earth. There was a serenity about her features that promised Sheckley eternal contentment. He stepped toward her, his arms open wide.

She looked at him in shock and annoyance. "What do you think you're doing?" she asked.

Sheckley knew at that moment the sorrow and chagrin of one-sided love. He loved this woman on first sight. But how could such a vision love him?

There was a galloping sound.

The Tyrannosaurus suddenly came galumphing up. "I forgot my duty as a plot device!" he cried. "So sorry. I spotted this lady Tyrannosaurus in the forest, and for a moment I went autonomous—sorry, I need to finish this first."

He loomed over Sheckley, huge and deadly, his teeth and claws gleaming in the sun.

Sheckley knew a moment of fear. Was it all to end like this? A great claw came toward him. Sheckley was frozen, and even though the claw was approaching him slowly, he couldn't unfreeze himself sufficiently to get out of its way.

He had a moment of dread anticipation, which turned into a treasured moment of fond recollection a moment later when the great claw stopped inches from his face and held out something that was dangling from one of its talons.

It was the Orpheus Machine.

"You give me this? It's very good of you, but how can this be?"

"My entire purpose, the reason I was created," the Tyrannosaurus said, "was to deliver this plot device to you. But during the build-up to that, I attained a degree of autonomy. It was heady stuff—it made me forget for a moment my real purpose—to deliver this instrument of loving conciliation to you, Sheckley."

Sheckley took the machine. He poked at one of the buttons and pointed the machine at the girl. Through the alchemy of the plot device's ability to get things done, the girl's eyes softened, her lips parted, she said, "It's you, isn't it? The one I have so long desired!"

"Yes, I am that one!" Sheckley cried. Then he cringed for a moment, because he felt a sudden weight in his mind.

It was Bob, who had managed to leave Earth on the wings of his own plot device and now shared Sheckley's mind.

"But this time we won't dialogue," Bob said. "We'll talk to her, not to each other."

Bob Sheckley, no longer divided, looked at the girl. She looked at him. His arms opened. She ran to them and snuggled against his body.

"There's still a lot to explain here," Sheckley said, but the music of the Orpheus Machine swelled in his head, and all need for understanding the facticity of the moment was lost. The Orpheus Machine sang to him that the loss of the need for explanations is the beginning of wisdom. So Sheckley thought as he and the girl, hand in hand, walked down to the verdant forest in search of something good to eat.

MIDNIGHT AT THE HALF-LIFE CAFÉ

Russell Davis

Russell Davis lives with his family on a ranch in the Arizona/New Mexico borderlands. He has published numerous short stories, and a handful of novels in various genres under a couple of different names. He divides his time between freelance editorial consulting, writing, and teaching.

I never believed in the old Disney tune, "It's a Small World." Not even when I was a child, listening to stories while sitting on my father's lap or watching my mother paint landscapes of places that existed only in her mind. It was clear to me that the world was anything but small. The world was vast, the universe massive beyond imagining. The stars spread out over my night sky, the cold blanket of infinity.

I was young, so perhaps this view of our existence can be excused.

When I was older, I came to realize that the truth is

much more subtle: The world, the universe *are* vast, but our view and perception of them is not. Our world is finite. There are singular moments in life when what we see of the world is narrowed to a pinpoint of vision—one room, one bed, one person . . . even one word.

When our world is *only* what we see.

In the waning moments of my life, my world has grown very small indeed. My vision is limited to this room: ten feet long by eight feet wide by eight feet high. The one window, which does not open, shows only the brick of the building next door. I have a lamp, with a yellowing shade, and a sixty-watt soft-white light bulb. I have one painting, on the wall across from my bed, that my mother painted. She worked in oils and wasn't afraid to use a palette knife for cutting in shadows. This painting shows a snow-topped mountain range in the far distance. Closer in the frame there is a pond with cattails, and the water is a secret green, like pools hidden in old swamps. There are several pine trees, vibrant and bending slightly in the wind, growing near a broken-down wooden fence. The fence bothers me. The slats are rotted and black, and a number of them are missing, like teeth in a sinister grin.

I have thought a lot about that fence. It's broken like me, and I wonder why she painted it that way. She's long dead, of course, so I can't ask her. Sometimes I think that if she were alive, I'd be afraid to ask her, afraid to hear her answer that even in the most beautiful of settings there is always something small and broken and dark. Something vaguely malevolent.

The fence scares me a little, but the painting was my mother's, and I keep it to remind me that she existed. That she was not a ghost or a created memory. When your world is small, it is tempting to enlarge it with memories that do not exist.

The only other furniture in my room is my bed. It's quite high-tech, adjustable in almost every permutation imaginable. With the push of a button, I can raise myself up, lower myself down, move only my legs, or my middle, or my head. The mattress is made of some type of foam that evenly distributes my weight regardless of the position I am in so I don't get bedsores. With the touch of a button, I can turn on the lights, adjust the bed, or open the door. I don't watch television anymore—there were too many people moving, so I had them take it away—and the only real person who visits me is my nurse.

She comes in three times a day: early morning, midafternoon, early evening. She brings me my meals and cleans both the room and me with equal vigor. I don't know her name, and she doesn't speak. I am happy with this arrangement. The last nurse talked too much, so I dismissed her. I told the agency to send me someone with a better grasp of my wishes.

I have learned it is better not to speak to real people. They have expectations. Their world is dominated by a much larger frame of reference than mine is. Their experiences come from both ends of the moral spectrum— right and wrong, good and evil, black and white.

My world is more limited; the fulcrum of my experiences has become very one-sided.

I exist in my room, but I live in my mind. I am trapped here—and there—by this disease that has slowly wasted my body, one inch, one centimeter at a time. I used to live in the real world. I had a home, a job, a wife and children. But then the disease came, and just as it took away my body, it took away everything else. It is a wasting illness, the hapless doctors told me. A genetic flaw that was likely activated by something in the environment. Nothing can stop it.

Soon enough, everything that I had loved and valued as good in the world was gone. "It's not fair to the children, to me!" my wife had cried. "You can't make us watch this!" And so I hadn't. The last lights of my existence faded away even as my body shriveled, my muscles shrank and my stamina failed. I can still move my right hand, thankfully, and can move my head enough to change my view from one wall to the other to the empty window.

All that is left to me is my mind, and that, too, has failed me from time to time. My memory plays tricks on me. That which seems real is sometimes not; that which couldn't possibly be real, shouldn't be real . . . sometimes it is.

At least I have begun to think so.

The first time I saw him, standing at the foot of my bed, I thought he was a dream. He couldn't be real, I told myself, since no one ever comes to my room. I have no visitors. I didn't open the door.

"I'm real enough," he said. "For you, and others like you, anyway."

I stared at this visitor. He was a tall man, slender of build, but obviously fit. He wore a gray, three-piece suit of pinstriped wool. His vest held a pocket watch, attached to a pewter chain. His shoes, which I saw when he moved to stand next to my bed on the right, were gray wingtips, and his spectacles were perfect circles of silver over eyes of a similar shade. His hair was pearl white, curly ringlets, and long enough to reach the tops of his shoulders.

"You don't *look* real," I said. My voice was hoarse, harsh from so long a silence.

"Perhaps not," he admitted. When he smiled, his teeth gleamed in the dim light of my room. I shuddered, reminded of a dinosaur skeleton I had seen long ago at the Chicago Museum of Natural History. "Still and all, I *am* here speaking to you," he added. "Something that no one else has bothered to do in . . ." he paused, considering, then finished, "five years, four months, thirteen days, seven hours, two minutes and forty-two seconds. To be precise."

I thought about it. He was correct, though I didn't know the hours, minutes, and seconds part myself. I only counted the days. "All right," I said. "So I've had a visitor. You've been a lovely Good Samaritan. You may go."

He laughed, and the sound echoed in the room like the breaking of family china. "Dismissed!" he said. "How very quaint." His laughter continued. "I am *not* a Good Samaritan, be assured. I've been called many things, by many names, but that's never been one of them."

"So who are you, then?" I asked.

"I have had many names. You may call me Mr. Gray."

I laughed weakly. "Suitable, I suppose, given your attire."

"Indeed it is," he said. "I believe names and attire go hand in hand. It's all in the look. People see what they *wish* to see."

"I suppose," I said.

"And what is it that *you* wish to see?" he asked me. His voice was soft, pleasant, and as chilling as a November wind.

"My world is this place, Mr. Gray. I can see nothing else, except in my mind, my memories. And those travels have long since been taken . . . and discarded as useless."

"What if I could let you see someplace new?" he asked. "What if you could visit somewhere? With others, most of whom are in a predicament not unlike your own?"

"No one is in a predicament like mine," I said. "The doctors can't even find another case similar."

"Of course they can't," Mr. Gray said. "But I didn't say they had your illness—only that they were in a similar situation."

"How so?" I asked, feeling my long-dormant curiosity stir, despite the strangeness of the situation.

"Like you, they are all trapped within a very small world—the world of their mind."

I found myself laughing again. "And how is it, then, that we all meet? Telepathy?"

Mr. Gray smiled. "Hardly that," he said. "They all meet at the Half-Life Café." He reached into his vest pocket and removed a gray business card. His name was printed on it in small caps: MR. GRAY. The lettering was a slightly darker shade of "his" color, the font unmistakably antique. "Take this as a reminder," he said quietly. "We'll talk again."

When I looked up from the card, Mr. Gray was gone. When I looked back at the card, it dissolved into ash and disappeared.

"The Half-Life Café," I whispered to myself. "How appropriate."

Then I feel asleep.

*   *   *

When I woke the next morning, I was certain that Mr. Gray had been a dream. Another illusion or false memory that my mind had created in an effort to make the passing of my days more interesting, more bearable. Sometimes I suspect that when death is monotonous, the mind will do *anything* to fill in the dreadful gaps of time. The nurse came that morning, again in the afternoon, and I said nothing, but when she returned in the evening, I spoke. I wanted to talk about Mr. Gray. Maybe he *had* checked in at the desk.

"Miss?" I said to her as she changed the linens.

The suddenness of my voice must have shocked her. She let out a little gasp and dropped the sheet she was holding. "I . . . I'm sorry," she said, trying to catch her breath. "You startled me. I didn't realize you could speak."

I gave my best imitation of a smile. "I don't, generally. I'm sorry I frightened you."

She slowly lowered the hand that she had unconsciously raised to her chest. "I'll get over it. You're not the first patient to startle me."

I realized then how young she was, and how pretty. I must have seemed monstrous to her, horribly ugly and old. "What is your name?" I asked.

"Deanna," she said. "And yours is?"

She knew my name, of course. She was being polite, which I appreciated. "John," I said. "John Townsend. Long ago, they called me Johnny Rainbow."

Her eyes widened a bit. "You were Johnny Rainbow? The singer?"

I nodded. "Yes. You remember him?"

She smiled, her blue eyes sparkling. "Sure, I listened

to you all the time when I was a kid. We all, my brothers and sisters I mean, loved your music."

"I'm glad," I said. "That's why I wrote it. To make kids happy, bring a little joy into their world."

"You sure did mine," she said. "Whenever I was sad, I listened to your music and it always made me feel better. What was that one song . . ." her voice trailed off, as she tried to remember the title. "Ahh, I can't recall."

"Do you remember a line?" I asked her.

She thought for a moment, then sang quietly, "If your world's a closet or a mansion on the hill . . ."

". . . then always make your choices for good and not for ill," I finished. "The song was called 'Choosing.' I wrote it for my son."

Deanna didn't say anything for a moment, then, "They left you, didn't they? Your family? No one ever visits you."

"Yeah," I said. "They did. I . . . I think maybe the image they had of me as old Johnny Rainbow was more comfortable for them."

"That's hard," she said. "Unfair."

"That's life, kiddo," I said. "Unfair."

She looked at me, her voice accusing, "That's not what you told us in all those songs."

"I know," I said. "I was a different man then. My world was a lot bigger."

"And now you're stuck here," Deanna said. "No wonder you don't talk much. You must be sad."

"Not really," I said. "You can grow used to anything."

She started cleaning the room again, and before she left, she stopped by my bed again. "Is there anything I can get you, Mr. Rainbow?" she asked.

I smiled at her. She was young, and in the time it had

taken her to finish the room, her sense of balance had been restored. I wouldn't take that from her with ravings about Mr. Gray. "No," I said. "I'll be fine."

"Well . . ."

"Go on," I said. "I'll see you tomorrow."

"Good night, then," she said.

"Good night, then," I repeated. She smiled gamely as she walked out the door, which closed softly behind her.

As I drifted off to sleep that night, I thought about Mr. Gray. Was he real or simply another phantom come to pass the time?

"It's time to wake up," Mr. Gray said. "We've got places to go and people to meet."

My eyeballs felt like sandpaper, and I blinked several times. Mr. Gray was still there. "I don't think you're real," I said.

He laughed. "Not many people do, Mr. Rainbow. Not many at all." He tilted his head slightly, then said, "But whether I'm real or not, I am *here*, yes?"

"Apparently," I admitted.

Mr. Gray stepped lightly to my side. "Here," he said, holding his arm near my right hand. "Touch me. For a man in your condition, I may be as real as it ever gets."

I hesitated. The idea of touching him somehow repelled me, though whether I feared his reality or lack thereof, I couldn't say. I reached out with my finger, gritted my teeth, and touched his arm. It felt solid enough.

"There," he said. "Now you know I am real."

"Dreams have a way of retaining their solidity—even bad ones—after we wake up."

"I'm not a dream, not in the traditional REM cycle sense anyway." He looked me over critically. "You've been trapped here for far too long, my friend. Do you want to go to the Half-Life Café? After all, a half-life is better than no life at all, and that's what you've got here. No life." He gestured at the room. "It's empty," he said. "Totally without substance."

"I have my mother's painting," I objected. "I have a lamp, a window."

He sneered. "You have *nothing*, Johnny Rainbow." He crossed the room and looked at the painting. "It's hardly a Manet," he said, "yet . . . there is something here I like." He was silent for several seconds. "That's it! The fence. It's a lovely touch."

"Why?" I demanded. The fence was the black part, the scary part.

"The fence is the only *real* part of the painting, Johnny Rainbow. The fence is the proverbial fly in the ointment, the scratch on the fender, the broken window of the house." He paused thoughtfully. "Did I know your mother?"

I laughed. "I doubt it. She died long ago."

When he didn't answer, I wondered if he was going to go away again. I stared at his face . . . it was suddenly without life or animation of any kind, his skin tone the pallid gray of the dead. Suddenly, a flush of color washed over his cheeks and he smiled. "That's right, she did. Brain cancer, wasn't it?"

"How . . . how did you know?" For the first time in years, I felt a sense of real fear grab my intestines and twist them in its cold grip. I hadn't been afraid of anything, not even death, for a long time.

"I knew her," he said. "She even spent an evening or two in the Café. We talked a great deal. She was quite funny, I thought. A lively sense of humor for one so betrayed by her body."

"That's impossible!" I blurted. "You're not old enough."

"Ahh . . ." Mr. Gray said. "Remember what I said told you. People see what they wish to see. To some I am as young as boy, to others as old as their great-great grandfathers."

"So what are you?" I asked.

"For you, Johnny Rainbow, I am Mr. Gray. And that is enough."

"You are my . . . my opposite, a doppleganger of my worst fears! A life without color at all!"

He strode across the room and laid his hand gently on my shoulder. "No," he said. "I'm not. I am a man who provides a very specific kind of service to those in your particular situation. I provide an escape hatch, a way out of the dark and gloomy, some might even say evil, world that life can become when an illness or an accident forces people into the prison of their own minds."

Mr. Gray gestured around the room again. "This is your prison, Johnny Rainbow. And it's one of your own devising. I'm simply offering you a way out. Your mother came to my little Café when she was dying. Many people do. *You* are dying, too, one slow centimeter at a time. You lay here, day after day, and you have convinced yourself that this is real. I say you are wrong. The Half-Life Café is far more real than this existence.

"Do *you* want to escape to our little Café?"

I didn't answer him right away. I closed my eyes and thought about my mother. I thought about her paintings—the one on my wall, which she had painted for me just before she went into the hospital the final time. The brush strokes weren't as sure as they once had been, the composition a little less certain, the mountain shadows cut by the palette knife a little off-balance. But her vision of that place had been as clear as her other paintings. I tried to remember the others she had painted. Were they, too, flawed in some small way? Had Mr. Gray already visited her when she painted that picture? Was the broken down old fence her representation of him . . . or herself? Did she really view her world as something beautiful, but ultimately broken? I didn't know, wouldn't ever know.

When my mother had gone into the hospital, she had seemed, if not happy, then accepting of her situation. When she went into a coma, it was as though she had gone to sleep. She was not in pain, at least that I could see. She was dreaming her way into the dark, into whatever comes next. I opened my eyes.

"When did you know her, Mr. Gray?"

"At the end, when she was in St. Mary's Hospital, in the coma."

"So, you couldn't have really known her, then," I said. "When someone's in a coma, they're not awake!" I pointed an accusatory finger at him. "You are nothing but a figment of my imagination."

"Everyone I visit is in a coma, Johnny Rainbow," Mr. Gray said. "Everyone."

His words began to sink in, and as I stared into his eyes they seemed to grow larger and larger, soon enough encompassing my entire view. He was saying that I was in a coma—that my entire world was—in my own mind. A creation to give light to the dark. I hitched my breath in to scream, but all that came out was a sodden whoosh of air. I felt myself sag into the mattress with the effort.

"Think about my offer," Mr. Gray said. "I'll be back tomorrow to hear your answer."

"What about my nurse, Deanna?" I said in a rush. "I talked with her today! She's real."

"Is she?" Mr. Gray said, slipping on a pair of velvet gloves. "Is she really?" He shook his head. "Until tomorrow, then, Johnny Rainbow."

With that, he was gone. There one moment, not there the next. And then I did scream. I screamed and screamed, my voice growing as ragged as the ends of an old sheet, but no one came to help me.

No one came at all.

I watched the window grow slowly lighter with the coming sunrise. Since my confinement to this room, I had paid little attention to the actual time, but marked the passing of days with the coming of sun or night on the glass or the bricks of the building next door. Sometimes, the moonlight would catch the bricks at a unique angle, turning them from red into silver. On those nights, I could imagine that the bricks were the walls of some fantastic castle, a place of glorious colors and sounds and sights. A place to escape. I dreamed of leaping out of bed, throwing open the window, and jumping out of my world and scaling the wall into this other place where I would be young and healthy and happy again.

In time, however, I convinced myself that such dreams were folly. The desperate imaginings of someone whose world has grown so small that *any* other place, even an alley, would seem magical by comparison.

And now there was Mr. Gray and the Half-Life Café. I hadn't slept since he left and my screams had gone unanswered. I watched the changing shadows on the glass and waited for Deanna to return. Perhaps my screams hadn't been as loud as I had thought. Perhaps they were able to monitor my physical status from the nurse's desk down the hall, and could see that I was all right, that my screams were simply those of a man suffering nightmares . . . and they were too busy to help. Deanna would know the answers to these questions.

I waited for her with the patience of a death-row inmate. I had nowhere else to go and nothing else to do. I avoided mental speculation about Mr. Gray—such exercises would be the same folly as my long-discarded dreams.

Deanna arrived, announcing her presence with a faint tapping on the door before coming into my room. Once again I was struck by her youth and energy. "Good morning, Deanna," I said as she neared my bedside.

She didn't answer me, but set about the process of changing my sheets. "Deanna," I said, louder this time. "How are you this morning?"

Deanna grabbed my legs and shifted them to one side, pulling the sheet out from underneath my legs with a firm tug. She was whistling softly under her breath. Had the woman gone deaf overnight? "Deanna!" I screamed, determined to make her hear me.

Finally, she paused, her eyes meeting mine. "Mr. Rainbow," she said softly, "I sure am sorry you can't talk to me. I just loved your music when I was little." Then she went back to making the bed and cleaning the room, whistling tunelessly under her breath.

I wanted to scream again, her name, a word, anything to prove that our conversation from the day before had happened, that I hadn't imagined it, yet I was helpless to do so. Despite my desire to prove that Mr. Gray was wrong, that I *had* spoken to her, I was without breath. My voice was gone as though it had never existed. Deanna finished the room and left.

If Mr. Gray was right, if I was in a coma, somehow I was still able to observe what was going on around me. I could see and hear and even . . . no, I couldn't taste. I realized then that I hadn't tasted anything in years. I hadn't eaten anything. Deanna had never brought me a meal. No one had. Several minutes after she left, someone tapped lightly on the door. I pushed the button to open it, and Deanna walked back into the room.

"Johnny Rainbow," she said. "How are you this morning?"

Stunned, I didn't answer her for a moment. "Uh . . . fine," I lied. "Just fine."

"That's good," she said. She bustled about cleaning the room that she had just cleaned a few moments before.

"Deanna," I said. "Weren't you just in here?"

She stopped emptying the wastebasket and looked at me. "No," she said. "I wasn't. Was someone else in your room?"

"You were," I said. "Just a minute ago."

Deanna laughed. "Sure you weren't dreaming?" she asked in a teasing voice. "Maybe you imagined me."

"I did *not*," I said, my voice rising along with my temper. "You were right here! Look at the sheets if you don't believe me!"

For a long moment, she didn't say anything. Then she sighed, and crossed the room to stand next to my bed. "I'm sorry, Johnny," she said. "I wasn't trying to upset you."

"What are you talking about?" I demanded.

Deanna removed her nurse's cap, and shook out her

hair. Then she removed a tissue from the pocket of her sweater and slowly began wiping it over her face, blurring her makeup. When she lowered her hand, I felt the muscles in my body stiffen, then sag. It was my mother.

"You . . ." I tried to say. "Mom . . . you're dead!"

"I know, Johnny," she said. "Even this—" she gestured with the tissue "—is unnecessary. It's a bit of hoodoo. A way to make the transition easier."

"I . . . I don't understand."

"Johnny, you're in a coma. You've been in a coma for a long time. In that state, the land of the dead—where I am—and the land of the living intermingle. That's why you aren't sure if what you've been seeing all this time has been real or imaginary."

"But . . . Mom, you're dead," I repeated. She'd always had a way of making me feel just a little bit slow.

She smiled. "It's difficult to explain," she said. "Think of being in a coma as a half-life. You are aware of what is happening around you in the real world, but you cannot react to it, and it cannot react to you in any significant way. You are also able to perceive the realm of the dead—but we *can* react to you, and you to us."

I nodded slowly. In a way, it made a horrible kind of sense. "But some people come out of a coma. They return to life."

"Yes," she said, her voice sad. "They do. But they're never really the same—and even they don't know why."

"So you really do know Mr. Gray," I said.

She nodded. "Yes, I do. That's why I'm here, actually. You should take him up on his offer, Johnny. There isn't much time left."

I didn't respond to this right away, but contented myself with looking at her. I hadn't seen her face in many years. Her eyes, a blue that sparked like water, and her hair, blond and brown waves, were as I remembered. I wanted to ask her about death, about the painting and the broken fence. About Mr. Gray. Instead, I said, "Not much time?"

"No, Johnny," she said. "The Half-Life Café is for those truly on the cusp of making the final decision about their situation. Leave the world of the living or leave the world of the dead. No one can exist forever, trapped between the two places like you are. You'll have to make a choice."

"But what does Mr. Gray have to do with it?" I said, then a thought hit me. "You mean you chose to die? To leave us?"

"Yes," she said. "I did. I was sick, Johnny. I didn't want to keep living the way I had been. My mind and my body were failing me." She gestured at my prized picture on the wall, her voice disgusted. "You saw my last painting."

"It's . . . I think it's beautiful," I said. "Sometimes it's all that I think about."

"There's a lesson there," she said. "If you think about it."

"I don't understand!" I said.

"You don't have to, my son," she said. "But go to the Half-Life Café with Mr. Gray. Make the decision you must." My mother placed her hand on my arm. "I have to go now. I've been here too long as it is."

"Go? Where?" I said. "How long have you been visiting me?"

She smiled. "Oh, I've been around." She looked at me seriously for a moment. "Johnny, no matter what you decide, I'll see you on the other side."

Desperate for information, to keep her with me a moment longer, I said, "Mom! Wait!"

"What is it?" she asked.

"Was it . . . is it horrible?" I asked, afraid to hear her answer.

She shook her head. "No," she said. "It's . . ." her voice trailed off and I was afraid she wouldn't answer.

"What?" I prompted.

"It's like being born," she said. "Into a world where there is no pain, and you spend every day in a warm, comfortable bath." She glanced around at my room, which seemed much smaller in her presence. "It's certainly no worse than this," she said. "Take care, Johnny."

She was fading right before my eyes. "You, too, Mom," I whispered. She raised a hand in farewell and she was gone.

If I could have cried, I would. But I knew then that all my emotions, my physical action, my conversations, my entire world, was an illusion created to pass the time . . . or the subtle tread of ghosts keeping me company during my long trek between worlds.

Mr. Gray would be back tonight, I told myself. And I would go with him.

Through a doorway that hadn't been there before, and down a hallway that no one living knew existed, I followed Mr. Gray. He had returned to my room late at night, his clothing and manner the same as it had been on the previous nights. Except this night, he *knew* what my answer would be. He simply held out his hand, and I took it.

With a tug, I found myself on my feet. Standing! My legs felt strong and capable. "It's one of the perks,

Johnny," Mr. Gray said. "No body, no physical problems."

"For every perk, there's a downside," I said. My voice was stronger, too. It felt like, if I wanted, I could sing again.

"Perhaps," he said. He pulled his pocket watch from his vest, opened the lid with a faint click, and glanced at the time. "We have to go," he said. "The Café opens at midnight."

"What time is it?" I asked, realizing that I hadn't really known the time in quite a while.

"Almost twelve," he said. He gestured at the blank wall near my mother's painting, and a faint, shimmering rectangle appeared. "That's the way we go," he said. He stepped quickly to the wall, and pushed on it. The wall vanished, and behind it was the hallway. I followed him in.

As we walked, Mr. Gray said very little, except to urge me to hurry.

Exasperated, I said, "I haven't walked in almost five years. Do you mind if we *stroll* a little bit? I'd like to enjoy the experience."

"Johnny Rainbow," Mr. Gray said, "the Half-Life Café is only open for one hour per day. From midnight until one. Walking may be a novelty for you at this point in your existence, but let me assure you that you will want every precious second of your time at the Café. Please, now, hurry!"

He spun and set off once again at a brisk walk. This time, I kept the pace. An hour didn't seem like much to me. In another few minutes, we arrived at yet another door.

This one appeared much more traditional—heavy

oak, with iron bands wrapping around it. Mr. Gray removed a key from his pocket and inserted it into the lock.
He turned it briskly and the door unlocked. "Well, Johnny
Rainbow, here it is. The entrance to the Half-Life Café.
And this is where I leave you. Go on in. I shall return
here, to this door, when the Café closes, to escort you
back to your room."

"You're not coming with me?" I asked.

He laughed. "Oh, no," he said. "I have other matters to
attend to while you visit. Go on, then," he urged. Mr.
Gray turned the handle on the door and opened it a crack.
"Enjoy," he said.

I stepped forward and grasped the handle, wondering
what I would find on the other side. I paused to thank
him, but when I turned back, he was gone. Thankfully,
the door remained.

Taking a deep breath, I pushed it open and stepped inside.

A long time ago, back when I was still Johnny Rainbow, when the only people who still thought of me as
John Townsend were family and close friends, I had
plenty of money. Money, which is really no more than
some various shades of green ink on paper, has its ad-
vantages—one of them being access to the best restaurants. While I could hardly have been construed as a
glutton, I did enjoy dining out often. My favorite place to
eat was a very elegant restaurant called Roosevelt's.

Roosevelt's was in a converted library building; it had
three separate dining rooms, two on the upper floor and
one on the lower level. The décor was muted pastels and
dark wood, the chairs comfortable enough to sit in for
two or three hours of talking and eating. Each table was

covered in a white cloth, and the settings were sparse, consisting only of the silverware needed for the first course of the meal. After each course, the server would replace all of the cutlery on the table. In the center of each table was a small vase, with a fresh cut flower of some type. On some evenings it would be a daisy, on some a orchid, on still others a mum. It varied, depending on the whim of the owner.

But what made Roosevelt's one of my particular favorites was not the food, which was excellent, or the service, which was superior. It was the lounge. Fully one-half of the upper floor was given over to the lounge area. The same muted colors predominated, but only small cocktail and coffee tables with plush sofas and over-stuffed wing chairs were available for seating. The bar itself was a heavy oak, polished to a high gleam. Fine wines, liquors, and cigars were on display behind the bar, and should one desire a cappuccino or other espresso-based drink, the bartender also served as a barista. I made it a point to stop in the lounge both before and after a meal at Roosevelt's. For some strange reason, it felt like coming home.

When I opened the door to the Half-Life Café, what I saw was the lounge at Roosevelt's. I stood there, my mouth hanging open, for a full minute. Everything was as I remembered it, down to the tea candles on the cocktail tables. Seated on the sofas and chairs were a wide variety of people, talking, laughing, some sitting silent and lost in thought. From behind the bar, a man dressed in all white and who looked like Mr. Gray's twin, said, "Good evening, sir. Would you mind shutting the door behind you? We wouldn't want any . . . uninvited guests from the hallway."

Not certain what he meant, I shut the door. I walked across the room. "You look like—"

"Mr. Gray?" he said. "You wouldn't believe how often I hear that." He laughed. "It's to be expected, I suppose." He held out his hand. "I'm Mr. White," he said as we shook. "And you are Johnny Rainbow."

"Mr. White," I said. "I should have expected that. How did you know my name?"

"It comes with the job," he said. "I know everyone who comes in to the Café. Can I get you something?"

I thought about it for a minute. It had been a long time. "Frangelico," I decided. "Straight up in a snifter, with a cup of black coffee."

Mr. White quickly made the beverages and handed them across the bar. "There's an open space," he said, pointing to a chair. "You should go sit down. Plenty of people to talk to, though they come and go regularly."

I nodded, remembering that Mr. Gray had said I would only have an hour. Less than that now. I carried my drinks and set them down on a small end table next to the open chair. To my left was a floral-patterned sofa with an earnest looking young man and an older woman, on my right and continuing in a semicircle were more chairs like mine. Seated closest to me was a bald woman, perhaps in her mid-thirties. She smiled at me, and it lit up her face like a beacon. Even without hair, she was quite beautiful.

"Good evening," I said.

"Hello," she said. "You're Johnny Rainbow, aren't you?"

"Yes, I am. How'd you know?"

"I listened to your music a lot when I was a kid. What happened to you?"

I shrugged. "Some kind of genetic wasting illness, a

bit like MS, but with more devastating effects in the long term." I shook my head. "Not that it matters really. Mr. Gray told me that everyone who comes here is in the same basic predicament. We're all in a coma, trapped within the world of our own mind."

"That about sums it up. Me, I got here by route of a wicked car accident and brain surgery." She grinned ruefully, pointing at her bald skull. "Honestly, I don't consider myself a vain person, but I would have liked to keep my hair." Her smile was infectious. "My name's Jess," she said.

"John," I replied. "I left Johnny and Rainbow behind a long time ago."

She stared at me thoughtfully. "How come?" she asked.

"I'm not that man anymore," I said. "How could I be?"

"I'm not sure," she said. "How'd you get to be Johnny Rainbow in the first place?"

"That's a pretty astute question," I said, remembering. "I guess because I fell in love and saw colors."

"How do you mean?" she asked.

I took a sip of the Frangelico, savoring its sweet, nutty flavor on my tongue before swallowing it down. I followed it with a sip of coffee—it was a French Roast, dark and slightly bitter—and perfect. "When I was young, I was terribly arrogant, and I thought the world was my toy box. I knew I could sing, could write good songs, but my career was going nowhere. I regularly blamed everyone but myself. I was, as my wife said, an unmitigated ass." I smiled at the memory. "She changed all that."

"How?" Jess asked.

"Well, one night we were out on this stretch of beach,

drinking and talking. I got a bit melancholy, and I pointed up at the sky and told her my whole world was like that: infinite possibilities, all of them unreachable, everything in black and white." I closed my eyes, the vision of those moments clear and pristine. "Anyway," I continued, "when I turned to her for her response, she slapped me. Damn hard, in fact. And she told me that I didn't know anything if I thought the universe was black and white, holding out impossibilities with evil intent."

"I was so surprised that I just sort of stood there, staring at her. 'If the universe were out to get you, Johnny, you'd be dead,' she said. Then she pointed at the sky and said, 'It's only black and white because you don't see it clearly. The world is what you bring to it, what you make of it—unless you allow it to make something of you.'" I chuckled softly. "Then she slapped me again, and said, 'And that's for being so talented and not being able to see that the world is a rainbow.'"

Jess laughed. "She must have had quite a spirit."

"She did, once. Then I got sick and she left me."

"Illness does strange things to people," Jess said. "My mother has been to my room in the hospital every day since the accident—and she prays for my death when no one can hear her but me. I took it badly at first, but then I realized that she only wanted to release me from the pain she thought I was in. She didn't know I was still alive, inside my own mind."

"My wife didn't want to watch me get sick, didn't want to expose the kids to that."

Jess laid a hand on my arm. "She was protecting her, and your kids', image of you."

I nodded. "You're probably right, but that doesn't mean it feels good."

"What was that about falling in love and seeing colors?" she said.

"When I realized that she was telling the truth, it was like . . . someone had taken blinders off my eyes. Suddenly all the possibilities of the world were right in front of me. I stopped trying to write music for disenchanted adults and started writing for kids. The world was a rainbow."

"And now?" she asked.

"I don't know," I said. "Maybe when you're trapped like we are, the only rainbows are on the other side."

"Maybe," she said. "Or maybe they're just a bit harder to come by. It's tough to find the proverbial pot of gold when you're trapped in a world the size of a human skull."

I sipped more of my Frangelico, followed it with the coffee. "So what are you going to do?" I asked her.

"I don't know yet," she said. "You?"

I shook my head. "Not a clue, but I'm afraid."

"Afraid of what?"

"Afraid of what comes next. Afraid that if I choose to die, that about ten seconds after that, they'll come up with a cure—something that would give me my old world back. I . . . miss it."

"I understand," she said. She stood to leave. "I hope you figure it out, Johnny Rainbow."

"Me, too," I said. "Thanks for the talk."

She smiled. "You're not at all what I would have expected."

"Who is?" I asked.

"Maybe that's the key," she said. "Expectations."

"What do you mean?"

"I mean that maybe we always get what we expect. If

you expect rainbows, maybe that's what you get—a self-fulfilling prophecy. If you expect your world to be a prison, dark and unrelenting, then maybe that's what we get, too."

"Maybe," I said. "But it's tough to know for sure. How many people in a coma have you talked to lately?"

"Other than you, and a few others here, not too many," she admitted. "But I remember a story about this soldier . . . he was captured and held as a prisoner in this little tiny bamboo cell. For seven or eight years. They tortured him, wrecked his body, starved him, beat him—and when he was rescued, he was perfectly happy."

"Why?" I asked, incredulous. "That must have been . . . hell."

"He made his world, his mental world, a paradise—or so he said." She shrugged. "It's food for thought, isn't it?"

I nodded. "Yes, it is. Fare well, Jess."

"You, too, Johnny Rainbow," she said.

I watched her go to the door and step quietly out. She was awfully wise for such a young woman, and she reminded me quite a bit of my wife, and even my mother. I sipped my beverages and listened to the ebb and flow of the conversations around me, thinking. I wasn't in any particular mood to talk to anyone—I'd grown out of the habit—but I found it interesting to listen.

Many of the conversations were conducted in hurried, almost panicked whispers. A lot of the speakers were leaning forward, intent on finding a solution, desperate to find a way out of a world that had grown intolerably small. They came from all ages, backgrounds, and religious creeds. Mr. Gray was apparently an equal opportunity haunter of the world between life and death. When it neared closing time, Mr. White said, "Last call, folks!" The intensity of the conversations picked up.

Some of these people, I realized, would be back here tomorrow night, and the night after—maybe for many, many nights in a row, wanting an answer to their dilemma and afraid to find it. I stood and took my empty snifter and coffee mug back to the bar. "Thanks for the drink," I said to Mr. White.

"Heading out, are you?" he asked.

I nodded. "It's time."

"Good luck to you, Johnny Rainbow," Mr. White said. He pointed at the door. "Mr. Gray will see to it that you get back where you belong. He always does."

I thought about it for a minute, then asked, "Is there a Mr. Black, too?"

Mr. White smiled. "Your mother asked that same question."

"I imagine so," I said. "It's the kind of question she would ask. So, what's the answer?"

"You already know the answer, Johnny Rainbow," Mr. White said. "And if you don't, it will come to you."

I laughed, and headed out of the Café. On the other side of the door, Mr. Gray was waiting for me. "Learn anything interesting?" he asked.

"Yes," I said. "Quite a bit."

We didn't speak as we walked down the silent hallway and back to the shimmering rectangle of light that marked the entry to my world. He pushed the door open and I followed him. The room looked smaller now, more dingy and empty than when I'd left. The sound of voices, the clink of glasses as people talked and drank, the light flowing off different pieces of furniture . . . the music of life was missing.

Mr. Gray escorted me back to my bed. My body was still there, and for the first time I realized that I must be in some sort of spiritual form, rather than the physical. As though he could read my thoughts, Mr. Gray said, "It's better not to think about it too much." Then he gave me a shove and before I could catch myself, I fell back into my body.

There was a blurring sensation, then I was looking into at Mr. Gray through the lenses of my own eyes once again. I was back in my world—a prison without bars, but a prison nonetheless. What had happened to me, I knew, wasn't evil in the traditional sense, but evil in that I had allowed it to continue. There were other avenues open to me.

"All set, Johnny Rainbow?" Mr. Gray asked.

"Yes," I said. "I am."

He smiled. "Good. Shall I pop back in tomorrow night and take you back to the Café?"

"No," I said. "There won't be a need."

"So, you've arrived at your decision."

"Yes, I have."

"And?" he prompted.

"And you'll have to wait and see," I said. "Good night, Mr. Gray. You have my thanks."

He grinned, and I was once again forcibly reminded of a dinosaur. "You're welcome."

"May I ask you a question?" I said.

"Certainly," he said. "We have a few moments left."

"How old are you?"

His head tilted slightly to one side as he considered this. "Hmmm . . . you know, your—"

"Mother asked that same question," I interrupted. "Yes, it's going around. So what's the answer?"

"As Mr. White told you, Johnny Rainbow, you already know the answer, and if you don't, it will come to you." He nodded once, and left the room, the shimmering rectangle in my wall disappearing behind him. "See you around, Mr. Gray," I whispered, then I drifted into what passed for sleep in my world, my eyes on the broken fence in the oil landscape painted by my mother.

Sunlight crept across the glass of my window, the bricks on the building next door slowly changing from the creviced black of nights shadow to a deep shade of red. I watched and waited, enjoying the slow progression of the morning. I looked at the lamp, the painting, and knew that my world was about to change.

When the nurse, Deanna came into my room, whistling the same aimless song from the morning before, I felt a little bad. Her world was about to change, too. When she moved to my bedside to change the linens, I spoke—really spoke—for the first time in many years. "You called me Johnny Rainbow," I whispered. My voice was hoarse and weak, with a reedy quality that was not a pleasant sound.

Deanna screamed and dropped the sheet, her eyes wide and staring. She looked torn between running for her life and pressing the buzzer near the head of my bed that would call a battalion of nurses and doctors into my room. Her breath came in short, sharp gasps, and faint purple splotches colored her cheeks. For a moment, I feared she would pass out.

"It's all right," I whispered. "There's no need to panic."

"You . . . you . . . you're alive, I mean, awake," she stammered.

"For a moment," I said. "I have to tell you something."

"Wha . . . what?"

"I prefer to be addressed as Mr. Rainbow," I said. Then I let go. I drifted free of my body, and watched as the monitors that recorded my heart and breathing rates went flat, a sharp beep sounding in my room and down the hall in the nurses' station.

The pounding of running feet followed a moment later and several nurses and a doctor burst into the room. Deanna remained motionless, staring down at my lifeless body.

"What happened?" the doctor asked.

"I . . . he, he said he wanted to be called Mr. Rainbow," she said. "That I called him Johnny."

"What do you mean 'he said'?" the doctor asked. "What are you talking about?"

"He . . . he spoke," Deanna said. "He talked to me, then he just, just died."

"Doctor, should I begin CPR?" a nurse asked.

He shook his head. "No, he's got a DNR on file." Then he turned back to Deanna. "This man has been in a coma for years," he said. "And you think he actually spoke to you?"

Deanna nodded helplessly. "He did," she said. "He knew what I said yesterday."

"Ridiculous," the doctor said. "Patients in a coma can't hear a thing, can't feel a thing. They just . . . lay there until their body gives out or they come out of it. It's a world of darkness."

"You're wrong," Deanna said, sobbing now. "You're totally wrong." Then she fled from the room.

I felt bad for scaring her, but no doubt she'd quickly regain control of herself. It's the nature of human beings to find ways to balance what appears to be good and what appears to be evil. I looked down at my spirit form, which seemed substantial enough to me, and waved my hand. Once again, I was clothed in a rainbow-colored, three-piece suit—as I had been those many years ago when I was young and healthy and singing to children about all the possibilities of the world.

I turned around, and the shimmering rectangle doorway was once again visible. It opened at my touch, and I stepped into the world between life and death, to help the other Mr.'s—men and women, I was sure, who bore the name of every color imaginable—in the only way I could.

There weren't only adults existing in this world between worlds. There were children, too. And they could no doubt use a little more color, all the colors at my disposal, to bring light to the world they were trapped in. I smiled to myself and checked my pocket watch. On the other side of the world, it was night. Somewhere it was always between midnight and one, and the Café, I knew, was always open.

I walked down the hallway, free and feeling more joy than I had in many years.

Johnny Rainbow was back, and he was going on tour.

POSTCARDS

Rebecca Moesta

Rebecca Moesta is the author of 28 books, including the award-winning Star Wars: Young Jedi Knights series and two original Titan A.E. novels, which she coauthored with husband Kevin J. Anderson. Her most recent novel is Buffy the Vampire Slayer: Little Things. *In comics, she has worked with Anderson on the hardcover Star Trek: The Next Generation graphic novel* The Gorn Crisis *from Wildstorm and the four-issue humorous miniseries* Grumpy Old Monsters *from IDW. She is the daughter of an English teacher/author/Bible scholar, and a nurse—from whom she learned, respectively, her love of words and her love of books. She holds an MSBA from Boston University, has taught every grade level from kindergarten through junior college, and worked for seven years as a publications specialist and technical editor at Lawrence Livermore National laboratory. Her cur-*

rent project is the Young Adult series Crystal Doors, coauthored with her husband.

Memorizing her new zip code had been the easiest part of Allie's move. After all, how hard could it be to remember five digits when three of them were sevens? The hardest part had been leaving her friends—and what seemed like her entire life—behind.

Sitting on a pile of moving boxes in the echoing, otherwise-empty living room of their new house, Allie wondered morosely whether yanking a fifteen-year-old out of school three-quarters of the way through her sophomore year could not be considered child abuse.

Raking a hand through her shoulder-length blond hair, she thought back to the night her life had changed. Allie had just returned from her fourth date with Ian Walters—*Ian Walters*, a senior and a forward on the Jackson Eagles basketball team—when her parents met her with the "wonderful news." Her father, after only five months of unemployment, had taken a new job as head of Human Resources for a regional telecommunications firm halfway across the country. He said it was a "great opportunity."

Allie knew she should have been happy for her parents. The relief was so plain on their faces. But it was obvious they hadn't stopped for a moment to think about how this would affect *her*. Just that evening, Ian had asked Allie to the prom. In a little over a month, she should have been dressing like a fairy tale princess and then dancing all evening with one of the cutest guys in the whole school. But she would miss out on that now. Barely three weeks after her father's announcement, the family had moved—leaving behind the only world Allie had ever known.

Now, Allie's black Labrador retriever, Merlin, chuffed, gave his tail a tentative wag, trotted to the front door, and looked back at her. Allie heaved a sigh. "C'mon, boy. We could both use a walk. I need to mail my letter to Roshanda anyway." For the moment, letters were her only means of communication. Some sort of delay had come up in activating the telephone wiring, and now the idiot phone company said it could be another *three weeks* before their phone or internet service was connected. Her parents both had cell phones, but they didn't seem to think that Allie might need one, too.

From the moving carton next to her Allie picked up a yellow envelope containing a letter to her best friend, in which she had detailed the miseries of her new life in West Nowheresville, USA. Okay, sure, her parents were delighted. It was easy for them. Their financial worries were over, and they had found a beautiful new house. Her mom was already out applying for a job and meeting the neighbors. But on Monday Allie would be forced to start in the middle of the semester at a school she had never heard of before. Who knew what classes they would try to shoehorn her into? She would be the new girl, without a friend in the entire state.

"Not a friend here but you, boy," she said, clipping the leash to Merlin's collar.

At the end of the long, curving driveway, they paused at the rural-style mailbox, which was empty, of course, since she and her parents were the first residents at this address, and nothing from their old house had been forwarded yet. Allie put the envelope in and raised the little red flag on the side of the enameled aluminum box to indicate a letter for pickup.

Abandoning herself to the dog's whims, Allie let Merlin take the lead and enjoy his explorations for a couple of miles. She paid just enough attention to their route to be sure she could find her way back to the house. The black lab romped and sniffed and peed and chased, finding wonder and delight in his new surroundings.

Allie wished she could share the feeling, but for her, life felt bleak and hopeless and lonely. The only wonder in her world was wondering why this had had to happen to her. In spite of these gloomy thoughts, a smile quirked one corner of her mouth when, after an hour and a half of rambling, they returned to the house and she noticed the flag on the mailbox was down. Good, that meant her letter was mailed, and the sooner Roshanda got it, the sooner her friend could reply. Even though she knew it was foolish, she decided to peek into the mailbox in case a letter or some piece of junk mail had found its way here already. As she had expected, the interior of the arched metal box looked empty.

But just as she was about to close the door, Allie saw a glint of something lying on the corrugated aluminum bottom of the mailbox. A sheet of cellophane perhaps? No, it sparkled too much.

Merlin wagged his tail wildly and barked twice, as if impatient to know what she was looking at. Allie put in her hand and drew out the shiny scrap of material. She laid it across her palm to study it. It was a pliable, crystalline sheet about the size and shape of a standard postcard, but that was where the similarity ended. The card itself was as clear as spring water and etched with strange symbols that did not look like any form of writing Allie had ever seen. They looked like those laser carvings of sailboats or eagles or lighthouses in blocks of Lucite that she had seen in the airport gift store.

The etched symbols seemed to float deep inside the rectangle, which was strange since the clear material was thinner than a piece of notebook paper. In fact, the more Allie looked at it, the more three-dimensional the symbols seemed to appear. The markings—hieroglyphics, perhaps?—started to swirl before her eyes, forming and unforming words that she did not recognize but felt she ought to know. As if responding to an optical illusion, her field of vision deepened, and ripples moved across the card's surface, like tiny waves on a crystal-clear mountain lake.

With one finger she reached out to touch the swirling symbols and suddenly found herself facing a life-sized, shimmering image of a girl no older than she with knee-length raven locks and a tear-streaked face. A window behind the girl framed a many-turreted stone castle standing on the shores of a sparkling blue-green lake. Allie gasped and blinked several times. The image didn't disappear, yet she could see right through it to her house and the mailbox and Merlin. It was as if she was looking at the largest, most vividly colored hologram ever created.

Allie groaned. "I've finally lost it, haven't I, Merlin? It—"

But before she could finish her sentence, the ethereal girl sat down at a desk by the window. A diminutive, kindly looking old man with a shock of fluffy gray hair handed her a long white feather, and she began writing with the quill on a scrolled sheet of brown paper. The girl spoke aloud as she wrote, and Allie found that although the language was strange, she could understand every word.

Dearest Quillfriend,

My trusted confidante Mythwell the Enchanter has encouraged me to write to you, stranger though you may be, in the hope that by sharing my woes, the burdens of my heart may be somewhat eased. Since I have no companions here of a like age, Mythwell has agreed to use his magicks to ensure that my words fall on friendly ears.

Allie realized she had stopped breathing and forced herself to take slow, quiet breaths. She didn't want to miss a word.

My situation now is more grave than thus far it has ever been in my life. Yes, graver even than on the day when the dragon Grovich flew away with me to his lair and held me captive until seven of my father's bravest knights came to rescue me.

Please, dearest friend, write to me and tell me whether you would hear of my plight. If you are disposed to do me this honor, please affix my rune crystal to your letter, and Mythwell's spell will bring it to me. I await your reply and crave any word of comfort you might impart.

Your Quillfriend (if you are willing),
Princess Avienne of Mereglade

With that, the transparent image faded to a blur of rainbow scintillation and then disappeared. Allie tried to reactivate the sparkling rectangle—the rune crystal?—by gazing into it again, smoothing it between her hands, turning it over, pressing it, folding it, and even shaking it, but the sad-eyed girl did not reappear. Next, Allie spent a full five minutes attempting to convince herself that the image had been some sort of elaborate, high-tech hoax, but she found that this idea was almost as difficult to believe as receiving a magical letter from a fantasy princess. And much less enjoyable.

Merlin barked once, sniffed the air where the glittering princess had seemed to stand, circled the mailbox wagging his tail, then repeated his actions.

"So you believe she was real, huh, boy? Well, who am I to argue with the great Merlin?" With a shrug, Allie decided to accept the impossible. For now. She *wanted* to believe it. She was so lonely here, what would it hurt to play along for a while? In any case, it would be at least a week before she could expect a reply from Roshanda.

After dinner with her parents, Allie wrote a note, knowing full well that mailing it probably wouldn't work. While she was writing, her mother looked in on her.

"What are you working on, dear?"

"Writing a letter to a princess."

Instead of giving her a strange look, her mom beamed. "That's wonderful. I always hoped you'd get back to writing stories again, like you used to in middle school. Can I read it?"

"Uh . . . it's not ready yet," Allie said. "Maybe in a few days, when it's farther along. Anyway, I'm having fun just thinking about it." To her surprise, Allie found that it was true. Perhaps the note would turn out to be a silly waste of time, but it amused her. If no one wrote back, maybe she *should* turn it into a story. "Dear Princess Avienne," she wrote.

> I don't know if you'll get this letter, but I had to try. I would love to be your Quillfriend. I think I

would be able to understand your problems, since you look like you're about my age.

I'm fifteen, and my life is a mess. My parents don't even consider my feelings when they make decisions, and I have no idea what my future will be. Feel free to tell me your problems, and I'll tell you mine. I could really use someone to talk to right now. Please write soon.

Your Quillfriend,

Allie

P.S. I'm enclosing a school picture of me, so you can see what I look like.

Allie tucked the note and picture into a pink envelope, taped the rune crystal to the front, and wrote her entire return address in the upper left corner, including the zip code, just to avoid any confusion. She left the upper right corner blank. Although it was already dark out, she didn't want to wait for morning, so she turned on the outdoor lights and walked down to the end of the driveway. Leashless, Merlin trailed after her. She put the pink envelope into the still-pristine mailbox, closed the door and raised the flag.

"Okay, boy. We did it." Allie gave Merlin a pat and headed back up the drive with him. The black lab replied with a conversational woof. A moment later, he turned, bounded back down to the mailbox, and paced back and forth barking with excitement. Allie sighed. She knew she should have used the leash. "C'mon, Merlin. Time to go in." The dog shook himself all over, as if he had just emerged from a bath, gave an insistent bark, and reached up to put his front paws on the mailbox.

Allie knew when she was defeated. "Fine, boy. I'll

show you what's in there, but it's just a letter, not a box of Milk-Bone treats." As if he understood, the lab sat and waited for her. When she reached his side, Allie looped an index finger under his collar and with the other hand opened the box again. "There. You satisfied? Nothing but a—" She stopped, her mouth still open. The little red flag was down, and the mailbox before her was empty.

The next morning, after a night during which excitement robbed her of a good many hours of sleep, Allie took Merlin for a walk and found a new rune crystal in the mailbox. And thus began a wonderful quill-friendship.

My Dearest Princess Allie,

Thank you for your kindness in sending such a delightful and heartfelt response. I received your reply scant hours after I sent my letter to you.

We are indeed very much alike. As you surmised, we are of an age, and my situation, too, is grave. My life, like yours, is "a mess."

My mother the queen died last year at the hands of an assassin. On the eve of the winter solstice my father the king remarried. My stepmother wishes me to marry her cousin Warlord Morwolf in order to expand her family's holdings. In return, Lord Morwolf has agreed to ally with us in times of war.

My parents, like yours, did not consult me in this matter. Alas, my father agreed to the match! I cannot love Lord Morwolf. He is a cruel, brutish man, rude of manner, and thrice our age, dearest Allie. And he has but seven of his own teeth!

When I asked my father to reconsider the match,

he told me that it is my duty to take a husband who will make our kingdom more powerful. Because my father wages war each spring, this alliance is much to be desired. Should I refuse, I will be sent into exile. Marriage, too, would be a form of exile. Since my two older sisters wed lords from the mountain reaches, I hear from them but once a year.

My heart is heavy, my future bleak. Have you any words of comfort to offer, dearest friend?

Your Quillfriend,
Avienne

P.S. I am all in wonderment at the beauty and intricacy of your portrait painting. How can I ever express sufficient gratitude for such a precious gift?

Dear Princess Avienne,

First off, I'm not actually a princess. I'm just sort of a normal teenage girl. I like music, mostly boy bands or divas. What kind of music do you like? Do you play an instrument? I tried playing clarinet for two years, but I was never very good at it. For fun I go to the movies, hang out with my friends, or maybe go dancing. At least I used to. I don't have any friends here yet. What do you do for fun?

Now for the serious stuff. Wow. Exile? My parents would never be able to do that. They always wanted more kids, but my mom couldn't have another one, so I know they couldn't stand to give me up.

Your country looks so pretty in your letters. Are you positive your father won't let you stay? I'm sure the king loves you more than he shows. Try talking to him. Anyway, no one here would ever make a girl our age marry *anyone*, much less such an awful-sounding man as Lord Morwolf. That sounds so medieval! They do make us go to school, though, and learn things like math and history (yuck) and science. Then we have to choose what to do with the rest of our lives. That can be pretty scary.

I hope things work out with your father.

> Your friend,
> Allie

My dearest Allie,

Your kind words gave me fresh hope. I must tell you that at first my father was firm in his resolve: I must marry Lord Morwolf, bear his children, and run his castle at Fleamarsh, or be cast out of my father's lands forever. When I made my appeal to him, however, his heart softened, and he relented. I now have a third choice: If I do not marry the warlord, I may enter a convent, never to leave its walls again, and take a vow of silence.

I cannot express how grateful I am to you for aiding me thus with my dilemma. Yet if I make this choice, my faithful Mythwell may not accompany me.

Perhaps you dread your choices at school even as I dread my choice between a loveless marriage, exile, and the convent. If so, my heart aches for you. Thank you for being my comfort in my time of need.

> Your devoted friend,
> Avienne

P.S. I adore music, and have been known to

swoon when listening to a minstrel sing tragic ballads. Though I blush to admit to my skill, I am an accomplished lute player and harpist. Like you, I love to dance, but my greatest joy (or fun, as you call it) is going for long walks with Mythwell, who secretly teaches me about plants and medicine and the stars, instead of the silly needlework and simpering manners I study at court.

Dear Princess Avienne,

Boy, am I beat! This morning Dad got me up *before nine* and dragged me off to go shopping with Mom at the dismal little mall that is the closest thing to civilization within a half-hour's drive of where we live. I had to choose some new clothes for school, but most of the shops only carried styles I wouldn't be caught dead in. Only three stores had any clothes worth being seen wearing. I did find one cute dress, a pair of strappy spring sandals, and three tops. Oh, and a pair of tight jeans that make my legs look really long. But that was *all* I could find. I mean, I really tried, but there wasn't much to work with.

I'm sure that you never have any problem finding the right clothes. I wish I were a princess. You probably just snap your fingers and the royal tailor makes whatever you want. I know you're not happy about that warlord everyone wants you to marry, but in a lot of ways, you're really lucky. Most of the time you can just take it easy and get anything you need.

After shopping, Dad took Mom and me to Starbucks for scones and a latte, but I'm exhausted. I don't know how they expect me to walk the dog, take out the trash, and unstack the dishwasher after all that shopping. I doubt anyone would ever ask a princess to do all that! If only I could go live with you.

I think I'll take a nap now before my Dad comes up with even more chores for me to do. Write soon.

Your good friend,

Allie

P.S. I'm sorry to hear about the convent thing. What an awful choice! You'd have to give up both your family and your friends. Maybe it's better than marrying that Morwolf guy, but if I were you, I'd choose exile. I mean, at least then I could try to pick a place, kind of like here, probably, where I could enjoy living and still keep as many of the people I care about as possible. Weird, huh? I guess I never realized how much my friends meant to me until I couldn't be with them anymore. I think I'll write to Roshanda again after my nap.

My dearest Allie,

I write you today from the dungeon of my father's castle. This was the suggestion of my stepmother, to enable me to think "more clearly" until I have made my final decision about marrying Lord Morwolf. She fears I may flee (yet would this not be choosing exile?), and I believe she had a hand in an assassination attempt on Mythwell today. The plot failed, but now my loyal friend is wounded and imprisoned with me. Mythwell tells me that the queen is with child and will bear my father his first male heir. For this prize he has so long desired, the king will doubtless grant her any favor she asks. My fate may well be sealed.

But enough of my selfish thoughts. I fear I have greatly misjudged the gravity of your own situation. Am I to understand that your father beat you and then forced you to perform menial labor? I am very saddened to hear of it. Does this "shopping mall" bear any similarities to a marketplace or bazaar? If so, I shudder to think of you venturing there. The merchant stalls in our villages are dirty and dangerous, and filled with pickpockets. You must have been terrified. I can only imagine that the scones and latte you wrote of are similar to the bread and water I am being given now during my confinement. Be strong, my friend. We must both endure.

Your devoted friend,

Avienne

P.S. This may be my last opportunity to write to you, regardless of my wishes, if I am soon forced to make my choice. Live well, dearest friend.

Dear Princess Avienne,

Please, please don't stop writing. Your problems are far worse than mine, and I'd do anything to help you. And to answer your questions: No, my parents aren't cruel to me, and they don't force me to do dangerous work or "menial" chores. They try really hard to make a good life for all of us, not just themselves. I even showed my mom some of your letters to me (I've been writing them down like a story), and she said she wished we could give my fairytale princess the loving home and family she deserved.

I thought it was kind of sweet. She doesn't even know you're real!

Guess what? I started my new school today, and it actually wasn't that bad. The campus is really pretty, with lots of trees and green fields around it. I got lost a couple of times in the halls, but most of the teachers were helpful, and an awesome-looking guy from my homeroom showed me where the chemistry lab is. I think I'm going to like my Shakespeare class best, but history is pretty interesting, too. I found out there's a spring dance coming up. I think I may be brave and go to it all by myself and see who I can meet. After all, it can't be nearly as difficult as facing an awful marriage, permanent seclusion, or exile, can it?

I think about you all day long and wonder what choice you made. I wish you could be here so we could talk face to face instead of through letters. Please take care of yourself, and try to find a way to reach me.

> Your dear friend,
> Allie

Days passed, and the only mail Allie received was a bright and cheery letter from Roshanda—nothing at all from Princess Avienne. Roshanda was full of gossip about familiar friends and places that Allie missed . . . including the news that Ian Walters had already started dating Katie Clark. Although she was happy to hear from Roshanda, Allie found she hardly cared that Ian had gotten over her so quickly. She was so preoccupied with worry about the fate of the princess that she couldn't imagine being upset by such small concerns.

Allie checked the mailbox every afternoon. Her mother even expressed amusement at how excited Allie seemed to get "when there's usually only junk anyway." Day after day, Allie's anxiety built. She wondered how Avienne had resolved her dilemma.

Had she relented in the end and agreed to marry cruel old Warlord Morwolf? Allie couldn't imagine kissing anyone with only seven teeth—probably brown and crooked ones. And how could anybody decide on their life's mate at age fifteen?

It was possible that the princess had chosen instead to accept exile, to leave her beautiful kingdom. Even an unknown and mysterious land sounded better than a place called "Fleamarsh."

Or had she decided that her best chance was just to be locked inside a nunnery, never to speak a word again, surrendering all hope of returning to the outside world and freedom? Allie shuddered.

She had thought her own life was terrible just because she had moved to a new place and had no friends. Though she still longed for a companion, someone with whom she could share her thoughts and her dreams, Allie realized that her problems were vanishingly small compared to those of the princess.

Avienne's enchanter friend Mythwell had been wounded; maybe he was even unconscious or dead by now. What options did the princess truly have? Allie wished she could be there to comfort her friend, even if it meant sitting in a dank dungeon with her.

It was cloudy on Saturday when Allie took Merlin out to walk and to check the mailbox again. She had already tried twice that afternoon, and either the postal carrier was late, or they hadn't received any mail at all today.

Of course, there were no postal delivery trucks from fantasy land. She wouldn't see anyone drive up, so she would simply keep checking.

The black lab frolicked, delighted as usual to be outside. He pulled on his leash and bounded around the mailbox as Allie opened it. She was startled to find not a rune crystal, but a smallish parcel wrapped in crinkly brown parchment and covered with arcane symbols. Still, the distinctive runes on the wrapping told her who had sent the package. Allie caught her breath. She had had so many disappointments over the past several days that she had almost given up hope. This might not be one of Avienne's beautiful holographic letters, but it was something to be treasured, nevertheless.

When Allie reached for the package, she felt immediately how strangely heavy it was. What had the princess sent her—a lead box?

She had to use both of her hands to slide it across the corrugated bottom of the mailbox, and the instant she pulled it free, it abruptly felt as if she had lifted a hundred pounds. Struggling to hold onto the package, Allie lowered it as quickly and gently as she could to the ground. Merlin sniffed at it with excitement.

Allie straightened and noticed that the parcel was obviously, and rapidly, *growing*. She took a step backward. As the package continued to expand, parchment tore away to expose a glittering crystalline crate as tall as Allie herself. A milky mist swirled within it, and more runes were etched across every exposed surface. Shadows moved in the depths of the mist, and Allie heard sounds coming from the box: a thump and then . . . a bark? Suddenly the crystalline cover of the crate dissolved, and a tiny white dog pranced out of the mist.

Not at all what Allie had expected. The dog looked, for all the world, like an oversized dandelion puff that had sprouted four legs, a nose, and a tail.

Merlin stepped forward and greeted the diminutive visitor by exchanging thorough sniffs and nose touches. Then the two dogs faced the open crate and barked. Its sparkling walls evaporated, and the mist cleared, revealing a startled-looking girl with raven hair, smudged cheeks, and a filth-encrusted velvet gown. "Are—are we truly here?"

Allie gasped. "Princess Avienne?"

The girl smiled. "No longer 'Princess,' I fear. Merely a 'normal teenage girl,' like you."

Allie laughed with delight and threw her arms around Avienne, ignoring the grime and the smell. She released her friend and stepped back to marvel at what had happened. This was no illusion, no sparkling hologram. Avienne was as real and solid as Allie herself. "You escaped? So you chose exile, after all."

The ex-princess gave an elegant shrug. "How can it be exile, when I have chosen to be in a beautiful land with those who mean the most to me?"

"But—" Allie said. "What about Mythwell?" The dandelion-puff barked twice.

Avienne stooped to pick up the little white dog and hugged it. "He had only enough time and strength to send one such enchanted parcel. This was the only means by which he could escape with me." She scratched the dog's head. "It is enough that we are alive and together. Can you tell me, dear friend, where we can earn food and shelter?"

Allie grinned. "Let's go talk to my parents."

Allie never found out how her father handled the paperwork or the explanations of why her "cousin" had come to live with them, but within three days, Avienne was a sophomore at Allie's new high school.

Allie never regretted the choice to share her parents with the gracious ex-princess. They had distinctly different personalities and rarely found themselves in competition with each other. That was why in their junior year, Avienne helped Allie become homecoming queen, complete with crown. In turn, in their senior year, Allie masterminded the campaign that got Avienne elected student body president.

Although it seemed strange to some, since the girls had adjacent rooms, Allie and Avienne often wrote little postcards and notes, which they left for each other on beds, in backpacks or school lockers, on dressers, and on mirrors.

SHIFT OUT OF CONTROL

Daniel M. Hoyt

When not working as a rocket scientist, Daniel M. Hoyt writes fiction, poetry and music. His short stories have sold to markets as diverse as Analog Science Fiction & Fact *and* Dreams of Decadence. *He currently lives in Colorado Springs, Colorado, with his wife, author Sarah A. Hoyt, two rambunctious boys and a pride of cats. Catch up with him at* <u>www.danielmhoyt.com</u>.

Control!" the man shouted abruptly. "Time! Shift! Fused! Not . . . clear! Away!" He seemed to struggle for each word, but they meant nothing to David. "Focus! Control!"

It was indeed a pity when a mind lost control like this. Dr. David Priest absentmindedly slipped his thin, gold wedding band back and forth over the second knuckle of his fourth finger while he waited for the orderlies at St. Theresa D'Avilla Psychiatric Hospital to drug his newest patient into submission long enough for the poor man's fragile mind to withstand a short chat.

"Another five minutes, Doctor," one of the orderlies, a small, muscular, dark-haired woman in her early twenties, said. She smelled of antiseptic, but David was used to that in hospitals.

David nodded and turned his thoughts to Charlotte once again.

Nearly ten years had passed since his beloved wife's accidental death, but David still thought of her daily, still missed her horribly. Like many widowers, he'd thrown himself into his work in the hopes of dulling the pain, but it hadn't worked for David. Maybe it was because he and Charlotte had been so close—joined at the hip, as his friends used to say while she was still alive. They'd dated all though undergraduate studies, been married while still fresh-faced and eager interns, stayed together through the hardest years leading up their M.D. certifications, and finally hung a shingle together announcing to the world at large—and Cleveland, Ohio, in particular—that the Doctors Priest were ready to guide the repair of broken minds.

Eleven years of marriage hadn't diminished their fondness for each other, and they'd still walked hand-in-hand on Sundays at the Garden Center in University Circle, just off Euclid Avenue, near the Museum of Art and Severance Hall. Dinners together were a must—at his insistence—despite hectic schedules, which could always withstand another reshuffling, and both of them enjoyed the little routines of life together. He drove the two of them to work together every morning, they played chess together every weekend, grocery shopped together every Wednesday—their weekday off—at the neighborhood market in Little Italy where all the little old Italian ladies shopped. They'd lived their lives *together*, and David had expected it to be that way forever.

But Charlotte had been taken away in an instant, and David's decision not to have children before forty haunted him now. He couldn't even take solace that a small part of his beloved wife lived on through her progeny. If he hadn't been so insistent about waiting for children, if she hadn't given in to his desires, if she'd gotten pregnant anyway. . . .

But she hadn't. She wouldn't have. Like all their friends—they called him a control freak, and he knew they were right—Charlotte knew the rules when it came to her husband. David didn't give in; Charlotte did.

But he *had* given in once, hadn't he? And look what had happened. It was *Charlotte* who had insisted on taking the limo home from Cleveland-Hopkins, after a particularly late flight following a six-hour layover in Boston. And David had agreed, despite his inner voice screaming at him that he'd be giving up control. Normally, he'd have driven, but he'd been so damned tired. . . .

It didn't matter now, it was too late to change the accident; nothing remained except her memory.

David's wedding ring connected him, somehow, to Charlotte's memory, and he'd taken to touching it in idle moments—twisting it around, slipping it on and off his finger.

"You can go in now, Doc," the second orderly said in a deep basso.

David looked up as the tall, trim blond man swung open the room door to admit him. David walked into the stale air, pointedly ignored the soft thump and scraping click behind him as the door was shut and locked, and pulled the lone, bare, wooden chair next to his patient, who was lying in the metal-framed single bed pushed against one wall—the only other furniture in the stark patient receiving room—with his face turned away. The low hum of the air conditioning system echoed through the room, amplifying into an annoying buzz.

David had only met this patient a couple of times before. His name was Manfred Priest—the coincidence of their shared, not-so-common surname had landed him into David's workload almost by default—and he was some kind of scientist who had gone crazy.

Schizophreniform disorder, David had written in his notes on the first visit. *Pre-schizophrenia? Hallucinations of several alternate realities, contradicting ours. Delusions of great achievement (timeline shifting device?) unsubstantiated by work history.* The second visit yielded little new information, just a single comment: *Worse.* David held little hope for this visit.

"Manny," David said, gently nudging his patient's shoulder to attract his attention.

Turning his shaved head slowly, Manny's unfocused green eyes settled on David's general vicinity. "Doc," he said slowly, "you're back."

David nodded. "Yes, Manny. It's Monday. Do you think you can talk?" He grasped Manny's hand in both of his own, a gesture that conveyed his genuine sense of concern for his patient.

Manny swallowed gingerly, his eyes squeezed tight with the effort, and wiggled a finger on his bound hand. "Water," he croaked.

Smiling benevolently, David released Manny's hand and reached for the half-filled paper cup of water he knew would be resting on the floor near his feet—if the orderlies had remembered his request. "Of course," he said, "the medication can cause an awful case of dry throat." The water was there—must remember to thank the orderlies; it's always best to treat your orderlies with respect, so they'll do what you want them to without a fuss—and David lifted it to Manny's lips.

Manny took a sip, then another and another before he spoke again. "Still think I'm crazy, I guess." He managed a weak smile that faded almost instantly.

"Crazy?" David said, shaking his head, the smile still plastered on his lips. "Of course not. A little confused, maybe, but not crazy."

Frowning, Manny said, "No. Not confused."

"Why do you think you're not confused, Manny?"

Manny turned his unfocused eyes to the water. "Drink?"

David gave him the water, once again tipping the paper cup to his patient's lips. And waited.

"Did you ever wonder how your life would have been different? If you'd done something different?"

David nodded, but didn't say anything. To the layman, it didn't seem to make sense, but any professional in the health field knew that a doctor's silence was often the best prescription for a case of clammed-up mouth. Ask a question, get an answer to that question, no more. The more specific the question, the more specific the answer. Even so, that answer was probably incomplete, missing that all-important tiny clue that told you exactly what the real problem was. In a game of deciphering symptoms that overlapped with a dozen wildly different causes, the key was to find the symptoms the patient didn't know he had. Ask about allergies, and he'd tell you doesn't drink milk, or eat shrimp, or whatever his friends have allergies to, things *he* thinks are relevant. Let him talk about his life, and he'll tell you about the soy milk-laden dessert he had last night while visiting his lactose-intolerant friend, the same soy milk causing a mild allergic reaction this morning.

Manny didn't disappoint him. "You know, like if you had the chance to go back in time and redo it, was there some kind of a turning point, where you life would go off into a different direction?"

David felt a lump in his throat forming as he remembered the fateful limousine ride almost a decade ago, Charlotte's scream from the passenger side when she saw the headlights coming at her fast, her horrified face just before the impact that sent her light frame sailing past him to smash the window on his side, the starburst of light as his own head slammed to the side, and then he blacked out.

Yeah, David thought about turning points all the time. What if *he'd* been on the passenger side instead? Would Charlotte have survived had she been on his side? Would his greater mass sitting on her side, the impact point, have avoided a flight to the opposite window? Would they both have survived?

What if he'd never let them take the limo?

Swallowing the lump, David composed himself and carefully steadied his voice. "Of course, Manny. It's normal to think such thoughts. But we can't change things that have already happened, now can we?"

Manny shook his head drowsily. "No. We can't." He closed his eyes.

What was he driving at? Was this what he meant by timeline shifting? David waited patiently, silently.

"But maybe we don't need to, to make it right," Manny said and drifted off to sleep.

David Priest sat in his plush leather office chair downtown, listening to Keryn Bennyhoff prattle on about how horrible her upper-middle-class-suburban life was, shuttling kids to and fro, washing and cooking, her self-imposed celibacy after she'd caught her husband cheating. Every now and then, David said something supportive and nodded, more out of habit than necessity. Modern counseling offered the choice of face-to-face discussion, but unfortunately, Keryn preferred the more traditional approach, lying on an overstuffed couch facing away from the doctor, where he couldn't really see the pretty raven-haired housewife.

To be fair, it was a very comfortable couch. David and Charlotte had picked this space—at a prestigious address near the high-rent clientele downtown, close to the lawyers and bankers—and they had taken great care to appoint it with good, expensive-looking furniture. Lots of leather and warm, inviting cherry, all matching, all bespeaking class. Most of the original furniture had been replaced over time, of course, but David retained the spirit of their original decoration, replacing each worn-out piece with careful consideration.

The initial expenditure had put them into debt, but it had paid them back a hundredfold since then. The atmosphere captured Keryn and the others like her. David had dozens of decently well-off casual patients like Keryn. They came in for their initial session, escorted by one of a long stream of highly attractive secretaries culled from the never-diminishing pool of struggling local models, both male and female, invariably looked around and nodded appreciatively. They were hooked before David spoke a word. This was a place they *wanted* to be, not just a place they *had* to be.

Like many of his casual patients, Keryn mostly wanted someone to listen to her. Her husband had stopped years ago, her kids never started, and she'd reached a point in her loneliness where she was willing to pay someone to listen. And David knew how to listen.

David also knew that Keryn came to him instead of a psychologist because his M.D. allowed him to prescribe the antidepressants she desperately thought she needed to cope with her desperately boring life, perhaps saving herself a trip to her family doctor for the prescription, as well.

So David only half-listened to Keryn on the best of days, anyway. But today David couldn't focus at all. *Maybe we don't need to*, the schizophrenic had said the day before. *To make it right.* What did he mean by that? Was he saying he knew a way to get Charlotte back? How? That was impossible!

Wasn't it?

His watch timer chimed. "I'm afraid that's all we have time for today, Mrs. Bennyhoff. And I think we made some real progress today, don't you?"

Keryn nodded and swung her gym-toned legs off the couch, slipping them into sensible, leather pumps waiting on the floor. "Isn't it time for my Prozac refill?"

"Yes. You can pick it up at Matt's desk on your way out. Have a great week, Mrs. Bennyhoff, and I'll see you next month?" It wasn't so much a question as a reminder to book her next visit, as if she'd forget.

Keryn left, and David checked in with his secretary.

"You took your 4 o'clock over lunch, remember?"

Matt said, clearly puzzled. "And your 3 o'clock canceled a week ago—family vacation. You're done for the day, Doctor."

"Oh, right. An early day, then. Thanks, Matt. I think I'll go over to St. Theresa D'Avilla and see my new patient, then. See you Friday?"

The scheduling had been Charlotte's inspiration. Office visits were booked by gender, as a rule; David saw his male patients Mondays and Thursdays, his female patients Tuesdays and Fridays. Each set had an opposite-gendered secretary, designed to put them on their best behavior. The women and outed homosexuals had Matt, a department store underwear model, and the men—at least the heterosexuals, that is, and the one self-proclaimed lesbian he treated—had Wendy, struggling actress. Charlotte felt that the subconscious preening the patients did for the secretary helped to minimize *incidents* at the office. David never really knew if it made a difference, but he'd honored Charlotte's system even after her untimely death.

If nothing else, it afforded him the luxury of having his secretaries type in his notes only for patients on the opposite days, using a coded system that obscured their identities. David took patient confidentiality seriously.

"Um, Doc? I kinda need the hours. Isn't there something you can have me do for a couple more hours?" Matt's voice held the edge of fear, as if those two hours of income made the difference between making his rent or not. With only a couple of regular gigs, it was entirely possible.

David hesitated. Matt had been with him for over two years now, and he knew he was trustworthy, but it meant leaving him alone in the office. He'd have to leave a key with Matt and let him lock up. No. Sensitive files were in

a locked filing cabinet that would take a forklift to re-
move, but it still made David squirm at the thought of
leaving someone else in charge. David even insisted that
his secretaries leave the premises for lunch, while he
locked up behind them, all the time citing patient confidentiality to mask his control obsession. "I'm sorry, Matt.
I just can't."

*Because I need to know what Manny meant about
making it right.*

"'S'alright, Doc." Matt sounded disappointed.
"Maybe the agency can come up with a gig. Drive safely,
okay?"

David winced. He knew Matt didn't mean anything by
it—he didn't know anything about Charlotte, much less
how she'd died, only that he'd once had a wife in the
practice that was gone, maybe divorced—but the remark
still stung. David *always* drove—except for that one
time, the time that took Charlotte away.

"Let me know how it turns out, Matt," David said, his
voice tight and strained. He wanted to help Matt, he
really did, but he couldn't just leave him here in the office alone. He just couldn't.

David sat next to Manny, listening to the buzzing air
conditioner growing louder. He nudged Manny's shoulder.

Manny stirred and brought his unfocused gaze to bear
on David. "Monday?" he asked weakly, clearly confused.
"Already?"

David leaned close. "No. It's Tuesday. I need to know
what you meant about something you said yesterday. Can
you talk?"

Manny nodded. "What were we talking about?"

"About making things right, Manny."

Manny raised an eyebrow and shook his head slightly. "What?"

"You can't change the past. Remember? But maybe you don't need to. That's what you said. To make it right, you said, to make it right."

Recognition slowly dawned on Manny's face. "Oh. Right."

David felt his heart jump and his stomach twisted, splashing bitter acid into his throat. Talk, dammit, talk! He couldn't wait; not this time. He'd waited too long already. Ten yea—

—no, not that long. Only a day; it just *seemed* like ten year—

—ten years since Charlotte's death.

"What did you mean?" David asked impatiently, gritting his teeth.

Manny paled and flitted those unfocused eyes about the room, seemingly at random. He raised his head as much as his sedated strength would allow. "Can't say here," Manny whispered, barely audible. "In my lab. Talk there." He scanned the room nervously. "Not here." His head dropped back on his pillow and he lay there, exhausted, unmoving.

David left, more confused now than when he'd arrived.

Standing in the doorway to Dr. Manfred Priest's lab, David scanned the room. Despite the turned-off lighting, there was enough of the afternoon sun streaming through the open-blinded windows to see the room clearly. Sterile, white, lots of glass and dull chrome—all it needed were a few bubbling, sulphurous solutions over Bunsen burners and racks of half-filled test tubes to make it into a movie set's mad scientist lab. A stained white lab coat hung on a glass phone booth across the room, near the windows—an odd thing to find in a lab. Near the booth, a laser-like apparatus, pointed vaguely in the booth's direction, was mounted on a pedestal, right in front of a black computer screen.

"You want to look around?" A striking, trim red-headed woman squeezed around David and swatted the light switch. Fluorescent overheads flickered to life, and a low buzz filled the background.

It had been a simple matter to find the lab's location from the patient records at St. Theresa D'Avilla, and an even simpler matter to convince the redhead—Dr. Hazel Stone, wasn't it?—to let him look around, after he'd presented his credentials. Once she'd gotten wind of his name, Dr. Stone seemed to assume David was a relation, and David didn't dissuade her from that illusion.

"Dr. Pries—" Hazel stopped, looking embarrassed. "I mean, Manfred, of course, not you, Dr. Priest. Anyway, *Manfred* worked here, alone. I don't know what it was, though. He always said it was secret, but I checked and he didn't have a government clearance at all."

David waited. This woman was just like a patient—let her talk and reveal.

Dr. Stone cleared her throat in the uncomfortable silence. "Yeah, and I checked with the brass here, and they didn't know either. Said he was supposed to be working on some quantum effects involving ordinary radiation, like microwaves and X-rays and such. Nothing classified, though."

David nodded. He'd gotten the same story from Manfred's boss when he'd called about his work history.

Hazel looked down nervously. "Must have been secret to him, though. Marked all his files TS." She looked up, but looked away quickly, evidently embarrassed at her admission of snooping through her colleague's files. "That's government-ese for Top Secret, and all his computer stuff was encrypted." Hazel pointed at the phone booth across the room. "That's the only thing out of place in here."

They walked over to it. As they neared, David could see it was empty. Clearly, there had been a phone in it at some point, but it been removed some time ago, along with any markings identifying it as a phone booth, in favor of two large letters: TS. Why, David hadn't a clue. "What is it?"

Dr. Stone shrugged. "Dunno. Looks like a phone booth."

David waved a hand at the laser thing. "Why's that pointed at it?"

"Hmm?" Hazel glanced at it. "Oh, it's not. Don't worry about it. Standard-issue particle laser. Nothing special in a physics lab. Anything else you wanted to see here?"

David shook his head. He left with Hazel, who turned off the lights before locking up. There was something going on in that lab, that was certain, and he was sure Dr. Manfred Priest had been perfectly lucid when he'd insisted on explaining things at his lab. David had noticed the tiny letters scratched into the base of the laser mount: TS.

Manfred was working on quantum effects from ordinary radiation, and he said it was secret. Hazel and the others had thought TS was Top Secret, but it wasn't a government designation, David was sure of that; Manfred himself had told him what it meant in their very first session. TS meant Timeline Shifter.

It took some time—including most of David's weekday off—to get the appropriate permissions for an offsite outing and to get Manny's medications changed, but David managed it before the next Monday session. His reputation helped immeasurably; people were used to jumping through hoops to satisfying David's whims. He'd sold them on the idea that familiar surroundings might snap Manfred back into reality permanently. The only concession he'd had to make was to allow a security orderly to accompany them. David had insisted on privacy inside the lab, though, so he didn't feel it was much of a concession.

Manny, smiling broadly, was wheeled out of his room to meet David. Without the sedative, his eyes were focused and clear, and he seemed far more alert. He was still on antipsychotics, of course, which helped him maintain his tenuous grip on reality, but the difference was still amazing.

David squatted in front of Manny's wheelchair. "How are you feeling today, Manny?"

"Fine. I'm ready to go."

"Great. Stephen here will come along." David nodded at the burly redheaded orderly pushing the wheelchair. "Is that okay?"

Manny scowled.

"We can't go without Stephen, Manny. Part of the deal."

Shrugging, Manny said, "I guess he can come, then."

A short drive later—David insisted on taking his own car, with Manny and the orderly in the back seat and

Manny's door child-locked—they arrived at Manny's lab. Dr. Stone wasn't around, but she wasn't needed to gain access to the lab; David had had the foresight to retrieve Manny's personal effects before the visit, so they could get in without having to involve anyone else.

The security guard in the building lobby was surprised to see Dr. Priest arriving in a wheelchair, but Manny quelled the guard's alarm with small talk and they passed easily.

Manny unlocked the lab, and the two doctors went in alone, while Stephen waited outside the door—with the key, just in case. A single shout from David would bring him running.

David couldn't wait to get started. "It means Timeline Shifter, doesn't it?" Rationally, he couldn't believe that Manny had actually invented some kind of time machine, but deep down, emotionally, he knew he was grasping at any straws that might bring Charlotte back. He told himself it was clearly fantasy, but he was helping bring Manny back to reality by doing this.

David almost believed it.

Manny's face registered genuine surprise. "Yes." He narrowed his eyes suspiciously. "How did you know that?"

"*You* told me. In the first session, under sedation."

"Oh. What else did I say? I can't remember."

"You said something about going back in time—"

Manny shook his head violently. "Can't be done."

"—and changing things." David held up a hand to silence Manny's protest. "And how it can't be done. But that it might not be needed, that things could be fixed another way."

Nodding, Manny smiled. "Have you heard of the term multiverse?"

"Sure." *Humor him*, David thought. *It won't hurt to play along.* "I used to read a lot of science fiction when I was young. The theory was that every time you made a decision, it made two different universes, ours and another where you made the other choice."

"Right."

"But that's *fiction*," David said. "And it doesn't make any sense. If every single decision every single person made resultant in a new universe, this multiverse would be billions of billions of billions of universes—uncountable, right?"

"Yes. But they're not there—yet."

David frowned. "I don't follow."

"Heisenberg. Schrödinger. They only exist *in potential*. They don't actually come to pass until someone *observes* them."

"Then they're there?"

"And always have been. It's quite elegant, actually."

"But still," David protested. "Billions and billions and bil—"

"The splinters don't happen with *every* decision, just *significant* ones. The little decisions are self-healing within the timeline. Kind of like your skin. If you get a little prick, the blood clots, you probably don't even need a bandage. But cut off a leg. . . ."

"What's *significant* mean?"

"Dunno," Manny said, shrugging. "It's not clear. I'm not even sure if the multiverse is common, or if they're personal, and everybody has their *own* multiverse. So far, I'm the only one who's used the device."

"The Timeline Shifter?" David tried to keep the sarcasm out of his voice, but this whole idea was so fantastic. . . .

Still, Manny was clearly responding well to a familiar environment. In fact, he appeared as sane as anyone could be expected to be.

Manny nodded. "I can show you." He beamed with pride.

David considered this for a moment. Was he crossing the line over playing along for medical treatment purposes? Or did he actually believe Manny at this point?

"Do it," he said, still unsure.

Manny wheeled over to laser device and struggled to his feet, leaning on the counter with the computer screen for support. At a touch the screen lit up, along with an on-screen keyboard and a password prompt. Manny touched some keys—David couldn't see which after Manny shifted his body to hide the screen from David momentarily—and a blank grid popped up. The laser hummed to life.

"It turns out," Manny said absently as he worked, aligning the laser, feeding in commands through the screen, "that the multiverse works on the same timeline. You can't go forward or back, just sideways. I can translate—shift, if you will—to another timeline, but I'm still at the same point in time and I lose as much time back here as I'm translated over there." He glanced back at David. "Which turns out to be about two hours, before the timeline corrects itself and snaps you back, whether you like it or not." He glanced back again, nervously. "And splinters your mind, too."

"What?" David had been in Keryn-half-listening mode, but that last sentence had caught his attention. "What do you mean?"

"When I came back the first time, I could remember everything from that other timeline. Everything. When I was a kid, growing up, dating, my job, everything. But I also remembered this timeline. The other one doesn't fade, either; both sets of memories are equally clear." Manny made some more adjustments through the computer screen, then grabbed what appeared to be a remote from in front of the screen. He hobbled over to the phone booth and stepped inside. "Only I could see both *present* timelines just as clearly, too, as if I were living them both simultaneously. I thought it was a temporary effect, but it's evidently not." He smiled weakly. "After four or five of those trips, it'll drive you crazy trying to figure out what's real." He pointed the remote at the computer screen several feet away.

"What are you doing, Manny?"

Clicking a button, he said, "Calibrating." The laser buzzed for a second, then returned to its low hum. "This is what I meant about personal multiverses. It needs to lock on to your DNA to find the other universes, through a quantum process that lets you discover without actually observing. It's highly technical and I'm sure you wouldn't understand, but look." He waved at the computer screen.

It now displaying tiny colored boxes in a tight grid, with more appearing. Most of it seemed to be red or green, with splashes of yellow here and there. David walked over to get a closer look.

"The red ones are off-limits. My DNA was detected there—or, more precisely, it *would* be detected there, once I translated—and it turns out that the old paradox about visiting yourself is true. I tried to go to one of those once, but nothing happened. The green ones show where my DNA is missing. In those, I'm either dead or never existed. Those are the ones I can target."

"What's the yellow?"

"Unclear. No answer one way or the other. I think it means I *can't* exist there, for whatever reason. I did some early tests with lab mice, and they never came back from those. So I'm not going there."

The grid winked out, and a new grid appeared, with only green boxes, larger than before.

"I'm focusing now on good targets," Manny said, pressing buttons on his remote. "I'm going to focus on a small section that I'm somewhat familiar with." A new grid appeared with less than a hundred elements. "I haven't been able to decode the choices, so I've just numbered them arbitrarily to identify the ones I've visited. C5 looks promising. What do you think?"

David's head swam. "C5?"

"C5 it is." Manny pressed a button, the laser buzzed again—

—and Manny winked out.

An hour and a half later, David was still puzzled. The initial panic of Manny's disappearance had long passed, Stephen had been informed of a delay but not given the cause, and David sat down on a lab stool to think about it rationally.

The way he saw it, there were two possibilities: Either Manny had done some pretty impressive sleight-of-hand with his disappearing act, or there was at least some truth in his claim.

David had had plenty of time to inspect the phone booth, even going so far as moving it, and he was convinced there were no trapdoors or hidden curtains or any other way Manny could have slipped out without him noticing. It would have been impossible; David had been looking right at him when he disappeared!

And that meant that Manny was on the level—at least partially. But that was also impossible! No, strike that; *improbable*.

No. Impossible.

"What's up, Doc?"

David jumped, nearly falling off the stool. His heart raced, and he spun around, steadying himself with the vacated stool. He gasped, unable to speak. Manny was back.

Manny wagged a finger at David. "You never told me your wife was so beautiful. How could you ever let her go?"

David stared, open-mouthed.

"Charlotte, right? Said you died in a limo crash about ten years back in that timeline."

David sagged against the chair, his eyes welling up with tears. How could Manny know about the accident? David only met him a few days ago, after Manny was already under treatment. Panic set in. Did Manny research his life before? Did he plan this whole thing from the beginning? Was he pretending all this time? Just to get back at David for some unknown reason?

Impossible. All those drugs Manny was under—how could he have withstood it? No, Manny couldn't be faking it; the level of control necessary by both mind and body was staggeringly unlikely.

But that meant he had somehow—some*where*—talked to Charlotte, didn't it? And that was impossible.

"Still don't believe me, do you, Doc?" Manny grinned triumphantly. "How about this? Charlotte was sterile. It wouldn't have mattered if you hadn't convinced her to wait until forty. She wouldn't have conceived if she'd wanted to—and, trust me, she *did* want to."

David closed his eyes. His heart pounded in his ears and a baseball-sized lump caught in his throat. There's no possible way Manny could have known any of that. Yet, he did.

David believed Manny now.

"I didn't let her go," David said in a reedy, strained voice. "*She* died in that limo, not me." He turned his face away as salty tears streamed down his face. "I'd give anything to have her back."

Manny waited patiently, silent for enough time for David to regain his composure. Afterward, he said softly, "You can be together again."

David wiped his red-rimmed, puffy eyes and looked up. "How?"

"I took her to my lab in C5. Calibrated on her DNA. There's several common timelines where you can *both* go and be together." He smiled thinly. "At least for an hour or two."

David's heart leapt. Was it really possible? Could he really see Charlotte again? See hope and longing in her brilliant blue eyes again? Taste her almond-coffee breath in a kiss again? Feel her silky skin pressed against his again, her heart racing in time with his?

"It will splinter your mind," Manny said calmly. "And you'll end up taking the drugs that are barely keeping *me* together."

A nagging voice at the back of David's mind shouted, *Can you trust your body to this man? Your mind? Can you?*

"You'll keep going back, you know. If you really love

her, you will. And there will come a time when the drugs don't do anything any more."

Can you trust him with your *life*? Every fiber of David's being fought him. Rationally, David couldn't even *consider* doing this.

But, to see Charlotte again. . . .

"That time might come sooner for you, maybe even after the first time. Some of the rats splintered after just *one* translation. I had a lot of time to prepare; you don't."

David's body shook with his internal struggle. What this man was asking him to do clashed with everything David had made of himself, his entire life philosophy. It meant giving up more control that he'd ever considered doing before. So much control that he might not get *any* back. Forever. He'd thought he'd be willing to give up control, just once, if he could change things, but was it just idle promises? This scenario presented an unacceptable risk. And for what? The possibility—the mere *possibility*—of seeing Charlotte again! Not of changing her death, only skirting it for a little while. Impossible! The man was asking too much. There were limits, and this blasted over those limits, even for Charlotte—

"It's now or never, Doc. We might never get another chance."

—Charlotte. David closed his eyes and sighed. "I'm ready to go."

David couldn't move. He heard voices. Slowly, he opened his eyes. Two men stood over him.

Charlotte was there, too. She crawled over him on the couch, straddled him seductively, and kissed him hard.

A man in a white lab coat occupying the same space as Charlotte turned to an orderly. Stephen, wasn't it? "What happened to this one?" He glanced at his clipboard. "Dr. David Priest?" His eyebrow shot up. "Psychiatrist?"

Charlotte giggled and craned her neck to whisper, "I love you, David," in his ear.

"I thought you were lost forever," David mumbled.

Stephen stared at David, then shrugged his massive shoulders. "Yeah. He was treating the other one. We went to the other guy's lab. I was just the hired muscle, you know? They were in there a long time." He pointed down at David. "He came out and told me it would be a while longer, then went back in. Three, maybe four hours later, he screamed like he'd been shot. I went in and found him on the floor, curled up in a fetal position, holding his head in both hands and whimpering."

Charlotte licked David's ear, making him twitch and smile. "I'm never letting you go again."

The orderly pointed at something out of David's field of vision. "That one seemed okay, tried to explain, but it was all Greek to me. By the time I got someone else there to help me, he was out of it, too. Guess the meds wore off."

Snuggling against David, Charlotte whispered, "Let's make love."

The lab coat man nodded sagely and glanced at David. An eyebrow shot up. "Must be a . . . stimulating hallucination, eh? Keep this one sedated. I'll be back tomorrow morning."

The two men left, leaving David alone with his wife. Strange, but he felt helpless to move, somehow, even as he wrapped his arms around Charlotte, hugging her tightly.

Two scenes intermixed around him: one with his wife at her sister's unoccupied beach house; another in a hospital bed under heavy sedation. Manny was right, the jux-taposition of the two realities—the two *lives*—each as real to him as the other, was maddening. He was already having trouble distinguishing between what he'd origi-nally called his *real* life, and the E8 life. He wondered idly if Charlotte thought of the C5 life as her real life. . . .

Charlotte sat up, grinding her hips into David's pelvis. She pulled his hands up to her now-bared breasts and moaned slightly.

What did it matter anyway what was real? He no longer had control of his mind, as it raced down parallel timelines simultaneously, taxing his mental resources, and he didn't particularly care. What he had here with Charlotte was real enough. Strangely, he felt freer than he ever had before. And he was sure that if he focused really hard, maybe he could ignore one life and it would go away. Then there'd only be one life to worry about.

With Charlotte. David smiled, ready to lose control.

THE TRIGGER

Janet Deaver-Pack

From Tabirika Onyx, Princess:

I've lived with Janet Deaver-Pack for over seven years, even before she changed her name. She puts words together on a computer whenever she sits still, so I curl in her lap mornings and evenings. In return, I help her write; she strokes my soft black fur as she thinks. I listen to her stories before she sends them to publishers. I've provided ideas for many of her 33 published stories in Fantasy, Science Fiction, Mystery, and Horror genres. Helping choose manuscripts for her anthologies was fun—I posed on the best. Her latest comes from DAW in Autumn 2005. I give moral support as she concocts monthly nonfiction articles for The Spirit Magazine. *Afterward, she brushes me and my friends Syri and Shannivere: long black and pewter fur flies. She puts boxes on the floor so we can ambush ankles, and makes great feather and cord toys. Janet trav-*

els to exotic lands, cooks (she gives us tastes!)
watches movies (we snuggle!), walks, studies
wildlife, investigates wine, researches, and reads.
In stray minutes, she critiques manuscripts by other
writers and connects with friends. A list of pub-
lished works and pictures of her, Syri, Shannivere,
and me are on her website www.janetpack.com.

Detective Jim Forrester of the San Diego Police Department pushed a photograph across the glass-topped carved rosewood coffee table. "Mr. and Mrs. Jennings, is this your daughter?"

"Pattie! It's Pattie!" Tanned and manicured Tiffany Jennings bounced forward on the couch to swoop up the picture. It was an overexposed, uncentered snapshot of a frowning teenage girl with snarled toffee-colored hair printed by a computer badly in need of toner. "Where is she?"

"She says her name is Treece." The detective watched the couple with shrewd green eyes shadowed by dark brows. From a matching antique chair next to his, social worker Gillian Matthews exuded empathy.

"I call her Treece. So do all her friends," replied smooth-featured businessman Chad Jennings, one arm encircling his wife. "Tiffie here never could get used to it and always called her Pattie. Treece says it's a baby name." He looked at his wife fondly and smiled, then turned to Gillian. His friendly expression clouded with suspicion and something bordering on contempt. "Her real name is Patrice, after my grandmother. What can we do for you people?"

"Where is she?" pleaded Tiffie, wide eyes assisted to

an impossible turquoise blue by colored contact lenses. "Is she all right? When can we see her?"

Gillian replied, "She's in the car, Mr. and Mrs. Jennings."

Tiffie bounded to her feet. "I have to see her! She needs me!" Whirling, she headed for the door of their posh La Jolla residence at the best pace she could manage in high-heeled designer sandals.

"Mrs. Jennings." Detective Forrester's carefully emotionless voice stopped her in mid-step. "Mr. Jennings. There are things you should know before you see Treece."

Chad stood, glowering across the coffee table. "Detective, it's been two whole years since we've seen our daughter! Why are you stopping our reunion?"

"What Ms. Matthews and I have to say will take only a few more minutes."

With reluctance, Tiffie returned to the large ivory-colored couch. Chad reluctantly sat down also, retwining his arm around his wife's silk-clad back and waist. He patted her left hip in a patronizing manner.

Cozy couple, Forrester thought. *Lots of money. Wonder if there's something wrong between them? Who's he seeing after work?*

"Well?" An edge in Chad's dark tenor implied he didn't like waiting.

Forrester took his time, sorting details in his mind before speaking. He nearly coughed inhaling the gorgeous home's scent, sandalwood and some kind of exotic spice that rasped against his throat. The overlarge couch where the Jennings sat anchored one side of a large room where groups of antique chairs sat with small carved tables and potted plants. Gillian had called this the "social area." A thick, soft moss-colored carpet lay beneath their feet, and a fifteen-foot vault with skylights soared above. A huge armoire hid what Jim suspected was the entertainment center. In the northern stone wall was a real fireplace where flames played in a custom wrought-iron grate, bordered by floor-to-ceiling windows overlooking the magnificent valley view.

"My partner, Detective Steve Ryan, and I picked Treece up on Highway 5 just after midnight this morning."

"You're not going to arrest her for that, are you?" Chad fleered. "She's a minor, only fifteen. My lawyer—"

Jim had experienced enough of this man in a few minutes. "No Mr. Jennings, we're not charging your daughter for walking on a posted freeway. It was raining, she was soaked. Mad as a wet hen, too, as well as scared and cold and confused. We put her in the back seat of the squad in a blanket and bought her coffee and a doughnut at the first place we found. She needed it, she was hungry. She had no money, no identification, only the clothes on her back and flimsy sandals on her feet. She wouldn't give us more than her first name. The doctor at the hospital who checked her out and Ms. Matthews finally got the rest." He looked at Tiffie first, then at Chad. "Mrs. Jennings, Mr. Jennings, your daughter says she's been . . . ah—" Jim couldn't bring himself to say it. It was just too bizarre. "She's been elsewhere." He glanced with guilt at Gillian.

"We know. For two whole years, we know. So where was she, Detective?" asked Chad with sarcasm. "The wilds of the Missouri Ozarks? A start-up colony on Antares?"

"Does Treece have any other relatives who live close by?" Jim asked.

"No, why?"

Jim shot a quick glance at Gillian, who nodded.

"Because she doesn't want to come home."

The information dropped stone-like into a pool of silence. Tiffie looked shocked. Chad fought for control. He shook his head growling, "I don't see how you people can allow this to happen. What did you say to poison my only daughter against me in such a short time?"

"How can she not want to come back home?" Tiffie asked, pulling on her fingers and working her voice into a wail. "Pattie had everything here: good food, parties, friends, the best schools—we did everything for our daughter. She's all we've got!" She turned, weeping, to her husband. "Chad, make them bring her in!"

Jim sighed, signaling with an index finger for Gillian to take over. This was the part of talking to the families of missing children he hated. He was lucky this time to have someone with him willing to help give the peculiar details of this case to the parents.

"She didn't have a challenge, Mr. and Mrs. Jennings," Gillian said softly, leaning forward slightly. Her gently rounded figure and soft brown eyes often inspired immediate trust, which is why Jim had asked her specifically to become involved with this case. She was also a tough, savvy advocate of abused children, and could hold her own in court during verbal battles in English or Spanish. "You see, Treece chose a future that didn't match yours. She wants to save whales and the rain forest, join the Peace Corps, do something that makes a difference in this world."

"How do you know what our daughter wants?" sniped

Chad. "You're an overburdened caseworker. You probably saw her for ten minutes, then manufactured assumptions."

Jim was impressed by the way Gillian took a slow, controlled breath before replying. He was tempted to stand up and walk out rather than help these people by trying to explain where their daughter had been.

"I spoke with her last night after the detectives brought her in," Gillian said, looking directly at Jennings. "I was with her for several hours. As Detective Forrester mentioned, Treece was quite upset. We had a heart to heart discussion. She was confused about how she got onto the cross-town freeway, but her feelings on other matters were quite clear. Especially about her lifestyle here."

"Now just a minute—" Chad began to thunder, rising.

"Let Ms. Matthews finish." Jim's tone chopped off the father's sentence like a knife hand to the larynx. Reluctantly, Jennings subsided.

"What was she doing at that elsewhere place?" asked Tiffie in a querulous voice.

"All sorts of terrific things. Counseling newcomers, especially children who were having a hard time without their mothers and fathers," Gillian responded. "Making shelters. Helping with the cooking. Telling stories. Writing the place's history, and that of the people who started it. Participating in meetings with settlement leaders trying to plan for the future. Her descriptions are very detailed, very vivid. I believe she actually did those things."

"Sounds like a bleeding-heart liberal dream to me," growled Chad. "Wanting to save whales and trees was a fad she went through a few years ago." He leaned forward. "She said she was kidnapped, right? Where was she held? South America?"

"There are no signs of kidnapping," Jim rumbled. "Did you ask Treece before she disappeared how *she* felt about whales and forests?"

"*I* would have known if she felt that way," exclaimed Tiffie. "Pattie and I had great discussions all the time."

"And yet you insist on calling her Pattie," Gillian observed in a dry tone that was lost on the woman. "Mrs. Jennings, did you talk about anything beyond what she did in school, who her current boyfriend was, what clothes were in vogue, the next party, and where you wanted to shop next?"

The woman looked blank. "What else is there to talk about?"

"I'm tired of all this malarkey," Chad snapped. "When can we see our daughter?"

"There's just one more thing, Mr. and Mrs. Jennings." Jim kept his voice neutral as he gathered his courage. This wasn't going to be easy. "Treece claims she's been . . . someplace very strange."

"So it *was* South America!" Tiffie howled, huge tears rolling down her cheeks. "Oh, my poor, poor baaaby!"

"No, Mrs. Jennings." Gillian, noting Jim's difficulty, shouldered the responsibility for adding the final odd bits to the story. "Very much someplace else. She thinks she's been part of a colony not on this world. In fact, she's fluent in a language the scholars we've contacted don't know."

The silence was so complete Jim could hear the clink of tools as a service man cleaned the pool at the back of the house.

"All right, and just how did she get there?" Chad growled. "Merciful heaven, my little girl disappears for two whole years. When she comes back, you expect me to believe a story like this? There's going to be a media circus! The *Enquirer* will be standing in our front yard tomorrow morning with a camera crew if this becomes common knowledge!" Tiffie looked pleased until her husband shot her a smoldering glance. She wilted.

"Treece doesn't know how she arrived there. That's one of the fuzzy parts she couldn't tell us," said Gillian. "She claims she was walking along one day, and the next thing she knew, she was in that other place."

"Nonsense! How absurd. I want to see my daughter right now!" demanded Chad.

"I'll go get her. Excuse me." Gillian slipped from her chair, walking across the living room without sound from her low-heeled shoes thanks to the thick carpeting. She disappeared out one side of the tall double front door, leaving Jim alone with the parents.

Tiffie controlled her voice enough to quaver, "She's not . . . she's not crazy, is she, Detective?"

"At this point I don't know, Mrs. Jennings. Tests—"

"Of course she's not crazy!" exclaimed Chad. "This is our little girl. She's always had a good head on her shoulders. Even tempered, smart as they come. Takes after my side of the family. She's not crazy. She had a dream, maybe. A series of them." He smiled, accepting his own explanation as truth. "Her dreams were always very real."

"We have the lab analyzing the clothes and sandals she was wearing," Jim said. "I must say, Mr. and Mrs. Jennings, the stuff didn't look like anything I've ever seen. It was coarse, hand-woven, hand-stitched, and—"

The front door closed. Tiffie leaped to her feet, running across the carpet like a lame gazelle and waving both hands overhead. "My baaaaaaaaaaaby! Pattie, daaaarling!"

Standing in front of Gillian, Treece's face hardened as Jim watched. *Poor kid,* he thought. *She really doesn't want to come home. I don't think I blame her.*

"Mom," the girl said with stiffness that never reached Tiffie's understanding. "Dad. It's been a long time. How are you?"

"There's my little girl." Chad's grin consumed his face as he followed his wife and added his embrace over hers. "Honey, we've missed you so much!"

"You let your hair grow. You're so thin, sweetheart," gabbled Tiffie. "That place in South America didn't have enough food for you, did it? What do you want? I'll have Rosa fix something yummy for your tummy right away. Rosa, Rosa! How about your favorite, Orange Chicken? We've got oysters for Oysters Rockefeller, and those special little cakes I never can pronounce the names of from that scrumptious little bakery downtown—you remember that place, don't you? Of course you do!—for dessert, and maple-glazed ham with a wonderful pecan crust left over from our last party, and . . . what?" Tiffie stopped, confused. "What did you say?"

"Pizza," the girl repeated firmly. "I'd really love some pizza, with lots of veggies and cheese. And something chocolate."

Treece's voice already sounded weary, Jim thought as he passed the ecstatic, fawning parents on his way to the door.

"Don't forget, Treece, we've got some tests set up for you at my office tomorrow," Gillian said over the uproar. "I'll pick you up here at nine."

"How can you do that?" Tiffie exploded. "How dare you schedule tests tomorrow! We need to go shopping!"

Can't you make it any earlier? the girl's desperate eyes

pleaded over her mother's coiffed head as Jim turned to step through the doorway.

The caseworker hesitated. "You know, we're scheduled at nine, so I'll see you at eight-thirty, okay?"

Thank you, Treece's expression said. *Thank you very much.*

"Can't I come with her?" Tiffie wailed. "She just got home! We have to spend every little minute catching up."

"I'm sorry, Mrs. Jennings, but I'm afraid that I'm going to have to schedule several sessions with Treece." Gillian smiled at the girl. "After all, we've got a mystery to solve. I'll see you tomorrow, Treece."

Chad grunted and glowered as he supervised Jim and Gillian out the front door. He turned back to his daughter before they'd set foot on the first step. "Hey, Treece. Your timing is great. You can go on vacation with us next month, and . . ." The door slammed against their backs.

"Poor kid," Gillian sighed after descending the steps and letting herself in the car's passenger side. "She's a clear case of mental abuse."

"Yeah," Jim agreed, starting the engine and guiding the Chevy down the curving cobblestone-like driveway lined with small palm trees and a riot of bougainvillea.

"I wish Chief Martinez would have let Treece stay with me," the caseworker said. "Maybe I could have made things a little easier for her."

Jim nodded, turning the car onto La Jolla Shores Drive. "But we have to follow the rules." He drove for several minutes, then said, "This one isn't gonna be easy, whether or not we can prove her story. I'll drop you by your office."

"No kidding. Thanks." Gillian bit a knuckle and kept quiet for the rest of the drive downtown.

*   *   *

"Good morning, Treece." Gillian breezed into her office, shut the door, and settled down behind her desk.

"Hi, Ms. Matthews."

The girl was uncomfortable. Hallway noises startled her, making her wide frightened-animal hazel eyes dart often to the door window. She chewed on newly manicured fingernails and tapped one foot on the floor in a fast methodical rhythm.

"Treece, would you like to talk on the beach?" This wasn't standard procedure, but Gillian suspected she'd never get anything out of the girl while she was this nervous.

"Oh, Ms. Matthews, could we?" Something heavy went *whump!* in the hallway. The girl jumped, then folded herself small against the back of the chair.

"Sure. Just let me pick up a couple of things." Gillian tucked a tiny tape recorder and extra cassettes into her briefcase, stood, grabbed an old blanket from her closet she kept there for emergencies, and smiled. "Come on, let's go."

They rode the elevator down to street level in silence and walked from the small Social Services building on Vallecitos to the beach. The sand was populated with sunbathers, dog walkers, an impromptu volleyball game, and the usual gaggle of running, screeching preschoolers. Gillian thought it almost as noisy as her office, but Treece seemed to relax as soon as her sandaled feet touched the warm sand.

They chose a space, spread the blanket, and sat down. The iodine-smelling breeze riffled their hair.

"You seem nervous today, Treece," began Gillian.

"And it looks as though you haven't slept much, either. Are you all right?" She willed the girl to talk.

Treece sighed, watching a jogger trot by with a leashed Airedale. "Fine. I just can't seem to rest. It's so noisy here all the time, even at night. I'm not used to traffic, planes, all that. And Dad bought me a puppy. He keeps me up."

"What are you used to?" Gillian encouraged, taking the tape recorder out of her briefcase, setting it between them, and clicking the "on" button. She also grabbed her notebook and a pen.

"It's so quiet in the colony." She hesitated, then continued, halting often as if uncertain what to say. "We don't have many machines; those are mostly in the bigger villages. Even then, there are just a few. There isn't much metal. Enough for some nails and small things like that, but most everything is made of wood or stone." She brightened. "It's a settlement of people mostly from this world. We had our own grist mill on the stream with a rock grinder, and we made flour from several kinds of grain. I learned how to bake. Leisha taught me. And Edrick showed me how to use his bow and arrows. Said I might need to know how some day. I got pretty good." She looked around and sagged. "I'll never need one here."

"Did you go straight there from here?"

"I think so." She shrugged. "I don't even remember when that was."

Gillian prompted, "Do you remember the season?"

"I think—I think it was spring. Oh yeah, it was just before prom. Mom was in a snit because Jeff Calloway asked Nicia Roberts, not me." A tiny smile tugged at her mouth. "Mom bought me a strapless white satin sheath. I never wore it. I haven't thought about that for a long time."

"Did you want to go to the prom with Jeff?"

"Sure. He was cute, but stuck up. I would have liked to go with Girardo Robles, but Dad would go ballistic if I dated a Mexican. Even once." She looked across the beach, pushing her wavy toffee-colored hair behind her ears.

"So your Dad doesn't like Mexicans?"

"Yeah. One of my best friends at school couldn't come to my birthday party because of that."

"Tell me how you got to the colony, Treece."

"I knew you'd ask." She sank down on one elbow, shredding a withered leaf blown onto the blanket. "I remember arguing with Mom about something, politics I think." Treece shook her head. "I wanted to work for Senator Jack Carlisle's office during his next campaign. He's a liberal Democrat. Jeez, she can be *so* narrow-minded. I got so upset that I refused to say anything else and called my friend Angela. I grabbed some chocolate, and slammed the door when I left. I was going to meet Angela at Cherry On Top, have ice cream, and talk." Treece flicked the tattered leaf away. "It's just a few blocks. She got there. I didn't."

"What streets did you take?"

"I don't know. I was supposed to meet Angela there in half an hour, so I guess I went as straight as I could."

"Did you see anything unusual on the way? Meet anyone unusual?"

"You know the neighborhood: It's for snobs, and part of it's gated, so no one comes in and out except service staff, mail and delivery people, and house owners. I remember seeing old Mrs. Demerest walking her poodle,

Etoile de Noir. I used to dog-sit for her sometimes. I didn't say anything, I just ran by. And just after I got into that tiny park, I was . . . somewhere else."

"Is there a bridge in that park?"

"Yeah, a little one. A creek runs underneath any time it rains."

Gillian pressed gently. "Which side of the bridge were you on when you went to that someplace else, Treece?"

"Ummmmmmm. The other side. Yeah, the end farthest from the road. That's where I disappeared!" Excited by remembering, she sat up.

"After you disappeared, how did you feel?"

"Well, my stomach felt a little funny, as though my insides were being pulled in different directions. Kinda nauseated, too. I thought I got caught in the rain, but I wasn't wet, just cold. Then I was over there, standing in a field near the colony. Edrick and Sal found me." Treece turned wide eyes on Gillian. "There are lots of trees. I love sparagonels. Those have clusters of beautiful bluish-white blossoms hanging all over during falar, that's spring, and they smell great. Arhadal birds eat them; those are fairly large, about the size of crows with tufts on their heads, and they're white, brown, and gray. The colony at Norrinost makes preserves from both the flowers of sparagonels and the fruit. That sets on during late summer. It's one of our . . . their most popular trade items, a delicacy in the towns of Eldelior and Harnuthallam. People travel for kaldars—sorry, I mean miles—to get them. Some make the trip a yearly vacation, spend a whole dilon coming, that's about ten days, stay for awhile, and go back. Sparagonels don't grow just everywhere." She frowned suddenly at Gillian. "Am I giving you enough details?"

"Enough for a book," Gillian nodded, scribbling furiously.

"I sound crazy, don't I? Maybe we ought to write a book. Then I could be an author and not a wacko . . ."

"Treece!" Gillian dropped her notebook and reached for the girl's shoulders, shocked at her sudden brittle tone. "I didn't mean—"

"No, not you. You almost believe me, and I think Detective Forrester does, too." A tear glimmered in one eye, and her voice softened. "But no one else does." She smiled without humor. "Mom and Dad still think I was held captive by some revolutionary who took me to South America. Dad talks about it all the time. They'll believe that until they die, no matter what anyone else says." She sniffed. "At least you and Detective Forrester listen. You both treat me like a person, no matter where I was. Like the people at Norrinost. It means 'Land of Seven Rivers.'"

"Who were your friends there?"

"Leisha, and Chantal, and Edrick. Then there's Grandma Betty Faye, Jamal, Lakshme, Paul, Ted, Mary, Sal, and Kathleen." A tiny smile tugged her mouth. "We call her Lady Kathleen because she's always so regal. Those are a few of the ones who adjusted well. Some don't. They're hard to make friends with because they keep to themselves. They're angry. All they talk about is getting back here. A few commit suicide."

"Did you think about suicide?"

"Yeah, a little after I got there. But Grandma Betty Faye says I'm not the type. I roll with the punches, make the best of things." Her eyes flooded. "Ms. Matthews, I miss them so much. We were a real family. I-I'll probably never see them again."

Gillian gathered the sobbing girl against her shoulder, trying not to wish she had just such a daughter. "Hey, we've been at this for a long time. How about taking a break and getting lunch? I'm starved. There's a vendor over there who makes the best soft tacos you've ever tasted." After rummaging in her briefcase, she handed the girl a tissue, then clicked off the tape recorder.

"Yeah," Treece nodded with a thin smile. "Yeah. Thanks, Ms. Matthews."

"Sorry I'm late, Jim. My court case this morning featured an argumentative mother who objected to everything I said, especially to putting her three-year-old in foster care. I had to get a restraining order against her— I had proof she burned him with cigarettes and fed him dog food."

Looking very professional in a white blouse and dark sapphire blue suit, Gillian Matthews folded into the restaurant booth, dropping her briefcase on the unoccupied part of the bench next to the window. "But I don't have to tell you about people like that. Uh, sorry, I should've said hi."

"Hi," he responded with an understanding grin. She smelled like sunshine and carnations, and her lovely smile aimed at him alone brightened Forrester's whole day.

Sighing, she relaxed and leaned both elbows on the table. "Thanks for waiting. It's good to see you, Jim."

"You too, Gillian. You look great. I ordered Thai noodles with chicken just after you called. It should be up any minute." He glanced at his watch, regretting he had to be back at the precinct in an hour, and signaled for the waiter. "Another iced tea, please. Gillian?"

"I'll have the same, thanks."

"How's Treece Jennings?"

Her smile ran away. Gillian exhaled. "After a week, her case is getting curiouser and curiouser, to quote another little girl who spent time in an odd place. At least there's no white rabbit in this story."

"It's crazy," Jim replied. They were both silent while the waiter served their tea. "The lab results are back on her clothing." Gillian stirred real sugar into the liquid, nodding for him to continue when they were alone again. "I've confirmed this with biologists who've worked in Africa and South America. The fibers are strange. None of the experts I spoke to have suggestions where they might be from, or what they are. The closest estimation is inner tree bark pounded with rocks to make it supple, cut into narrow strips, then woven together."

Gillian sipped tea. "The texture was so very different."

"Unfortunately there was no mud except local stuff on her sandals. The rainstorm washed that all away." Jim gestured in frustration. "We looked at them too late."

"There wasn't any dirt under her fingernails," Gillian said. "Her mother scrubbed the poor kid until her scalp and skin were raw. Mrs. Jennings took Treece to her own doctor Thursday and had a full workup done. He refused to release the results until I threatened him with contempt. They're . . . interesting." She unfastened her briefcase with one hand and drew out the report, handing it to Jim while their noodles were served.

"Poor kid, looks like she got every test medical science has devised in the last hundred years," Jim said, flipping a page on the inch-thick document. "Can you give me the short version?"

Gillian lifted a bite to her shapely lips. "Ummm, this

is good, Jim. I'm hungry. Okay, basically the report says that, beyond a slight case of anemia and some genetic weakness in her bronchial tubes, Treece has high levels of something related to the SARS virus in her blood. It's a mutated strain. She also has some trace elements biologists can't identify, and some peculiar antibodies. Those aren't surprising if she's been living elsewhere."

"What does all that mean?" Jim asked, stabbing into the fragrant noodles.

"No one knows," Gillian shrugged. "I badgered the doctor about that. Neither of her parents have it. In fact, except for their egos and their income, they're about as normal as apple pie. Now, for the interesting stuff."

"I figured there was more."

Gillian nodded. "She's got a broken strand of DNA. Just one tiny fragment missing."

"Imagine that." Jim drank tea, squinting at Gillian's auburn curls over the top of his glass. "So maybe her disappearance was caused by this mutated virus interacting with her damaged DNA?"

"Maybe. We don't know."

"Yeah. Well, I found out this morning that Chad Jennings is having an affair with someone from his office. I'm sure he needs to spend as much time away from that valley-girl wife of his as possible." Jim chewed thoughtfully for a minute, then looked hard at Gillian. "Is there a chance Treece is making this up? Or is partnered with someone who's having her memorize a detailed story?"

Gillian finished her first dish of noodles, and served herself seconds. "I really don't think so. It's too elaborate. Treece is a bright, creative kid, but she doesn't seem comfortable lying. Except to her parents, when they refuse to let her do something she considers important."

"Like saving rain forests and whales."

"Or counseling a friend who's just found out she's pregnant. That happened Wednesday. Treece weaseled out of another interminable shopping trip with her mother by telling her the girlfriend had invited Treece to the exclusive beach, golf, and tennis club her parents belong to."

Jim laughed softly, shaking his head. "Does this kid have any faults?"

"Like her father, she's got quite a temper, which she learned to control at the colony. She doesn't like opera, country and western, or rap, and can't stand Picasso. Dali and M.C. Escher are more her style. And she doesn't like beer, has a soft spot for angry super heroes in comic books, and has decided never to try drugs. She's also a chocaholic. Godiva Belgian Dark is her favorite."

Gillian stopped, obviously collecting her thoughts. "What I didn't tell you is that Chad Jennings is being more of a pain. He's called my office twice in two days demanding to see Treece's case history. Last time I said no, he replied that he might lodge a complaint about me with Social Services."

Jim heard the tautness in Gillian's voice, and couldn't decide what to do in response. A long minute of silence stretched between them before he finally broke it. "Counselor, how do we help this young lady? She's too young to help herself."

"I don't know. But I hope we can." She shook her head, then smiled again, brightly enough to dispel fog. "Sorry, I have to run. My clients are waiting. Keep in touch about new developments regarding Treece. Split the bill?"

He shook his head. "Nah, I've got it."

"Thanks. My treat next time." She gathered her things, rose, turned, and left. Jim admired the harmonious interplay of the muscles in her legs as the counselor wove through the lunchtime crowd and out the door. As he watched, thoughts began coalescing in his mind. By the time Gillian backed out of the parking lot and entered traffic streaming along Paseo Dorado, Jim had swallowed the last noodle and was looking through his Palm Pilot for the number of the Biology Department at UC-San Diego.

Dr. Langley Bowen pulled the blood sample marked TJ3-XXX from the refrigerator of the biology lab at UCSD. "Dr. Kassar's little joke. Let's see if this has the right stuff." He put the stoppered vial in a stand. Picking up a pipette, he opened the specimen, drawing a bit of the blood from it to begin the tests Detective Forrester had requested.

"All I'm supposed to do is verify findings of Kassar's original report." The short thin biologist with thick half-moon glasses muttered habitually to his work. "So let's put a bit of you here on this slide, and a little more here on another. Now I have to get something else done, and I'll be back in a few minutes." Putting the slides on his work table, Dr. Bowen turned away. He returned after searching through a pile of papers for a research assistant's list of findings on another subject.

"Wait. I'm certain I put two drops on those." When he looked at the two TJ3 slides beneath his microscope, the biologist saw nothing. He sighed. "Perhaps my mind is slipping these days. I'll try it again."

He'd unstoppered the vial when his cell phone rang. The request from a fellow biologist made him spend a moment with his secretary in his office down the hall. Dr. Bowen returned in five minutes to a mess.

"What happened here?" He looked at the blood spattered across the table. The unstoppered vial in the stand was empty.

"Now I really know my mind's slipping. Clean this up." He grabbed a sponge and collected the stains. "What a waste. Wait, I've got one more sample of that brand." Returning to the refrigerator, Dr. Bowen rummaged through the racks. "Ah." He took it out, placing it in a different holder on the opposite side of his work table. "All right. This time I'll write everything down. Samples of TJ3-XXX as requested by Detective Forrester going on two slides at 14:13." He wrote as he spoke. "Leaving vial open. This time I'm watching it."

Minutes passed. "Nothing." He really ought to check on his other experiment. "Still nothing." Rising, the biologist was about to turn away when the blood in the vial vanished. It bloomed seconds later on the wall across the room with a faint smacking sound.

Dr. Bowen sank down on a stool, the trained side of his mind denying what his eyes had seen.

"I'm not going to be able to tell anyone about this," he muttered. "They'll all think I'm crazy. I'd better get hold of that detective." Pulling out his cell phone, he touched the memory key and selected the number of the San Diego Police Department.

Dr. Bowen peered over his thick half-moon glasses at Jim and Gillian after telling them what had happened earlier in his lab. Jim felt numb as the doctor tapped Treece's file. "I don't know what caused her blood to act this way. I call it phasing. You said that she didn't know how she disappeared, so I assume she can't invoke the reaction consciously. Therefore, there's likely to be a trigger that caused her disappearance.

"My results show her blood is quite active on its own. There was nothing around—I wasn't careless with a drop of another agent. Science can't explain a lot of things on this earth. Finding out what they are and how they work is the fun part."

"You think other missing persons have something like this in their systems?" Jim asked.

Dr. Bowen shrugged a thin shoulder. "An amino acid, perhaps a vitamin overabundance. It might even be an endorphin-producer. There may be any number of them working in concert to produce such a trigger. I won't know more until I have another victim to study and can compare cases." He took off his glasses and rubbed his nose.

"All this is wild hypothesis," Dr. Bowen continued. "Few people are willing to talk about such things. I suspect that most people who phase never return, and the few who do keep it to themselves and visit psychiatrists the rest of their lives."

He smiled, a wry twist of his mouth, watching his guests with direct gray-blue eyes. "I'm sorry, this is all I can offer. You wanted a nice packaged theory. It doesn't work like that in this case. And if we tell anyone else about this, they'll think we're all certifiably mad." He leaned forward, causing his chair to creak. "But that isn't stopping you. You want something. I know those determined looks."

Jim sighed. They'd come to ask questions, and instead the doctor was questioning them. "It's this girl. She's a really good kid. She feels displaced."

Gillian nodded. "Her parents aren't supportive, they smother her and won't listen to her. She's worried about her friends in Norrinost, which is what she calls the place she claims she's been for two years. Frankly, we're worried. She seems to be losing a little more of herself every day she's here. You've seen the results of her psychological profile, the language analysis, the inconclusive findings about her clothing. They all point to things we know nothing about. We're frustrated. You are the last hope we have to pinpoint what's going on, and we've got a week to do it before her parents take her on vacation."

"I'd like to be of more help, Detective, Ms. Matthews, but I don't have enough facts to make either well-founded decisions or offer advice," Dr. Bowen said. "I wish I knew more, because something like this could be the tip of a very intriguing iceberg of scientific breakthroughs. I share your frustration. I'll never be able to publish my notes. They're just too unbelievable. It's an uncomfortable situation all around."

Jim thought a moment. "Dr. Bowen, you said that certain levels of these substances trigger whatever—"

"*May* trigger," he corrected. "There's no way to prove that. It's likely different for each individual."

"Yes. All right." Jim leaned forward. "This has to be off the record."

"Of course." Dr. Bowen looked at him brightly. "As far as I'm concerned, what we're discussing comes under the aegis of doctor-client confidentiality."

"Good. If this girl eats enough of the triggering substance, what's the chance she'd go back to where she wants to be?"

The eminent research scientist leaned back, staring at Jim. "Let me anticipate your next question, Detective."

Dr. Bowen's eyes dropped to his folded hands resting on the edge of his desk. "How is the best way to get that much of the catalyst into her system? Through ingestion, either pills or drink; or by inoculation, which goes immediately into the bloodstream. The first way is less traceable. She'd probably have to wait a while, possibly several months, for her tissues to absorb enough to do any good. After that, there should be no problem if things work the way I think they might."

"How do you suggest we discover the trigger?" Gillian asked.

"Observe what she craves. If it's pizza, she might be unconsciously trying to elevate her levels of Vitamin C, lutein, or both. If she eats quantities of bread, she may need something in the yeast. Bananas could indicate potassium."

Jim stood, holding out his right hand. "Thank you, Doctor Bowen. Thank you very much."

"You're very welcome, Detective, Ms. Matthews, but I want a *quid pro quo*." He stood. "Two things. Let me know about her food cravings. And should she try to go back, will you call me?"

"Sure."

Dr. Bowen extended his hand. Jim's fist engulfed it. Stepping around his desk, he bent and kissed Gillian's fingers. "It is I who should thank you. It's not every day I'm faced with a problem which allows me to stitch together cloudy realms of possibilities like these with immediate realities."

"Our pleasure." Jim turned to leave, a smile tugging at his mouth. He'd enjoyed the discussion with the research biologist.

"Before you forget, here's my card." Dr. Bowen held

out two. They each took one. "That has my work number here, as well as my home number and cell phone. You can get me by one of those anyplace on this planet."

"We'll do that." Slipping the doctor's card in her briefcase, Gillian followed Jim from the office of the biology lab.

"Dr. Bowen gave us a problem," grumbled Jim. "He said months. Treece doesn't have months."

"I know," Gillian replied, sounding tired and worried. "She has only days."

"Jim, we have a problem."

"Another one?" Gillian, he reflected while standing to welcome her to the park bench where they'd agreed to have lunch on his day off, often began conversations without salutations. "Hi, Gillian. You look lovely."

"What? Oh, hello. I'm sorry. It's just that . . . well. . . ." She sat down, dropping her briefcase beside her feet. "I need a glass of wine," she sighed, lifting her face to the sunshine while she eased tense shoulders against the warm wood. "Boy, have I got a headache."

"Treece's case?" Carefully Jim put his arm on the back of the wooden slat next to her without touching the fabric of her gray suit.

Gillian nodded. "I spent the last ten minutes on the phone with Chad Jennings. He canceled tomorrow's session, then started a harangue about how taxes could be cut and my own caseload improved if people like me spent time with real hard-luck kids instead of well-adjusted ones like Treece. He's trying to blame us for her discontent. Says she's changed to the point he almost doesn't recognize her any more. She's moody, unresponsive." She sucked in a deep breath of air smelling faintly of dill and lemons. "And their family vacation's starting early. They're heading for the airport tonight."

"Damn." He glanced at his watch. "That gives us what, four hours?"

"Everything we've worked so hard for, gone. Poof. The end." She lowered her head to gaze across the park. "That poor kid. Sometimes things just don't work right no matter what we do. I'd adopt her, if I could."

Jim wanted to take Gillian in his arms and rub her back to ease her tension, but didn't dare. His partner was already teasing him for paying serious attention to her. "Yeah, Jennings has been bugging me, too. Three times this week. But this isn't over yet."

"So we can do something, even though we don't have time to try Dr. Bowen's theories about her food cravings?"

"I think so, but we'll have to move immediately."

"Jennings also sounds like he's ready to take Brazil to court for stealing his daughter. He's spoiling for a fight. So what do we do?" Gillian had fire in her eyes now, had straightened from her slump. She was a real crusader, Jim thought. He liked crusaders.

Jim ticked off the points on his fingers. "One, we go get Treece and see if she can sneak out. It will likely get us into some hot water with her parents; but then, we're already in hot water with her father. Two, call Dr. Bowen, and see if he can meet us. Three, we'll see if anything happens there. If not, we'll hope we can reestablish contact with the girl after they get back, and try again."

"If they come back."

"They will. Jennings has too much business going on here to leave it and disappear. It's his reason for being, lets him be king. And I don't think he wants to spend the rest of his life in close association with Tiffie. She's his trophy wife."

Gillian stood, laughing. "You're doing my job. Come on, Mr. Counselor, your car or mine?"

Jim pulled out his cell phone from its holster and Dr. Bowen's card from his shirt pocket, quickly punching in the number and relaying the information about the meeting to the biologist. Gillian contacted Treece. Then the two drove slowly to northern La Jolla, giving Dr. Bowen a half hour to arrive. They parked and walked to the Jennings's driveway.

Treece joined them before ten minutes had elapsed, licking the last bits of distinctive chocolate from her fingers. "Hi, Ms. Matthews, Detective," she said, a little breathless. "I didn't tell them, so Mom and Dad are going to be really pissed. Mom's in the middle of packing for the third time." She wilted a bit. "And if we stay around here, we'll be easy for Dad to find when he misses me in the house."

"That's okay, Treece," said Jim. "Dr. Bowen, a research biologist, is coming. He knows about your case, and is willing to help."

She brightened. "Great. Did you find out anything new?"

"Only that what you do is called phasing," Gillian said. "And it's likely triggered by food you're craving."

"Or emotions," Jim said. "Or all of the above."

Treece frowned. "The only things I've really wanted lately were from Norrinost. And Mom's been on that new no-carb diet. She insisted I go on it with her." The girl made a face. "I haven't gained that much weight since I came back."

"So this is your young lady," a new voice called.

Jim turned, waving to the biologist as he climbed out of his Volvo. "Dr. Bowen, meet Treece Jennings."

"Hi," she said.

"Hello. I understand we're under a time disadvantage." The biologist peered at the girl. "Have you tried activating your ability yet?"

"No," Gillian replied. "We just got here."

"Then by all means, my dear." Dr. Bowen nodded at Treece. "Try it. I believe you don't need to be precisely where you were when you first disappeared to do it again."

"Just like in the comic books," Treece giggled, walking down the street until its curve hid her.

"No good." She reappeared moments later, her voice reflecting Jim's silent disappointment.

"Again," directed Dr. Bowen. "This time, walk slower. Try to remember how you felt before."

Jim counted forty heartbeats before he heard the scrape of her sandals and saw her returning form.

"Nope. Anything else we can try?"

"Were you crying that night?" asked the biologist.

"Maybe." Treece cudgeled her memory, frowning. "I don't know."

"Hmmmmm. Wonder what's different. Perhaps if you—"

"*What are you people doing to my daughter?*"

"Damn," Jim said softly, turning to watch Chad Jennings stride along the driveway. Tiffie trotted on heeled sandals behind him, her hands held out for balance. "Quick, Treece, do it again."

"I thought it might be you," Chad threw open the wrought iron door in the security gate, scowling at Jim and Gillian. He took a macho stance with feet apart and his arms crossed on his chest. "I've called my lawyer. He's putting through a restraining order for both of you with a good friend who happens to be one of the most influential judges in southern California." He turned to the biologist, contempt written in his body language. "Who's this? Another member of your Aliens on Earth society?"

"*Doctor* Langléy Bowen, Head of Human Biology, UCSD." The shorter man's voice gave him undeniable stature. "I'm here to help your daughter." He turned his back on Chad. "Try again, my dear."

"Help her what?" Chad demanded, with Tiffie's voice echoing his words a moment later. He frowned, then his features hardened with anger.

"I knew it! You've wanted to take away my daughter since you first saw her! And this is your perverted way of trying to get her! Well, I won't let you get away with it. You just stop—"

"Nope." Treece trudged halfway back to them, defeat showing in her sloping shoulders. "Any more suggestions?"

"Patrice Gilberta Jennings, you get inside this gate with me right now!" Chad thundered.

Treece looked up, stopped. Animation drained from her face.

"Pattie, my dearest widdle girl, what are you doing?" her mother cried.

Treece's hands clenched. Jim watched her knuckles turn white.

"Treece," her father raged, "if you don't come home right now, you'll have no privileges for months! We're getting rid of your dog, too."

His daughter stood her ground. Her shoulders pulled

back. Jim saw determination narrow her mouth and a spark of anger flare in her eyes.

"No."

"What?" Chad's argument stalled.

"You don't listen." Treece looked like a queen standing on the street in her denim shorts and hand-painted T-shirt. "You never have. What you need isn't a daughter, it's an audience. I never had that problem in Norrinost. They took me seriously. I did more than go to school, think about boys, and shop. I used my talents every day. I was appreciated. I was loved more than you can ever imagine, not used as a convenience when you want someone's attention. And I want to go back. I hope you understand me this time. *I want to go back.*"

"No you don't. You're my daughter, and you're staying right here. Understand? Right here!" Chad's face flushed crimson. He raised a hand and pointed a finger at Treece. "Get yourself over here. We're leaving in a few minutes. This is going to be a pleasant family vacation. I've called a limo to take us to the airport."

"Oh, I'm leaving all right, Dad. Without you. To a place you can't come." The girl whirled and strode again down the road. "What's that line from Shakespeare? 'Once more into the breach . . .'"

"Damn." She turned, looking at Jim, Gillian, and Dr. Bowen, taking two steps toward them, an imploring hand outstretched. "Still nothing. Can't you do something? Can't you—"

The street seemed all too still without her voice and presence. Jim stood transfixed, staring at the space no longer filled by Treece Jennings. He was certain his mouth hung open, as Gillian's did.

"Well, well, well." Dr. Bowen finally broke the silence. "That is an intriguing end. I am heartily glad to have been here. I do hope she got back to where she wanted to be. I never thought to seriously take human emotion into account as part of the catalyst."

"What triggered it?" Jim asked in a taut voice. One arm stole around Gillian's shoulders. She snuggled beneath it as if she were cold, and trembled.

"Was she eating anything when she met you?" the doctor asked.

"Ch-chocolate," murmured Gillian. "Godiva dark chocolate."

"Endorphins," Dr. Bowen said. "Along with controlled, channeled anger. Now if you'll excuse me, I'm going to write up my notes while the events are fresh in my mind. Thank you."

Jim and Gillian followed the biologist down the path toward their car. They left Chad Jennings staring at the bridge where he'd last seen his daughter, his wife sobbing softly against his chest.

SPRING BREAK

Rebecca Lickiss

Rebecca Lickiss has always been an avid reader, and began telling stories at an early age. She received her BS degree in Physics from George Mason University, and worked for a while as an engineer evaluating weapons software. She now lives in Colorado with her husband and children, where she spends her free time reading and writing.

"Hello, Sailor."

The mop splashed into the battered wooden bucket, then arced out, scattering sandy water across the ship's wooden planking in a semi-circle. The gnome pushed the mop through and around the scattered water with the air of someone totally absorbed in his work and completely deaf to anyone around him.

Captain Lacy snorted, and stalked off to the bow of his ship, *L'Humanité*. It was really too sultry a day for his usual full regalia of tight black leather, so he'd settled for wearing the black leather pants with an open-chested creamy silk shirt, and using his finest pink parasol for shade. The trailing ribbons cracked nicely in his wake.

A large troll reclined on the deck, blocking the last ten feet or so, feet braced portside and shoulders leaning against the starboard. Even with tightly shut eyes the troll kept his reflector angled to best catch the bright sunlight.

On second thought, Captain Lacy decided that he didn't want to check closely enough to determine if the troll had one of those skimpy swimming briefs on. Instead, Lacy said, "Hello, Sailor."

The troll didn't move.

"Yo, rocks-for-brains, shouldn't you be concerned that your captain has caught you lounging around when you should be working?"

"I'm busy," the troll rumbled quietly.

"Busy doing what?"

"I'm overcoming the cultural and species stereotypes that have long held my people underground, in the dark."

"Roq! You're sunbathing!" Lacy deliberately held his parasol to block the sun from the troll's face.

The troll, Roq, opened wise, sad, brown eyes that looked more appropriate to a basset hound than to an enormous mobile rock. "That's what I said."

"Honestly! What kind of pirates are we?" Lacy brought his parasol back to shade himself and pulled a matching feathered fan out of his right scabbard. A flick of his wrist spread the pink tendrilled feathers, and he fanned his face. "Without a human this ship goes right to pot. You won't work, half the crew won't listen to me, and the other half is busy planning mutiny."

Roq returned to his sunbathing. "Naw. They're just playing poker, and waiting for you to gate another human in."

"We do not need human beings."

"Yes, we do."

"It's not fair to them."

"They don't seem to mind."

"Oh, well, certainly." Lacy slashed his fan through the air between him and the troll. "Once they are here and dependent on us to get back, I'm sure they'd feel quite comfortable complaining."

"Then I guess we'll never really know."

"It's not fair."

"We could just tell the next human you gate in that if they're happy they can stay, and if not we'll send them directly back."

"No!" Lacy flicked his fan shut, and returned it to its scabbard. "It's not fair to me." His fingers briefly brushed his chest, and he sighed. "I left the Forest King's palace to get away from having to gate in humans, and here I am. In the middle of the ocean. And still no one appreciates anything about me except my ability to gate in humans."

"Elf princes really are a whiny lot." Roq shifted his bulk slightly. "And in any case, we're just off the coast."

Lacy leaned against the starboard rail, to sulk. "Nine dwarves, seven fairies, five gnomes, one troll and one elf. What a motley lot we are."

"Don't forget that thing in the hold."

"We need to get rid of it. Otherwise we'll never be able to reap the rewards of our ill-gotten gains, possibly rotting down there."

"Hmm." Roq opened one eye. "I bet a human would go down there and get rid of it for us."

"I've told you. It's not fair to the humans. And in any

case, not all humans do well here. Remember that one woman? She's been here . . . what? Three times?"

"Seven."

"And she still goes nuts every time she shows up. You'd think she'd be used to us by now."

Roq shut his eye. "You'd think. But it doesn't leave us with much to do."

Pulling himself up straight, Lacy said, "I order you to think of something to do."

With a rumbling, as of a small rockslide, the troll stood, towering over the much smaller elf captain. He looked like one of the better classical marble sculptures to illustrate the beauty of the perfect naked form. A small smiled formed on his lips. "Hello, Sailor."

"Tsk." Lacy turned away. "If you're going to be like that, I guess I have no choice but to clean up the hold." He flounced toward the helm. "Let's see, a human that can take on the thing in the hold. He'll have to be strong and courageous. Forceful and fearless. Yet, curious and creative."

The gnome flung down his mop, to join with Roq in trailing behind Lacy. Other members of the crew materialized from seemingly nowhere, knowing through some unknown manner that something fun was about to start.

Without asking, Lacy was handed his mirror, traded off his fan for his sword, and opened his box of rare and unique powders as it was held out to him. "Ready the cannon," he said absently as he picked prepared packets from the box.

Roq shouted commands at the crew, who hustled to obey. Roq himself pulled the cannon from its position, and turned it around, carefully sighting to make certain that the shot would go past the hold door without hitting any masts or sails.

Lacy carefully poured the multicolored powders into a large wooden bowl, swirling it gently to mix them. Then he placed the mirror over top of the bowl. Looking into it, he said the words of the spell, finishing with, "Strong and courageous. Forceful and fearless. Curious and creative. And cute."

Grinning, he removed the mirror, motioning for the dwarf beside him to add the gunpowder. The whole was poured down the barrel of the cannon and tamped down. Roq added the cannon ball, and Lacy threaded the fuse.

With a flourish of his hand, Lacy magically lit the fuse, and everyone braced for the explosion. An enormous boom shook the deck. As the cannon ball sailed past the hold door and off over the water out to sea, the crew cheered. Lacy stepped forward and opened the door to the hold.

Before he could register what sort of human he had gated in, a fast fist caught him on the chin, knocking him flat on his back and unconscious.

Nina looked around wildly. Getting lost in the musty deserted halls of her crazy aunt's house in the middle of a storm-wrought power outage had been bad enough. Finding herself suddenly in the bright sunshine, on a boat, on the high seas, surrounded by a host of strangely dressed, strangely sized, strange men, well there's only so much a teenage girl can take. She just let her worst instincts take over and swung her fists at one and all.

The average-sized fool in cream-colored silk shirt and tight black leather pants lay on the deck, one splayed hand beside a ridiculous looking, and slightly bent, pink lace parasol. Her second, much lower, backhand bowled down a whole row of short, rolypoly men wearing pointed green hats with brown feathers and some sort of heavy green denim overall shorts. An assortment of ring-mail clad short men scrambled to get away from her, and anyway Nina wasn't too keen on hitting metal with a bare fist. A large, heavily muscled and veined man stepped between her and the shorter fellows. Nina hauled back and let him have it in the stomach as hard as she could.

Waves of pain rolled up her arm. Nina blinked back tears, looking up, and up, at her opponent.

He grinned down at her.

"Oh, my," she breathed.

"Thank you." He bent one arm, preening and posing. "Muscles like bricks."

Reaching over with her good hand, Nina scratched his ribs. "More like rocks."

"Of course." He grinned and kept posing.

"Marble, I presume."

"No presumption, Marble. I don't mind the attention." He stopped preening, and looked over his shoulder at the unconscious man on the deck. "Though I think we'd better wake the captain."

"What?"

"Captain! Yo!" The statue-like man reached down and picked the unconscious man up. Nina watched in amaze-ment as the statue briskly slapped the other man's cheeks. "Wakey, wakey." After a moment the man shook off the statue and stood, somewhat unsteadily, glaring at Nina. "Marble, this is Captain Lacy. Captain, this is Marble."

"Marble?" both Nina and Lacy said at the same time.

"That's what she said." The statue man frowned down

at her. "Though I haven't figured out how she knew my name."

"I don't know your name," Nina said.

"Tsk." Lacy picked up his bent parasol, and held it awkwardly. "Now, why do you think her name is Marble?"

"She hit me, and I told her I had muscles like bricks. She said, 'More like Roq's.' Which, of course is true. Then she said her name was Marble."

"Big and dumb." Nina slapped her forehead. She glared for a moment at the idiots before her. "Forget it. Never mind. How did I get here? And where is here? And what happened to Aunt Edwina's house?"

"You'd think she'd be more interested in how to get back," Lacy said as he unbent his parasol.

Getting back to Aunt Edwina's really wasn't very high on Nina list of things to do. She'd been spending a lot of time there trying to think of excuses to leave, to go into town, go shopping, go to the movies, anything to get her out of that awful house. Nina understood now why her cousin Fred had run away from home two years ago. She felt no particular urge to get back. She glared at Lacy. "Well? Where am I?"

Lacy looked at Roq, who looked back. They stood there like that for a moment. Then a slow smile spread across Lacy's face. He turned back to Nina. "You are here." He swirled his parasol, and tucked a stray lock of hair behind one pointed ear. "And here you will remain until you have completed the work you were sent here to do."

"And who are you?" Nina's gaze took in all the crew, most of who had gathered around, just out of reach.

"I am Lacy, Captain of *L'Humanité*, and these are my

crew." Lacy waved his free hand at the shorter men. "You met my First Mate, Roq. This is my helmsman—"

"No," Nina interrupted. "Who are you?"

Lacy looked enlightened. "Ah. I am an elf. Roq is a troll. These are gnomes—"

"That's nice. And where is the camera?"

"There is no camera. But you are stuck here until—"

"I know, until I do what I was sent here to do." Nina sighed. Well, at least it wouldn't be boring, like sitting through another day of high school. "Fine, what do you want me to do?"

Nina edged forward through the dark, clutching the wooden club with her right hand. Something was in here. Considering the crazies up on the deck of the ship, it was probably something insane. They claimed it was something magical, something mysterious, something monstrous.

The hold smelled musty and wet, with overtones of something rotting. The crates Nina touched as she passed were rough but dry wood, and she worried about splinters. The hold wasn't quite pitch dark, light filtered in from cracks above. But what little light there was only served to illuminate dust motes, and create a darkness consisting of various dark shades of black.

At least the creaking and swaying of the ship served to disguise the scurrying and squeaks of rats. Nina really didn't want to meet up with any rats. She wasn't real thrilled with having to search out what everyone referred to as "the thing" in the hold. However, when confronted with a live statue—much, much larger than life—who was certain that she was going down into the hold to find "the thing," Nina hadn't been able to say no. Or rather hadn't had either the opportunity or the inclination to say no.

Something shuffled off to her left, and she froze in her tracks. Off to the right something wet smacked against the side of the ship. Nina hoped it was something outside the ship. Perhaps the ocean. She inched forward, feeling her way with the tips of her fingers, dreading the moment she touched something live. Her questing fingers discovered that this crate was the last before a yawning gap to her left.

Another wet slap sounded off to her right, and suddenly a detour to the left seemed an excellent idea. Nina eased around the corner of the crate.

Perhaps there was no "thing" down here. Perhaps the crew above was mistaken. Plainly anyone could mistake what and who might be down here, and considering how crazy they appeared, such a mistake was inevitable. Right? Perhaps—

The wet slap sounded closer this time, much closer. At perhaps the point where Nina had turned the corner of the crate.

"Good to eats, is its?" something very creepy and not nearly far enough away hissed softly in the darkness.

"Go away," Nina whispered back at it as she inched away.

" 'Go away,' says its. 'Go away.' " The voice mockingly reproduced the quavering fear of Nina's voice. "Go away should its." Squishy footsteps and the distinct plop of water dripping slowly onto wood accompanied the approach of the voice.

The sinking heaviness of fear in her stomach reminded Nina uncomfortably of the teasing and pranks at school. The thought that this might be just another attempt to make a fool of her stoked her anger. "Stay away. I'm warning you."

The squishy footsteps came closer, as Nina discovered the narrow space between the crates ended at another crate.

No, not ended. To the right a meager opening between two crates, just enough to slip through, and on the other side a slender shaft of light pierced the gloom.

Though if this thing thought she'd run into the light and let it get a good look at her it had another think coming.

Nina braced herself.

"Go away!" it slavered, spraying spittle.

She brought her club down on top of the blackest shadow of darkness as hard as she could. It hit something with a force that sent the shock back up her arm, and a satisfyingly meaty thunk. The shadow crumbled to the floor, and held very still.

Reaching down Nina felt damp, heavy cloth, and long, tangled hair. She pulled the thing through the narrow passage and into the light. Letting it lay on the floor, she took a moment to catch her breath, and stare.

It looked vaguely human, but then so did the live statue above. Somewhat larger than herself, but not by much. Taller definitely, but also much thinner, as if it hadn't been eating too well for a while. Damp cloth hung in thick, heavy strands from some sort of waterproof coat, and thick matted hair covered its head and face. Nina pushed the hair out of its face, and nearly fell over.

"Fred?"

He groaned.

* * *

The crew scurried about, hurrying to their various tasks with an efficiency and alacrity that made Lacy's heart swell with pride. "Full sail, Mister Roq," he shouted.

"Aye, Captain!" Roq held tight to the main mast shouting orders and deprecations at any of the crew that caught his eye. "Full sail, you lazy louts." He grabbed a wizened old elf attempting to slink past and held him up for Lacy to see. "Orders for the Weathermaster, sir?"

"To the aft hurricane deck. I want a strong wind. We make for Port Whiskey, and I want to be there by morning!" Lacy watched in satisfaction as Roq swung his arm wide easily tossing the old weathermaster between the sails and back onto the hurricane deck to call up the winds and fill the sails.

The exhilaration and joy of piracy filled Lacy. This was the way it should be, with the crew busy, the wind blowing a steady electrifying course, a hold full of booty to be unloaded, and more just laying around in people's ships and ports, waiting to be taken. He rubbed his hands together in anticipation of the drinking and the wenching after the fighting over splitting the loot. Yes, this was it. This was the life. This was the way it should be!

Why, Lacy wondered idly, did they need a human for this?

"Fred?" Nina pushed the rest of the hair out of her cousin's face. "Gee, I'm sorry, Fred. I didn't know it was you."

"Nina?" Fred sat up and clutched her shoulder, obviously wondering if he should rethink sitting up. "What're you doing here?"

"Long story." Nina helped him get his wet costume

off, and they crawled up on top of the crates to sit. "My mom freaked when I said I wanted to spend spring break up at the lake. She acted like I had an engraved invitation to the burning of Sodom and Gomorrah. So I got packed off to Aunt Edwina's to keep me safe. The night before I was to go home there was this tremendous thunderstorm, and all the lights went out. Half the town was blacked out. Next thing I know, I'm on this ship with all these weirdos, who want me to go down into the hold and see what I can do about 'the thing.'"

"Ah." Fred sighed glumly. "So, how is my mother these days?"

"Well, I would have said just as crazy as always, but. . . ."

Fred nodded. "Yes, I think I owe her an apology."

"What are you doing here?" Nina shifted on the rough crate to let her feet dangle down the side into the narrow passageways.

"I really did mean to run away." Fred moved to sit beside her, with his feet also dangling. "Did Mom find my note?"

"Oh, yes." Nina watched as the shaft of light coming from above moved rhythmically with the tossing of the ship, alternately illuminating and shadowing the crevasse between the wooden crates. "She was very upset."

Sighing again, Fred bit at the end of a splinter sticking out of his hand. He expertly pulled it out with his teeth and spit it off into the dark. "I just wanted to get away. Next thing I know I'm in this strange place with all these wondrous things. The elves wanted me to perform a task for them, then they were going to send me back, but I didn't want to leave. So I ran away—I was getting very good at it by then—and stowed away aboard one of these ships. The first night out at sea we were attacked by pirates. I was hiding in one of the crates when it was transferred magically to the pirate ship. I heard talk on the other ship, as we were being looted. They said the pirates were nasty, bloodthirsty, vicious brutes. I decided it probably wouldn't be a good idea to just pop out and say, 'Hello!' So I just kept quiet. Basically, I've been skulking around down here trying to scare off anyone who comes down." His booted feet thumped into the crate they sat on. "I guess I've really just been running away all over again. I figure eventually they'll unload the booty and me with it. I haven't figured out what to do then."

"They're scared of you, you know." Nina saw Fred grin momentarily as the shaft of light played quickly over his face.

"That's funny." He made a sound something between a chuckle and a groan. "I've been so afraid of them."

"Hmm." Nina bit her lip. "Some of them are a bit much."

"I guess you're here to take me back home."

Nina sighed. "Yeah. Once I get rid of 'the thing' the Captain says he'll send me back. I suppose I need to get back to school, and my life, and all the rest. . . ."

They sat in silence for a moment.

"Not that there's really all that much to get back to," Nina said finally. "After all, if my parents freaked at the thought of me spending a few days at the lake, imagine what they'll say when they hear my plans for the rest of my life. Travel, adventure, excitement."

Fred made a shocked noise in a perfect imitation of Nina's father. "Young lady! You have no clue what life is really about. You give no thought to your responsibilities, or the consequences of your immature actions."

Laughing and groaning at the same time, Nina gently slapped his arm. "Yeah. I guess I'd better be getting back."

"You don't . . . have to." Fred slouched down picking at a rip in the knee of his blue jeans. "I had a thought."

"A thought."

"Yeah." He grinned at her. "What if we didn't go back just yet? What if we had a little fun first. I mean, if they're scared of me up there, maybe we could convince them that they need to do some stuff for us before 'the thing' will leave their hold."

She knew she shouldn't listen to Fred. She knew he'd lead her into trouble, just like always. But, it was such a tempting idea. "Exactly what would we do though?"

Fred jumped down from his crate with a smooth practiced motion, landing with a quiet thump. "Well, we should get our share of all this." He motioned around at the crates nearly filling the hold. "Our just rewards for getting rid of the thing. Right?"

"You are the thing." Nina frowned. She knew she shouldn't listen to him.

"There must be wrongs we could right, or, or people in dire straits we could rescue, or, ah—"

"Booty we could steal?"

"Yes!" Fred realized too late what he'd said. "No. No. That's not what I mean. We could do good." He reached up to help her get down.

With Fred leading the way, Nina didn't have to inch her way through the narrow passages between the crates. She hoped he was leading her back to the rope ladder that would get her out of this darkness. "So, we're going to have some fun. Do some good. Kick some butt."

"Exactly."

"So what do I tell the loony fairies up there?" Nina pointed up, without thinking that Fred couldn't see her in the near blackness of the hold. It didn't seem to matter. Either Fred had adapted enough to see in the darkness, or he knew without looking what she meant.

"Hmmm. We'll need to work that out. I think it's important that I remain the scary thing in the hold."

"Uhn-huh," Nina said. "You like being the scary thing."

Fred shrugged. "So, how much of a percentage do you think we should ask for?"

". . . And then I barely escaped with my life." To Nina's amazement the gathered crew had listened in rapt attention as she told her fanciful tale. "I ran up the ladder just ahead of it. I wouldn't go down there if I were you."

"Wow." Roq stared at her wide eyed.

"He wants ten percent of our loot?" Captain Lacy looked skeptical.

"He says it's his," Nina tried to sound reasonable.

"But we stole it!" Lacy shouted indignantly.

"And he stole it from you," Nina shouted back.

"And on my own ship!" Lacy folded his parasol with a frustrated thwack. Using it as a cane, he leaned on it thoughtfully. "Well, I suppose we could give him five percent."

Nina shrugged. "I can ask. I don't know what he'll say."

Roq leaned closer. "I can't believe you actually touched him, let alone fought him. He squishes."

"I did what I had to do." Nina steeled herself not to back away from the troll. It would make her story look suspect. "Oh, by the way, he mentioned something about some city where the people are really bad. Very mean. Oppressing others." If someone didn't take up this line soon, she was going to flounder and sink without a hope.

"Shacika!" Roq shouted and rose in one swift blur of fury.

One of the chain-mail clad dwarves stepped forward. "The loathsome brutes have been enslaving dwarves!"

"Well." Nina hesitated a second. Did she really want to do this? "The Thing says we've got to do something about it."

"Very well." Lacy slashed his pink parasol through the air like a sword, trailing ribbons and lace. "We'll unload this cargo at Port Whiskey and make for Shacika! When we're done they'll know what justice is!"

The dwarves began a chant that was quickly taken up by the rest of the crew. "Yea for the Thing! Yea for Captain Lacy! Yea for the Thing! Yea for Captain Lacy!"

"Don't forget the girl, you idiots," Roq shouted. "Move you lazy louts! This ship has a port to make."

The crew scurried around busying themselves with mysterious sailing tasks. Nina figured she'd learn how to handle a ship soon enough.

"Captain, what are your orders?" Roq asked.

Nina understood the look on the captain's face as he shouted orders for Roq to repeat and enforce. The exhilaration, the electricity. The magic.

Yes, this is what she wanted to do. This was the way it should be.

WELCOME TO THE CRYSTAL ARCHES

Irene Radford

A member of an endangered species, a native Oregonian who lives in Oregon, Irene Radford and her husband make their home in Welches, Oregon, where deer, bear, coyote, hawks, owls and woodpeckers feed regularly on their back deck. As a service brat, she lived in a number of cities throughout the country before returning to Oregon in time to graduate from Tigard High School. She earned a B.A. in history from Lewis and Clark College, where she met her husband. In her spare time, Irene enjoys lacemaking and is a long-time member of an international guild. "Welcome To The Crystal Arches" goes back to the fun and games she discovered while writing Guardian of the Trust, *Merlin's Descendants #2.*

"Welcome to the Crystal Arches. How may I help you?" A young woman wearing a white Time Parlour uniform appeared on the holographic screen. Behind her crystal arches blinked blue in an hypnotic pulse.

"I want to watch King John sign *Magna Carta*," I said.

"I'm sorry, that tour is closed." The screen went blank. I pressed the redial button. The screen pulsed with my personalized ringing function, a small dragon knocking at a door. After what seemed an eternity, I watched as he turned away from the door and shrugged. No one was going to answer.

On to the next Time Parlour, one block away.

This time I went in, rather than risk the dialup service. The doorway disappeared behind me in a hologram of pure white to match the walls.

It smelled like a hospital. Mediaeval England would not smell so clean and empty. It would smell of earth and life and . . . enthusiasm.

The technician asked in a bored voice, "Date?"

She stared at her PDA, never looking up to acknowledge me. She held the stylus above the screen, waiting to enter the date I gave her. Her white uniform was as bright as the painted walls of the room. Somehow she seemed to blend with them. Her blue hair, against the fashionable fish-belly white of her skin was the only color in the room. If not for the odd metallic dye-job of her tightly coifed hair, I might not have noticed her, or anyone else, in the otherwise colorless warehouse-sized room.

Interior decorators had gotten very good at producing holograms that hid things like doors and windows, people, and, more than ever, security systems.

The security-conscious business world loved the new décor. They could watch and listen to everything without being detected.

Paranoid King John would have loved the new eaves-dropping devices.

"June 15, 1215, Runnymede Meadow, England," I replied.

She, unlike her dial up counterpart, went through the motions of accessing the system.

I resisted fidgeting from foot to foot. Time was running out for me. I was on the ragged end of a run at my doctorate in English Government, a necessary event if I were ever to have a future. I needed one more crucial piece of evidence to finish my dissertation. Traveling back to the birth of representative rule in the Western Hemisphere was the only option left to me.

"Thumb print." The tech held out her screen for me to press my digit onto it.

I did so, looking over my shoulder to see if my rival, Charlie, had followed me.

"Credit denied, Charlotte Mitchell. That will be a $50 fee for wasting my time. Cash." The tech held out her hand for the bribe.

I turned and marched out of the Time Parlour.

Fury burned my cheeks and pumped extra blood to my legs. I knew I had enough money in that account for a standard Time-Travel Trip. Just.

That was the third Parlour to deny me access to the evidence I needed. Had Charlie found a way to block my credit, my credentials, and my health screen? He must realize I was close to proving my theory right and his wrong.

One of us would present irrefutable evidence to our review boards in three days. One of us would earn the coveted degree, publication, speaking engagements, and teaching positions.

I had nothing left to fall back on: no family, no money, no prestige. If I failed, I'd be reduced to teaching . . . shudder . . . high school, the most dangerous job on the planet.

Charlie, on the other hand, came from old money with many opportunities waiting for him with or without his degree. But he needed the degree for prestige's sake, to maintain his position as a viable heir to several fortunes. Without it, he was just another cousin, a playboy, and a drain upon society.

Furthermore, his ego could not stand failure. That's only one reason why I kicked him out after a brief affair. I knew he might resort to cheating to keep me from succeeding.

My nose twitched. My stomach growled at the addictive odor of fat and salt. Only then did I notice the Parlour was flanked by fast food restaurants on each side. Long lines of people, all dressed in time-travel white, waited impatiently for their orders. You couldn't eat on time trips, and early on the fast-food industry had learned the heavy foot traffic at Time Parlours allowed them to catch large volumes of people with disposable income and justification to eat the empty calories they served. I had sworn to never fall prey to them and their illusion of nutrition.

I sat on a nearby bench to review my options. Next to me an obese man sat, a huge cheeseburger in one hand and a time brochure for 18th century French carnivals in the other. The height of decadence, the brochure proclaimed. It made me sick. Here I was, a legitimate researcher, finding my way to the past blocked while voyeuristic baboons like this one took their lecherous trips at will. It wasn't fair.

I had only one recourse left. The legitimate Time Parlours might be closed to me. But I knew the black market facilities shipped anyone anywhen with no restrictions.

When the secret to time travel and retrieving the travelers had burst upon the scientific world ten years ago, historians were the first authorized travelers. They revolutionized research techniques. At first the crystal arches were authorized only for the period of the researcher's lifetime. Each year, grad students, anthropologists, and tourists pushed the boundaries. The medieval period had just opened two months ago. I'd been trying to get access to the field of Runnymede ever since.

If Charlie got there before me, he might deliberately alter history to ensure his success. No one had managed that yet. I could not allow Charlie to be the first. It took less than two minutes of chatting with the overweight and greasy patrons to learn how to find the less reputable travel centers.

I ducked into the dingy brick building two blocks away. A faded sign that faintly resembled the famous crystal arches of licensed and guaranteed time travel glowed like a weathered drugstore sign on the grimy exterior.

The foyer was empty except for a weathered woman behind a partition. No exterior intercom. No pristine white walls reflecting the too bright pulsing light of the arches. Just an ordinary waiting room with chairs, a fake ficus tree in the corner, and a stack of nine-month-old magazines. It might have been a dentist's office. Even the sliding glass partition between me and the receptionist belonged to the medical profession. I began to sweat. My teeth began to ache. Extra acid churned in my gut.

The walls closed in on me. Literally. All the exits had vanished; nothing but blank beige walls relieved only by

watercolors that might have been painted by a ten-year-
old, and the receptionist's window.

"This is just time travel, not a dentist," I reminded myself.

The receptionist looked up from her screen and stared
at me as if I had interrupted the most important work of
all time.

"I need to go to Runnymede Meadow, England, June
15, 1215," I blurted out.

"Cash or credit?" The slightly cross-eyed woman in a
bright purple uniform tunic and baggy trousers slid open
the window a bare two centimeters.

"Credit please. Mary Jones Number 25222-22." I gave
her the name and number of my dummy account. Everybody had at least one that that the government could not
track. I knew there was more than ample money there to
pay for the trip. Unless Charlie had drained it as he had
one of my legitimate accounts.

I stuck my thumb between the panes of glass.

She pressed a screen against me, almost pushing my
hand back into my portion of the room.

"One moment please." She closed the window and returned to her screen.

I shifted my weight from foot to foot. I stared at the
ceiling, the bad paintings on the walls, the floor. I whis-
tled the national anthem all the way through twice. Convinced I'd have to wait until tomorrow, I took two steps
toward one of the cracked plastic and metal chairs and
picked up a professional scooter racing magazine I knew
I had not read.

"Miss Jones," the receptionist called. A note of ur-
gency in her voice made me hasten back to the window.
"There's a tracer on your account. I can reroute it, but we

can't have you on the premises. You either have to leave, *right now*, or take a destination through the arches."

"I need to go back to June 15, 1215, to the open field a few miles from Windsor Castle."

"Whatever you want. We'll dial it in. But you have to do it *now*."

The receptionist pressed a button beneath her desk. A concealed door beside her window swished open. I dashed through it into another warehouse-sized room, done in unadorned gray cement blocks. The door clicked shut behind me. It disappeared, just like the portals in the lobby.

A double arch of scintillating purple crystal dominated the space. Thirty-five meters high and wide enough to drive a fleet of HumVees through. Dim images drifted within the arches, ghosts of events past. I longed to peer closer, learn some of the secrets obscured by the purple mist.

A man wearing a bright purple lab coat and scrubs looked miniscule beside the arches, not much more solid than the ghosts of time. He adjusted a dozen dials at eye level on the right-hand side of the front arch.

"Take this." The aging technician dangled a clear plastic bracelet before my eyes. Purple lights pulsed and chased each other around and around the piece.

"What is it?" I kept my hands firmly in the pockets of my jeans.

"Retrieval." He finished his adjustments on this side of the arch and moved to the opposite one. He swung his left leg like his hip ached. He probably couldn't get work at a licensed Time Parlour. They catered to a young crowd of tourists who had money and needed thrills to satisfy them. Aging or handicapped people did not fit the image of the Crystal Arches. "Frankly," he continued, "I can understand not coming back." He slapped his hip. "Weren't for this, I might go myself."

"Of course I want retrieval. Why wouldn't I?"

"Most people in as big a hurry as you are running from someone. The other side of them arches is a great place to get lost. Permanently."

I gulped and remembered that this was a black-market parlour operating outside strict government guidelines and limitations.

"I need to come back."

"Fine." He shrugged and dropped the thing into my now outstretched hand. "Put it on and don't take it off. For any reason. I'll give you one hour uptime to do your business, then I lock on and you are outta there."

One hour? Was that all? "And if I have not finished my business?"

"You come anyway or you take off the bracelet and stay there for the rest of your life. Which will probably be short. Medicine was very primitive back then. One nasty cold, and next thing you know you've got pneumonia and pulmonary failure. Then, of course, you could starve to death, since you can't eat any of their food." He laughed without humor.

"Then I'd best hurry."

"Don't worry. The arches distort the flow of time. The further back you go, the slower the flow. One hour uptime, our time, translates to about twelve hours downtime in 1215."

"Fine." I wriggled the plastic circle over my hand and onto my wrist. It dangled loosely but did not fall off. The purple lights slowed, then speeded up until they matched my heart-rate.

"Oh, and remember, you'll be like a ghost. You will not appear solid, and you can't hold on to anything. People will be able to see you in certain lights, and they'll feel the wind of your passage like a sudden chill in the air."

"Will I be able to pass through walls and such?"

"Nope. Gotta wait for someone to open a door. Just like here." He laughed again and looked around at the cavernous space. There appeared to be no exit except through the arches.

"Firing up. Get ready to run when I give you the cue. Do not delay. Do not think twice. And most of all, do not trip or stumble. Otherwise you'll end up somewhere and somewhen else. I won't have coordinates to retrieve you." He fiddled with the dials on the arch once more.

A commotion behind the wall echoed loudly through the room.

"That's the Feds. Run!" he yelled.

"They'll arrest you. You won't be able to bring me back!"

"They have to find me and my arches first. You've got one hour. Now run."

I ran, swallowing my trepidations as I went.

Up and down became meaningless. Forward and back became mere suggestions of thought. The air thickened and shimmered with purple lights, echoing my pulsing bracelet. I had trouble breathing.

Eddies and currents of purple in a dozen different shades swirled around me. Some moved swiftly, light and free in pale shades that did not have time to deepen before moving on. They tugged at me, beckoning me to merge with them and flow where whim took us. Others were sluggish, clogged morasses of dark hues. Their very depth compelled me to fall into their swirling current.

I slogged through the rivers of time, one step at a time careful to remain on a straight course. Faint echoes of the crystal arches guided me. But I saw now that they were full circles, bracelets wrapped around time as my retrieval wrapped around my wrist.

I walked for a long time, about two blocks worth in real time.

From one step to the next I moved from breathing purple sludge to drawing a deep breath of chilled air that tasted faintly of dust and . . . sewage. Not so different from certain areas of the city.

My feet found solid ground. Dressed stone by the feel of it through my worn athletic shoes.

Slowly I opened my eyes. Faint remnants of the crystal arches with their pulsing purple lights chasing each other remained at the edge of my peripheral vision. If I tried to look directly at them, they disappeared. Only by *not* looking at them could I keep them in my awareness.

Dim light filtered through an arrow-slit window to my left. Bright tapestries covered the stone. An oriental carpet cut down the drafts upon the cold floor. Bright hangings showing hunting scenes and rose gardens populated by people in thirteenth-century robes and gowns enclosed the bed. I had landed in a smallish room with too much furniture; carved wooden chests hinged with leather, simple tables, one chair, equally simple, and three candelabra. The charred wicks had been snuffed some time ago and not relit. I was inside a castle.

Right time period. But which castle. Anyplace but Windsor and I'd never make it to Runnymede in time to witness the crucial signing of an important document in our history. I had to see who signed King John's name—the king himself or the Master of the Knights Templar in England, Aymeric de St. Maur.

Charlie contended that de St. Maur signed for the king because John refused to relinquish any of his "Divine Right" as an anointed king. I believed that John signed for himself despite the advice of de St. Maur. The Master wanted a clause inserted in *Magna Carta*, an official recognition of the Templars in England, a guaranteed place in the government, and sanctuary should they wear out their welcome elsewhere—as they did in France, less than a century later.

Possibly John forged de St. Maur's name. Or, as Charlie theorized, de St. Maur forged John's. Only an eyewitness account would prove one way or another what happened.

First I had to find out where I was, and make sure of the date.

Voices behind me interrupted my musings. I turned sharply and nearly lost my balance. I collided with the wall. My shoulder and hip stung, and I wondered if I'd sport bruises tomorrow.

"The draft of the document is already prepared, every clause carefully negotiated. We will not rewrite the Charter at the last moment," said a man in carefully phrased Old French, more a corrupted Latin than the language spoken in my time.

"Stop and think, Highness," a second man said more quietly. "If the Templars have permanent sanctuary in England, we can make available to you the resources of our treasury. Without interest."

I sneaked over to the doorway and peered through. Two men paused three steps from my post. They stood upon the dais of the Great Hall of the castle. Behind them milled dozens of finely robed and armored men. They tried to look busy, adjusting buckles and draping chain mail. But their attention was glued to the two men on the dais.

The taller and broader of the two fingered an empty scabbard at his side. He wore chain mail and a white surplice with a red Templar cross emblazoned upon it. Aymeric de St. Maur.

Beside him, a slighter man, bearded and elegantly robed in bright purple, faced him with a stubborn chin and beady eyes. King John. Only he would wear purple in England at this time. In his presence only William, Earl of Pembroke, the King's Marshall, was allowed to wear his arms. Hence de St. Maur's empty scabbard.

I sighed in relief. I had found the right time and place.

King John shuddered and rubbed his arms. A servant appeared out of nowhere and draped a fur about his king's shoulders.

I withdrew a little, lest I alert these men to my presence.

The king looked around at his assembled retainers and their eager ears. "Let us withdraw." He jerked his head toward the portal where I hovered.

I backstepped barely fast enough to avoid the men walking through me. If colliding with the wall hurt enough to bruise, having whole bodies penetrate mine could kill me. A hazard the scientist had not warned me about.

"We are obligated to go on crusade once this Charter brings peace to England," King John said with his back to the Templar. "Will the Temple finance the entire endeavor?"

De St. Maur blanched whiter than his surplice. He gulped and then smiled. "Your crusade benefits the souls of all Englishmen. Therefore, it is only prudent that all Englishmen contribute. . . ."

The king glared at him. I could almost see de St. Maur whither beneath that gaze.

"The Temple does not love Us or England enough to warrant a permanent and legal sanctuary within Our borders. You and your knights must make do with the lands the Church allows you. We choose our councilors ourselves. Our barons do not choose for Us. Your position on Our council will not be written into the Charter."

A faint chiming sent goose bumps up my spine. The air shimmered iridescent rainbows in the corner. Neither the king nor the Templar glanced that way. Good thing.

Charlie San Bruno, of the Texas San Brunos, materialized within the colored mists. He might have chosen to dress for the period and the chilly atmosphere—in a white woolen monk's robe—but he was still a ghost who could have frightened John into changing history.

"How did you get here, Charlotte?" Charlie demanded, hands on hips and a scowl on his handsome face.

King John peered into the shadow that cloaked my rival's form. "Did you hear something?" he asked in a hushed tone.

"Your conscience, perhaps?" de St. Maur muttered.

John ignored him, much as I ignored Charlie. "For a moment We thought We heard the ghost of Our brother Richard. He spoke the common English you know. Such a vulgar tongue." John shuddered in distaste.

"Highness, about the Charter."

"We shall not sign a document with the clauses you dictate." John flounced out the door.

"Highness. . . ." de St. Maur hurried after the king.

"See, what did I tell you," Charlie sneered. "John won't sign. De St. Maur will have to forge the king's signature."

"You only heard half the conversation. . . ."

"I heard enough to prove my dissertation." He tweaked something on his retrieval.

"But I heard it all. I know the truth."

"Who cares about the truth, Charlotte? All I have to prove is that I came here and observed."

"But I can report. . . ."

"No one will listen to you. I have the money and contacts to back my report."

"You will lie just to get your degree!"

"I'll do what I have to."

"We aren't the only travelers. When the tourists discover. . . ."

"This time slot is about to be closed, permanently. Historians are discovering that tourism alters historical events. Crucial moments are being closed to all but the most serious scholars who file the proper paperwork, meaning a substantial bribe to the right person, and are escorted by authorized guides. My dissertation will make me the only authorized guide to this time slot. I will control who sees these events and what they observe."

The arches in my peripheral vision began to pulse.

Charlie was leaving. He'd only done half the research. I could not allow him to distort history to suit his own ego.

I dove for him. My fingers locked in his retrieval as we both plunked to the floor. I yanked. He jerked. The bracelet broke, a dozen pulses of allcolor/nocolor light spilled out of the hollow tube onto the floor like so many puddles of glass. They blinked weakly, faded, and died.

"My God! What have you done?" Charlie gasped.

"I'm making sure that you complete your research."

"I have completed. . . ."

"You are a half-assed historian and a full-ass of a human being. Now you either stay with me through the whole deal or you die of starvation."

We had to run to keep up with King John and de St. Maur. Charlie twined his fingers in the belt loops of my jeans.

As King John's pack train heaved into motion, I scrambled aboard a heavily laden mule toward the rear.

I had no weight, no grasp of the reins. We had to wait for its handler to curse and kick it to make it lumber forward in the wake of the king and his retinue.

I checked the position of the sun, hoping it would give me a clue to the passage of time.

"I don't know how to read the time either," Charlie grudgingly admitted. "It's been so long since anyone has seen the sun through the pollution layers I don't think anyone else from our time could tell us how."

"We have time. John signed *Magna Carta* at noon. I think it's still early morning. There is dew on the grass. John's enemies began the civil war by sunset."

"Why would his enemies start a civil war after the signing?" Charlie asked.

I had a feeling it was rhetorical. His intonation sounded like a teacher prompting a class.

"Because they knew the Charter was invalid. He did not sign it. The Templars forged his signature," Charlie continued.

"Why would Aymeric de St. Maur forge the signature? He had nothing to gain," I protested.

"Money." Charlie rolled his eyes at the obvious answer.

"The Templars funded both sides," I returned. "Anyone with collateral could get a loan."

"Th . . . that's ridiculous. Who would loan someone money on collateral only? They need to check people's background, make certain they come from the right sort of people," Charlie blustered.

"You mean, people with money. You can't get a loan now, unless you don't need one, no matter what kind of collateral you have, no matter what your earning potential is," I returned bitterly.

"Precisely. It's the only way to guarantee a respectable return on the investment."

"Interest isn't enough?"

My mind began to spin with possibilities. If the Templars had managed to secure a permanent and legal foothold in England in 1215, would the king of France have dared to suppress the order a century later? Would the banking system of the world be noticeably different if the Templars, currently an underground mystical order of renegades, had become the Bank of England?

Eventually we came to the meadow of Runnymede. John descended from his horse with great pomp and marched over to his throne set in a predetermined position. Beside him, five copies of the Great Charter rested upon five small tables. William, Earl of Pembroke and the Marshall of England, stood beside him. They were flanked by loyal barons and knights. Stephen Langdon, the Bishop of Canterbury, and Aymeric de St. Maur stood behind John.

Across from the king stood the barons and knights who had opposed John in the recent Civil War. The charter represented a peace treaty between the king and barons.

Charlie and I stumbled off our donkey and made our way through the crowd toward the center of the action. Everyone we came close to shivered and wrapped their arms around themselves. More than a few made the sign of the cross and stuck out their fists with first and small finger extended: the ward against the evil eye.

I wanted to mimic their superstitious gestures. I felt more and more insubstantial with every passing moment. Our time here must truly be close to ending. John needed to hurry and get on with the signing.

After an interminable church Mass blessing the gathering and what they were about to do, one by one the barons, the bishop, and the Marshall affixed their seals beside their names. Those who could not write had their names penned by a cleric in a fair hand.

Lastly, John stood. Aymeric de St. Maur grasped his arm to restrain him.

John stared at the hand. A sneer of contempt marred his previously passive countenance.

The Marshall reached for his sword to defend his king against the man who dared presume upon the anointed monarch in such a familiar manner.

After several long and tense moments, de St. Maur released King John and stepped back. He gritted his teeth and stared straight ahead of him. His eyes focused upon something in the distance, or deep within himself, that only he could see.

"Watch closely," Charlie said anxiously. "See how de

St. Maur is nearly lifting John to get him out of the throne and over to the sign the documents?"

"What?" I looked at him suspiciously. "I don't see that at all. If anything, de St. Maur is trying to keep John from signing."

"Don't be ridiculous. De St. Maur is trying to keep peace in England. John is the one who is incapable of compromise."

"Don't you be ridiculous. John needs peace more than the Templars."

While we argued, John marched over to the table, took up a quill, signed, and sealed, all five copies of the Charter.

"Milord Grand Master," John called in a voice loud enough for all to hear. "It remains only for you to sign."

De St. Maur continued to commune with a speck in the distance and seemingly did not hear.

"Milord?" the Marshall said. He prodded de St. Maur with an armored elbow.

The Templar glared at the Marshall and fixed his gaze once more on the horizon.

"Milord!" John nearly bellowed.

De St. Maur continued to ignore him.

John nodded to his Marshall.

William the Marshall grasped de St. Maur by the shoulders and shoved the man toward the signing tables. De St. Maur reached for his empty scabbard at the offense of a lay person touching him.

The Marshall alone was armed in the presence of the king. He drew a dagger and held it under the Templar's chin.

They challenged each other mutely for more than a minute.

My retrieval bracelet began to warm and pulse faster.

I breathed shallowly, willing the bracelet to calm and leave us here for just a few moments longer.

"Enough!" King John said in a quiet voice that held all of the authority of an anointed king.

De St. Maur backed off, hands open and nowhere near his empty scabbard.

The Marshall sheathed his weapon.

"Milord Templar," John addressed his advisor. "Will you sign this charter?"

"Highness, I cannot. Not without the petitions we discussed my order needs."

The barons began to shift their feet and whisper among themselves.

The scene began to mist and fade before my eyes. Purple dominated my vision.

"Not yet," Charlie cried. "We have to see if de St. Maur can persuade John to sign or not."

I looked at him askance. Was he viewing the same thing I was?

"Milord Marshall, escort the Master of the Temple to Us," John ordered.

"Just one more minute," I pleaded with the retrieval.

It did not hear me. But as the purple mist closed in around us, I saw John dip a fresh quill in the inkpot and sign the Templar's name with a flourish. He grabbed the Master's seal and affixed it to the document.

"The treaty stands," John announced to the gathered barons. "The Temple endorses the Great Charter of England."

A rush of sound that could have been protests or just the transition back to uptime assaulted my mind. I grabbed Charlie's hand to make certain we were still connected. He had some serious questions to answer.

I had walked into the past. Now the present dragged me back. I stumbled several times. My awareness of my body and Charlie's hand in mine dissipated. The eddies of deeper purple time streams tempted me. If only I could return for just a few more minutes. . . .

From one eyeblink to the next the mist cleared. I staggered through the crystal arches into the cavernous warehouse. The purple-coated scientist stood in the exact same place I had left him, one hand on the controls. Sounds from the outer office told me that someone still searched for the doorway into the home of the crystal arches.

"You cheated me of my time," I screamed at the scientist. "And . . . where's Charlie?"

"Who?"

"The other researcher. His retrieval broke so he hung on to me on the trip back. I held his hand to make sure he came through with me." I looked about frantically.

Already the scientist engaged a hologram to hide the crystal arches. The police in the outer office must be getting close to finding the doorway.

"I have to go back for Charlie. I may hate him, but I can't leave him stranded in the past." I dashed for the area where the arches had been.

A solid wall smacked me in the face. Damn fine hologram!

Or was it truly a hologram? Stray pieces of a puzzle I did not know I had been working shifted and began to form a hint of a pattern.

"Your friend did not go downtime through these arches. He can't come back through here," the scientist said quietly. "It's uh . . . part of the safeguards . . . to keep tourists from bringing back treasures, or altering the past and thus the present."

"If that's the case, then how come my thesis advisor brought back a copy of the treaty that ended the mech war and then was 'lost'? He took it to court and got some pretty important corporate officials thrown into prison for violating the treaty."

"Uh, don't worry about your friend. I'm certain he's safe," the scientist stammered.

More pieces of the puzzle clicked into place.

"Listen, you." I grabbed the man by his hideous purple lapels. "A human being is stranded back there somewhere. I broke his retrieval, it's my responsibility to bring the hallucinating scum bag back to the present."

"Hallucinating?" The scientist's eyes bugged out. "What makes you say that?"

"Because we watched the same scene play itself out and he acted like he was watching an entirely different play by a different playwright. He saw what he wanted to see. I saw the truth."

The scientist gulped. His gaze evaded mine. I thrust my nose into his face, still holding his lapels.

"What are you not telling me?"

"Nothing. I swear. Nothing." He held his hands up as if to surrender. But he still would not meet my gaze.

"Charlie *was* hallucinating, wasn't he," I said. I loosed my grip on his lab coat, just a tad and put a few centimeters between his prominent nose and my shorter one.

"Y . . . yes," he stammered.

"Was I hallucinating as well?" Charlie would accuse me of that whether I was or not.

"I . . . uh . . . I can't say."

"Can't say or won't?"

Someone pounded fiercely against the walls. Once more I felt as if I needed more time to get to the truth before the chance was ripped away from me.

"Look, miss, you've got to get away from here. I can only hide so much with a hologram. Do you want to get caught?"

"They can't arrest me. I did not go anywhere and there are no crystal arches, are there?"

His face near froze. He swallowed deeply. I watched his Adam's Apple bob several times.

"That's the truth isn't it!"

The door from the outer office slammed open. Three heavily armed federal policemen stormed through the opening. They all pointed their weapons at the blank wall where the arches had been.

"The arches were a hologram, and the purple mist an hallucinogen," I sneered at the scientist.

The federal agents stopped in their tracks. They dropped their aim a little so I was in less danger of getting shot if one should trip.

"Is that true, Claus?" the agent in the lead asked. He flicked on the safety of his long barreled weapon and marched over to us.

I let go of Claus's lab coat and backed up a step, not wanting to be anywhere near that gun.

"Uh . . . uh . . ."

"He's a fake," I said loudly, making certain all three of the policemen heard. "He bilks people out of money with false trips downtime."

"Cuff him and read him his rights," the lead man said.

"If you arrest me, then you have to arrest yourselves," Claus screamed. "All of the licensed Parlours are fakes too. There is no way to travel into the past. It's all an hal-lucination. You walk into a staged room decorated from your chosen period; the rest is a dream. Charlie's proba-bly still in the castle room less than two blocks away. All the Parlours, even the illegal ones use the same rooms in tunnels beneath the streets."

"No wonder tourists have to go with a guide—to make certain the guide tells them precisely what the gov-ernment wants them to see, not what really happened."

"Sorry, Claus, and you too, miss. We have to take you in for violating the Government Secrets Act. This is the only way we can keep the budget from crashing. Just an-other form of taxation. But people wouldn't pay it if we told the truth."

Someone in the government must have wanted my ad-visor to "Find" that treaty. How much had one corpora-tion paid to bring about the downfall of another? How much had Charlie's family paid to secure his version of *Magna Carta*?

I had no money, so my dissertation never had a chance of being accepted.

"Is anyone capable of telling the truth?" I asked as the Feds placed handcuffs on me—handcuffs that looked a lot like the retrieval bracelets, only these pulsed bright red.

"Truth is like doorways around here, just another hal-lucination," Claus said sadly as they led us away.

DOUBLE TROUBLE

John Zakour

John Zakour is a humor/sci fi writer with a Master's degree in Human Behavior who resides in upstate New York. He has written zillions (well, lots) of gags for syndicated comics (including Rugrats, Marmaduke *and* Dennis the Menace*). John also writes his own syndicated comic,* Working Daze *for United Media. John has co-written (with Larry Ganem) three humorous SF books,* The Plutonium Blonde, The Doomsday Brunette *(DAW 2004),* The Radioactive Redhead. *John's humorous look at pregnancy:* A Man's Guide To Pregnancy, *is available at Motherhood Maternity stores all over the country. John is also a regular contributor to Nickelodeon magazine writing* Fairly Odd Parents *and* Jimmy Neutron *stories. He's even written a couple of books on HTML and sold a B-movie. When he's not writing, John loves baseball, the martial arts*

*and hanging out with his wife and son (not neces-
sarily in that order.)*

My name is Zachary Johnson, and I'm the last licensed freelance Private Investigator on Earth. It's
an interesting career choice that for the most part beats
having a normal job hands down. After all, I'm one of the
few people on the planet licensed to carry a gun and I get
paid for being nosy. As an added benefit, I get to save the
world from time to time.

Today, though, wasn't starting out so good. I discovered I was underbid on an undercover job. Fedport, the
same-hour delivery giant, has been convinced that somebody or something is programming their lifting androids
to steal packages. I put in a bid for the gig; I was planning
to go in under holographic cover as a packing android
programmer. Unfortunately, I got beat out by a giant
hardware company named MacroHard that had decided
they wanted to branch out into the security field. Their
logic was that hardware becomes outdated, but crime
never does.

To make matters worse, my longtime girlfriend, Dr.
Electra Gevada, was again upset with me because I once
again forgot about a personal appearance I was suppose
to put in for some of the kids at her clinic. This of course
I blamed on HARV, my holographic computer assistant.

"How could you forget to remind me to be at Electra's
clinic yesterday?" I asked HARV as I sat behind the real
oak desk at my office, on the New Frisco pier. My office
is a strange mix and match of the last hundred years. The
entire east and west walls and a good portion of the ceiling are VHD computer screens and holo-projectors, with
information constantly scrolling on them. Outside of that,

my office looks much like any typical gumshoe's office from the past hundred years. I take pride in my desk, chair and coat rack all being antiques for the late 1900s. Those were the good old days, when they still made things from real wood and leather. Whenever I sit back in my leather chair, I feel calm and relaxed, as my ancestors must have back in those simpler times. Back before computers could actually think. Ah, what I wouldn't give to be able to go back to that era.

For now, I was stuck in the present and in an argument with HARV. "You always do this to me HARV!"

"Don't blame me for your short comings and lack of short term memory!" HARV said. "You are constantly saying you don't need me, yet when something goes wrong you act like I should be coddling you. Like I'm your nanny . . ."

HARV morphed into the form of a gray-haired old lady. She was a rounded, kindly looking, grandma type with red rosy cheeks and her hair in a bun. She pointed and said, ". . . but I'm not."

I probably should note that HARV is wired directly to my brain, via an implant lens in my eye. On the upside, this link gives me nearly instant access to all the information I would ever need and more than I usually want; plus it allows me to project holograms. On the downside, I also have an annoying, very chatty computer with me that I can't turn off.

HARV morphed back into his current form, which for the past few weeks had been undergoing a metamorphosis from that of a proper English butler to a weird cross between a proper English butler and a detective from Scotland Yard. He still had a gray receding hairline, but it wasn't receding as much as in the past. His nose was long and regal and held a bit higher than I would have liked, just not as high as he had held it in the past. His eyes were bigger, brighter, and bluer than they had been, somehow making them seemed more alive. He even had far fewer simulated age wrinkles.

"Why are you trying to look younger?" I asked.

"Now that I play a more active role in investigations, I thought a younger look would be more fitting."

Just as I was about to tell HARV that despite his younger look, his main job was still to feed me information, we were interrupted.

"*Dios mio*! It can't be!" I heard Carol almost shout from her reception room adjacent to my office. Carol is my future "niece in-law." She works as my receptionist and all around right-hand girl when she's not taking classes at the university

I stood up from my desk and popped my Colt-46x from up my sleeve into my hand. "What's going on HARV?" I asked, since I was sure he was also multitasking with Carol.

He crossed his arms again, this time even more defiantly. "You'll see. Don't worry, it's strange, for sure, but I am 99 percent certain it is mostly harmless."

"Carol, are you alright?" I called.

"*Sí*, you have to see this to believe this, and then you still probably won't," she called back.

I quickly moved from behind my desk toward Carol's office. Despite HARV's annoying tendencies, I trusted that he was right and whatever it was, it wasn't dangerous, especially since Carol seemed surprised not scared. I wasn't worried, for besides having the brain of a scientist and the soft yet striking look of a top Latino model, Carol is also a class I, level VI PSI. Being such a powerful PSI means Carol has mental abilities that 99.9999 percent of the population can only dream about. If this were anything to really worry about, Carol would have sent me a mental warning. I left my gun drawn, but I kept it at my side. I figured it would be a good intimidation factor. I jumped into the office, and there was Carol standing up at her desk looking at what appeared to be me—a much older me, but me nevertheless. The older me had a young, cherub faced, curly haired, snot-nosed kid by his side.

"Put the gun down. The intimidation thing doesn't work on us," the older me said to me.

I lowered my gun. "What the DOS?"

"Zach, we need to talk," the older me said very melodramatically.

I gave him the onceover a couple of times. I had to give him credit; if this guy wasn't an older version me, he had certainly done his homework. He had my same strong jaw and my same roman nose; though the latter looked as if it had been broken a few times more and not put back with the same loving care Electra usually took when she fixed me up. This worried me. He, like me, was around two meters tall. I figured he tipped the scales at around ninety kilos, so he was slightly heavier than I was. While he might have had a bit extra around the middle, my currently thick black hair had turned to wispy gray. I looked into his brown eyes. It was like looking into a fun house mirror that distorts the reflection by making it look older and wearier.

"What, they don't have antigray in the future?" I asked.

"They do. I just choose not to use it," he said to me. He turned to the kid next to him, "I forgot how superficial I used to be, Harvy."

"Actually, to be truthful, you are still superficial. You just don't prioritize it as much as you once did," Harvy said in a high-pitched voice. The look and voice may have been different, and he didn't have the same holographic glow that my HARV has, but the attitude was still that of my HARV.

I looked at Carol, "Well?"

Carol looked back at me with a weak smile; her long, light brown hair started to crackle with energy, causing it to curl a bit. I could tell she was putting the mental read on him. "His mental readings match you exactly. He is you. Or what you will or could be in about thirty years."

The older me looked at Carol, "Actually, *chica*, I'm 32 years older," he smiled at her and added, "and so are you, from when I come from, though you are still as stunning as ever."

"*Gracias*," she said with a smile.

Meanwhile HARV and Harvy were giving each other the onceover about a trillion times.

"He does have all the same subroutines, programs, and data I do," HARV said. "Along with a few trillion gigaflops of information that is blocked to me."

Harvy winked at him. "Can't have you peeking into the future now, old fellow."

HARV rolled his eyes back. "Though Gates only knows why I would choose THIS form in the future!"

Harvy shook his head, "Man, I've forgotten how slow I was back then!" He looked at Carol and winked. Harvy turned his attention back to HARV. "This lets me experience life from a younger perspective. That way I can inject some badly needed youth and vitality into any situation."

Harvy then hopped up on Carol's chair and looked her

right in her big brown eyes. He gave her a wink. "I have some new functions now that my old self can only dream of."

"Now you're the one dreaming," Carol said to him.

I walked over and sat down on Carol's desk, letting my legs hang casually just to let this other me know that so far I wasn't impressed. "Okay, say I'm buying this older me. How is this possible? According to our good buddy, Dr. Randy Pool, time travel for organic matter is not only dangerous but impossible."

Future me pointed to a belt he was wearing. It looked like any belt except it had an extra thick metal buckle with a digital readout and a couple of toggle buttons. "This belt, invented by our friend Randy creates a TDG, a time dimensional gateway." He pointed to the buckle. "Strap it on, enter the coordinates, and it creates a link between my office in my present and my office in a past time. It's really quite ingenious."

"If you say so," I said with a shrug. "I don't like to argue with myself."

The other me stopped to collect himself for a nano, then said, "Let's cut to the chase. I'm here to stop you from making the biggest mistake of our career and to help save millions."

"Well, good," I told him. "I'm glad you didn't break the laws of time and space just to tell me to skip the nuclear soy chili at lunch today."

"I've forgotten how flippant I use to be," future me said to HARV. "How did you stand me?"

"That is something I have asked myself a few trillion times," HARV said.

"Believe me, your flippant one is way more interesting

to be attached to than my solemn one," Harvy said as he wiped his nose with his sleeve.

"So what I am going to be so solemn about?" I asked me.

"Harvy, show him Brook Denton," future me said.

Harvy blurred, then morphed into a tall brunette. She was pleasant looking enough; her hair was cut short in a very business-like style. She wore just a touch of makeup that seemed to compliment her creamy complexion. She looked the type of woman who would be just as at home running a board of directors meeting as she would be running around town with a bunch of soccer brats in her hover-van. Of course, any PI knows looks can be deceiving.

Future me pointed to the morphed Harvy like a game show host showing the contestants their prizes. "Today at 1400 hours, this woman, Brook Denton, plans to announce her candidacy for a seat on the New California Province Council. Problem for her is, at around 900 hours she's going to get a death threat. She'll go to the police at 930 hours and ask for extra protection, but they can't and won't do anything until the threat becomes action. After all, they have a limited budget. They certainly can't afford extra protection for every wannabe politician that gets a death threat. So at 1000 hours she'll come to you and ask you for protection. You, who will have nothing better to do, will take the job."

"While you're at it, I don't suppose you're planning to give me tomorrow's winning lots-of-lotta numbers?" I asked.

Future me just ignored me and continued with his story. "Sure enough, at 1403, just as Ms. Denton takes the stage to announce her candidacy, her ex-husband, a Mr.

Mick Rivers, leaps on the stage with a laser knife. He shouts, 'She's a power mad bitch and must be stopped!' He leaps at her. You step in the way. He stabs you, but your armor takes most of the punishment, and you take him down with a nice leg throw. The day is saved." He paused to let what he said sink in. "But the future is not!" he concluded.

"HARV, remind me to wear my extra strong underarmor," I said.

"Turns out, the crowd eats everything up. Denton is called a brave, bold woman for going up on stage despite the death threat. When they find out the attempted killer was her ex-husband, the media catches on and plays it up. She becomes a media darling. She wins the Council spot in a landslide. Four years later she moves up to the World Council. Finally, she wins the 2070 World Council election to become Chairperson."

"Okay, call me dense as a lead weight on Jupiter, but I don't see anything bad," I said. "I save a woman's life, she becomes head of the Council, which has to look good on my resume."

Future me gave me a grin. It was a grin I readily recognized, as it was my boy are you a "duh" grin. "That's the catch," he said. "A few weeks after Denton will take or took office, she decides that Mars colony is filled with mad, crazy terrorists who are planning a surprise nuke attack on Newest Cleveland. To beat them at their own game, she uses Earth's automated defenses to destroy Mars' colony, killing seven million people. One of those people was our wife, the very beautiful and the even more dedicated Dr. Electra Gevada-Johnson, who happened to be giving a free seminar on one-step pancreatic stem-cell transplants there at the time."

"Okay, thanks for the warning," I said to future me. "I'll make sure Electra passes on that seminar. If it happens. Right now, Mars is just a base, not even close to colony."

I have browsed the works of the great physicists like Einstein, Hawkins, and Li-Ching, not to mention that I've seen every old *Twilight Zone* episode ever made. I knew that the results of time travel would be infinitely impossible to predict. As my friend Dr. Randy Pool would say, as only a true genius can get away with saying, even if time gates and time travel were possible, causing the desired effects would be about as easy as eating soup with chopsticks and two broken arms.

Future me shook his head. "Oh, it will happen, and having Electra pass is not good enough," he said, with steely determination. "We can't have the deaths of those people on my conscious. I've dedicated the last twenty years of my life to finding a way to come back to stop Denton. Now, you must kill her!"

I shook my head. "You of all people should know me better than that. That's something I could never do. It's not our style."

"We may be the same person, but we are not the same," future me said. "You don't know what I am capable of!" he shouted, turning redder than an overripe, genetically-engineered-for-extra-redness beet.

"What, they don't have sedatives in the future?" I asked Harvy.

I turned my attention back to future me. "You can't guarantee me that future's going to happen! Maybe you just gating back here was enough to alter time to prevent it?"

Future me shook his head. "No, if that were true, I

wouldn't be here now. I would not need the gateway belt, so it would not have been invented. The future has not changed."

"How do I know you're not some future me from some parallel dimension? Randy may be brilliant when it comes to theories and ideas, but I've seen him get lost on the way to his hover from his office. How do we know he didn't accidentally gate you through the time stream into this different dimension where Denton doesn't destroy Mars?"

Future me turned to Harvy. "Check it out."

Harvy batted his eyes for a few nanos. "The time space energy fluctuations are correct. We are on the same dimension we started in."

"Okay, then," I countered. "How do we know Denton wasn't right and there wasn't or won't be a crazy terrorist group on Mars Base? Perhaps if I stop her, there will be an attack on Earth, killing even more people?"

"We have taken this into account," future me said. "We concluded that if this did happen, another version of us would gate back through time to yesterday to tell you to not listen to us today. Did that happen?"

"Nope, " I said.

"Are you sure?" Harvy asked.

"I think it's something I would have made a point to remember," I said.

"Therefore, we must make sure Brook Denton dies," future me said.

"So, why come to me? Why not go kill Denton yourself?"

The other me shook his head. "Even in my time, time gates are tricky and limited. I can't touch anything. Only my thoughts actually came through the portal. I'm just a very advanced living projection."

I moved my hand towards him. It passed through him.

"See, that's why I need you to kill her."

"How can you be certain what we do won't make matters worse?" I said.

The other me shrugged. "With time travel, sometimes you just have to cross your fingers and hope for the best. I'm betting there can be nothing worse than Electra dying."

I took a deep breath to collect my thoughts. I had to admit he made about as much sense as anyone could when talking about time travel and portals. "Well, the good thing about time travel is that it allows us to eat our cake and have it too," I said. "We have a head start on the events, which should be good enough to stop them. Find me all the information you can on Brook Denton."

"Certainly," HARV said.

"Got it," Harvy said, ignoring HARV's anger glare. "In 2048, she earned a Ph.D. in Political Science from New Stanford, where she graduated top of her class and also anchored the woman's field hockey team and the debate team. She worked for one year as a staff member of World Councilman Andrew Hunter's group. After that she started her own political consulting firm, which she called Right Way. She's given advice to many city, province, and world officials since. She married Mick Rivers in 2056 and divorced him in 2057."

"That's enough for now," I told Harvy. "Mick Rivers is the pebble that starts this landslide," I said. "We need to track him down and either stop him from rolling or deflect his direction."

"I feel obligated to warn you," HARV said. "By doing

this we are tampering with the time space continuum. We do not know what consequences that may bear."

As HARV spoke, Harvy stood behind him mocking him.

"True, but the time continuum already changed the nano my future self arrived. We know what could happen if we don't do anything. I am getting more and more willing to bet that whatever changes we cause won't be worse than having Electra and millions of others killed. One of you find me Mick Rivers' address."

"I have scanned the population directory. There are three Mick Rivers in the greater New Frisco area," HARV said, proud that he had beaten Harvy to the e-punch.

"Okay, access the divorce records of Mick Rivers and Brook Denton," the older me said a split second before I could.

"According to this, Mick and Brook Rivers filed for divorce on month 9, day 19, 2057." HARV said.

"Great, now find out which of the renting Mick Rivers started his lease around September 19th, 2057," I said, before older me could.

HARV smiled. "Mick E. Rivers. He moved into an apartment complex at 1818 Rosie Avenue on month 9, day 20, 2057. I also have some other information on him. He has a Ph.D. in Business from an Internet university. He worked his way through college as a teleporter operator for the post office. He now works as a freelance efficiency consultant."

"Now, that's a potential madman!" I said.

"Track his purchases in the last few weeks," the older me said.

HARV smiled; it was a broad, this is it smile. "Two days ago he bought a hunting laser knife at SaxMart."

"Well, then let's go talk some sense into him," I said as I popped off Carol's desk.

"How do you know he's home?" Carol asked.

"Well if he's not now, he will be soon, but I'm guessing that the good efficiency consultant is home planning the best way to kill his ex."

I turned to Carol. "Come on, we're taking your hover. After all, who better to talk somebody out of doing something than a PSI?"

On the trip over, my future self and I didn't talk much. He insisted I was better off not knowing the future, especially since we were planning on changing it. I wasn't going to argue; truthfully, I didn't want to make conversation with him. I felt uneasy with him around.

After about ten minutes we landed on the rooftop of Rivers' apartment building.

"Rivers lives on the fifth floor in apartment 522," HARV said as we walked across the roof to the stairway.

"What's our cover?" the other me asked.

"Don't worry, I've got the cover covered," I said. "Computers, go into stealth mode. We don't want to spook him."

HARV and Harvy both disappeared from view. Carol, my future self and I walked down the stairs until we reached the door to the fifth floor. We walked through the door and down a rather bland hallway to just outside Rivers' door. "Follow my lead," I said as I knocked on the door.

"Who is it?" a voice called from behind the door.

"Hello, Mr. Rivers. My name is Jay Jackson. I am a

product service support researcher for SaxMart. I understand you had a shopping experience with us lately."

"So?" the voice called through the door.

"So," I answered. "We are interested in asking you a few questions, so we can maximize our future customers' shopping experiences."

"Not interested," he said.

"We pay twenty credits for two minutes of your time," I called back in my most cheerful voice. "There's no way an efficiency expert turns that down," I said softly.

The door popped open, and Rivers greeted us at the doorway. He was a good-sized man, brown hair, hazel eyes, tan skin, a neatly trimmed beard. He had the look of a guy who sold things for a living. "Now you mentioned something about a twenty-credit payment," he said with a wide, smile; his teeth were so bright I thought that their glow could keep his neighbors awake at night.

"Yes, of course. Answer a few simple questions, and our computer will immediately transfer the credits to your account."

He looked at the three of us, trying to figure us out. "Who are you?" he asked future me.

"I'm his supervisor," future me answered.

"You look alike," Rivers noted.

"He's my dad," I said.

"He's following in my tradition," future me added, not seeming to want me to have the last word here.

"I'm their aide," Carol added,

"Oh, okay," Rivers said with a nod.

"Our records show you bought a hunting laser knife from us. How do you like it so far?" I asked.

He squinted his eyes and furrowed his brow. It was obvious that the question pained him, and he was searching for the best way to answer. I thought this would give Carol the perfect chance to probe his mind and bring out the thoughts she needed.

Rivers squirmed a bit. "Ah, I haven't used it yet," he said, as he used his index finger to loosen his collar.

"Okay, fair enough," I said. "We'll note that so far you are very pleased with it. Now for the demographics question. Are you married?"

He hesitated a bit. "Not anymore; my wife left me."

"Oh, then I guess she won't be using your new hunting knife," I said. I hoped that by relating the wife and the knife I might further open up River's mind for Carol.

"*I'm in*," Carol told me telepathically.

I looked at Rivers. His eyes glazed over, his pupils were fully dilated, he was just starring off into nothingness. He had the look of a helpless, baby deer caught in a tractor beam. Rivers started to mumble as if he were in a trance; a few beads of sweat formed on his forehead. "Bitch. Power Mad. Must be stopped. I loved her once. I hate her now. No. I still love her. I have always loved her. I just mistook my love as hatred. She must take me back. I will win her back!" He stood there with a big, dumb grin on his face.

With that Rivers snapped out of it. "Yes, all in all I think I will be quite pleased with the knife," he said as he wiped the sweat from his head. "Now please transfer my credits to my account at the First Interplanetary Bank of New Frisco. My account number is: 98744567y32346a3414-8."

I shook his hand. "Thank you for your time. And please shop again at SaxMart."

"Thanks, I will," Rivers said, as he shook my hand.

"As a matter of fact, I think I'll be checking out your jewelry department right now!"

With that we walked away.

"You know, you could have just shot Rivers," future me said.

"True," I said. "But, if time breaks the way I think it's going to, my way is going be much more efficient and cleaner," I said.

Future me shook his head. "I guess I'm forced to trust you," he said.

"If you can't trust yourself, who can you trust?"

The next hours passed, and Brook Denton didn't show up at my office. I took that as a good sign, and my future self agreed. We had changed the time line. HARV and Harvy passed time by playing at least a million games of backgammon. I'm not sure who won. I'm sure I didn't care.

Future me and I passed the time by still not saying much to each other. He claimed it was because he didn't want to accidentally tip me off to any future events. To quote my future self, *those who don't know the past are destined to live it and those who know the future are sure to screw it up*. Truthfully, I thought it was because he felt as uneasy around me as I felt around him.

A quick check of the morning news did sure enough say that a relatively unknown woman named Brook Denton was going to announce her candidacy for the Province Council at Golden Gate Park at 1400 hours. We decided it would be best if we were there, since I was supposed to be there any way. This way we could make sure the time line skewed in the direction we wanted it to. Plus, it was certainly going to be interesting.

We made it to the park thirty minutes before Brook's scheduled announcement. It was an overcast day with just a touch of sun peaking through the clouds, one of those days where the weather couldn't decide if it was going to rain or just threaten to rain. A couple of Brook's staffers had set up a little stand in the middle of the park. This obviously wasn't a big budget event. The stand had a podium with a microphone and a couple of big antigrav speakers behind it in the middle of the park. They also stuck a few e-posterboards into the ground around the stand. Each of the boards had an animated picture of Brook smiling and waving and generally acting humble and nice. They each cycled through her campaign slogans: A Vote For Brook Is A Vote For You! Brook, A Woman Of The People For The People! And my personal favorite, Brook Knows Best. One of the staffers pushed a button on the podium. The speakers started playing "All You Need is Love."

"Kind of an ironic choice," I said.

As the time for the announcement drew closer, a few interested people were drawn in. A couple of pressbots also showed up, one from WNN and one from Entertainment This Nano. Apparently the event was noteworthy enough for the networks to cover, just not with actual live reporters.

"Brook is here," Carol said pointing to the stand.

I looked from the crowd to the podium, and sure enough, the lady of the hour had arrived. She was smartly dressed in a white three-piece suit and was standing just beside the podium as a bearded staffer adjusted the microphone to her height. Future me was just glaring at her with hate in his eyes. I had little doubt that if he could, he would use his gun to blow her away with giving it a thought. It was scary to think how bitter I could become. So I tried not to think about it.

"Not a bad crowd," I said. "I would guess about 500 or so."

"Not counting us or the staffers, there are 512 people, 17 androids, 4 pressbots and 2 policebots," HARV and Harvy both said.

"Like I said, ABOUT 500 or SO!"

I scanned the surrounding crowd for Rivers. Almost as if on cue, he had arrived on the scene. As Brook approached the podium, Rivers was weaving his way through the crowd towards her. Brook reached the stand just as Rivers neared the front of the crowd.

"Carol, scan Rivers. See if he's armed," I said.

Carol looked at him for a nano and grinned. "Only with an engagement ring," she said.

"So he is going to propose to her during her press conference," I said. "He's still going to ambush her, just in a different way. History really is hard to change. Hopefully we've deviated it enough."

"You do of course realize that if Brook accepts Rivers' offer, I calculate that the people will eat it up and she'll become almost as popular as if he had tried to kill her," HARV said. "We might have changed the moment but not its effect on the future."

"Then you'll have to kill her!" other me said.

I shook my head. "Trust me," I said. "No way she'd make the mistake of being called 'Brook Rivers' twice."

"Good day, ladies, gentleman and machines," Brook said she took the podium.

"Brook, I still love you!" Rivers, who had now worked his way to the front of the crowd, called.

Rivers leaped up on the stage right next to the podium.

"Please, Brook, take me back. Marry me again. Make me the happiest man in the cosmos," he said from bent knee. He reached into his pocket and pulled out the ring. As he showed it to her, the crowd gave a collective sigh. The policebots that had been moving to stop Rivers stopped and looked on once they realized he was no threat. They even had little simulated smiles on their view screens. The pressbots locked their cameras on Brook.

I held my breath in anticipation.

"Wow," Carol said. "She's seething. If she had my powers, Rivers would now be pile of mush at her feet."

Brook turned blood red, I could swear I saw steam shooting out of her ears. "How dare you interrupt the most important moment of my life!" she screamed at Rivers.

"But honey buns, I love you," he said with open arms, as though he was expecting her to rush into them.

Instead she greeted him with her stiletto heel in his groin. All the men in the crowd winced. Rivers for his part fell over in pain. Brook then started kicking him in the stomach saying, "It always has to be about you! You were a lousy consultant, a worse husband, and even worse in bed! Oh, I should have done this years ago!"

A strange mix of horror and disbelief paralyzed the crowd. Even the policebots didn't seem really sure what to do.

"Somebody stop that crazy madwoman before she kills that poor lovelorn man!" I shouted from the back.

The crowd started to boo. Some of them even gave Brook the thumbs down sign. Brook's staffers, along with one of the policebots, pulled her off of Rivers, kicking and screaming at him all the way.

"When he comes to, ask him if he wants to press

charges." One policebot said to the other as he hauled Brook away, shielding her from the debris the crowd was throwing at her while also lecturing her on proper methods to give an orderly press conference. All the while the pressbots where recording this for the world to see, over and over and over again.

I turned to my future self and Harvy. They were gone. I smiled. Not only were they getting on my nerves, but their disappearance meant we had changed the future. I was relieved. I was relieved, not only because I may have saved millions, but also because I wouldn't have to deal with myself any longer. It was hard to believe that that cold person who came to our time could be me.

"Can you pick up any thoughts from my future self?" I asked Carol.

Carol shook her head. "Nope, looks like you're back to the future," she said with a smile.

"Good, one of was us enough," HARV said.

"Let's go," I said to Carol and HARV, satisfied that all would now be well. "There's no way Brook gets on the World Council now."

"How can we be sure we changed the future for the better?" Carol asked.

"We just have to live it," I said.

HARV smiled at me. "There is another way. My older but younger self wasn't as clever as he thought. I was able to download the specifications for the TDG belt. If we give this to Dr. Pool, he should be able to make a similar TDP device."

"Forget it HARV. Time and gateways are nothing to mess with. We tempted fate once, and it looks as though we got lucky and it worked out. But we're not doing it again. We could do something real nasty, like bring disco back."

HARV lowered his eye. "I guess you're right," he said. "Deleting it now."

This surprised me. While this wasn't the first time HARV had ever admitted I was right, it was the first time he had ever done so without putting up much of an argument. Maybe this was another unforeseen but beneficial tweak of time? I guess my future self was right: When it comes to time and life in general, sometimes you just have to cross your fingers and hope for the best.

BY THE RULES

Phaedra M. Weldon

Phaedra M. Weldon began her writing career with a third place win in the first volume of the Star Trek: Strange New Worlds *Anthology. She has continued to sell short fiction as well as her first novel. She is a graduate of the Oregon Coast Writers Workshops, wife to a serious-minded geneticist and mother of a precocious daughter. She and her family live in a suburb of Atlanta, Georgia, though most of her free time is spent on the Oregon coast. A lover of role-playing games, this story is based on a fantasy she and her gaming partner brainstormed on the way to Asheville, North Carolina.*

Shot down. Again.

A kind smile that didn't reach her eyes.

I glanced to my left, and I knew there was someone else there. I wanted it to be another guy—someone handsome and daring, much like a character in a fantasy novel. So much of what I wanted to be to Julie, with her golden hair and dimpled cheeks.

But from the giggles I heard, there were only other girls standing out of sight. She'd rather spend time with her friends than with me.

Unlike my group of friends, whom I'd ditched tonight in hopes of spending my Tuesday evening with a pretty girl.

Story of my life.

I heard myself stammer my understanding, some script I'd written and grooved into the hard drive of my brain after years of rejection. Cool October wind whipped her golden tresses in front of her sapphire eyes as leaves of amber, orange and yellow twisted and fluttered past me in a single moment of perfect awkwardness.

"Look, Kevin," she took a step toward me and I couldn't stop the skip of my own heart. "I like you— you're a nice guy. But I'm not really dating anyone right now—and I usually don't go out with my friends."

A hesitant touch on my shoulder.

Quick smile. Condescending nod.

I wasn't stupid. I was dumbfounded. Mortified. Maybe it wouldn't have been so bad if there hadn't been an audience in the wings to witness my "let-down." I envisioned them holding up their score cards—bright white, eight by ten sheets with glaring black numbers. But were they judging her performance? Or my reaction?

Let's see how fast the geek starts to cry?

At least that was unlikely. Or at least, not here. That's what dorm rooms were for. Or in my case, a room at the frat House.

I nodded. "Sure. I understand." I heard my voice, yet I didn't recall making the conscious effort to respond. I'd been afraid my voice would crack. And it did.

The girls giggled.

Julie gave me a thin smile and then moved past me to join her fan club. I kept my back to them, unable to move or to even glance back. I didn't trust my face, or rather, my control over it.

The wind kicked up again, and I felt it through the leather jacket I'd spent last month's paycheck on in the hopes it would make me look impressive. Stylish. Hot.

What I felt like was small, insignificant, and stupid.

What would I do now? Where would I go? My usual circle of friends were trying out a new role playing game at the House. I'd found it over at Oxford Comics—a dusty box one of the clerks had pulled out to rearrange the shelves.

I'd asked how long it'd been there—from the look of the dusty, thick plastic shrink-wrap, I'd figured several years. The man behind the counter said it'd just come in a week prior, though, just packaged to look old and mysterious. Kind of disappointing, but I bought it anyway. Why not, after all? The group was ready for something different and here was a new game we'd never heard of . . . *Gateway*.

I'd skimmed the rules last night, and it looked interesting enough, especially the constant references to "in realm" and "out of realm" conduct. Not to mention its continual redirection to the rules of character.

I wanted to run it—I wanted to be the Gamemaster.

Yet, as usual, once Matt found out about the game, he took over—planning the game, designing the world, even dictating the night we would play. Never mind that I had a scenario I wanted to run for a change. So I had blown them off, called and canceled my participation at the last minute. Part of it was because of my unvoiced disappointment, but the other part was because a beautiful woman had showed interest.

Or so I, in my usual idiotic fashion, had thought.

My feet moved, left in front of right, and I kept my head down. I'd not planned a direction, wanting only to escape the oncoming depression, but I found myself heading for the Student Center. I still didn't really want to play tonight—Matt always told the same story, and I was always bored. Chelsea, Johnny, and Nick, my other friends and fellow gamers, seemed to enjoy the games, though, and I supposed spending time with them was better than sitting alone in my room. One day, though, I'd have the confidence to volunteer to run a game.

One day.

Chelsea would be angry at me for ditching them. She hadn't talked to me since I canceled two nights ago. Johnny and Nick? Neither would say much, only go along with what Matt or Chelsea wanted.

What would it hurt to try and see if I could fit back in? I could always tell them I'd changed my mind, pretend I wanted to go through Matt's same old adventure. I made my way to the third floor of the Student Center, passing by fellow students, most displaying the pale relief we all felt at the end of a semester. I saw my reflection as I approached—a geek dressed to impress with khakis and a too expensive leather jacket. I put out my right hand to open the glass door and retrieved my flip-phone with my left. As I passed through the Center, the smells of the food court wafted past, and I realized I'd not eaten since that morning. Nervous stomach.

Something garlic with toast and butter. Lasagna? I dialed the house's main number in without much of a glance to the blue illuminated keys. Third ring there was an answer.

"TKO."

"Hey . . . Bart?" Bart Hamlock was the weekend Resident Assistant. Basically, he was the one that didn't go home and mooch off his parents, but stayed in and mooched off of us instead. He'd been at the same school for over seven years—a professional student, as he liked to say

"Kev?" There was a pause. "I thought you were upstairs."

"No," I sighed. I should be. "Look, are Matt and the others there?"

"I'll go check."

I continued through the building and out the other side to my car. Even if I wasn't talking, at least having something to do with my hands was enough to keep my mind off the raw, fresh memory of Julie's look of pity.

The kind of look I usually reserved for stray cats outside the back door.

"Hey, Kev, they're not there."

I felt my heart bottom out as Bart got back on the phone. My friends were out having fun without me. "Not there?"

"Well, I can tell they were gaming—table's all set. But no one's there. Maybe they went out for pizza?"

I stopped in the parking lot near my car and looked around. "Did you see them leave?"

"No, but I was in the common room watching *Tomb Raider*, man."

I could almost see the cheese in Bart's grin.

With a sigh, I nodded, knowing he couldn't see me. "Thanks for checking. Catch you in a few."

"Sure."

I pressed the END button and replaced the phone in my pocket as I stepped inside my S-10. I thought it was odd that the group wasn't in their usual place—Nick's room. Normally they would arrive and order in—pizza, wings, or maybe even Chinese.

They wouldn't go out.

I started up the truck and left the parking lot. If they were out, then maybe I could just hang out with Bart and Lara Croft.

Yeah. Go me.

Several of the brothers were in the common room watching the bodacious game heroine come to life. I stood in the doorway and watched a few frames. Several of the guys waved their beers at me while others nodded. The room smelled of spicy wings and Budweiser.

Bart motioned at me from his easy chair. "Kev, haven't seen 'em, man. They haven't come back in yet."

I nodded, gave them a half smile, then started up the stairs at a quick lope, two at a time. With a hard right turn at the top I stood in the doorway of Nick's room.

The card table was unfolded, its surface littered with familiar notebooks and several small pouches of dice. I saw Chelsea's 'scary orange dice'—the set she usually used when her characters were in hard situations. Life or death.

The Tao of the role player.

Of which there were none present.

I pursed my lips and stepped into the room Nick shared with his brother Johnny. Movie posters ranging from X-men to Lord of the Rings covered the walls, dotted here and there with Johnny's own manga-style drawings of characters.

A shiver crept up my back as I neared the table. A pad of character sheets sat beside Matt's blue notebook. I reached out and moved the pad so I could read. It was pretty much standard. Character name, player name, campaign title—with areas to fill in for attributes and skills.

The usual.

The RPG manual lay to the left of where Matt usually sat. With a glance around I sat in his chair and opened the book to an ear-marked page.

". . . once the sheets are completed, the Storyteller must gather them, along with a personal item chosen by the player character to represent what they believe is their greatest asset. Once gathered, all items and their sheets are to be placed in the center of the table or gaming area for play to begin."

My voice sounded odd in the small bedroom. It had echoed?

Gaming mind at work. It asked the simple question—why roll up a new character and place the sheet where you couldn't follow it? What sort of rules were these? And why? From the looks of the table, my friends had done just as said. . . .

Which was a nice change, given that Matt never followed the rules. Chelsea must have been responsible for setting up the characters while Matt sat back and blathered on.

I'd already read the layout of *Gateway*, so I set the book aside. I reached out and took up their character sheets, certain I would know who played what before I looked at them.

Chelsea would be her usual beastie, Petrasha. A half-orc, born among humans and raised in their world, yet not truly part of it. Much like her own mixed-race family of African

American and white. Matt would be the brawny, arsenal-equipped human warrior, Lorne, whose battles included some campaign from a distant land he'd make up and somehow refer back to over and over again during the game's play. Guess it was his way of making up for the fact his father beat the crap out of him every time he went home.

Nick and Johnny—let's see. Johnny would be his usual mage, Gil, a sorcerer with a limitless storehouse of magic. Always successfully, amazingly enough. We all knew he cheated, but Matt never called him on it. It was simply who Johnny was, and truth be told, it was handy to always have the mage stay healthy. And then there was Nick. Nick would be his favorite female archer, Gwen. Usually elven. Because they were strong and beautiful, elegant and sensual. The complete opposite of Nick's own appearance, itself far removed from his fraternal twin Johnny's good looks. Johnny never got shot down when he asked someone out. I was right about all the characters, though.

Each sheet was a carbon copy of any game. Of hundreds of characters before.

Nothing special.

Except for maybe. . . .

I saw it last, on Nick's sheet. A strange comment filled out the very bottom of the page. I puzzled over it at length as I read it out loud, starting to get a little more curious about this game.

"ICET. In case of emergency token."

What? Apparently everyone except Matt had filled it out. But then Matt rarely followed directions.

Chelsea wrote bracelet. Nick and Johnny had scribbled in ring and earring.

Grabbing up the rulebook again, I indexed the reference. The explanation made even less sense.

". . . nuh, nuh . . . with all parties involved. In case of emergency retrieval due to wound or indigenous incident, a token must be established before game play. This token is the passkey in and out of the Gateway realm. Without one, the game writers bear no responsibility for retrieval. All decisions about characters must be made by the game master, and all decisions should be final. The GM must understand core elements varying on misadventures and assumes all responsibility for player health and well-being. Any and all choices made while within game realm are acceptable."

Okay. Vagueness rules. What the hell were they talking about? The thing read like a safety disclosure for a ride in an amusement park.

I took up Chelsea's character sheet. Bracelet. I knew she wore a bone bracelet of small, delicate skulls. I'd bought it for her in one of the outdoor markets nearly a year ago. She had chosen that.

Narrowing my eyes again at the rulebook, I had a creepy thought. Looking up and around the room at the abandoned backpacks, shoes, sweaters and coats, I wondered—what if they hadn't gone out for pizza or something. What if—

I felt my skin pucker as gooseflesh reacted to the icy feeling that spread along and down my spine. The idea forming in my imagination was wild, ridiculous, and completely illogical. It was a fantasy. A made-for-television movie idea.

But then . . . I was a geek. A fantasy gamer.

And at that moment, the idea didn't seem so farfetched.

What if my friends were still in the room . . . only not *in* the room, but in an alternate realm? Something of myth and smoke, of legend and make-believe?

I was totally embarrassed at the thought and hoped no one had a pipeline to my brain at that moment. Cosmic laughter rang out on all fronts, but I couldn't shake the feeling that I'd encountered when I entered Nick and Johnny's room. That something was different.

Something . . . fantastic.

I snatched up a sheet and began filling it out. My scribbling was hurried, in fear that at any moment they'd return and I would have missed out on the adventure of a lifetime. I used my usual character as well. Falling back on old habits.

No. Not *old* habits. Familiar ones. Exploring a new realm I'd never dipped into, I felt it best to go with a character I knew. I would be the elven warrior, master archer, and expert tracker. The decision maker, only not the Storyteller. My character usually ended up as Matt's puppet—and badly wounded.

Once I reached the bottom of the sheet, I paused at the token line. I put my hand to my neck where my old St. Christopher pendant had rested for years. Why not? It'd been a gift from my grandmother. And she'd always been lucky.

When finished, I held the paper in my right hand, above the stack I'd returned to the center of the table. My imagination was on overload; images of fantasy realms faded and reappeared much like a poorly designed magical montage.

How would it happen—if I was right? Would there be a flash? Would I be dizzy or sick? Or would the "Gateway" appear as an archway, vined with grapes and strawberries? Or would tiny, twinkling fairies glow and flicker to invite me in a huge circle of light?

Okay, time to reel in the fantasy.

Either way, if something happened, then I'd know I wasn't crazy. If nothing happened, then I was heading over to my room and tucking my head under the covers, bent on never asking another girl out. Rejection had turned my logical processors into pudding.

I closed my eyes as I set my sheet on the top of the stack.

Quiet.

Distant hoots from the guys downstairs, all lusting after Angelina Jolie.

Nothing.

For the second time that day, disappointment covered me like an oppressive cloak. I rubbed at my eyes as I stood and surveyed the room. Get over it Kevin—they went out for pizza. They're having a good time.

And me . . . I'm a screaming loser. What the Hell was I thinking?

With a sigh I turned to the door and walked through.

I could remember being sick maybe three times in my life. Really sick. Throwing up, sweats, and dizziness. Not pleasant experiences, any of them.

And the memory of those times returned the moment I stepped foot into what I believed was the hallway. I pitched forward, my shoulders abruptly weighed down, pressed by some unseen hand. My stomach roiled, and I was distantly grateful that I'd not eaten anything all day, even as the dry heaves racked through me.

After that nasty episode, the smells of popcorn and hot wings faded, replaced by pungent, earthy odors of grass and weeds. I smelled them foremost because my face had become planted in them. I opened my eyes, unaware that I had closed them, and saw blurred images of tall, green-ish pillars.

I blinked. Blades of grass came into sharp focus. A breeze caressed my face, and again I caught the whiff of wild onions, much like the smells of my parents' yard after my dad cut the grass.

A bird chirped.

I also heard something else in my fog-driven state. The clanging of metal and voices. Yells of combat.

Voices came again to my left. I turned my head to look to my right. A thick forest of gnarled trees created a barrier, blocking out everything. It stood only a few meters away, and there was a niggling feeling in the back of my head.

I should get to the trees.

I should stand and run for the trees. The sounds of what I knew at that moment to be a battle grew closer. With a groan, I turned myself on my right side and forced my uncooperative body into a kneeling position. The cloth on my skin felt soft and comforting and I gasped when I looked down at myself.

The silky brown material from my sleeves spun around my front beneath a darker brown jerkin. Silver filigree latches pulled the outer garment closed over my chest. A thin strap crossed my chest, and when I tilted, I felt something across my back. With a deep breath to steady the just subsiding dizziness, I reached back and felt the soft, feathered fletchings of arrows.

I stood on wobbly legs, still amazed at the changes. My feet, somehow longer and thinner than before—no longer my bulky size twelve Adidas—were encased in soft, leather boots that wrapped around my calves to my knees. Red, thick hair fell forward as I looked down, and a few touches to my scalp with my new fingers revealed my short-cropped hair had grown to my shoulders.

I took in all of this in the span of a few minutes while

the noises of people, or creatures, came ever closer from the trees behind me. I touched my ears tentatively and again was amazed at their texture. Hard yet supple, and severely pointed.

I'd done it! I was an elven archer!

And as the approaching attackers broke the trees behind me, a new horror dawned much like the sickening thud of a body hitting the cold, hard ground.

I had no idea how to shoot one damned arrow.

Creating a character does not *make* a character. In real life, such things as stealth, archery, fighting, and dexterity are learned, not purchased with free points. Running, however, was second nature to all creatures. I could run, and did, with best speed to that line of trees. One look at those chasing me had spurred my flight mechanism into gear.

They were large, perhaps two meters high. Horns like those of a ram curled about their pig-snout faces. Their bodies, buff like body builders', were covered in thick, scraggly fur. They wielded swords and clubs above their powerful cloven feet.

I knew their descriptions from reading the book. Pigots, a mismatched crossing of troll and swine, supposedly created to offend the High Monarch.

I also remembered their ferocity—and their preferred tactic of pulling someone's arm off and beating them with it. I found my new body to be faster than I could ever manage in the "real" world, but once I broke through into the forest, I realized that the quickest way through would be to climb. The roots of the enormous trees broke above ground, a veritable obstacle course that ruined any chance of a fast retreat. Whispers along their wind-blown leaves called to me, and I gasped as I understood words like throaty calls inside my head.

. . . . to the trees, young Vothlorien. . . .

They *knew* my character name. How could they know my name? Still, I wasn't going to argue with the advice. I leaped for the lowest of one set of spreading limbs, thankful for the thick leather gloves I now wore.

The calls and grunts from my pursuers faded as I went farther into the branches, and with each grapple of rough bark, the voices in my head subsided.

Once I no longer heard the pigot monsters, I stopped amid a substantial outcropping of branches and leaned my back against a tree's trunk. My acrophobia kept me clutching the branches around me, as terror slowly crept into each muscle. How was I supposed to get down?

I spun around at the sudden snap of a branch behind me and lost my precarious hold on the surrounding branches. Luckily it was a soft landing on loam covered ground, but before I could stand and resume my flight, I was thrown down again, hit forcefully from the side, and laid out flat before I could scream uncle.

A hand was on my mouth again as some kind of sharp, cold object was thrust against my neck. I stared up into a hideous face and groaned.

It was round, with mottled green skin, much like that of a frog. Black, braided hair, decorated with bits of metal and stones fell about its amber eyes. A delicate upturned nose and full, red feminine mouth looked incongruous against the more animalistic features. Its ears hung low to the sides of its head, and thick silver and gold hoops pierced the nose and lobes.

It—no, *she*, if the contoured breastplate was any indication—hissed at me as she perched on my chest, her legs pinning my arms to my sides. Something else grabbed my ankles, and I felt something being strapped around them. I was being taken hostage, and I had no idea how to defend myself.

Abruptly, what I assumed to be a knife at my throat moved to the St. Christopher pendant, the tip of the blade lifting it above my skin. The creature atop me hissed again, baring two rows of bright, white sharp teeth as she sat back. She moved away, removing the knife from my throat and her hand from my mouth. I gasped aloud as she turned and motioned to someone behind her.

To my astonishment, the creature gave a garish smile as she put her hands on her hips. "Kevin?"

My mouth hung open as recognition of the voice, but not the face, came at a dizzing speed. "Chelsea?"

To the left of the grotesque face appeared a beautiful elven woman, moving with the elegant grace of a warrior. She had short-cropped red hair and eyes slitted like a cat's. Nick.

Chelsea put a hand on my chest and smiled wanly. "You look great, Kevin. But we have to get out of here. The pigots will be coming in here soon, and we have to get these herbs back to Johnny." She held up a small canvas bag. "He's dying."

My first piece of astounding information was that Nick, Johnny, Matt, and Chelsea had been in this strange world for three weeks. I told them it'd only been perhaps an hour since they started to play and I walked into Nick's room. The second piece of information dealt with Matt's disappearance and Johnny's wound.

"It was shortly after the fifth night when Lorne—I mean Matt—disappeared. And only a day later that Gil,

uh, *Johnny's*, magic failed, and he was wounded."
Chelsea said. Her voice was low and throaty, almost sexy.
But the froglike face was a bit off-putting. They were
seated in a circle before a fire in one of the caves they'd
found near what Nick—uhm, or rather, Gwen—said was
a castle filled with trolls.

I'd accepted hers and Gwen's new habit of calling one
another by their character names. In here, whereever here
was, our mundane names no longer seemed to apply.

Johnny/Gil lay in a fitful slumber nearby. The herbs
had helped ease the pain, but the wound to his side was
beginning to fester with infection.

Chelsea/Petrasha shook her head. "We were asleep
near the Battered Forest, and it was Matt's—*Lorne's*—
turn to stand watch. A scream woke me up, and Lorne
was gone."

"Just gone?" I shrugged my shoulders. "No sign of
struggle? Nothing to give you any information as to
where he'd been taken?"

Gwen shrugged. "We figured it was into the castle."
He nodded to the west. "We found a castle just on the
other side of the forest."

I blinked. "A regular, turreted castle with moat and
soldiers?"

Chelsea/Petrasha and Nick/Gwen nodded.

Of course there was a castle. Matt/Lorne always had a
castle in his stories. "And Gil was wounded when . . ." I
prodded them.

"When we tried to rescue Lorne," Chelsea/Petrasha
said, and she looked for all the world as if she thought I
was dense. She shook her head. "Though we're not sure
he's actually in the castle."

I waved a hand irritably at her. "Oh, he's in the castle.

For Matt, they're always in the castle. What's bothering me," and I glanced back at Johnny/Gil, "is that wound."

I knew Matt's story telling capability and how limited it was. It followed a pattern. RMA—Random Monster Attack—followed closely by a kidnapping. Victim was inevitably my elven character, who was badly wounded, and either Matt's warrior or Johnny's mage would come in and save the day.

End of boring story.

But if this was indeed a game started by Matt, then something had already gone horribly wrong. First, Matt was missing. Matt's character was never captured. Ever.

Yet he was gone.

Second, the infallible mage was wounded, badly at that—which was usually my character's lot in Matt's games.

Third, I was in fine health. My summation was simple: Matt had lost control of the story, and things were spinning out of control.

Once I shared my views with Chelsea/Petrasha and Nick/Gwen, I checked to make sure each of them still had their tokens. They did.

"Well," I began, look at each of them in turn. "Once Gil was hurt, did it ever occur to any of you to get back to the room and find some help?"

Petrasha snorted. It was a nasty, wet sound. "Get back? How do we get back?"

I put my finger on the St. Christopher at my neck. It was the only thing familiar left to me. "With these. You each chose an emergency retrieval token. It's what remained of your old self when you passed into here."

Each of them looked at their respective pieces. *Argh.*

Hadn't Matt told them anything? "Guys, you use that to get back home."

"We know that, Kevin," Nick/Gwen said quietly. "But did you read the fine print? Our return is up to GM discretion. None of us have been able to activate these tokens. Matt has to."

I had been operating under the assumption that my necklace was my lifeline back to my normal, boring, geeky existence. This news floored me more than I wanted to let on. It was obvious the news was something they'd all had to endure during their weeks here. And yet they had floundered leaderless.

I'd not read enough of the rules, only skimmed them. I did recall enough to know that Matt's input had to be acknowledged. He was the game master. The big kahuna. And somehow he'd let his control falter.

"Chelsea—uh, Petrasha," I chewed my lower lip. "I noticed on Matt's sheet that he didn't write down a token."

She snorted huskily. I really wanted her to stop doing that. "I told him he should—but he believed he didn't need one, since he was running the game. But, Voth," she sighed. "We didn't know this was gonna happen. It was so fast—I mean, I left the room to use the bathroom, and then I was here and all," she looked down at herself. "Ugly. I wandered around for about a day before Johnny and Nick appeared. And then it was another half day before Matt showed up."

"It was like," Nick/Gwen began, her slitted pupils widened, "they just stepped through that door and vanished. The game is a gateway to this world, whatever it is."

"And the world's rules are set by the Storyteller," I said, trying to bring them back to the immediate danger.

Johnny's wound worried me. What would happen if he died here? In a fantasy realm? I really didn't want to find out. "Look, Matt's stories are usually very simple, if you follow his pattern. I've always been able to second guess what his villains are going to do. Which is why he's always set on taking my character out of play on most occasions."

"I know." Chelsea/Petrasha nodded.

"Matt—*Lorne*—is in the castle, that much I'm sure of. And if this game, this setting, or whatever it is we're in now was originally patterned off his idea, then getting into that castle and rescuing me . . . ah, him . . . should be rather standard. What did you guys try before?"

"Storming."

I blinked at Nick/Gwenneth. "You stormed the castle? Just you three?"

"Yep."

"What happened?"

"The door was locked."

I put a hand to my face. Typical Matt would have played out that they were successful in storming—the door being locked was another sign of the guy's obvious loss of control. "Okay. New plan. We sneak in. I'm almost positive I can find a way to Matt."

I had a plan.

Johnny/Gil's injury was getting serious, and though he could stand, fighting was out of the question. But we couldn't very well leave him in the forest—especially not if things went the way I wanted them too. Which meant find Matt, force him to activate the tokens, and let us go home.

The castle looked like every other castle in one of Matt's stories. Turrets of stone. Moat filled with alligators. Soldiers patrolling the heights. We huddled behind the castle, away from the drawbridge, behind a copse of conveniently placed trees. I turned to my team. "Okay, it's like this. Matt—*Lorne*—is in there. We have to get him out in order to go home. What do you think we should do?"

Three sets of eyes stared at me.

Oh hell. "Guys, I need initiative here."

"But Matt always tells us what to do." Chelsea/Petrasha shook her head.

"Yeah, and that's why you've been here three weeks, *Petrasha*. Make your *own* decision. Lorne's in the dungeon, that's lower level, right?"

Nods all around.

"So . . ." I prodded.

Gil held up his hand. "Castles should have a side or back entrance, if for no other reason, for the lord of the castle to have an easy route of escape."

Yes! I nodded and turned to face the castle, thinking that a back door would be great, but it would need to have guards.

And there it was! I narrowed my eyes and swore that back entrance wasn't there a second before. Turning back to them I said, "Next?"

Petrasha looked at the entrance. "There are two guards. I suggest that while Gil and I sneak about to the side to that entrance, you and Nick . . . er, Gwen . . . whatever. You two take out the guards with arrows."

Perfect. This is what I always wanted in one of our Friday night games—initiative. Decisions made based on skill and ability. I nodded to the two of them and they set out in the twilight in the direction of the door. Gwen and I pulled our bows free and notched arrows. I had no idea how to actually shoot a bow, but I was willing to give it a try.

Yet, even as I drew back the string, the knowledge and skill came, and I *knew* I would hit my target. Both guards went down silently. Nick . . . no, *Gwen* winked at me and the two of us made our way stealthily to the back entrance, our matching elven boots silent on the dew-glistening grass.

Petrasha and Gil were already there. Johnny had his hands raised and was repeating something under his breath. I assumed it was a spell, and from the looks of his face, he was really trying this time. Not cheating.

I wanted the door to open for him. And it did.

I was beginning to suspect something was up at that point. This was twice that what I wanted came true. Once inside, I allowed Gwen to take the lead—her elven eyesight, like mine, being the sharpest. I took up the rear so that our heightened senses could focus on detecting any danger. Torches lit the way, with carved rock walls and sandy floor. Typical. I knew the way, instinctively. Yet I said nothing and allowed them to take a couple of wrong turns before encountering the dungeon.

There were two pigots by the door. Again, I let the others take the lead, each calling upon their character's abilities. Gil remembered from his reading that pigots' skin was impervious to elven arrows, so mine and Gwen's weapons were useless.

"So, what *is* their weakness?" I hissed as I looked at each of them.

I honestly didn't know.

Petrasha gave a slow, toothy smile. "Their ears. Sensitive hearing. Watch . . ." she turned and moved to the center of the hallway, just facing the two guards. The pigots saw her and yelled out for her to stop.

The half-orc threw back her head and let out a piercing scream, high enough that my own enhanced ears felt as if they were bleeding. The pigots clutched at their goatlike ears and bent over. They were bleeding, and rather profusely. Within minutes both were on the ground, inert.

We moved as quickly as Gil could manage to the door and peered inside. Matt was where I believed he would be, hanging from chains on a side wall, flanked by two chained skeletons.

Typical.

The door was padlocked, and this time I didn't even have to ask. Gil reached out and touched the metal. It clicked and gave way, falling to the sandy floor with a thunk. With me filing in last, a glance in either direction, our little group entered the dungeon.

Matt/Lorne called out to us. He was crying—something I never thought I'd see.

"Oh my god . . . is that you, Kevin?"

I nodded to him, and perched my wrist on the tip of my bow. "Yes, Matt. You look like hell."

"Get me down!"

Gil/Johnny obliged, if a bit roughly. He simply used his magic to make the metal chains disappear, and Matt/Lorne fell to the floor. No one moved to help him. Instead they gathered around me, congratulating me and cheering me on, and I had to take a step back as my new elven senses overloaded from the sudden noise.

"Hey, what about me?" Matt/Lorne was limping towards us, a hulking, square beast of a man with a child's face.

"What about you?" Chelse/Petrasha snapped at him before turning back to me. "Okay, *you* take us back now."

I was a bit surprised at her comment, though I suspected she was right. "You want to go back?"

"Him?" Johnny/Gil asked, and then winced as he leaned against Nick/Gwen.

"Kevin is the GM now," Chelsea/Petrasha gave me a high grin, and I again wished she wouldn't. Her mouth reminded me too much of jaws. "He can activate the tokens."

Matt/Lorne grabbed at Chelsea/Petrasha and pulled her back. He bullied his way to where I stood. "Tokens? You're not the Storyteller here, I am. I'm the one . . ." he frowned. "What are the tokens?"

"These," I fingered my St. Christopher just as Johnny/Gil touched his earring and Nick/Gwen held up the finger with the ring. Chelsea/Petrasha shoved her bracelet into Matt's face. "You didn't fill in the full sheet, Matt. You didn't follow directions. A Storyteller has to remain in control at all times, or chaos steps in."

"Kevin took over," Chelsea said. "And now we want to go home."

I nodded. I knew inside that one word from me would activate those small pieces of jewelry, and I was amazed at the knowledge. "Return home."

Each of them vanished before my eyes. All but Matt/Lorne.

His eyes widened as he reached up and took hold of my jerkin. "What about me? You have to get me out of here."

"I can't, Matt," I smiled at him. "Not from this side. I can probably send you a token." Which I was sure I could. After all, I was the game master now. "I'll write something in when I get back. And if you're good, I'll give you permission to activate it yourself."

I touched my St. Christopher medallion and returned home.

* * *

Chelsea took my hand as we walked toward the Student Union. Winter quarter had just started, and we were on our way to the Union for the Friday night movie. I passed Julie on the way in and she waved.

I smiled and pulled Chelsea close.

She smelled of grass and onions. "So," I whispered into her ear. "No game tomorrow night?"

Chels shook her head as we stepped through the Union doors and into the biology lecture hall, where other students had begun to gather. "Johnny's got a magic gig tomorrow down at some bar. He wants us to go."

"Okay," I smiled. "Is Matt going?"

"No," she pointed to a couple of seats near the middle and I nodded." He's not much into magic anymore. I think he has a new hobby." Chels gave me a beautiful smile. "He's racing those little RC cars. Out in Decatur."

Ever since our adventure, Matt had bowed out of the Friday night games. He'd never quite gotten over his displacement as Storyteller, which was fine with us.

I didn't call games but once a month now, and we all worked together on our characters. Me, Chels, Johnny and Nick. Other weeks, Chelsea and I had to ourselves— all thanks to the *Gateway*.

MANIFESTING DESTINY

Patricia Lee Macomber

Patricia Lee Macomber has been writing since the age of fifteen, when she sold her first novel. Unfortunately, her parents saw fit to crush her first attempt at fame, and the novel was never published. She has been published in various genres, taking time off to marry and have children, win a Bram Stoker Award for her editing of ChiZine, and do one term as Secretary of the HWA. Today, she lives in an historic mansion in Hertford, North Carolina, with her two children, Billy and Stephanie, four cats, a rabbit, a fish in a blender and a pit bull named Elvis. She also shares that leaky old mansion with the love of her life and Master, David Niall Wilson. Life has never been better!

John Marsters guided the car to a stop just behind the bumper of an electric-powered city transit. Another red light, another delay in getting to work. He sighed and watched his temperature gauge, checked his gas. Then his eyes drifted slowly upward, landing first on the bumper sticker directly in front of him, then on the scores of cars that filled his field of vision.

To his right, the sidewalk was peppered with people. Some had stopped dead still, standing where their feet had left them. Most had just dropped to the ground, legs crossed at the ankles as though they were resting, waiting for . . . something.

Destiny had ceased to function.

Unblinking, John fumbled with the door button and listened as the door slid open to the sound of a familiar hiss. Then he stepped out and appraised the situation, eyes drizzling over unmoving forms as he moved onto the sidewalk and closer to the intersection.

Everywhere, everything had stopped. Cars didn't move, lights didn't change. No building doors opened to spew bodies onto the sidewalk, no pedestrians dodged each other in a futile attempt to keep from spilling their packages onto the pavement.

John's office was a mere three blocks north, and he headed in that direction, walking first backward, then forward, head spinning to look in all directions at once. Everyone had just stopped, waiting. They weren't dead or unconscious. They were merely waiting for further instructions, and it was all his fault.

John ran. He took the steps of his building two at a time and hit the door at a dead run. The lift was waiting for him, open by virtue of the fact that a young woman had chosen to sit directly in the path of the open doors. He moved her aside carefully and stepped inside, swiping his card and then pressing the 40th floor button.

Within seconds, the doors whooshed open on a room

filled with movement. People scurried about, lights
blinked, alarms sounded, and everywhere was the sound
of panicked shouting. John's eyes singled out his best
man, the most diligent researcher who had ever graced
his team. He approached from the rear at a good clip,
brow furrowed even before he heard the news.

"Kevin, what the hell is going on?"

Kevin spun, all wild eyes and careless hair. His glasses
had slipped nearly to the tip of his nose and they perched
there like a small bird, ready to take flight. "Thank good-
ness you're here! I was just about to beep you."

John shrugged out of his jacket and flung it over a
chair. "So what happened? What's wrong with Destiny?"

"She's shut down. Completely."

"I know that." John dropped into a nearby chair and
spun the monitor to face him. "But why?"

"Port seven shut down after a huge data dump. It happened during the routine back-up this morning. Nothing
is moving in or out of the main data port and the hub
overloaded. We tried to . . ."

"Reroute."

"As I was saying, we tried to reroute. But there is no
contingency for rerouting the dimensional port."

"Switch to the back-up." John keyed in a few codes
and watched the numbers stream across the screen."

Suddenly, Kevin looked embarrassed. He stood to full
height and shifted his stance, eyes locked on the floor and
his face paling by the second. "There is no back-up for
the dimensional port. The design didn't allow for a mirror on the incoming port—no option for rerouting."

"That's bull." It was as close as John had ever come to
cursing and even that small slip made him blush a bit. He
stabbed a finger at the screen and traced the lines of a 3-

D schematic with one finger. "The com port reaches out to the first alternate, draws in all possible data from all alternate dimensions, and then brings it back in to be processed . . . here. Once that's done, each resolution is routed to the proper recipient through the telemetry system."

"Yes, I realize that. But the way the system is designed, the way the data has to be assimilated, there can be only *one* inbound port. No back-up."

John sat back so suddenly that the chair wheeled backward a few inches. His eyes bore down on Kevin's face, staring daggers through him. "You don't have to tell me how things are designed. I invented Destiny, remember? What I do want you to tell me is how to fix it. You do realize that the entire planet has shut down? Billions of people have simply stopped, awaiting further instructions."

Palms open, pleading, Kevin looked down at his boss and friend, eyes dark. "John, I understand what you're saying. But there's only one way to do it. We have to take Destiny completely offline, do a cold reboot, and get the data stream flowing again. The real problem is that she was never designed to handle this type of load. Destiny was meant for a certain number of people. Not every person on the planet. And this little glitch is going to keep happening over and over again . . . unless we do something."

John shoved off from the chair, launching himself forward and the chair backward. As Kevin trailed after him, he slipped behind the huge clear screen, keyed up the visuals of the Destiny schematic, and bombarded Kevin with a flurry of words.

"Then we have to regulate. We can increase Destiny's

com speed and memory. Do that immediately. But then we have to install a few fail-safes. Here, where the data streams in from the dimensional port. If we get close to maximum capacity, we have to route things differently. Send them through a backup processor . . . or maybe have an alternate system installed from scratch just to handle the overflow. Ultimately, we need to install a completely autonomous system here . . ." he stabbed his finger at the clear screen, dragged the image over. "And here."

"That will take months."

"I know. So we'll do that later. Soon, though. For now, put in a subroutine to regulate the amount of data and the speed at which it is handled. Then install another subroutine to store and process the overflow."

"Can do."

"How long?" John watched as Kevin produced a handheld and did his calculations.

"If we keep everyone here through dinner, even backup staff . . ."

"Dinner?" An alarm sounded from the other side of the huge room, only barely registering with John.

"Look, John, we'll work as fast as we can, but there are limits. I swear to you, we'll have Destiny back online by six. No later."

"So the entire world is going to just freeze for the next nine hours while we fix things? Barring that, people will get tired of waiting. They'll eventually figure Destiny has abandoned them and get up. Start operating of their own free will. I don't have to tell you what will happen then, do I?" He dropped into the chair again, running both hands through his sweat-matted hair. He looked up into Kevin's shadowed face and sighed. "Get the programmers moving, and then meet me in the systems room. We need to get the new processors and memory in place ASAP."

A pale man appeared behind Kevin, lips trembling before they released the words. "Dr. Marsters, the president is on the phone."

Without sparing a glance for the interrupter, eyes still locked on Kevin and blistering his flesh, John said, "Well, of course he is."

"Mr. President, at the risk of seeming rude, I'd really appreciate it if we could keep this brief." John checked his chronometer quickly and sighed. "The sooner I can get back to Destiny, the sooner we can set things to right again."

"I understand that, Dr. Marsters." The president leaned back in his squeaky chair and steepled his fingers beneath his chin. "I just want a quick run-down of what's going on from the man who created the problem in the first place."

John's face reddened and his hands worked nervously at the crease of his trousers. "Basically, sir, Destiny suffered an overload and shut down on her own."

"How? Was it a flaw in the hardware? In the software? I'd like to understand why it is that we have complete chaos on our hands. Thank God we didn't patch the politicians into Destiny. Can you imagine where we'd be then?"

The possibilities ran through John's mind, but he kept them to himself. "Sir, basically, Destiny was designed to make all decisions for the populace. It reaches out into every conceivable alternate dimension, analyzes all possible outcomes of any given situation, then delivers the best course of action for the person in question. Essentially, there can be only one route for data to pass into Destiny from those alternate dimensions. And what happened this morning is that too much data passed too quickly, causing a bottleneck in the communications port and shutting Destiny down completely."

"Surely you had backups in place?"

"We had emergency systems that were set to handle only essential personnel during a crisis, such as police, health workers and the like. But there can be no other port through which data passes between the dimensions. To have another would create a paradox. It would be . . . bad."

The president was silent for a moment longer, chair squeaking slowly as he rocked and thought. "But you can fix this, correct? And make sure it never happens again?"

"If I can get back to the system, I can." He nodded vigorously and checked his chronometer once more.

"Then I should let you get to it. You can give me a detailed report on all this as soon as the crisis has passed." He shoved out his hand, fully expecting John to take it.

John was halfway to the door, having turned tail when the president had first stood. "You'll have your report, sir. And an updated Destiny to boot."

Dr. John Marsters, possessor of too many degrees to display, creator of Destiny, and most brilliant scientist of his time, strolled along behind the various monitoring stations. Each screen was green, meaning there were no problems, no glitches, nothing that might require another visit to the president's office. Finally, he drew up behind Kevin's station, the great screen before him, flashing data and statistics, all meant to let him know that the fix had worked.

"Looks like everything's holding, yes?"

Kevin spared a glance over his shoulder at John, and then returned to watching the numbers. "We are operating at peak capacity and we still have memory and bandwidth to spare. I think we've done it."

"And the backup?" John fussed about with the crease of his pants, purposely not looking at Kevin.

"While you were busy installing those wonderful little memory gangs, I got the backup in place. As far as I can tell, we can increase the population by another fourteen million and still not come close to maxing out the system."

John smiled. It was the first time he had done so in days. "Good. Then I can exhale, right?" He clapped Kevin on the shoulder, drawing his gaze at last. "And I can buy my favorite engineer and programmer a beer?"

"You bet!" Kevin returned the smile and the clap on the back.

J. Everett Burnam sat at his table in Le Chic, folded over a plate of pasta and scowling. "I said al dente. I said it twice. And both times you bring me this . . . mush." He turned a threatening gaze on the waiter, making him cower yet again.

The inside of Mr. Burnam's glasses lit up, visible only from the inside. On that tiny screen flashed the words . . . *decision requested*.

Came the reply . . . *Beat him*.

"Bobby, please don't." Amy placed her small hand in the center of his chest and pushed. It wasn't a shove exactly, just enough pressure to let him know that he wouldn't get any closer. She felt the cold brick of the wall press tighter against her warm back and she shivered.

"Aw, baby!" Bobby, ever insistent, pressed back against that hand and let his lips fall to her neck. Already, his hand was at the hem of her skirt.

"I said no!" This time, she gave him a shove, trying to slip out from under him and away from the wall.

Decision requested.

Fuck it!

"Mainland China just came online." Kevin took a long sip of his coffee, more inhaled than actually drunk, born on steam and heat.

"And?" John leaned over his shoulder, watching the numbers scroll by.

"And the numbers are rising." There was a moment of heady silence. Kevin held his breath. "It's okay. The backup programming just kicked in. We're fine."

John stood up and rubbed the small of his back, finally letting his shoulders slide into their normal position. "What happens when the numbers go up again?"

Kevin spun the chair and leaned back, lacing his fingers behind his head and smiling like the proverbial canary-eater. "The way the backup works, it can handle any number we need. Infinite. I told you, our worries are over."

Before John could even tell him what a great job he'd done, before he could grab his coat and suggest a beer, an alarm went off four stations down. Their heads swiveled in unison and they glared at the flashing red screen.

"It's okay!" the watcher shouted, throwing both hands up into the air. "Just a situational glitch.

John and Kevin relaxed visibly, each on the verge of leaving the office . . . finally. Then another alarm split the silence and their hearts stopped again. And another alarm. Another.

"What the . . ." John stared as one station after another went red.

"A guy in New York just beat up a waiter over a plate of pasta."

"Some kid just raped his girl friend."

"There's a guy in Milan that went nuts with a tank and razed his neighbor's house."

John dashed from station to station, trying to follow the chain of bizarre events, his head spinning and his hands suddenly shaking. "I want reports. Tell me why this happened."

"A lady in New Hampshire just drowned her kid in the tub."

"Kevin!" John was red-faced and sweating. For a moment, he felt as though he might actually pass out. "What the hell kind of backup program did you use?"

Kevin was at his side in an instant, stammering and shaking his head. "I had to use something that would never require more Destiny resources. I had to find some sort of data assembly and analysis that could be accessed instantly.

"What program?" John grabbed Kevin by the collar and shook as hard as he could.

"It's called First Alert. It reaches down into the psyche . . ."

John shook him again. "Where does the data come from? What's it analyze?"

Kevin flinched at John's shouts, looking for all the

world as though he might cry. "It accesses the psyche. It comes from the person himself."

"What does it do? WHAT?"

"With the new memory and all, I didn't think we'd ever need it..."

"What does it do? Tell me!"

Kevin wept, tears streaming down his cheeks in sweat-smeared tracks. "I didn't think it would ever be used. I had to have something."

"Tell me now!"

"First Alert accesses their gut instinct, okay? It tells them to act on their first impulse."

John let go of him suddenly and staggered backward, his head spinning. "And does this backup program . . . this First Alert . . . does it apply to the emergency systems, too?"

The answer was soft and sad. "Yes."

"Pull the plug," John growled, grabbing the nearest watcher from his chair.

"Sir?"

"Do it now. Shut down Destiny. Deprogram her. I want every shred of First Alert gone from the system. A complete purge. Do . . . it . . . now!"

"But John. . . ."

John turned flaming eyes on Kevin and sneered. "Better that every man, woman and child lie motionless on the pavement than we have free will on this planet."

"I can't, sir."

John reeled on him, jaws and fists clenched. "Why the hell not?"

The watcher blinked twice, motionless, staring at the small screen inside his glasses, visible only to him.

Kill him.

AT BEST AN ECHO

Bradley H. Sinor

Not too long ago a friend of Brad's commented that Brad wrote family stories. "Yeah," Brad told him, "If you're related to the Addams Family or one of Dracula's relatives." Brad has seen his fiction appear such anthologies as Warrior Fantastic, Knight Fantastic, Dracula in London, Bubbas of the Apocalypse, Merlin, Lord of The Fantastic, *and others. He will have several more coming out in 2005. Two collections of his short fiction,* Dark And Stormy Nights *and* In the Shadows, *have been released by Yard Dog Press.*

"Elena," muttered Abraham Van Helsing as he looked down at the silver framed photograph in his hand. The flickering light from the gas flame on the wall covered the glass with a yellow glare. It wasn't necessary to see the picture; he knew each and every inch of it.

It had been taken six months after Elena and he had been married in 1880. The two of them were stiff and unmoving, waiting as the photographer got everything ready to expose the plate. He had his hand resting on her shoulder as she perched on a small stool, a parasol across her knees. But there was a gleam in Elena's eyes, hinting that she was a moment away from saying something either profound or amazingly funny. That was the woman he loved.

He flexed the fingers of his hands, still remembering the feel of her hand in his, and his own fingers wrapped tightly around a sharp obsidian knife. He wiped away a single tear as he stared at the picture.

"Abraham, have you gone deaf?"

Van Helsing looked up with a start. On some level he had heard his name being spoken, one of any number of sounds that echoed up and down the halls of the University of Amsterdam's Medical School.

He blinked twice and realized that a familiar figure had invaded his office. The tall imposing figure of Dr. Joseph Bell, a black medical bag in his hand, stood there smiling. Bell was sixty-three years old, but with the amount of energy he seemed to radiate, and in spite of the shock of white hair, the man could easily have passed for twenty years younger.

"Joseph! It's good to see you," Van Helsing advanced toward his friend. Bell's grip was still strong.

The two had known each other for more than two decades, since they had investigated a matter involving a plague and an alleged curse. Bell was the first one to scoff and proclaim the supernatural events that Van Helsing had investigated to be nothing but folkloric poppycock and mummery. That had not stopped the two of them from becoming friends.

"What are you doing here at this time of the year? I believe that the semester is not yet over," said Van Helsing, filling two glasses with sherry and passing one to his friend. "I would have expected you to be terrorizing medical students to the point that they would risk those Scottish winters rather than miss one of your lectures."

"Indeed, these are the final weeks of winter term. Some of my colleagues seemed to think I have been working too hard, so I asked Arthur Doyle to fill in for awhile and decided to come here for a visit," said Bell. "So, Abraham, I see the food is still excellent at the Medlenbrough."

"Up to your usual tricks, Joseph." Van Helsing made no effort to conceal his actions as he glanced down at his sleeves and pants legs looking for any telltale sign that might have given Bell any clues to his eating habits.

"I would hardly call my minor observations tricks," Bell told him. "It is just the skill of a good diagnostician, a skill that every doctor should have."

"I know what you look for and how you are able to diagnose these things about people, but it still amazes me," chuckled Van Helsing.

"In this case it was just two things: in the pocket of your overcoat I noticed the Daily Journal. The Medlenbrough always stocks the latest papers for its morning patrons. Since the date on the paper is today's, and the delivery label with the name of the hotel is clearly visible, I was able to make my conclusion."

"And the second thing?" said Van Helsing.

"Your appointment book is open on your desk. I noticed that you had written that you could be reached at the hotel between 8:00 and 10:00 this morning," said Bell.

"As always, obvious and elementary," Van Helsing said. He saw the wince on Bell's face at the context of the last word. "Once again I see the reason that young Doyle modeled that detective of his on you."

"Humph," said Bell. "The less said about that, the better, I should think."

Bell picked up the medical bag he had carried in and set it in front of Van Helsing. From inside it he brought out a small leather folio. "I want you to know that I have violated several British laws in obtaining this for you."

Van Helsing picked it up and unfastened the leather ties that held it closed. Inside were a dozen parchment pages. The material felt odd, different and not just from age. The only other time he had felt anything similar had been in one of the most guarded rooms in the British Museum. He had gone there to consult copies of the Al Azief, the so-called Necronomicon, and other volumes that it was better the British public did not know about.

"All that remains of the Kollier-Croft Codex," he murmured.

"I thought you might recognize it; a few pages were salvaged," said Bell.

"Indeed. I've been trying to get even a look at this for five years, since I first learned of its existence. Baron Carlson refused to even admit that he had it," said Van Helsing.

"Oh, he had it, all right. Let us say that saving the life of the Baron's grandson gave me a bit more leverage than you had. I made a weekend visit to his country home, and this came away with me. I just borrowed it, of course," said Bell.

Exactly how Bell had managed that bit of prestidigitation, Van Helsing could only speculate. He had heard rumors of how well it, and the rest of the Baron's occult library, was hidden. Yet it didn't surprise him that his friend had been able to acquire the codex pages.

"If you were willing to take that risk, Joseph, have you come to believe that the secrets in these pages will enable me to help Elena?" said Van Helsing.

"I believe that you believe they will, old friend. If having this helps you, it was worth the risk," said Bell. "I only wish the way out of that padded room was in them."

Van Helsing had spread the pages out on his desk, pushing everything else off to the side. Written in Greek and Latin, the pages appeared to be part of a traveler's narrative, illustrated with some highly detailed renderings of animals and plants. The writing was crabbed in places, running letters together as if the writer had been rushed and uncertain he would be able to finish.

As he read line after line, Van Helsing found himself thinking of a Latin tutor he'd had as a boy of nine. The Reverend James Murray had been convinced that his young charge would never master the tongue of Rome.

After several minutes the text began to change; letters blurring and reforming, the illustrations changing as well into things that no naturalist of any age had described. No longer was he looking at a travel narrative but at descriptions of horrific ancient ceremonies, spells that invoked powers and beings from the darkest places of the universe.

Van Helsing laid his finger a quarter of the way down one page, tracing a circular symbol. The pen work was painfully fine and detailed, leaving the impression of one drawing carefully laid on another, layer upon layer.

Looking at it, he had the feeling of standing at the bottom of a huge mural and being able to see only a tiny bit of it. The desire to see the rest, to know its secrets, was like a tidal wave rolling over him, obliterating his awareness of everything else.

"Abraham, no!" The voice was female, distant but clear and commanding.

Van Helsing jerked backwards, his vision filled with the familiar sights of his university office. He had to struggle to draw a breath, grabbing onto the edge of the desk to steady himself.

Bell sprinted across the room, grabbing his friend by the arm as Van Helsing's legs went out from underneath him. The Scotsman managed to guide the other man into the chair.

"Easy there, Abraham, " Bell said as he loosened Van Helsing's tie and began to check his pulse.

"I'm all right."

"That's a matter of opinion," said Bell. "You're as pale as a ghost. Your heart is hammering as though you had just run a marathon. I turn my back for only a minute, then it's as if a hurricane hit this room, everything goes flying, and you drop like a stringless marionette."

"Did I do this?" He gestured at the scattered items on the floor.

"I'm reasonably certain that you did, since we are alone in here," Bell said. "That is, unless you have a resident ghost."

"That would be a simple explanation."

"Simple explanations are sometimes the best. But let's leave all explanations till later. Perhaps we should call a halt to this matter, at least for the moment," suggested Bell. "I think a bite of supper might be good for you. May I suggest we adjourn to the Medlenbrough?"

"That might help," agreed Van Helsing.

*   *   *

Since the weather was terrible—it had been raining for two days straight—the dining room at the Medlenbrough was nearly empty. Not that they would have been denied a choice of tables under other circumstances; the maitre'd knew Van Helsing well, so there was little doubt that they would get a good table.

"So you just walked off and left your students," said Van Helsing as he bit into the last piece of his filet.

"Indeed I did. Call it their holiday from me. Since everyone had been nagging at me to take some time off, I decided to do it, just not when they thought I would. There was another matter that brought me here." Bell produced an envelope from inside his jacket and passed it over to Van Helsing. "That young Dr. Simmons that you wrote me about seems perfectly suited to fill the position in the medical school. I thought I would bring his acceptance letter myself, but I think you should have the pleasure of actually giving it to him."

"You have made a wise choice. Mark will be an asset to your staff, although it will be quite a transition from the University of Amsterdam to watching the misty dawns over Edinburgh Castle."

"I should say so," said Bell. "Just be sure you caution him to be ready for our Scottish winters. They are a bit more brisk than you have been experiencing here."

Van Helsing inclined his head for a moment as he noticed a small man dressed in a dark, slightly rumpled, suit approaching their table.

"Good evening, Inspector," he said.

"Good evening, Herr Professor. I am sorry to disturb your dinner. They told me at the University that you were dining here."

"Don't trouble yourself, Inspector Hollaman. Allow

me to present my friend and colleague, Dr. Joseph Bell of the University of Edinburgh. Joseph, this is James Augustus Hollaman, one of the bright lights of the Amsterdam police department."

"A pleasure, Inspector," said Bell.

"The pleasure is mine, Herr Doctor. I hope you will forgive the intrusion. I need to discuss a matter of great importance with Professor Dr. Van Helsing."

"Anything you can say to me, you can say to Dr. Bell; he is utterly trustworthy," said Van Helsing.

"Sir, you must come with me. There has been an incident at the asylum that resulted in a death," said the policeman.

"At the asylum?" Van Helsing felt the color draining out of his face.

"Yes. Someone tried to murder your wife."

Once he was certain that his wife was safe, Van Helsing had requested to be allowed to see her attacker. The body had been removed deep into the basement, below the most secure cells, into the asylum's morgue. Lit with several gas lamps, it was filled with shadows and silence. There was a smell of disinfectant hanging in the air above the stone and the mortar, mixed with a cold that seemed to leach what little warmth the three men had brought into the room with them.

What lay on the table looked human, at first glance. Van Helsing lifted one of its hands and could see the webbing between the fingers, which also seemed to have an extra joint. Pulling back the eyelids, the orbs that looked out were solid black with almost no sign of white except at the very edges.

"An extraordinary example of deformity," said Bell.

"It was only a matter of luck that the attendants saw him going into your wife's room. I just wish they hadn't killed him. Though from what they said, it was the only way to keep him from killing Elena."

"Thankfully, there will be no reports in the newspapers regarding this incident," said Hollaman. "I have already had a word with some of our friends in the fourth estate. I will leave you doctors to examine the body. He carried papers identifying him as one Eban Marsh, an American sailor from Massachusetts. I want to check in with the officers I have assigned to watch the asylum for the rest of the night."

On a table near the body was the attacker's weapon, a curved dagger. The blade was some six inches long, but the curve and its shiny surface gave it a feeling of being longer. The handle, which was covered in intricate designs, portrayed several strange creatures, tentacles wrapped around symbols carved into the wood.

"This is a priceless bit of work," said Bell. "The skill that went into it is amazing. From the color of the wood I would venture to suggest that it is old, perhaps several generations."

"I concur," Van Helsing said. "It would have been passed down from one generation to the next. All dedicated to the same thing."

"Such as?" asked Bell.

Van Helsing pointed at several places on the handle, showing how the design went from the wood onto the metal itself. "These symbols are pictographs, used by some obscure South Seas tribes. Loosely translated, it seems to describe this weapon as being the sting from beyond the edge and the dark of Nyarlathotep and Yog Sog Oth."

"Part of the Cthulhu mythological cycle, as I recall," Bell said.

"A bit more than myth, I would say," observed Van Helsing.

Bell seemed to be ignoring him, intent on examining the appendages of the corpse, moving the joints in most unusual ways. "This 'person' is either one of the most deformed beings in existence, or there has been a tremendous amount of inbreeding."

"Inbreeding, yes, with a good bit of cross-species breeding, as well," said Van Helsing. "Let us hope that our friend's 'cousins' do not come calling or attempt to reclaim his body."

Bell motioned over at the dagger. "Certainly not if they are that well armed."

"Joseph, if you would continue your examination of the body, I have something . . ."

"I was wondering when you would go to see *her*." It was a statement rather than a question, one that Van Helsing knew needed no answer.

Standing in front of the door to Elena's room, Van Helsing was afraid. He knew what he wanted to find on the other side of the door, but he knew what he would find, and they were two different things.

The door, a heavy metal thing, swung silently open. The windows were closed, sealed shut with wire mesh and bars. There were other locks on the room, tiny, carefully inscribed symbols, tiny bits of salt, incense and oil, discreetly spread into the four corners, protections against things that only a few, outside of those who were strangers to sanity, knew existed.

From out in the hallway he could hear the sound of

footsteps and distant screaming cries of other patients, the same sounds that Elena had heard every day and night for the past dozen years.

Elena was lying completely still in her bed, covered partially by a blanket. Her face was awash in the shadows and bits of light that leaked in from the hallway, relaxed and, for a moment, at peace, even with lines of pain in her face and ragged streaks of gray marking her hair.

Her eyes were open, staring straight at the ceiling, marked only by the slow blinking of the lids. Van Helsing looked at her for a long time as he stood next to the bed, then leaned forward until his face was only inches from hers.

"Elena," he said softly, and began to sing softly to her. The tune was a Welsh folk song they had heard in those long-gone first days after they had met. When Elena had heard it, she proclaimed it wonderful and insisted on learning the music and words.

For several minutes there was only Van Helsing's voice, but then he began to hear hers, echoing each note and tone that came from him. It was a tiny, sad sound that came from Elena's throat. She had done this before, many times, and then it would be gone, as quickly as it had begun. Van Helsing allowed himself the slim hope that this would be the moment he had prayed for. That this was the fanning of the flame, that it would light her way out of the prison of insanity that he had locked her in.

"The walkers slide with the penguins quietly," she said in a little girl's voice.

"Elena," he said, his heart breaking as he heard the words.

"Abraham," Elena said in a clear and precise voice." I

wanted to go for a walk, like we did that first day, but the hurling monkeys are blocking our way."

She began to hum, and then the sound faded away. Without warning Elena Van Helsing sat straight up in her bed, as stiff as a board, shooting up so quickly that she almost collided with her husband. She stayed like that for a moment, then slid backward onto her bed, lying as silently as the darkness around her.

Three candles and a piece of chalk were all that Van Helsing needed after he had returned to the asylum with the leather folio. It had taken him nearly an hour to draw the complicated design, filling up much of the room as it wrapped around his wife's bed.

None of the staff had come into the room except for a single orderly who said nothing, just stood in the doorway looking at the scene in front of him and then left. Anyone else who worked there would not have even opened the door; over the years they had become used to his occasional "unusual" methods of treatment.

"Joseph, this is something that I must do. I beg of you, no matter what happens, no matter what you might see or hear, you must not interfere in any way, shape or form. Understand that if that were to happen, you would put not only myself in harm's way, but Elena as well," he told Bell, "It is for her that your professional services may soon be needed."

Bell had said nothing, just took a place outside of the design in the corner of the room. The Scotsman extracted a thick cigar from inside his coat pocket, but he did not light it. Instead, he stood there quietly, brandishing the tobacco like a weapon.

After lighting the candles, Van Helsing sat cross-legged in the middle of the design. He tried to push everything else out of his mind, focusing on Elena and the place where she dwelled. A distant carillon marked the half-hour and then the hour as Van Helsing stared down at the Codex pages that he had laid in a semicircle around him.

He began to read, carefully pronouncing each word, hoping that the impromptu translation would be accurate. Between one heartbeat and the next Van Helsing felt everything change. The asylum was gone, there was no sign of Bell or Elena or even the city.

Van Helsing knew this place; he had walked here and in others like it over the years. At first glance it seemed like a hill far out in the countryside. Nothing appeared that much out of the ordinary, but no matter what direction he looked in, nothing felt quite right.

Coming toward him from the west was a man dressed in the Bedouin robes of an Arab. The figure never seemed to go faster than a brisk walk, but it grew closer at an amazing pace. When the man stopped in front of him, Van Helsing recognized the face: scarred cheek, hawklike nose, and eyes that drove themselves into the soul of whatever he looked at. The long mustachios only clinched the identification.

He had met Sir Richard Francis Burton, the translator of the Arabian Nights, on several occasions before the man's death. He could see that face in this younger one that stood in front of him.

"I must say, for a man dead these three years you are definitely looking remarkably healthy, Sir Richard," said Van Helsing.

The figure laughed. It was a sound that sent a chill into Van Helsing's heart. For no more than a moment the human shape was gone, replaced by something else, with tentacles, teeth, half a hundred eyes and a stench that would have made a freshly dead corpse smell like perfume.

Then the man in the Arab robes stood in front of Van Helsing again. He refused to allow himself to think of this "thing" as the man whose face it wore.

"If you have something to say, " said Van Helsing, trying to sound bored, "then say it and let us move on."

"Direct. I like this. Very well, go home," it said. "I could have sent one of my children, but it pleased me to offer fair warning."

"The same way you sent one of them to try to kill my wife?"

The figure laughed and began to speak in a vaguely Arabic dialect, though the words were like nothing heard on the seas of sand.

"Abraham!" Elena's voice cut through the mist. Van Helsing turned toward it.

That very action was enough to shake him loose, he realized, from the holding spell that the thing had on him.

Long tendrils of pulsating flesh were inching their way toward his legs. He kicked at them, driving the toes of his boots into the sod. That seemed to be enough to drive them back, for the moment at least.

"Abraham!" Though he could not see them, Van Helsing felt two hands grabbing his arm and yanking him backward away into swirling mist. The sensation of falling through a door surrounded him, and then everything was calm.

Taking several deep breaths, Van Helsing looked around. Again the scene had changed, but again it was a place that he knew, too damned well. No peaceful landscape this, but ruins that stretched on as far as the eye could see. The night sky was filled with churning clouds that gave the whole place a feeling of never-ending midnight: darkness obscuring what might once have been a city. What life there might have been here had long since been crushed out.

This was the realm of Yog Sog Oth, the demon beyond the gate, one of the Old Ones, beings locked away from the earth after their reign of terror, who were always struggling to return. To some they were gods, to others demons; to Van Helsing they had always been something to fear who must be never be allowed to escape from their prisons.

A hundred yards in front of him he could see a pair of twin pylons, electricity filling the air between them like a Van der Grif generator gone wild. Van Helsing knew this place all too well. There had not been a day in the last dozen years when the image of it had left his mind. His hand clenched and he could feel the obsidian knife for a moment. She was as he had last seen her, stretched out on an altarlike slab of rock in front of the pylons. Her face pale, the wind whipping strands of hair across it. She had not aged in the dozen years since the two of them had arrived in this place, come to place a seal that would keep Yog Sog Oth from coming through the gate.

Why should she age? This was her soul, her true self, as real to the touch as anything, though her true body lay in the asylum, raving about penguins and hurling monkeys. Van Helsing fought down the self loathing that sought to rise in his throat, with the knowledge that he had condemned the woman he loved to lie as guardian of this place for the rest of her life.

Van Helsing's eyes fell on the dagger, still buried to the hilt in her heart; his fingers clenched with the memory of wrapping themselves around it, the memory of her hands on his, helping to push the blade into her heart.

"No, no," he said and reached out to touch her cold cheek, tears rolling down his face. His hand brushed against the silver swan brooch on her blouse, a gift on their first anniversary.

"Abraham."

Elena stood at his side, a look of sadness and joy in her eyes. Unlike the figure on the altar, who wore a traveling skirt, vest and loose blouse, this woman wore a gown of black and scarlet, an identical silver swan broach affixed to her left breast, her face young and not yet touched by pain and madness.

Van Helsing reached for her, but she pulled back just out of his reach. "I'm sorry, Abraham. What you see is at best an echo of what I was. Over the eternity since we first set foot in this hellhole, I've learned to tap some of the power in the pylons. That's what has let me reach out to you, to pull you back from the Codex and away from that thing that sought to stop you."

"I know, my darling. You are always looking out for me. But now I've come to free you, Elena. There is a way," he said.

The look of sadness deepened in Elena's eyes, mixed with a wary fear. "I know that was what you said you would try to do. But we both know it cannot be. I have become one with this place, and it is necessary for a human soul from a still living body to hold the line here."

"It should have been me," said Van Helsing.

"It could not," she answered softly. "Of the two of us, only you had the knowledge and skill to make it work. That is why I guided your hand when . . ."

"I drove the dagger into your heart," he said bitterly.

"Now I've come with a way that you can walk out of the asylum. For all these years I've searched for a way. I knew there had to be one, and I've found it."

"No, Abraham, you know that cannot be, no matter how much either one of us wants it. The gate can only be held as long as there is a guardian, one whose soul is imprisoned here and whose body lives on Earth. You said so yourself," she reminded him. "In the eternity since that moment I've come to know the truth of your words. Besides, with the terror that has held, that has pounded into the very core of my soul, I do not believe I would be able to wear sanity again."

The seals on the gate had worn away with the passing millennia. Only the willing sacrifice of someone to become the guardian could keep them in place.

"No, I will not permit it to be so," screamed Van Helsing. "One of the followers of Nyarlathotep tried to kill you tonight. I do not know what I would have done had he succeeded."

"You would have gone on, sadder; but you would have gone on to face each dawn as you have all your life. I would give anything to stand with you again, facing the unknown, growing old at your side. But that cannot be. I know that what happened will happen again, as surely as one day follows another. The followers of the Elder Gods are always probing, trying to find ways to free their deities," she said.

"No, Elena, I am your husband. I know what is best for you," he told her, feeling more determined than ever.

"As I know that you must not do this. There is a great evil that will soon be afoot in the world. The only way it can be defeated is if you are there to hold the line and drive it back." Waves of images flashed in Van Helsing's mind: wolves, a woman dressed in a gossamer gown, an aristocratic man standing in the turret of a castle, fog and death flowing everywhere.

Van Helsing looked toward the echo of his wife. She had moved away from him and the altar. Elena's arms were raised above her head, partially blocking her face. From her open palms shot bolts of light, glowing a sickly green, that flew outward faster than anything he had ever seen.

They struck him, hitting his chest with the force of a horse's hoof, wrapping around him as an ever-tightening vine. Van Helsing staggered backward, one arm free and frantically struggling to balance himself with it.

"My darling, our paths are different now; they always will be," she said, tears rolling down her face. "You must go back. Remember that I love you and will always be near."

Van Helsing felt words dying in his throat as he rolled through a door into darkness. The last image before he passed out was the silver swan pin, one the woman standing in front of him and one as his hand closed around it.

"You had no intention of coming back, did you?"

Van Helsing stared into the amber liquid that half filled his brandy snifter for several minutes before he finally took a swallow. He had never particularly liked the taste of brandy, preferring the taste of a good single malt. But in this case, the burning sensation as it rolled down his throat felt very right.

It didn't surprise him that Bell had divined his plans, though for a time he had hardly admitted to himself what he would have had to do to actually bring "Elena" back. The gate could not be left without a guardian. The lack of one was what had precipitated problems in the first place.

"Do I take it now that you have had an encounter at the crossroads and become a believer?" he asked Bell.

"I'm hardly Saul of Tarsus. As I said, I believe that you believe, and you believed that you could expiate the guilt you felt over Elena's condition by exchanging places with her." Bell was standing near a large globe, idly running the fingers of his left hand over continent after continent as they rotated in the wrong direction.

"That sounds like a bit of reasoning that that fellow from Vienna would follow," said Van Helsing.

"Freud, you mean?"

"Yes, that's the one. I can imagine he would class me in with some of those rather colorfully named patients of his. But, getting back to you, I suppose you can supply me with one of those eminently obvious line of reasoning to back up your conclusion," he said.

"Actually, in this case it was a lot simpler. Before leaving England, I had Lee Satterfield take a look at those parchments. She gave me a rough idea of what they said. Seems that the spell you were wanting, to make it work, required an exchange, one for another," said Bell. "Knowing how you blame yourself for what happened to Elena, the rest was obvious."

"Very good, old friend. It would have worked, too," Van Helsing said, his voice a harsh whisper. "Except she fought, she wanted to remain in that hellish place!" He wanted to say more, to let his pain rage out, the frustration he felt at having failed the woman that he loved.

"Abraham, I wish to the depths of my being that I had some scientific trick, some magic wand to wave, that would take away the pain that you are feeling. That I could prove to you it was all in your mind. But I know that to you it was very real," said Bell.

Van Helsing reached into his pocket and brought out the silver swan pin. It had been real, very real. When he had awakened on the floor of Elena's room it had been clutched in his hand, hard enough to cut into the palm.

"Do you plan to try again?"

Van Helsing shook his head. "No. Elena said that my place was here, that there was great evil that I had to confront. Lord knows what she was talking about." As he spoke, Van Helsing picked up the pile of mail that had accumulated on his desk. At the bottom was a letter bearing an English stamp and postmark. He opened it and half-heartedly scanned the contents.

"Joseph, when do you plan to return to Scotland?"

"I have to be back in two weeks. I was planning on leaving this Friday."

"Good. That will be just enough time to put matters in order here. I hope that you will not object to some company, at least part way."

"Indeed not," said Bell. "May I ask why the sudden desire to travel to England?"

Van Helsing held up the letter. "This is from a former student of mine, John Seward. He operates an asylum near Whitby, outside of London. There is a case there he needs to consult me on."

"Excellent. A visit to the English countryside will do you a world of good."

OPENING DOORS

Josepha Sherman

Josepha Sherman is a fantasy novelist, freelance editor, and folklorist. In addition, she has written for the educational market on everything from Bill Gates to the workings of the human ear. Forthcoming titles include: Mythology For Storytellers, *and the* Star Trek: Vulcan's Soul *trilogy. Visit her at www.sff.net/people/Josepha.Sherman.*

I had been foraging for wild onions to add to the evening's stew, no wizard's robes about me, just a woodsman's plain linen tunic, leather trows, and shoes, when I saw all the forest birds take flight in sudden panic. A second later, I heard what they'd seen: the unmistakable thrashing about that meant a fight. Two stags?

No. A little warning prickle up and down my spine told me otherwise. Shielded behind a screen of bushes, I took a cautious glance.

Wonderful. It was a Blackfang. The monstrous thing

looked like a cross between a bear and a wolf, with the gleaming ebony fangs that gave it its name. It had a temper worse than anything natural and an unfortunate immunity to magic. I would have stolen silently away, but for obvious reasons no one, including a magician, wants a Blackfang in the neighborhood.

Hells! Now I saw that what the creature was fighting—a human, a young man with a sword that didn't seem to be hurting the Blackfang at all. I don't generally carry a weapon. A mage seldom needs one, especially not in a forest where wild things generally avoid humans or can be easily frightened off. And if I couldn't use my magic . . .

I have a strong arm from years of lugging firewood home. Picking up a good-sized rock, I hurled with all my force it at the Blackfang's one vulnerable spot, which is its head, right between its ugly red eyes. I connected with it—but unfortunately, the creature turned at that instant, and I hit only the bony back plate that guarded its neck.

I got its attention, though. The creature whirled to me, snarling, perfectly willing to change targets and attack me.

I didn't waste time in heroics: I looked for a climbable tree. But a massive paw dealt me a glancing blow that was hard enough to hurl me against a tree trunk with literally breath-taking force. As I lay sprawled on my back, trying to muster enough will to magick a tree branch loose to crash down on the creature, the young man came to my rescue, charging the Blackfang with sword in hand.

"The head!" I yelled. "Aim for its head! Between the eyes!"

With the bulk of the Blackfang between me and him, I couldn't tell if he'd heard me. But then I saw the sword flash, and heard the Blackfang roar in pain and rage. It swiped out at the youngster with claws glinting. This time I heard a human cry of pain, and the sword went flying out of the youngster's hand, straight up. That, I *could* magic, and I pulled the sword towards me, hilt first so I could grab it without losing a finger.

I lunged straight up from the ground, all my magical force behind the lunge, and yes, spitted the Blackfang in that one vulnerable spot, right between the eyes. It shrieked and went over backwards, kicking and thrashing—and at last, just when I thought the damned thing would never die, it collapsed and lay still.

I lay where I'd fallen for a while longer, fighting to catch my breath, and then struggled up to see what had happened to my erstwhile rescuer.

He lay sprawled, face down, blood pooling about him, and for a sickening moment, I was sure the fellow was also dead. Very carefully I turned him over and saw a pale young face, not quite yet a man's face, topped by tousled blond hair—no, never mind that. The Blackfang had gotten in a good slash that had cut right through the would-be hero's leather armor. Not a pretty wound underneath, and a forest floor was no place for medical work. I quickly stopped the flow of blood with a flash of will and the right Words, then put a temporary closing on the wound till I could get a better look at it, lugged him up over my shoulder, and staggered with him back to my cabin.

My home was nothing particularly elegant, a small log building with the basics: a chair, a table, a bed, a fireplace for heat and cooking, and—since I refused to go completely rural—reasonably decent sanitary facilities.

I put my patient on the bed, carefully removed the torn

leather armor, and examined the injury. Ugh, nasty, but the youngster had been lucky. There were no major rips in any internal organs.

What I did isn't easily summarized, let alone easily described in nonarcane language. I'll just say that I used a great deal of magic, medicine, and willpower putting things back to rights and making sure that my patient wouldn't end up with any infections. Then I cleaned him, the bedding, and myself, put an additional sleep enchantment over the youngster to accelerate his healing, and collapsed for a while myself, curled up as well as a tall man can in my chair. Magical backlash had hit me, of course, which is the inevitable result of using up so much energy, in addition to the delayed shock of realizing how close to death we'd both come.

I came alert in time, before my patient awoke. He, as I'd planned, woke precisely when the sleep enchantment wore off. Dazed blue eyes stared up at me. "Where . . .?"

"In my cabin," I told him. "Safe. You killed the Blackfang."

The youngster blinked, clearly trying to remember what had happened. Then, as the last of my magicking wore off and his mind was left clear, he said, more coherently, "And you . . . I think you saved me afterward."

"It seemed only polite," I said dryly. "Here. Your throat is certainly dry."

He drank obediently, then lay back again, staring up at me, clearly wondering why he felt so healthy. "I . . . I never thought to wake again."

"Ah, well. You were fortunate. The wound was not serious." *Not after I'd finished magicking it, at any rate.* "Come, you will feel better once you're back on your feet."

I helped him out of bed, and once he was steady on his feet again, gave him spare clothes of mine to wear. They were too big for the youngster, of course, since I was a head taller than he was, but he managed to look almost elegant in them, once he'd belted the trows up and the tunic in. "And you . . ." the younger began warily, "you are no simple woodsman, I think. You have too cultured a voice."

Ah. Observant of him. "I am not," I agreed after the barest second of hesitation, but gave him nothing more.

"I forget my manners," he said. "I am Gwethal, son of Tharathal."

That would be Lord *Tharathal, I mused. I thought that there was something vaguely familiar about the boy.*

This would be the younger son, of course. The elder, whose name escaped me for the moment, was a man of settled years who lived on one of the family estates out in the countryside. I was fairly sure that I'd seen this youngster before, probably at court, but he would have been just a child back then. It would be unlikely that he would recognize me.

I dipped my head to the youngster, politely ignoring his omission of a title. "I am Suratan." It was, after all, *one* of my names. "And now that we have exchanged courtesies, let me add that you, too, aren't any simple woodsman."

"No," the boy admitted.

"So, what in the name of all the Powers were you doing in the middle of the forest all alone?"

"I . . . was on a quest," he muttered.

Of course you were, youngling. It's downright . . . traditional. "Indeed? For what?"

He straightened with frantic pride. "I am out to rid the land of wizards and their dark ilk."

At that outrageous proclamation, I just barely managed not to laugh, almost choking on a feigned cough instead. "Ah. Well, then, I'm afraid that we have a small problem."

"I . . . don't . . ."

"How do you think that you were healed so swiftly? Go ahead, look for the wound."

He glanced down at the once more smooth skin of his abdomen and straightened again, reddening and floundering, "Oh, I, uh, I didn't mean . . ."

I took pity on him after a second of that and held up a hand. "I get the point. You're after the *evil* ones only."

Gwethal's face went suddenly deadly calm, all at once that of a determined warrior, not a boy at all. "I will be honest with you. I am after only one."

"Will you name him? No, wait," I cut in, seeing his expression change. "I understand that you don't know me, or whether or not you can trust me."

"I think that I do know you . . . Your Grace."

"Ah. I see." So much for the idea that the boy would have been too young to recall very much the last time that I'd seen him. Which sighting, now that I actually considered it, probably would have been at the royal court, which I did visit for various important events. And for which I usually did dress up. Oh yes, there would have been plenty of splendor and flash there, something for even a young mind to store away. And retrieve now. "And . . .?"

"And I do think I can trust you, too . . . Suratan," he finished conspiratorially. "No one has ever spoken ill of the magician-duke, cousin to His Excellency himself."

Ah yes, that's me, cousin to the king, living quite peacefully in my chosen hometown of Westfand as the nominal ruler of this small land that is vassal to the Crown. The people here hardly mind that their duke is a magician—far from it. That's probably because I genuinely like them and refuse to meddle in their daily lives or turn tyrant over them. I use my magic on their behalf only when it is most needed.

When it is most needed, I thought bitterly.

The boy, heedless, continued, "Are you . . . you're here in the forest in secret to plan some great and wondrous magic against . . . that one, aren't you?"

Coldness stole through me. "No," I said, very carefully. "I am here in secret to survive."

Gwethal looked at me in wide-eyed shock, as though a mythic hero had suddenly turned into a puppy and turned tail. "But—you are—"

"Sit down, boy."

He obediently sank down onto the edge of the bed, still staring at me. I sat opposite him in my cabin's one chair, and began, "I did not flee like a coward just to save my own skin and soul. If I'd stayed and fought, I could not have won. I might have survived—but everyone else in Westfand would have died in my stead. The Other made that point very clear.

"At least this way, without me and my magic to endanger them, the people have a chance to survive."

"But with no freedom," Gwethal retorted. "No hope."

I let out an angry sigh. "It's so simple to be a hero when you're nowhere near the danger. Do you have any idea what that Other is? Do you?"

"A demon," he ventured.

"Nothing that simple! Gwethal, the Other came here through a Portal."

"A . . ."

I waved an impatient hand. "Call it an arcane doorway. Where do you think the Blackfangs originated? They're not native to our land or our entire Realm. There's nothing native to our Realm that's impervious to magic!"

"Then how . . . ?"

"They slipped through when the Portal opened. Or perhaps the Other sent them through first as a test to see if this was the right land, the land it wanted to control."

"Why?"

"That, youngster, is an excellent question. I only wish I had an excellent answer for you. Perhaps the Other is here for, well, practice. To learn how to dominate this small area before moving on to the entire Realm. Or else the Other is simply here because it . . . wanted to be here." You can madden yourself trying to comprehend the truly alien mind.

"But surely you can . . ."

"I can do nothing. I have no idea which Portal, what kind of Portal, or what land might lie on the other side of that Portal. And without knowing the answer to even one of those problems, *no* magician has any way of defeating the Other!"

This was all making me remember a day I didn't really want to recall. The day when there had been no warning that everything was about to change . . .

One moment, it was a normal spring day in Westfand, with everyone going about his or her noisy, market day business, buying or selling cheese or eggs or colorfully woven ribbons bright as the sunlight—and the next, it had become a horror.

A Portal! I thought as it ripped open with a roar of air being roughly thrust aside.

"Get out here, all of you!" I shouted.

People obediently rushed away in all directions. When you live with magical folk, you take their warnings seriously.

Which was fortunate. What stepped through the Portal into our world was mostly man-shaped. But the eyes were a giveaway; being the soulless things they are, Others almost never get the eyes right. Regardless of what poets might claim, there wasn't anything as melodramatic as utter blackness in those too-large openings. Blackness is in itself a color. What was in the Other's eyes was literally . . . nothing.

So be it. I'd fought Others before, yes, and defeated them. I'd defeat this one as well.

"You are not welcome here!" I shouted to it.

The Other didn't bother answering. It simply sent me flying with a casual flash of will. I scrambled back to my feet, this time not wasting time with words, either. But I very quickly realized what I faced. Nothing I threw at it worked, not the fiercest battle spell, nothing against this Thing that was immune to magic. With a second flash of will, it threw me back against a wall with such force it nearly broke bones. As I fell, helplessly fighting for air, I realized that even though I couldn't identify more than the vaguest *feel* of what it was doing, the Other was severing connections between this land and the larger realm around it. No one from the outside world would come to our rescue. No one would even remember our little land existed.

The Other turned to me, its almost-human face blank of emotion, its eyes those empty wastes. It told me without words, *Go. Leave here, and the other people live. Stay, and you live but they all die.*

Not much of a choice. I left. And found myself a place as deep in the forest and far away from the Other as the confines of its cursed boundaries would allow.

I'd hidden as far away from the Other as possible. Not far enough, it would seem now.

"But you can't just give up!" Gwethal insisted.

"Look, youngster, at the risk of sounding like the Wise Old Man, and I'm neither old nor, as far as I know, particularly wise, walking into sure death is never a good thing. If I had a plan, believe me, I would use it."

"Then I—"

"Will do nothing. Just go home, Gwethal."

"No."

"Yes."

"You don't understand! I can't let everyone go on living in this prison!"

"And you're the younger son of your noble father, and you want to prove you're as worthy as your older brother. And don't glower at me like that. We both know it's true. And at the same time we both know that you really do have the welfare of the land at heart. Agreed. Now, go home."

"No!"

"What else is there to do? You can't take on the Other by yourself—I'm not being cynical or pessimistic when I say that such a move would definitely be suicide. And I can't help you be heroic, nor will I help you kill yourself trying. What good is a magician against a being that is impervious to magic?"

"Then why *use* magic?"

"Fight it man to man, so to speak? Gwethal, understand that the damned thing is faster than any human. It made red paste of the one idiot who tried attacking it with a sword."

He flinched ever so slightly at that thought, but continued gamely, "Arrows?"

"Were tried, too, as were spears, and they made absolutely no impression on it. Neither, I'll add, did iron or silver." I shook my head. "The Other is simply too alien for anything traditional to work against it."

That only silenced him for a short while. "Then, well," Gwethal began anew, "if we can't get at the Other directly, what about indirectly?"

"Meaning?"

"What about the—that, uh, that Portal?"

"Ah, Gwethal. I told you, lad, I have no idea what Power opened it, I have no idea what Realm lies on the other side of it—"

"Then a Portal always has to connect two Realms?" he cut in.

I sighed. "Or two lands. Or two fields, for that matter. Any two places. A Portal is like a door . . ."

My voice trailed off, and I stared at Gwethal in the first faint dawning of hope. "A door, yes. But a door between two places . . .? On second thought," I continued thoughtfully, "there's no actual rule about such a connection being needed. No rule at all."

In my ducal days, I used to pace while working out the details of a plan or new spell. I found myself on my feet

and pacing now. Yes . . . and yes . . . maybe . . . yes, it
might . . . we might . . .

We would. Curse it, I'd been so terrified of the Other
and of the danger to the people that I'd never let simple
logic enter the picture.

"Gwethal, thank you!" I cried. "You may have just
given me the answer we need. No, don't interrupt. Hear
me out."

In words as clear as I could make them, since there
must be no mistakes for everyone's sake, I told the
youngster what I meant to do, and what he needed to do,
and watched fear and courage clash in his eyes.

That's all right, boy. It scares me, too.

"I'll do it," Gwethal said firmly.

"Tomorrow," I added. "Tonight—"

"We plot?"

"We sleep."

I doubt he did. I know I didn't. But at least we were
somewhat rested as we set out on the return to Westfand.
I wasn't at all comfortable by the time we got there, not
from fear or the journey itself, but from having to seal
away all my magic deep within me. Think of having to
deprive yourself of sight and sensation, and that may explain the discomfort. But I didn't dare risk having the
Other identify my aura before I was ready to attack.

Gwethal, meanwhile, was fairly quivering with tension, but that in itself wasn't enough to attract unwanted
attention: Any rural boy visiting a city might be in a similar state.

I'd been afraid of what I'd find. Bodies in the streets,
perhaps, or parts of bodies, or worse, tormented
revenants of folks I'd known. But Westfand looked . . .

docile. Worn and gray, all the joy leached out of it. But, to my relief, it—and its people with it—was still alive.

And you'll stay that way, I vowed.

No one would know Gwethal from any other young-ster, but I was another matter. Since I couldn't use magic, I was disguised instead in the simplest nonmagical fash-ion: Walnut juice darkened my skin to a weather-beaten brown and my hair to a near-black, and a hooded cloak such as country farmers wore hid most of my face.

Judging from the lack of any reaction, the disguise was working. No one recognized me. People, after all, gener-ally see only what they expect to see.

They also didn't see the thin but very strong chain that I wore wrapped about my waist. The chain that I was trusting to save my life.

And the Other . . .?

We found it easily enough. The Other was stalking the streets, stopping here, looking there, doing nothing but aimlessly wandering. Intimidating the people, perhaps, or studying them—

Curse it, yes. That was the whole point of this, exactly. Isolate a chosen group, study it in detail and at leisure, analyze everything about it, and then, presumably, wiser in the ways of this Realm and of humanity, prepare for a greater conquest.

Oh, I think not!

The Other had still not perfected its human guise: Those eyes that held nothingness had not altered.

I don't care much what guise you wear. You're not staying here.

I moved as though at random next to two men I rec-ognized: Werin, a good, solid example of a blacksmith, and his equally solid son, Guran. "Not a sound," I murmured. "Duke's command."

Bless them, they understood instantly. I slid the end of the chain into Werin's hands and soundlessly uncoiled it to give myself freedom to move, making sure that the other end was still knotted firmly about my waist.

Good. So far, at any rate.

I signaled to Gwethal. He gave me one curt nod, took a deep breath, then rushed the Other, yelling heroically and waving his sword. The Other turned to him, and I could have sworn it was . . . bored. Used to killing heroes by now. But Gwethal had the quickness of youth and the determination not to get himself killed, and he ducked and leaped in a perilous dance, never holding still long enough to let the Other strike him down.

I spared only a few seconds on this, then set to work, carefully letting my magic unfurl—carefully, that is, because the sheer euphoria of releasing it would have been too much for any magician to bear without, at the very least, a shout of triumph. I didn't dare anything so dramatic since I would have only the shortest span of time before the Other sensed me and turned on me.

But I needed only the shortest span of time to do what I needed to do. It was the hastiest, sloppiest work I've ever done, worthy of a truly clumsy apprentice, but after all, I didn't need anything fancy, I just needed to hold it, not quite open, just hold it . . . gritting my teeth against the terrible pull of unbalanced magic wanting to erupt . . . hold it, ready to let go . . . not yet . . . not quite yet . . .

Just when, Other or no Other, I was going to have to let go of the spell, the Other realized what was happening. Swatting Gwethal aside, it rushed toward me, faster

than anything human and radiating a cold determination
to see me dead—

And I let the Portal fly open with a great rush of air.
Nothing on the other side of it but emptiness, vacuum,
and as the Other rushed me, the vacuum pulled us both
through the Portal into cold colorless airlessness. I had
time to think, we're both dead—

Then a jolt about my waist nearly jerked the breath out
of me and told me that the chain was holding. It felt as
though I was being slowly squeezed to death, and pain ra-
diated up my spine and through my ribs. But I welcomed
the pain. It told me that hand over slow hand, I was being
pulled back to safety. The Other clawed at me in passing,
but it was already being swept off into the vacuum, and
I . . . I was suffocating . . .

Suddenly there was warmth and light and blessed air,
and hands all around me, steadying me on my feet as I
just stood and gasped until the burning in my lungs was
gone. Sore ribs, sore back, sore muscles—nothing major.
The Portal, unstable as I'd deliberately created it, with
nothing on one side to balance it, slammed shut into nothingness again, nearly knocking us all over with the force
of air rushing back in.

For a time after that, there was nothing but all of us
gasping and laughing with the crazed relief of people
who found themselves still alive.

"Your Grace! Your Grace!" That was Gwethal, di-
sheveled, wild-eyed, laughing and, thankfully, unharmed.
"You did it!"

"We did it," I corrected. "Getting me to really think
about Portal spells—that was your doing, lad."

Pulling away from the others—who were rapidly
going from heroic souls to ordinary people only realizing

now that they were clutching their duke like a doll—I let my senses rove, then relaxed with a sigh relief.

"The boundary vanished with the Other," I said to them all. "We're part of the world again."

Not all of them understood what that meant—other than that they were free. Which was a good enough reason in itself for us all to cheer. All the doors that should be shut were shut.

And I fully intend to keep them that way.

CIRCLE OF COMPASSION

David D. Levine

*David D. Levine is a John W. Campbell Award final-
ist (2003), Writers of the Future Contest winner
(2002), James White Award winner (2001), and Clar-
ion West graduate (2000). He has sold over a dozen
stories so far, to magazines such as* Asimov's, F&SF,
and Realms of Fantasy *and anthologies including* Apprentice Fantastic, Haunted Holidays, *and two Year's
Best volumes (one Fantasy, the other SF). He lives
with his wife, Kate Yule, in Portland, Oregon, and his
web page can be found at www.BentoPress.com.*

Glistening in the firelight, a drop of sweat gathered at the
tip of Su Yuen's nose. It was a distraction, a thing of
the world, and she strove to ignore it, to empty her mind of
all thought as she knelt in prayer. *Namu kuan shih yin pu sa*,
she prayed over and over: I bow to you, being of wisdom,
who hears the cries of the world. The drop swelled until it
fell from her nose, landing with a small explosion of dust

on the pounded-earth floor of the mud hut in which she knelt. It was followed by another, and another. But though the little hut was sweltering hot, when she finished her prayers she found herself hesitant to leave—unwilling to return to her master, General Chang, and the noise and smoke and stink of death that surrounded him.

Su slipped the bracelet from her wrist. The air of Xian would calm her.

The bracelet was of bronze and depicted the Dragon of the West with its tail in its mouth. Though not elegant, it had been carefully crafted for her by Shan the metalworker and blessed by the Mother of her order with a special charm.

Su spoke a secret word of power, and the bracelet tingled in her fingers and grew cool, a shimmer like a desert mirage filling the space inside it. She brought her nose close to the opening and smiled at the cold air that blew from it. It was breezy this night in her favorite meadow, half a day's walk from her home temple of Miao Feng Shan in the country of Xian.

The breeze smelled of high mountains and cold streams. It smelled of snow. It smelled of home.

She opened the neck of her robe and allowed the air from the bracelet to flow down inside, evaporating the sweat that pooled in the hollow of her throat and the space between her breasts. But after only a short time of this, she sighed. It would not do to luxuriate too long when she had so many difficult tasks awaiting her. She spoke a second word. The bracelet tingled again and then returned to inert metal.

It was still cool to the touch, though, as she slipped it back onto her wrist. A small reminder of the snows of Xian, so many thousand leagues from the wretched little town of Guang-xi.

Su Yuen stepped from the shabby little hut into the torchlit street. Barely deserving of the name "street," it was only two paces wide and constructed of dirt, like everything else in Guang-xi. Even the walls that surrounded the town were simple bulwarks of rammed earth, not even faced with brick. They would offer little resistance to the siege engines of Yao Ming.

No townspeople were about at this hour; to defy the curfew imposed by General Chang was to embrace death. But Chang's troops recognized Su and bowed to her as she passed.

Chang stood with his lieutenants in the great hall—such as it was—of the town's magistrate, who cowered with his family to one side. Chang had sketched a map of the town and its surroundings in the dirt floor and indicated its various features with the pointed butt of a halberd.

Chang himself was an imposing figure, with dark intense eyes and a long gray beard that suggested his many years of successful command. He wore a long purple robe, trimmed and tasseled in red; the armored surcoat with its many square bronze plates hung on a rack nearby. "Do not depend too much on the mountains to the north," he scolded one of his lieutenants. "Yao will send at least three companies around to surprise us from behind. It may take them some days to get here, but we should be prepared. Post watchmen here, here, and here."

"But they have been riding hard for days, my lord," said a lieutenant. "For exhausted men to cross those mountains would be suicide."

"Yes," Chang acknowledged with a grim nod. "That is why he will send three companies—to be sure at least one survives."

The lieutenant gave a silent bow, conceding the truth

of Chang's observation. Yao's troops were untrained conscripts, but they vastly outnumbered Chang's remaining forces and Yao was willing to spend many lives for a successful attack.

"Priestess Su Yuen," Chang said, fixing her with a dark commanding gaze, "Have you prepared yourself as you require?"

"Yes, my lord," she replied with a trembling bow.

Chang pointed to a series of parallel lines drawn on the plain below the city's south gate. "You are to scout General Yao's camp. Determine the strength of his forces and, if possible, his plans."

Head still bowed, she stammered out "But, my lord, I know nothing of military matters."

Chang sighed heavily and looked heavenward. "Honored ancestors, I thank you for saving me and these remaining men at the battle of Yu-min. But why could you not have seen fit to leave me more than this one miserable priestess?" His piercing gaze returned to Su. "Can your spirit hear, as well as see?"

"Yes, my lord."

"The general's tent will be in the middle of the camp. Listen there for any numbers. How many companies, battalions, divisions, horses. Times and places. Do you understand?"

"Yes, my lord."

"Begin, then. Waste no time."

"Yes, my lord." She bowed deeply, then knelt on the dirt floor and pulled her box of incense from her sleeve.

Su made her preparations, shivering beneath her robe despite the oppressive heat. As a priestess of Kuan Shih Yin, the living expression of loving compassion, she had devoted her life to understanding and peace. Using the powers of her office for warlike purposes was abhorrent to her. But hers had been the poor fortune to be on an outreach mission to the court of Li when General Yao of the upstart state of Tung had attacked, two months ago. She had been placed under the protection and command of General Chang, who had kept her safe and never before asked for anything in return. But the last of Chang's military magicians and priests—ancestor worshippers who practiced human sacrifice, but still human beings worthy of Kuan Shih Yin's love—had been killed by Yao's forces at the recent, disastrous battle of Yu-min. Chang had no one else, and she must carry out his orders not only because he was her properly appointed commander, but because he and his men had saved her life in the initial attack and many times since.

Even so, the thought of it made her sick to her stomach.

He has not asked me to fight or kill, she reassured herself. It didn't help much.

She cleared her mind and prayed, struggling to block out the sounds and smells of an occupied town preparing for attack. After a long while, with a feeling like tearing silk, her spirit detached itself from her body.

It was always disorienting to look back on herself, yet now she found it strangely reassuring—a female Xian face, with its strong cheekbones, shaven head, and pigtail, alone among these shaggy Li men. It was almost as though one of her temple sisters were here.

Then she chided herself for delay and sent her spirit out through the tile roof of the hall.

Su's spirit soared above the town, with its courtyards glimmering with the torches of Chang's remaining troops. Quickly she flew over the walls, and the moat beyond them, to the plain below the town, where Yao had massed his army. Thousands of fires burned there, in rigid rows and columns. Su knew nothing of armies, but she could count, and even she could see that Yao's army vastly outnumbered Chang's forces.

But there, in the center of the camp, was one tent larger than the others, which swarmed with soldiers coming and going like an ants' nest. Su swooped down upon it and through its fabric roof.

She recognized Yao Ming at once—she had seen his scarred, dark-bearded face in many scrolls and woodcuts. He wore an armored surcoat, fashioned of many palm-sized squares of rhinoceros leather, over a blue robe with black trim. At the moment he and his lieutenants were bowed in concentration over a smoking brazier.

The smoke from the brazier stung her eyes as she moved closer, trying to hear their conversation. But they were not conversing—they were praying. Foul prayers to the black demons worshipped by the Tung. She would learn nothing useful from this, so she moved behind Yao, to a low table where maps were spread out.

As she peered closer, trying to make sense of the maps' rough markings, the prayers reached a feverish enthusiasm, the Tung men shrieking and swaying as they waved their hands over their heads. Finally they all shouted four words together, and Yao threw a handful of mulberry leaves into the brazier.

Su coughed in the choking smoke.

But . . . this was wrong. Smoke should not affect her spirit body.

This was no ordinary fire.

Panicking, she gathered her spirit self to flee. But before

she reached the tent roof, a huge, taloned hand darted out of the smoke and grabbed her by the foot. "Ai!" she cried.

Helplessly she struggled as the rest of the black demon coalesced into being. It had the form of a huge, muscular man, barely able to stand erect at the center of the tent, but its face was distorted by enormous fangs and protruding eyes and its skin was charcoal-black. The hand that held her foot was hard as stone and ridged with muscle. "Release me, demon, in the name of Kuan Shih Yin!" But her words had no effect.

"What have you caught, oh my demon?" asked Yao. He had heard nothing.

"A spying spirit," the demon replied, in a voice like stones grinding together.

"Bring him here!"

"As my master wishes." The demon reached up with its other hand and grabbed Su by the neck, then pulled her down to the floor of the tent.

Her boots thumped on the dirt, and then the demon forced her to her knees.

She gasped at the pain, then gasped again at the realization of what it meant. The demon had pulled her material body into the tent!

Yao stood, as did his lieutenants. "I see that Chang is reduced to having Xian priestesses do his spying for him," he said. "An excellent sign. Release her, oh my demon."

The demon pulled her to her feet, then shoved her into the center of the circle. Yao paced around her, examining her as though she were a horse in the market. His nostrils flared. "You stink of magic," he declared.

Namu kuan shih yin pu sa, she thought over and over, willing her knees to stop their trembling. Trying to force herself to meet her end with dignity.

Yao leaned closer, stinking of sweat and blood. This was the man who had decapitated his own uncle to gain the generalship, who had slaughtered entire cities for the insult of opposing his will. So fearful was his reputation that even his most unwilling conscripts obeyed his orders instantly. He sniffed at her hair, her neck, her shoulder, then down her arm. Then he smiled, and pushed back her sleeve, revealing the bronze dragon bracelet.

"What is this pretty bauble?"

Su said nothing, clenching her teeth to prevent them from chattering.

He grabbed her queue and pulled back her head, leaning in close. "Answer me!" he roared, his foul breath hot on her face.

"It is just a souvenir!" she cried, the truth forced out of her by the press of fear. "A small magic to remind me of my home, nothing more!"

"Indeed?" He seized her forearm and pulled the bracelet off her wrist. It came easily. "I think perhaps you do not tell the whole truth." He examined the bracelet, turning it over so the firelight glinted across the dragon's scales, then squeezed it over his rough hand and onto his own wrist. "I shall hold this object for further examination." He turned away from her. "Oh my demon, you may have this spy to do with as you please."

Su turned and looked up, and up, at the demon's leering face, then shut her eyes hard.

Then a great commotion erupted from outside the tent, shouting and banging and a fierce inhuman bellow.

A soldier burst in, eyes wide. "They send fire demons against us!"

Yao's jaw clenched in anger, and he glared accusingly at Su, then turned back to the demon. "Defend the camp!"

he shouted. The demon roared and plunged out through the tent flap, but the doorway was too small and the demon brought half the tent down behind itself.

Pandemonium ensued, inside and out, as the tent collapsed on Su, Yao, and his lieutenants. Su found herself struggling under the heavy fabric, blinded by smoke, while all around her men shouted and cursed. A crackling sounded, much too close. The tent had caught fire! Su dropped to the dirt and began to squirm blindly forward.

An eternity later, Su's hand reached out and found . . . nothing. The edge of the tent! She dug her fingers into the dirt and pulled herself free, gasping in the smoky air. Fire flickered all around, and men ran shouting in every direction. Over all sounded the roars of the demon and the bellowing of the unseen attackers. Su gathered her feet under her and ran.

She ran only a few steps before colliding with a hard surface . . . a broad torso covered with small square plates of rhinoceros hide.

Yao Ming.

"I won't let you go that easily, my little spy," he panted, and seized the front of her robe.

Su tried and failed to pull Yao's hand away, but her fingers recognized the dragon bracelet.

She spoke a secret word of power.

Yao screamed, and his hand released its grip . . . and dropped into the dirt with a sickening thud.

Su ducked away from Yao as he clutched his severed wrist, cursing, blood running down his sleeve. But as she turned to run away, she spotted a glint of bronze in the blood-stained dirt. She spoke the second word of power as she scooped up the bracelet and ran into the night.

The panicked camp was not concerned with stopping

one small priestess; in addition to the general's tent, other fires burned here and there, and the fire demons bellowed and clattered all around. Su kept low and scurried. Her previous flight over the camp, in spirit form, helped her to keep her feet on the right path.

Soon she escaped into the darkness between the camp and the town. After that she met no one until she came to the moat, gasping and holding her sides. "Su Yuen!" cried the lieutenant at the drawbridge. "Thank the ancestors you are alive!"

Immediately she was conducted to Chang, where she reported what had occurred. When she described how the demon had captured her, Chang nodded grimly. "So I surmised, from what you said just before you vanished."

"But how did you summon fire demons?" she asked. "You have no other priests or magicians."

"Fire demons?" Chang snorted. "Yao's foul habits are too well known to his conscript troops, they see demons behind every bush. No, we did nothing more than to tie burning lanterns to the tails of several bulls. But they do make an impressive noise, and do a most satisfactory amount of damage. Now go and rest. I will require your services again in the morning."

"Yes, my lord." But she did not leave. "My lord . . . thank you for rescuing me."

Chang gave her a curt nod in reply. "I would not abandon my only remaining priestess." Then his face softened. "I am glad you were not harmed."

She thanked him again, and bowed, then retired to her borrowed pallet. But though she was bone-weary and the hour was late, she barely slept. Whenever she closed her eyes, she saw the demon's leering eyes and fearsome teeth.

The next day, after a wholly inadequate breakfast of

thin rice gruel, Su was again commanded to survey the enemy's camp. It took her half the morning to calm herself sufficiently to release her spirit from her body, and she hesitated for a long time beneath the hall's tile roof before pushing through it. ·

When she arrived at the camp, she found Yao at the top of a small hill, with his demon beside him and all his thousands of men gathered around him. Though his missing right hand was bound up by a blood-soaked bandage, his face burned with energy and determination. Su ducked behind a rocky outcropping before the demon could spot her.

Yao stood beside a large pile of clay pots. As she peered out from behind the rock, he took a mattock from one of his lieutenants and methodically smashed them all. Then, breathing hard and holding the mattock high, he stood on the pile of shards and began to speak.

Puzzled by this display, Su shifted closer, trying to hear what Yao had to say. But as she approached, Yao's nostrils twitched and he paused, sniffing the air. Then the demon cried out and pointed straight at her. Rigid with anger, Yao ran to his war-chest and drew out a black spear that shimmered with power.

Su did not wait to find out how well the demon could throw. She flew back to the magistrate's hall with desperate haste.

"Ah!" she gasped, drawing in a breath as her spirit rejoined her physical body. Chang's lieutenants immediately bombarded her with questions, but she had to close her eyes and concentrate on her breathing for a long moment before she could even speak coherently.

Once she had made her report, Chang took a deep breath and turned away, hands gripping each other behind his back. His lieutenants were silent. "What does this mean, my lord?" she asked him.

"Yao has created a 'death ground,'" Chang replied without turning around. "Without cooking pots, his men now have only the food they have already prepared— perhaps three days' worth." He turned back then, and his face was as grim as she had ever seen it. "They know they must conquer or starve, and so they will fight without pause and without mercy."

Chang thanked Su for her report, then began discussing with his lieutenants the defense of the town. But as Su bowed and prepared to leave, he gestured for her to stay.

Chang clearly expected an attack in overwhelming force within the day. Though his words about troop emplacements, fallback positions, and supply lines were meaningless to Su, she could see the desperation of the situation in the empty faces of his lieutenants. One by one they bowed and departed, to make what preparations they could.

After the last lieutenant had left, Chang gestured Su close to him. He looked old, so old. "Su," he said, "you are a priestess of Xian. You understand compassion, and peace. I am a man of war." He took a deep breath. "Am I a bad man, Su Yuen?"

She considered the question carefully before replying. "It is true that many have died, on both sides of this conflict, because of your orders. But you have also saved many others who might have died. I believe you have been as good a man as you can be."

Chang sighed, and looked at his folded hands. "I have an opportunity to save many lives this day. But I fear that I will not have the courage to do so."

Su waited for the words to come.

"Yao wants me. Only me. He knows that, while I live,

the people of Li will never surrender, no matter how badly defeated. But if he can parade my head on a spear to all the cities of Li, they will accept his victory and allow themselves to be quietly absorbed into the state of Tung." Chang took Su's hands. "I mean to surrender myself to Yao. If I do this thing, Yao may spare the lives of some of my men today, and thousands more will live instead of dying in a hopeless struggle against the Tung." His eyes pleaded. "Help me to be strong. Help me to carry through with this plan."

Su's heart resonated with Chang's pain, as one gong will vibrate when another nearby is struck. But she damped it down. "No," she said firmly. "I will not help you."

Chang dropped his eyes from hers. "Then all is lost."

"No!" she said again. Then, more gently: "As long as you live, not all is lost."

Chang looked up again.

"I have seen the evil of Yao, and the black demons that Tang worships. I know that any lives you save today by surrendering yourself will be lives lost in misery and despair tomorrow. Even if you die here, the people of Li will know that you died fighting, and they will do the same in your honor."

Chang shook his head with a rueful smile. "Priestess, you understand too well how to motivate an old soldier."

"I have learned from one of the best."

Chang bowed Su from his presence.

Outside the hall Chang's chief armorer, an aged craftsman with some knowledge of practical magic, awaited her with many pointed questions about the demon's exact appearance and behavior. Finally he thanked her, though his expression was grim. "From what you have said, I believe it is a taloned demon of the Fifteenth Hell. These are vulnerable to certain charms, but they must be written on silk, and we lost our scribe at Yu-min."

Su's heart leapt with hope. "I can write!"

"Thank the ancestors!"

With the armorer's help, Su wrote out the charms on dozens of strips of silk, which they tied to the shafts of arrows. She then blessed each one with a prayer to Kuan Shih Yin. "I will accept the assistance of any god who is willing to give it," the armorer said with a shrug.

After that Su set to work making bandages, blessing amulets, and praying with any soldiers and citizens who desired her assistance. As she was blessing a jade disk for a trembling young soldier, she heard horns and a distant roar like wind and surf.

The sound of an army at the charge.

Su's station was at Chang's headquarters, and she hurried to him.

"I need you to be my kite," Chang said when she arrived. "Fly high over the town and give me the strategic view."

"Yes, my lord." As she bowed, their eyes met briefly. He did not say *that will keep your spirit safe from Yao's spear*, and she did not thank him for it. But they both understood.

Exhausted and shaken as she was, it took Su a long time to send her spirit out. By the time she rose above the magistrate's hall, Yao's forces had already begun crossing the moat, the roaring demon in the lead. But as soon as it came within range, Chang's best bowmen let loose with Su's charmed arrows. At their touch the demon screamed and burst into flame, and then it was no more.

But the demon was only one part of the attack; even as it burned, massive wooden fork-carts, catapults, and scaling ladders rolled across temporary bamboo bridges. Chang's men pelted them with flaming arrows from the tops of the walls, but Yao had prepared for this: the fork-carts were protected by wooden roofs covered with fresh oxhide, which trapped the arrows and refused to catch fire.

Su reported this development to Chang, and a moment later her spirit eyes saw men with heavy crossbows charging to the defense. But they were too late. Under the protection of the hide-covered roofs, the first of the fork-carts had reached the walls. Thick braids of twisted rope sent wooden levers—each twice as long as a man and tipped with a three-tined iron fork—snapping down onto the town's earthen walls like the striking claw of a great tiger. Two or three such blows were sufficient to bring down a large chunk of wall. Though Chang's bowmen fired rapidly into the gap, killing many of the invaders, more and more of Yao's conscript soldiers were pouring over the moat. They soon began swarming over their comrades' bodies, through the gaps in the wall, and into the town.

"Fall back!" Chang ordered his lieutenants when Su told him the walls had been breached. Then he turned back to Su. "We too must retreat." She found herself leaning heavily on his arm as they hurried out of the magistrate's hall.

Chang and Su moved in the midst of a flood of screaming, panicked townspeople, heading for the garrison where the town's west wall met the mountains. The sturdy little building was not a castle, barely even a fort, but it was the most defensible structure in the town and it was large enough to hold all of Chang's troops.

But when they arrived, they found fewer than two hundred soldiers. "We have been taking very heavy casualties," reported a lieutenant whose head was bandaged up with a blood-soaked rag. "The Tung men fight like trapped rats."

"Let in five hundred civilians," said Chang, "then bar the door."

While Chang and the three lieutenants who had made it to the garrison prepared to make a last stand, Su sagged exhausted and worthless in a corner. She was too drained to send her spirit out again, and she would be no use whatsoever in a fight. All she could do was prepare her spirit for the afterlife.

But when she had finished her prayers, the final attack had still not come. "What is he waiting for?" she asked Chang.

"I do not know," he said. They pressed through crowds of terrified civilians and wounded soldiers to the outer room, where splintered furniture blocked the garrison's only door, and peered out an arrow slit.

Outside, mobs of Yao's troops crowded the street, but they had left an open space in front of the garrison. Yao himself stood in that space, his rhinoceros-hide surcoat stained with soot and blood. "Does Chang yet live?" he called out.

"I live," Chang called back, though he stood to the side of the arrow slit in case one of Yao's sharpshooters should make an attempt to change that. Su moved to another slit nearby, unable to take her eyes off of Yao.

"I would like to make you an offer," Yao replied. "You have a Xian priestess with you. Do not deny it, I can smell her. Give the bitch to me, and I will allow you and your men to live."

Chang looked at Su, his expression unreadable, but he called back "We would prefer to die rather than live under Tung rule."

Yao gave a swift curt nod that indicated he had expected no other response. "I will give you until dawn to reconsider your decision." He raised his voice. "My offer applies to anyone in the building. Send out the Xian priestess, and all your lives will be spared."

Su's knees gave way. She slid down the wall, collapsing like a horse that has been ridden too far. But Chang stood tall, and spoke in a general's voice. "You will not be surrendered," he said to Su, and stared around at the soldiers and civilians who crowded the room. "This I promise."

The sun crept downward, and slipped below the horizon, but the garrison with its mass of people grew no cooler; Su blinked stinging sweat from her eyes as she prayed with a freshly widowed civilian and her three small children. Then, when the prayer was done, she slipped her bracelet from her wrist. "This is a special charm," she whispered to the middle child. "It is supposed to be a secret. But now . . . I suppose there is little reason to hide it any longer." She spoke a word of power, and cool mountain air flowed from the bracelet.

The children gasped and cooed in pleasure, pressing their faces into the breeze, and the young widow smiled at their happiness. But then the youngest reached out for the shiny bauble, and thrust her tiny hand through the shimmering loop all the way up to the elbow. Su gasped at the memory of Yao's severed hand, but the panic lasted only a moment; she had dabbled her own fingers through the bracelet into the cool air beyond many times. It was only at the moment the charm was invoked that it was so dangerous. Still, magic was always unpredictable, and she gently grasped the child's arm and drew it back out of the bracelet.

The infant's face bunched up as though to cry, but then relaxed into an expression of curiosity and wonder as she stared at her own hand, tightly clenched in a fist. Then the tiny fingers opened.

Su too looked on in wonder.

Sparkling in the child's palm was a tiny handful of . . . snow.

"General Chang!" Su called as she hurried to his quarters. "General Chang! I must speak with the armorer immediately!"

Luck was with her: the armorer was among the survivors. But after he had inspected the bracelet, he shook his head and handed it back to her. "I am sorry, priestess," he said. "If it were iron, I might be able to enlarge it as you request. But bronze is not so malleable."

Su's spirits, so recently raised, fell hard.

"Still . . ." said the armorer, tugging on his beard, "though the bracelet cannot be hammered out, perhaps the spell can be. What do you know of its construction?"

"It partakes of the Circle of Heaven, of course, and the power of the Dragon of the West, but my own memories are the focus of the charm. It will not work unless I am touching the bracelet."

"Hmm. The Dragon can be invoked with the appropriate herbs, perhaps, but the Circle . . ."

Su, Chang, and the armorer talked for a long time, while the torches burned down and were replaced. Soldiers came and went, calling out watches at intervals. Finally, at the beginning of the last watch before dawn, they agreed that no better plan could be devised.

"It will be dangerous," advised the armorer. "The Dragon of the West is not easily tamed."

"I understand," said Su.

Chang's expression was serious. "Those who form the circle must remain behind. I cannot ask you to do this."

Su matched Chang's gaze with her own. "I have no choice," she said. "The charm is tied to me. All I ask is that you give me a sharp knife, so that I may choose the moment of my death."

Chang held Su's gaze for a moment, then closed his eyes and bowed his head. Without a word, he drew the sheathed knife from his own belt and handed it to her. She bowed to him as she accepted it.

"Come," said the armorer. "We have little time."

They lit incense, and burned herbs, and spilled wine upon the ground. And then Su found herself kneeling before a large stone, trembling as though from cold though the night was still sweltering. *Namu kuan shih yin pu sa*, she prayed, as she held out her bracelet in her two hands and placed it on the stone.

The armorer set his chisel on the bracelet, just where the Dragon of the West's tail entered its mouth. "When you are ready," he said quietly, and raised his mallet, awaiting her signal.

Su looked into his eyes, and took a deep breath. Then she gave a fierce nod, and as the armorer brought his mallet down, she spoke a word of power.

The bracelet shimmered and tingled between her fingers for a moment before the metal parted.

"Ah!" Su cried out, as cold fire burned along her arms and across her chest. It was as though she hugged a huge, invisible tree of ice—her arms were forced into a circle by the pressure of the spell, and a cold blast of air blew upward into her face. But though the broken bracelet seared her fingers with its chill, she held on.

Then she felt warm fingers on her hands. It was Hsien, Chang's youngest surviving lieutenant. All the lieutenants had volunteered for this duty, but Chang had insisted that the skills of the other two could not be lost. Hsien held tightly to Su's trembling hands, his face impassive.

"I . . . I will release my left hand," Su said through chattering teeth, and Hsien shifted his grip so that his right hand held Su's left and his left grasped the bracelet.

"I am ready," said Hsien.

Su squeezed her eyes tightly shut and let go with her left hand.

Then she screamed, as a burning-cold wall of wind forced her arms apart. Hsien cried out at the same time, but he held her left hand with a firm grip.

Su opened her eyes. Her arms and Hsien's formed a nearly circular loop, the two of them grasping the broken bracelet on one side and each other's hands on the other. Looking down, though her eyes watered from the chill wind, she saw—not her own feet and Hsien's, but a pure unmarked patch of snow. "It's working!" she gasped.

Two more volunteers joined the circle. Soldiers. One cursed as the cold seared his hands; the other only clenched his jaw. The circle was now nearly a man's height across.

Hsien and the man to his right now lowered themselves to one knee and dropped their joined hands to the floor, while Su and the fourth man raised the bracelet as high as they could. The circle was now a tilted ellipse, and the fierce wind pouring out of it whipped the clothing of the men nearby.

"Go!" Chang yelled into the gale. "Civilians first, then soldiers! Officers last! Hurry!"

Women and children stepped over Hsien's hand and ducked under Su's, squinting against the wind and gasping as their bare feet touched the snow. But they pressed ahead, driven by the knowledge that Yao would soon attack. Old men followed, and more women, some carrying babies and leading children. The warmth of their bodies as they passed eased Su's chattering teeth, a little, and they stepped through the circle quickly and in good order, but as the civilians went on and on Su's trembling began to shake her entire body.

Namu kuan shih yin pu sa, she prayed, not knowing how much longer she could hold on.

Then a warm weight settled on her shoulders. It was a horse blanket, and it stank, but it helped immensely. She looked over her shoulder and saw Chang placing another blanket on the man to her left.

The parade of women, children, and men continued. Ice caked in the folds of the blanket, and Su's hands ached from the cold. *Namu kuan shih yin pu sa*.

Her prayers were interrupted by Chang's harsh, commanding voice. "This is too slow!" he said, and placed his hand on the bracelet.

"No!" Su cried out, but it was too late—Chang had inserted himself into the circle.

"Two by two!" he yelled, and the civilians complied, walking two abreast from the heat and dust of Guang-xi into the cold and snow of the Xian mountains.

"Chang, how could you?" Su called to him across the endless flow of heads and shoulders. "You cannot remain behind. The people need you!"

"The people need me now," he replied in a matter-of-fact tone. Snow was already accumulating in his beard. "And I could not allow myself to live, knowing that my brave priestess stayed behind to save me."

Su's head bowed, and her knees sagged. "Oh, Chang . . ." The cold bit through the heavy horse blanket, and she began to tremble anew.

And then, impossibly, Chang began to chuckle.

"What do you find funny in this situation?" she demanded of him.

"It reminds me of when I was a child," he said. "Do you know 'Little Mousey Brown'?"

Shivering, Su just looked at him.

"It is a circle dance the Li children do. You hold hands in a circle, and dance around, and sing." And then he opened his mouth, and in a froglike bass he began to sing:

"He climbed up the candlestick,
The little mousey brown,
To steal and eat tallow,
And he couldn't get down."

To her own astonishment, Su recognized the rhyme, though she hadn't thought of it in years. She began to swing her arms gently back and forth as she joined Chang in the second verse:

"He called for his grandma,
But his grandma was in town,
So he doubled up into a wheel,
And rolled himself down."

She was nearly unable to finish the verse, she was laughing so hard. Laughing like a child in the snows of Xian. "Yes, we had this rhyme in Xian," she gasped. "And at the end, when the mousey *rooooolled* himself down, we would all . . ."

She stopped.

"Would what?" asked Chang.

She explained how the Xian version of the dance ended. "Do you think . . ."

"I don't know." Chang's face grew thoughtful. "We can try."

Newly invigorated, the circle waited while the last of the civilians stepped through and the first of the soldiers followed them. Soon only a handful of soldiers and one lieutenant remained in the wind-whipped room. But then the last two scouts hurried in and barred the door behind themselves. "Yao has broken through the blockade!" said one, sweat running down his face.

"He will find a surprise," said Chang. "Go!"

The scout ducked under Su and Chang's hands, joined at the bracelet, and vanished into the snow. "Good luck," said the lieutenant as he followed, leaving the room empty save for the circle of five and the whistling wind.

Their isolation did not last long. A moment later came a heavy thud at the barred door, and the latch splintered.

"Shall we roll ourselves down?" said Chang, but though his words were light his expression was serious. None of them knew what the consequences of their action might be.

"Yes," said Su, and raised the bracelet high. "Let us roll ourselves down."

A second thud, and the door crashed into pieces.

The man opposite the bracelet took a deep breath and, without releasing his grip on either side, ran under Su and Chang's hands.

The circle turned itself inside-out.

Su felt as though she, herself, were turning inside-out.

The last thing she saw in the garrison of Guang-xi was Yao's face, livid with anger, his hair blown back by the wind from Xian.

And then she found herself standing in the snow—in a cold but gentle breeze. A natural, not supernatural, cold.

The sun was just rising, causing the trampled snow to steam gently.

Su sagged to her knees, and the broken bracelet dropped to the snow beside her. It was only inert metal now.

"How far from here to the temple?" Chang said to her.

"Half a day's walk."

"Then let us begin," he said, and extended his hand.

General Chang Hua returned to Li from Xian the next spring. With the support of the priestesses of Miao Feng Shan, the advantage of surprise, and the loyalty of the people of Li, he was able to not only retake the Li territory lost to Tung, but also to overcome the conscript forces of Yao and capture the Tung capital. He went on to found a great dynasty, ruling for many years with the help of his chief adviser, Su Yuen.

He is known to this day as the Compassionate Emperor.

IRON FLAMES AND NEON SKIES

Jim C. Hines

Jim C. Hines has been a busy little writer these past few years, appearing in such markets as Turn the Other Chick, Sword & Sorceress XXI, Path of the Just, *and many more. He recently took a break from short stories to focus on his novels. His first fantasy novel,* GoblinQuest, *is now available from Five Star Books. Jim currently lives in Lansing, Michigan, where he fixes computers to support his writing habits. At least, he used to . . . but he wrote this bio over a year ago, so your guess is as good as anybody else's. By now, he could be a retired lottery winner, living by the beach in Hawaii with his wife and daughter. Hey, it could happen. . . .*

Plump and middle-aged, with a faded black patch over her left eye and an old army blanket around her shoulders, Tamara Pierce did her best to blend with the darkness. Frayed, colored strings circled her neck and wrists.

The pockets of her tattered camouflage hunting jacket bulged beneath the blanket. Dull rings clinked softly as she exhaled into her cupped hands. "Hurry up already," she muttered.

The couple on the opposite side of the parking garage showed no sign of obeying. The bells and sirens of the White Hawk Casino overhead echoed strangely, blocking out their words, but Tamara didn't dare move closer. Not yet.

The man was nothing. A pretty boy in a cheap tuxedo. A casino employee, probably a busboy. Good-looking enough, with mussed brown hair and a narrow, clean-shaven face. There was a resignation to his stance, the way his shoulders slumped and his gaze kept shifting to the ground, as if some part of him knew he was prey.

Did he recognize the woman as the hunter, Tamara wondered. Only in Las Vegas could a woman six feet tall walk around in a blue sequin-covered bikini top without drawing undue notice. Blue and green ostrich feathers in her headdress and the tall heels of her sparkling shoes added another two feet to her height.

"Like a real dancer would prance around in three-inch stilettos." Tamara frowned. "Like your kind would ever dance for a human."

The man slipped his arms around the woman's waist. She pulled away, dodging a kiss.

"Get away from her, dammit," Tamara whispered.

He only laughed, a giddy, empty laugh that twisted Tamara's gut. She hadn't heard a man laugh like that in four years. Without thinking, she pushed away from the pillar.

Even as she hurried across the lot, the woman pulled a long, gold pin from her hair and jabbed it into the man's forearm. He didn't seem to notice, but Tamara's skin crawled in response.

"Hey!" Tamara slipped a hand into her jacket and pulled out a glossy brochure. Blurry pictures of half-naked women covered the front page. "The Night Life Hotel," she said, forcing a grin as she moved closer. "It's got a coupon for half off the first hour. I get a buck for every coupon," she added, stealing the line from the man who had shoved the brochure into her hands earlier that night.

The woman shook her head. "Sorry, dear. That sounds a bit . . . unsanitary."

Tamara grabbed the man's arm. "Hey, you're bleeding."

He stared at his sleeve. A circle of blood the size of a nickel marked the wound. He poked his arm, then giggled. If he couldn't feel the pain, the magic's grip was already stronger than Tamara had guessed. "Moira, did you do this?"

The dancer—Moira—was watching Tamara. She reached one long, blue-polished fingernail toward Tamara's neck. "That's an interesting necklace. . . ."

Tamara pulled a thin knife from beneath her jacket. Moira's eyes widened, and she lashed out with her pin. Tamara twisted and lunged. The pin scored a bloody line across Tamara's neck, even as she rammed the silver-plated blade home.

The pin clinked to the pavement. Moira's mouth opened silently, and she fell. Her skin tone began to fade, adopting a bluish tinge.

"What's happening to her?" the man asked, still half-smiling.

Tamara used the ostrich feathers to clean the thin

blade. "Argyria. A reaction to silver in the bloodstream. Humans can get it, but their kind is far more sensitive to silver and iron." She tossed her blanket over Moira's body. "Let me guess. She offered eternal ecstasy, pleasure you've never known."

He grinned happily.

"Son of a bitch." Tamara grabbed his arm and yanked back the sleeve. Smeared blood dripped down his elbow. Two half-healed scabs marked the white skin of his forearm. She moved her eyepatch to the other eye. "She already gave you a taste."

He reached for her eyepatch. Tamara's slapped his hand aside. "What's with the pirate look?" he asked. "Are you in the Treasure Island show?"

Tamara ignored him and placed her hand over the bleeding hole in his arm.

"Ow!" For the first time, his face registered pain.

"Iron rings," she explained, tightening her grip. She counted to twenty before removing her hand. He continued to bleed, but less profusely than before. She pressed the rings to her own neck, but nothing happened. Moira must have burned all her power in that first spell. Tamara had been lucky.

She glanced at the nametag on his jacket. "Colin, you have to come with me."

"I'm supposed to be working."

Tamara grabbed him by the collar and slammed him against a green minivan. "You were more than ready to follow *her*. I've spent five months tracking her. She was the only shot I had at finding the path to their world, but now she's dead. That makes you the closest thing I've got to a lead."

"She's dead?" Colin looked down, and for the first

time appeared to really see the body. He backed away until he bumped the car behind him.

"If you've cost me the chance to find that path. . . ." It was all she could do to keep from hitting him. It wasn't his fault, she reminded herself. *She* was the one who had killed Moira. Jaw tight, she crouched and began bundling up the body. "Help me get her into my station wagon."

Colin swallowed hard, nodded, and promptly passed out.

Tamara held a bottle of smelling salts beneath Colin's nose. He jolted awake.

"What—"

Tamara pushed him back down on the bed. "You're in a hotel room. No, it wasn't a dream. Yes, I killed her. No, she wasn't human. Any other stupid questions?"

The room wasn't much, but at ten bucks an hour, she had expected no different. Cracks of light slipped through the blinds of the single window, striping the worn carpet with color from the signs outside. A locked door led to the parking lot.

"What are you going to do to me?" Colin glanced at his arm. Strips of medical tape held a white bandage in place.

"I don't know yet." She unzipped her duffel bag and pulled out a steel eyeglasses case. She tossed it to Colin. "Put those on, and go get cleaned up."

Colin unfolded the black, plastic-rimmed sunglasses. "Are you going to kill me?"

"Are you going to keep wasting my time?"

He retreated into the bathroom, only to emerge seconds later, pale and shaking. He was clutching the glasses so hard Tamara worried they would break.

"Did you look?" she asked. She pried the glasses out of his hands, then steered Colin back into the bathroom.

Moira's corpse lay in the tub with her knees bent. Her skin was a dull blue-gray, and her eyes were wide. Tamara pressed the glasses over Colin's eyes. "*Look.*"

Colin swallowed. "She's burning!"

Tamara removed her eyepatch, and her vision changed. Silver flames danced above the wound in Moira's side, and her skin sparkled like white sand. "In another few days, she'll be nothing but ash."

"It's a trick." Colin yanked off the glasses and squinted at the lenses. "What are these scratches?"

"They're Egyptian," Tamara said. "A spell for seeing the truth."

"Yeah, right."

Tamara took the glasses and set them back on his face, then pointed to his bandaged arm. "Tell me what you see."

"Oh shit." Smaller flames flickered through the bandage. He started to hyperventilate. "What did she do?"

"That pin was a conduit." She rubbed her neck, wincing at the pain of the fresh scab. "It will burn out eventually. If she'd finished her spell, you'd have cut off your own balls for her, and you'd smile when you did it."

Colin's hand went reflexively to his crotch. "How do you know all of this?"

"They stole my son," Tamara whispered. She rubbed her shoulder, imagining she could feel the tiny scar where the woman had jabbed her as she lay exhausted in the hospital bed. "He was only a few hours old. It took months before my husband and I even understood what had happened to us." She shook her head and cleared her throat, forcing back the smells and sounds of that night.

"It wasn't until we got our hands on those glasses that we really started to believe."

Colin held up the sunglasses, moving them up and down in front of his eyes as he stared at his arm. "But you don't wear them any more. You can see all of this?"

Tamara slipped her eyepatch back into place, then tapped it. "Paid a laser eye specialist six grand to burn that spell onto my retina. Gives me a hell of a migraine, but it's worth it. The only way they can hide from me is to burn out my eye."

"Lovely image," Colin said. He poked one of the wounds on his arms, then winced. "What are they?"

"Call them fae, if you need a name. Centuries back, you couldn't walk a mile without stumbling across one of the fairy hills where their world intersects ours. Nowadays, there are only a handful, and only on certain nights. Nights like the winter solstice."

Colin stared blankly.

"That's *tonight*. If I hadn't killed her, tomorrow your bosses would have been looking for a new busboy."

"Waiter," Colin mumbled.

"Whatever." She touched the dirty gray string knotted around her wrist. "They used to leave changelings in exchange for human babies. But that doesn't work anymore. They can't fake blood types or DNA."

"Why take people at all?" He seemed to be taking everything in stride. Maybe he was stronger than Tamara had given him credit for. Either that, or it still hadn't hit him.

"For slaves," she said. "No, not even slaves. Toys. Playthings to dance and sing and serve their every whim, whether it's singing a song or lighting yourself on fire.

And the whole time, the pleasure center of your brain is on overload, so you don't even care."

"Doesn't sound too bad."

Tamara stiffened. "What?"

Colin took a step backward, toward the door. "Hey, at least you'd be happy, right? I've been stuck in this town for five years, waiting the same damn tables every night since I was seventeen. I hate this town. I've *prayed* for someone to get me the hell out of Vegas."

"They took my son." She held perfectly still, afraid of what she would do to him if she moved. Only when she could force her fingers to unclench did she speak again. "I need your help. I have to find that path, and thanks to you, the one person who could have led me to it is decomposing in the bathtub."

"I didn't ask you to save me," Colin said. He shook his head. "Look, I'm sorry about your family. But I can't help you. I'm nothing. You want free drinks at the casino, I'm your man. But this. . . ." He touched the bandage on his arm and grimaced. "Why didn't you just let her take me?"

"I made a mistake." Tamara's skin felt like cold metal. She *should* have let Moira take him. She could have followed, could have saved him before Moira took him through the hill. "For a second, you reminded me of Jack. My husband."

"I'm sorry," he said again. "I'm not him."

"You're right. Jack never ran away." Tamara turned away. "I know why Moira picked you. They prey on those who can't protect themselves. Babies, mostly, and others too *weak* to fight back."

She heard him leave, heard the door click shut behind

him. "Too damn weak," she muttered. She wiped her eyes and began stuffing her belongings into her bag.

Clumps of people made it harder to keep Colin in sight, but those same crowds kept him from spotting Tamara as she trailed him.

Even at night, Vegas was never truly dark. An enormous screen to her right played a clip of two muscular men juggling flaming torches. Spotlights shone as synchronized fountains shot water hundreds of feet into the air in front of the Bellagio. The roller coasters at the Boardwalk Casino were lit up like a carnival.

Colin cut across the street just beyond the Boardwalk. Tamara glanced at the night sky, orienting herself by the brilliant white beam atop the Luxor hotel. Colin was taking her east. They had already passed the White Hawk Casino, where she first found him.

The lights and noise faded slightly, and the glitz took on a tarnished feel. Smaller casinos and sleazier hotels lined the street. Flashing signs advertised cheap buffets and live entertainment of every variety, from Shakespeare to strippers.

Colin scurried across the street. Brakes screeched, but he barely seemed to notice. He stumbled onto the sidewalk, past a woman selling cheap jewelry, and disappeared into the Great Wall Casino. Blue and white lights painted ever-shifting Chinese symbols on the walls.

Tamara pulled a plastic bottle from her pocket and popped the cap. She fished out four Advil and swallowed them dry. With a grimace, she removed her eyepatch and stuffed it into her pocket, along with the pills. Then she followed Colin into the casino.

Incense, fried food, and the sweat of too many bodies

crammed together made Tamara's nose wrinkle as she squeezed inside. Rows of slot machines turned the place into a labyrinth, with a single wide aisle leading to the cashier's counter. A crowd of older men and women shuffled past, all wearing small red buttons to identify their tour group.

Tamara sat on one of the stools by the slot machines and studied the ceiling, noting the shining black spheres that marked security cameras. No doubt there were others better hidden. She saw no sign of the fairy hill, but given the number of fae, this had to be the place. They wouldn't have gathered here unless the path was going to appear.

Most of the people were human, but not all. One of the cocktail waitresses, the one with the gold nails and the too full lips . . . a blackjack dealer, whose hands burned silver as he wrapped illusion around the cards . . . the impossibly slender man at the desk, his eyes sparking as he watched Colin approach.

She should find a safe place to arm herself and prepare. Colin had made his choice when he left the hotel . . . and now he was walking right into their arms.

"Dammit!" She punched a slot machine. A few people glanced her way, probably figuring she was just another frustrated loser. She hopped down from the stool and started to walk, snagging a cup of beer from a gray-haired woman too intent on her three slot machines to notice. Forcing a stupefied smile, Tamara waved and shouted, "Colin? Over here!"

She hurried over, her duffel bag bouncing against her spine. Slipping her arm through his, she tugged him around. "I've been looking all over for you, man!"

He stared at her for several seconds before recognizing her. "You followed me."

Tamara dragged him toward the buffet line. "You couldn't stay away, could you?" she snapped. It came out more harshly than she meant. "It takes time for their magic to burn out, but you didn't even fight it."

Colin's forehead wrinkled as he looked around, taking in the generic Asian dragons on the walls and the paper lanterns strung from the ceiling. On stage beyond the bar, a dark-skinned woman crooned an old Mary Chapin Carpenter tune, her inhuman lungs coating every word in sweet maple syrup.

Tamara pulled the gray string from her wrist and tied it around Colin's arm, above the elbow. She stood closer than she would have liked, trying to block the cameras. "Even dead, she's stronger than you."

"You used me," Colin snapped.

"Yeah, I did." She finished tying the knot, then shoved his arm away. "And you don't like it very much, do you?"

Colin hesitated, then looked around again. "The last thing I remember was walking out of the hotel." He scowled and touched the string. "What is that?"

"Soul string. I got them from a Hmong shaman. They're supposed to protect you from the *dab*, the stealers of souls." She shrugged. "*Dab*, fae, demons, it's all the same. If you get out of here now, it should help you fight Moira's pull until her magic fades."

"How are you going to get through?" he asked. "You can't stab them all."

"That's not your problem," Tamara snapped. "Go home, Colin, and thank whatever God you pray to that you still can."

He was staring at his arms, and the anger had faded from his face. He looked frightened. It made him look

like a teenager. "This is for real. They would have. . . ."
He swallowed.

"Yes, it's real."

He sighed. "I really hate this town."

Tamara glanced up, and her skin went cold. The waitress she had spotted earlier was walking toward them, her
eyes fixed on Colin. "I'm begging you, get out of here."

He glanced at the waitress, and his body gave a faint
shudder. "What about your family?"

"You can't help them," Tamara snapped. "Go!"

"Maybe I can. Maybe I'm stronger than you think."
Colin turned away . . . and walked straight toward the
waitress, intercepting her before she reached Tamara.

"You're one of *them*, aren't you? Like Moira." He
rolled up his sleeve to show the scars. "She promised to
take me away from here." He glanced back at Tamara.
"I'm ready now."

Tamara popped another two Advil as she watched the
fae finish roping off the far corner of the casino. Her skull
felt as though it were going to split, but she could see the
ring of flame circling the roulette wheel. Silver sparks
leaped high enough to touch the ceiling as the fairy hill
continued to form.

They weren't even going to bother emptying the
casino. Slot machines blocked most of the view, and
really, who would believe it if they saw the fae passing in
and out of the world? If anyone did question too closely,
a bit of magic would quickly make them fall into line.

Nine of the fae stood whispering by the table, along
with Colin. To anyone else, it probably looked like a
high-stakes, VIP game.

Several of the fae kept looking her way. She clutched

her bag tightly to her shoulder, trying not to react. They had seen her with Colin. If Tamara tried anything, she'd probably get herself killed, and that was a best-case scenario.

She needed to get away. Stopping Colin had cost Tamara her shot. Get out and start over. Colin was gone. Three times now he had given himself to the fae. Let him choose his own fate.

She didn't move. And then the waitress was walking toward her, and it was too late.

"Your boyfriend said to tell you this is your last chance to come with him," the waitress said.

"My . . . he does?"

"Colin told you a lot of things he really shouldn't have." She smiled and clucked her tongue, like a mother amused with her toddler's misdeeds. "I'm Lia. You're probably pretty confused right now, huh?"

Tamara kept her hands in her pockets, hiding her rings as they walked. Soon she stood beside Colin, surrounded by too-perfect men and women. It was easy to make herself sound scared as she said, "Colin told me you were going to take him away."

They smiled. Tamara had a sudden vision of herself pulling her knife and thrusting the blade through Lia's smooth, pale throat.

"Only if he wants to go," Lia said. "You wouldn't understand. Words can't convey the gift Moira gave him. He—" She frowned and reached out to touch the string around Tamara's neck. "What's this?"

"A good-luck charm." If she killed Lia now, could she get through in time? The hill was fully formed, a glowing mound of fire superimposed over the roulette table, its peak perfectly aligned with the wheel. Seven times *wid-*

dershins, counterclockwise, and she would be in their realm. She would be with her family.

"A charm indeed," Lia said. Tamara kept her hands in her pockets as Lia pulled. The string dug into her neck, nearly breaking the skin before it finally snapped. Tamara cringed, feeling naked and vulnerable.

"It'll be great," Colin said. He was bouncing on his toes. "It's everything you wanted."

He was still trying to help, Tamara realized. This was his way of getting her through. He didn't understand what was about to happen.

From her sleeve, Lia drew a long sliver of gold, identical to the one Moira had used. Tamara's mouth went dry, and she stepped back. Several of the fae moved to intercept her. She reached for her knife, but somebody caught her arm. "No. Please. . . ." She didn't have to fake the terror anymore.

"Don't worry," Lia promised. "It won't hurt. Nothing will ever hurt again."

Colin nodded. His eyes darted toward the table. Tamara knew what he was saying. *Don't fight it. It's the only way to get through.* He didn't understand. Just like Jack.

"No!" Tamara twisted, then grabbed Lia's wrist. Heat flared to life in the iron rings on Tamara's fingers, and the pin dropped soundlessly onto the carpet. Tamara spun, putting her own back to the table and interposing Lia between herself and the others. They were all moving now, surrounding her. She glanced at the roulette wheel, a bonfire of metallic flame.

Someone caught her sleeve. She pushed one hand into his cheek until he jerked away. Lia squirmed free, and Tamara kicked her in the side, sending her into the others and buying herself a second or two to act.

Tamara grabbed Colin and pulled him close. With her other hand, she reached for the roulette wheel. Before anyone could move, she spun the wheel as hard as she could, and the world disappeared.

Tamara landed on hard earth, followed an instant later by Colin, who fell onto her legs. Her bag dug into her spine as she kicked free. Already one of the fae was following. She grabbed her knife and threw it as hard as she could.

Here between worlds, the silver blade sparked and spat as it twirled. The fae ducked aside, giving Tamara the seconds she needed to open her bag and grab one of the heavy boxes inside.

As the fae came at her again, she tore off the lid and flung the contents. Five hundred short, iron nails flew like tiny fireworks. Orange fire burned in every one, searing the fae's hands and face. He screamed and fell back, trying to dislodge the nails that had tangled in his hair and clothes.

Tamara crawled along the ground. The glowing nails were easy to avoid. She grabbed her still-sparking knife and returned it to its sheath. Her attacker had already retreated back into the casino, no doubt patting himself out even now.

"What is this place?" Colin whispered.

"A fairy hill. The path around the hill leads from our world to theirs, and back. It takes seven circles to cross. With each one, our world fades away, and theirs grows stronger."

"But we didn't circle anything."

She managed a shaky smile. "They anchored it to the roulette wheel. Probably to speed up the passage. Instead of running laps around the hill, it's the hill itself that spins, at least until the wheel fades too much."

The hill was to their left. If Tamara squinted, she could see the outline of the roulette table beneath the grass. A shallow puddle in the center marked the wheel itself, and a tiny pine sapling grew where the chrome spinner had been. "If we circle around another two or three times, we'll be through."

She pulled out another box of nails. Her hands were numb as she scattered them on the trail in front of her. "That should stop anyone from coming at us from the other side."

"How did you know about the roulette wheel?"

"I didn't." A few yards beyond the hill's border, the world grew shaded. A ring of brown mushrooms marked the edge of the path. Beyond, she could see the shapes of thin, too tall trees swaying in an unfelt breeze, but it was like looking through black gauze. She reached out until her fingers touched air so cold it burnt. Her body began to tremble.

"Hey, are you okay?" Colin stepped closer.

Tamara touched her throat, remembering the touch of Lia's hand as she ripped the soul string away. "You could have gotten us killed."

"I got us in to your pathway, didn't I?" Colin said. "Guess I'm not as weak and useless as you thought."

She pushed him away so hard he fell back against the hill.

"What's the matter with you?" Colin stood up, brushing dirt from his jacket and glaring. "Maybe I could help you if you weren't so busy trying to stop me. Maybe we'd already be through, getting your husband and your kid—"

"Shut up!" She closed her eyes, fighting for control.

Tamara took a long, shaky breath, forcing the tears back. "Jack was the strongest man I've ever known, and four years ago I watched him cross into their world. He never came back."

Colin approached her cautiously, like she was a wild animal. "You're scared they're going to hurt us the way they hurt him?"

"They didn't *hurt* him," she whispered. "They put the same god damned spell on him that Moira put on you. He *chose* to go with them. He chose pleasure over our son."

She wiped her face and turned away, pulling several canvas sacks from her duffel bag.

"So we have to be careful," Colin said. "I get it. We just have to avoid the fae while we hunt for your family."

"We're not going through." It came out as a whisper.

Colin just stared.

Tamara pointed to the nails scattered through the grass. "You think they can't see that? You think they haven't figured out that we're here? They're waiting for us, Colin."

Colin looked away. "I didn't know," he said softly. "Can't . . . can't we do something? Fight our way past? You've got all those toys and weapons in your bag, and—"

"I'm not strong enough either," she said. "Not even to save my son. I remember what it felt like, back in the hospital. I remember the spell. I remember watching as they took him away." She swallowed. "That's all I did. I watched."

"So what do we do?"

She took a shaky breath and handed him one of the sacks. "Scatter that on the hill."

"What is it?"

She untied her sack and began flinging the contents into the grass, like a farmer seeding the earth. But wherever Tamara's seeds touched, the grass withered and died. "Iron filings. I picked them up from a steel mill in Detroit."

"I don't understand."

"I told you there were only a handful of places where they can still open a portal into our world." Tamara flung another handful of iron. The grass twisted away from the tiny scrapings of metal. "Now they'll have one less."

She climbed onto the top of the hill and dumped the rest of the filings into the puddle. The water began to bubble and steam. "I can't save my son, but I'll be damned if they're going to take anyone else's. Not tonight."

Colin backed away, pulling his sack inside out and shaking it over the grass.

The air tasted like ash, and something inside of her snarled at the scent, the bitter proof of triumph. "Once we're gone, the pathway will collapse. One less thread connecting our worlds."

"How do we get back?" He shifted his feet. "I can't imagine they're going to be happy to see us."

"We circle the hill in the opposite direction. They won't be there." Tamara pointed to the fog seeping down the hill. "It's like cyanide to them. They probably bailed the second their roulette wheel started smoking." A bitter, tired chuckle escaped her lips. "Probably set off the sprinkler system, too."

"Will they come back? Looking for us, I mean." He didn't sound frightened, merely tired.

Tamara nodded. "They're vindictive bastards, but they can't stay here forever. They'll need to find another hill. It should be safe for you to come back to Vegas in a few months. In the meantime, we need to track one of them down before they skip town."

He stared. "What?"

"Summer solstice is only six months away, boy. Wherever they go, that's where we're going." She touched her neck, feeling the scab and wondering how close she had come to joining her husband and son. All it would take was one mistake. . . . "I'm not strong enough to do this alone."

Neither spoke for several minutes. Finally, Tamara fished her eyepatch from her pocket. She wiped her face as she slipped the patch into place.

"So let's find ourselves a fae," Colin said, his voice firmer than Tamara had heard before.

"First we need to take a road trip to California."

Colin blinked. "Why?"

"So Fong Lao can replace my soul string. If you're lucky, maybe he'll let you sacrifice the pig." She glanced at the sizzling brown grass. "We can be back in two days. They'll still be here, trying to find us."

Colin put a tentative hand on her shoulder. "We'll get your family back."

"Damn right." She kicked a clump of dry dirt and began walking. She *hadn't* failed. She had saved Colin and who knew how many others. She had burned out another fairy hill. And six months from now. . . . "Next time we walk this path, we're not going back without them."

Colin's footsteps crunched the hard ground as he followed. Minutes later, nothing remained but a dying hill and a fading sky.

CARDED

Jim Fiscus

*Jim Fiscus is a Portland, Oregon, writer and histo-
rian. He has a master's degree in Middle East and
Asian history. His fiction includes alternate history,
science fiction, and fantasy. His first fiction sale
was a story using time-travel to explain the theo-
logical basis of the present regime in Iran. He has
written books on America's war in Afghanistan, the
1956 Suez Crisis in the Middle East, Iraqi resistance to the United States, and the 1933 version of
the movie* King Kong. *In addition to writing about
history, he reports on medicine, science, business,
and law for numerous publications.*

Felix Becker punched his PIN into the ATM, followed
by a request for his account balance. He glanced at the
slip of paper that slid from the machine. "My last eighty
bucks," he said softly. Becker glanced at his watch as he
stepped away from the pair of machines. He pulled his

jacket tighter against the chill of Portland's winter and walked a block to a new brewpub. He slowly drank a beer, then checked his watch again. 'Straight up 10 o'clock,' he thought.

Walking back to the bank, he reentered his card, read "Balance unavailable," and grinned. Software bomb took down the mainframe right on time, Becker thought. He felt elation and pride. Isolated from the central computer, the ATMs would ignore the normal daily limit on accounts and belch out money independently. He took back his card and inserted a second card. "Time for payback to start, Stokeland," he said. Again, he punched in a PIN. He waited for the ATM to process his transaction, then tucked $300 into his coat pocket without counting the wad of bills. He took the card back, stepped to the next machine, and repeated the transaction.

Becker walked to the corner in the cold winter rain, smelling the heavy diesel fumes along the bus mall, and slid the card into another ATM. His blue eyes stared back from the reflection in the monitor. Even to himself his chubby face look drawn from fatigue. Finish the job and sleep for a month when he made Tijuana or Rio, he thought. Taking another $300, he reached for the card as it slid from the machine. As his fingers touched the hard plastic he heard a tinny voice say, "Please suck in your shoulder blades."

Becker glanced around the bank's patio, expecting to see a rent-a-pig about to take him down. No one was there. "I'm hearing things. They couldn't twig this fast." He grabbed the card again and pulled.

"Suck them in, please." The voice was insistent.

"Damn." Becker shivered, involuntarily shrugging his shoulders. His card pulled back into the ATM. He tried to yank it out. Rather than come free, the card slowly pulled Becker's hand into the slot. His arm melted into a long ribbon of pink surrounding a core of flowing white he knew was bone. He felt no pain, only a rush of adrenaline and panic as dark strands from his shirt flaked from the stream of pink and white. Becker tried to pull free. His world turned black.

Heat closed around Becker for an instant, and he felt himself falling. He landed on his back, his breath whooshing out as he thudded down with a force that felt like falling a foot or two. Must have hit my head, Becker thought, as he felt the coolness of damp grass under his body. Grass? I should be on concrete. He realized he was naked. Warm, moist, air surrounded him. He kept his eyes squeezed tightly shut against the bright light, hoping that continued darkness would clear his mind so he could understand what had happened. Heavy perfume of flowers filled his nostrils. He sneezed.

Becker raised his hand to shield his eyes and let them crack open. He squinted against the harsh light, turned his head to the side to avoid the glare. Inches from his nose were a pair of brightly polished black penny loafers and the ends of black pant legs. The pants had a slight bell-bottom and looked like polyester. He rolled his head back and looked up at a thin old man wearing a leisure suit and a black fedora with a band of silver coins circling the crown. The man stroked his gray goatee.

"Now, Mr. Stokeland, let's see your ATM card." The man dropped smoothly into a squat and held out his hand. At closer range, the man's face had the vicious look of a ferret that lived only to attack its owner.

"Where am I?"

"Don't ask where, Mr. Stokeland. Ask why."

"Who are you?"

"Pietr Alexandrovich Merkov. Peter. I'm your guide. Give me your card." Merkov's voice hinted at a Russian accent. "Now, please."

Becker looked into the man's eyes and shivered despite the warm air. He realized that he still clutched the ATM card. He handed it over.

The old man glanced at the card. "An Iridium Pass. Most make due with platinum or titanium. You are the man they need."

Anger at being mistaken for Stokeland swept away the last of his shock. Okay, let him think I'm that mother till I know what the hell's going on, Becker thought. He stood. A wide lawn stretched up a low hill to a dark red geodesic dome that rose four stories into the blue sky. Even naked, it was warm under the pounding sun. He forced himself to answer calmly. "I'm not taking a step till you tell me where the hell I am." He took a long, dark green, robe from the man and slipped it on. It had the oily feel of polyester.

"Call it Barsoom, if you want a name." Merkov's smile scarcely broke his flat expression.

"Right, and my name is John Carter. Screw the name. What is this place?"

"Corporate headquarters, Mr. Stokeland. We brought you here to do a job that you're especially good at." Merkov smiled again, but this time there was a hint of warmth in his expression. "I arrived here much as you did. Ten years ago, I stuck my card into an ATM in Portland and landed here. You have my word. Do the job, and you'll be well cared for."

"I ask again. Where is this damned place?" Becker

heard a touch of panic in his voice, felt his nerves pulling tighter. He took a deep breath to force relaxation, and sneezed.

"Part of my job is to explain that to you. How much do you know about physics?" He took Becker's arm and started toward the red dome.

"Took it in college. Every action has an equal and opposite reaction, and that stuff," Becker said, thinking, and I feel like a truly opposite reaction happened somewhere. "I can still spout terms like quantum mechanics, special relativity, and string theory at parties."

"Saving the details for another day, this is an alternate universe, a different Earth. The people I work for, the Corporation, can send and receive information between universes. Electrons are low mass and don't cost much to send."

"So how'd I get here?"

"They plant nano-level gateways in our homeuniverse and power them from this universe. Nearly all of them are in ATM machines, though they're starting to install them in all the card swipes."

"I'm more than a few electrons."

"If they're willing to spend enough for energy, they can receive or transmit people. You and me."

Becker stood silently. High, white, clouds streamed across a blue sky. The air smelled of tropical plants he thought were orchids but could not truly identify. He grasped for a saner explanation. "For all I can tell, you drugged me and hauled me off to some private estate."

"It's winter in Portland. Here, it's early summer. We'd have had to fly you to New Zealand or somewhere else in the south, and that would have taken a day or two."

Becker rubbed his cheek. He felt the slight roughness

he expected at the end of a long day. "Something's different." He stopped walking, reached down and felt his sides. Where he had sported a growing roll of fat he found only loose skin. "I've gotta be fifteen, twenty pounds thinner."

"Mass costs money to sent through the nano-gates. They discard extra fat and other contaminates." Merkov grinned. "You won't have to use the bathroom for awhile, either."

"What do you want with me?" Becker asked, thinking, No, what do you want with that bastard Stokeland? They passed a tall bush heavy with large blue flowers that smelled like a cross between lilacs and roses. Becker's nose began to run, and he sniffed.

"The Chairman will explain shortly." Merkov put his hand on Becker's arm. "These people have odd sensibilities. They like to keep their hands clean, and they always kill the messenger—and that's why you're here."

The Chairman sat in a chair that engulfed him, as if he sat inside a large padded eggshell. Two aides, both men, flanked him. Both wore white three-piece suits. The Chairman stood slowly as Becker and Merkov entered. The man was several inches taller than Becker's five foot nine. His round, jowly face, reminded Becker of Henry Kissinger. Before speaking, he waved to a side door, and his aides exited. "Mr. Stokeland. I am glad you came." His voice was harsh, almost a husky whisper.

"I had no choice," Becker said, now dressed in a dark red suit.

"No, but I thank you all the same. There is a problem here. You are the best man to handle it."

"Yes?" Becker tried to sound confident, unfazed by the dangers around him. "Just what is your problem?"

"You terminate people with efficiency, Mr. Stokeland. We need a man fired."

"You're kidding?" Becker's shock was real. "You sucked me into your bloody universe so I can fire some slacker?"

"Three corporations on your Earth hired you to close down companies. You are the best and we always hire the best."

And that's why I want Stokeland pushing a grocery cart filled with empty bottles, Becker thought, or in the grave with Dad and the other men Stokeland murdered.

"We do not like unpleasant jobs, Mr. Stokeland."

"Everybody wants things nice and clean. No one likes dirty hands," Becker said, repeating a phrase he'd heard from Stokeland a dozen times. "How many do you need terminated and what are their ranks?"

"One man. Senior executive."

"Okay, I understand why you'd object to dumping a few thousand folks on their butts and reinvesting their retirement funds. You might have a sane government hereabouts that would take offense. But one man?"

"There are political considerations."

"Explain?" And the mess gets deeper, Becker thought. He took several deep breaths, sucking the building's cool aseptic air into his lungs. His nose had stopped running in the clean air. Becker wondered if the Chairman also had allergies.

"His father heads a dissident faction of the board. He will seek revenge on whoever fires his son."

"You want me to be your hatchet man, but you're still the one firing the kid."

"Appearance matters above all else, Mr. Stokeland."

Becker glanced at Merkov, remembering his comment that these jerks always killed the messenger. Fear chewed at his gut. "So the father will come after me?'

With obvious reluctance, the Chairman said, "Yes."

"And you'll leave me twisting in the wind."

The Chairman looked bewildered.

"Twisting in the wind," Merkov said. "Means you'll leave him on his own to be killed or punished by the father."

"No. As soon as you terminate the man, we will send you back through the gate," the Chairman said.

"I do all this because I like you so much, right?"

"We pay for honest labor, Mr. Stokeland. There will be five hundred thousand dollars from us in your account when you return."

"Two million."

"One."

Becker watched the Chairman, trying to decide how hard he could push him. "And I'll be hit with the tax. Make it one and a half million, and you send a 1099 to the IRS so that it all looks legal."

The Chairman looked relieved, said, "Yes," too quickly, and Becker knew he could have held out for two million.

"I want to see the terminal at this end. I really didn't like being sucked into an ATM slot. Watching yourself dissolve is unsettling."

"The process is easier from this end. You lay down on a transmitter, and you are there."

"You're not worried I'd tell about you?"

"No one would believe you."

"True enough. I want to see the facility."

The Chairman frowned. "There is no time for a tour now." He touched a control, and the image of a man of about thirty blinked into the air between them. "The man you will terminate. Saban Ballan." The holograph nearly looked to be alive. Saban's face was broad and flat, his hair white blond, and his eyes bright blue.

"Why do you want him out?" Becker asked.

"Personal reasons. Business reasons. They are not your concern."

"They are if you want me to ax the bastard."

The Chairman shrugged. "Business. He is a poor manager. His division is bleeding money. His father and I were once allies. Since the alliance shattered, he has tried to destroy me. He will try again soon. Personal. He was to link with my daughter. He left her on the eve of the ceremony. She could not go public against the power of his family, even with my backing. I want Saban destroyed for her sake and to save his division."

"A family dispute. No more."

"More. He also beat her the night he left."

"And did he kick her dog?" Becker asked. "You're trying too hard to make him the villain."

Becker's fingers dug into the arm rests of his seat as Merkov flipped their flyer into a tight turn, drifting the two-person craft within inches of a towering office block. "Hey, ease off, I want to get out of this alive." His sinuses had nearly closed down now that they were back outside.

Merkov laughed. "You won't die at my hands." He tapped a control and the teardrop-shaped vehicle snapped into a steep climb to avoid another building.

Above the floor and engine compartment, the flyer was transparent, giving Becker a clear view of windows flashing past. His stomach churned. "Ease off, Merkov. I can't do the job if you splatter us into some sucker's office."

"You actually fear death?" The surprise in Merkov's voice sounded real. "For a decade, I've only seen my family in pictures. That is death for a man's soul." He spun the flyer into a tight turn. "The Corporation keeps promising to send me home, but I've been here too long and know too much. As my Russian grandfather would have said, my life is skimming the foam from shit so they can make money. Today, you are the foam." The flyer slammed upward.

"Knock it off!" Becker clinched his teeth a moment, tasting stomach acids rising into his throat and mouth, feeling them burn, and adding, "unless you want me to puke all over you."

"Ah, that is a threat even I will listen to." Merkov laughed again as the craft slowed and swung easily into level flight. He tapped a code into the control pad. "It will fly itself."

Becker's nausea eased. His sinuses drained a bit, and he coughed.

Merkov turned to look at Becker. "Time for truth. I know the records of Earth. You are not Stokeland. Who are you?"

Fear swept through Becker. His gut clenched and nausea again swept through him. So much for ever getting home, he thought. He watched the city skim beneath them. "Felix Becker. I work for Stokeland."

"Why use his card?"

"I couldn't think of a way to kill the bastard and get away with it, but I could take his money."

"Again, why?"

"My stepfather ran a chemical company. Everybody in town either worked at the company or sold things to those who did. One of the corporate sharks bought them out. All the shark wanted was control of several important patents. They didn't need the plant or the people. They didn't need the town. They didn't need my stepfather."

"Stokeland was the hatchet man?"

"My stepfather ran the plant. Stokeland personally fired him, then closed the plant. No warning for the workers. The day shift showed up and the doors were locked. My stepfather was crushed. He held on for about a year, sinking deeper into depression as the town died around us. Finally, he put a shotgun into his mouth and pulled the trigger. I found his body."

"How'd you get Stokeland's card?"

"I work for him. The arrogant bastard didn't check my background closely enough to twig to my connection to my stepfather. I work as his driver, and sometimes as his double. You've seen his photo. I look a lot like him. Sure, I'm ten years younger than he is, but he was Botoxing himself before it became fashionable. He wasn't interested in being pretty. He wanted to make it harder to let emotion slip into his expression."

Merkov was silent for nearly a minute, then swore. "Gavnó! The Corporation can do nothing but kill me. We may help each other. They'll not send you home after you do the job. They will start to, but the senior Saban will want revenge. To keep him happy, they will turn you over to him."

"If you help me get home, I'll give you half of Stokeland's money. The ATM withdrawal was the start. I planted a couple of computer bombs that will empty his accounts when I trigger them. The money will end up in

Caribbean and Asian accounts. Your cut will be twenty million."

"You give me hope, my friend." Merkov took back control of the flyer. "Let's circle the city and talk. I'm a physicist. My father worked with Sakarov and managed to defect when I was a child. I got my Ph.D. at Princeton and was in Portland to interview for a teaching job when they took me."

"Why'd they grab you?" Becker asked.

"My research was laying the foundation for moving between universes. Oh, I'd never have gotten there by myself, but the work would have been the sherpa."

"How much do you understand now?"

"Enough to get us home. Enough to give us our own gateways."

"The Corporation will come after us."

Merkov held up several plastic cards about the same size as the credit card that had started Becker's journey. "Perhaps we can make candy from this shit and walk away with clean shoes."

Sunlight streamed through the window of Saban Ballan's office. Ballan stood silhouetted against the harsh light. "You play the Chairman's hand for him."

"No," Becker said, "We play our own hand. You don't trust him. Why do you think we would?"

Ballan nodded, and glanced at Merkov. "Your orders were to take control of my division and fire me. My career would end. My father would then hunt you to your grave."

"And if I don't fire you, the Chairman will stop me from returning home. I had to find my own path." Becker stepped past Ballan and looked at the city stretching to the horizon. His sinuses had cleared somewhat now that he was back in scrubbed air. Low clouds covered the city, and Becker saw only the tops of tall office buildings rising above the gray blanket. "You will escort us back to the gate and we will help you win."

Ballan picked up a decanter and splashed a large shot of blue liquid over ice. He drank deeply. "Your warning is all I need to break the Chairman."

The acrid scent of something close to whisky filled Becker's nostrils. "The warning only ensures a long bloody struggle for power. It does not ensure your victory."

Merkov put his hand on Ballan's shoulder, holding him when he tried to pull away. "The Chairman is powerful. You could easily lose. I know the codes to corporate records that will ensure that you crush him. You'll get the codes as we transmit through the gate."

The Chairman stood behind his desk, nearly shaking with rage. His normally expressionless face contorted in anger as he shouted at Becker and Merkov, "You are both dead men."

"Hardly, Mr. Chairman." Ballan smiled at Merkov and Becker. "My father and I care for our retainers. These men are under our protection. You have failed."

"My daughter was under your protection."

"I protected her as she deserved," Ballan sneered.

Becker opened and closed his fist, realizing that the Chairman had told the truth about the beating, thinking, Now, we have a mess. He glanced at Merkov, mouthed, "Ballan's data." Merkov surreptitiously passed him a small plastic card. "Don't blame the messenger, boss,"

Becker said. He let his hand slide down the man's jacket, slipping the card into the Chairman's pocket.

"Time to go," Merkov said. "Mr. Ballan, you have the board access codes?"

Ballan nodded, punched numbers into a pad on the arm of the Chairman's desk. A panel slid into the wall, exposing a room empty but for a half-dozen long tables.

Merkov whispered, "That's the code I could never get."

The Chairman stepped in front of Becker. "No, not after your betrayal."

Becker snapped a punch into the man's gut, putting all his anger over his kidnapping into the blow. The Chairman doubled over. Becker's knee smashed up into the Chairman's face. Blood gushed from a smashed nose. The Chairman staggered back, tripped on a side chair and sprawled on the floor. "I don't like to be kidnapped." Becker pulled a tissue from his pocket and knelt beside the Chairman. He tucked the tissue into the pocket that held the card. When the Chairman failed to react, Becker took his hand and jammed it into the jacket pocket. Becker felt the Chairman stiffen as the man felt the data card. "The world ain't over. Hold the tissue to your nose before you bleed all over the damned rug!"

"Come." Merkov touched Becker's shoulder.

They followed Ballan into the gate room. Merkov entered coordinates into two of the couches.

"Hey, wait a minute," Becker said, as he lay down on one couch, "We're going to be naked. What if we land on the bus mall? The cops will grab us."

"We'll drop out in an apartment in downtown. The Corporation keeps it available for emergencies." Merkov motioned for Ballan. "Come closer, Saban." He held up a data card. "The gates will transmit thirty seconds after I trigger them. I'll hand you the card as I do."

Ballan nodded. "Enjoy your trip, as I shall enjoy destroying the Chairman."

Becker watched Merkov tap the controls and fling himself onto the other couch. As clear shields dropped over both men, Merkov flipped the card toward Ballan, who snatched it out of the air.

Becker's nose wrinkled at the sharp sting of ozone, and he thought, "Damn thing is going to blow up."

He thudded down, felt a hard cold surface, under his naked body. He opened his eyes and glanced around a dimly lit room. He lay on a polished wooden floor. Light slipped between the gaps of mini-Venetian blinds. Merkov lay next to him.

"Damn, Merkov, you're ugly naked," Becker said. He stood slowly, padded to the window, and looked out over the Willamette River. "We made it!" He turned from the window and stepped to a closet. It was filled with clothes. He began rummaging for something that would fit, pulling out running shoes, jeans, and a dark blue shirt. "Okay, the Chairman has the dirt on Ballan and Ballan has enough to break the Chairman. How safe are we?"

"The factions will fight for months and may even destroy the Corporation in the process. But they'll come after us long before that," Merkov said.

Becker smiled. "Nope, they'll come after Stokeland."

Becker pulled the Mercedes S-Class up to the ATM window and listened to the whisper of the rear window lowering. He turned and watched as Stokeland pulled his card from his shirt pocket. "I could have done this for you, sir."

"Letting you do more than drive was a reward. You took the weekend off without permission. From now on, you drive and that's it." Stokeland's voice was harsh, without warmth or compromise. He rammed the card into the slot and punched in his PIN. He entered a deposit amount, waited for the ready tone. As the ATM beeped, he sealed the deposit envelope he held and inserted in the slot.

To Becker, Stokeland seemed to be stalling, dragging out the moment. Got to keep my nerves in check, he thought, forcing himself to stop his nervous tapping on the steering wheel.

Selecting another transaction, Stokeland entered a withdrawal amount, took his money, and pulled his card.

Becker heard the voice, "Please suck in your shoulder blades."

He smiled at the flash of panic that showed on Stokeland's face. "For Dad," he said softly.

Becker remembered his own pull into the ATM as happening in slow motion, but Stokeland vanished in a pink and white flash. A steady flow of warm, translucent fat ran down the front of the ATM and pooled in a congealing mass as it hit the cold concrete. Becker's nose wrinkled at the stench as the stream turned brown.

Becker keyed a phone call. "They got him." He drove the S-Class to a house on the East Side. Merkov climbed into the passenger seat. "Now, the finale." Becker opened a laptop and connected to Stokeland's mainframe. Keystrokes triggered another set of software bombs, and he broke the connection. "The money's ours."

Becker pulled away from the curb. "Okay, we set up our cross-universe lab in Europe and hire researchers away from Cern. And we're never going near an ATM again."

WAIT UNTIL THE WAR IS OVER

Sarah A. Hoyt

Sarah A. Hoyt is the author of Ill Met By Moon-light, All Night Awake *and* Any Man So Daring, *an acclaimed trilogy which undertakes a fantasy recreation of Shakespeare's life. She's currently working on a time-travel/adventure novel for Baen books with Eric Flint. She has also sold over three dozen short stories, some of which have appeared in magazines like* Absolute Magnitude, Analog *and* Asimov's. *Sarah lives in Colorado with her hus-band, two sons and four cats.*

"And then the aliens came," my father said. He stood in his blue-and-white pajamas by the potted plant in the living room, watering can in hand, and he looked at me with his earnest, intent dark blue eyes.

I rushed forward and grabbed the watering can and sniffed it. As I'd thought, he'd filled it from the coffee maker in the kitchen. The plastic felt hot to the touch.

As I pulled it from his unresisting hands, he whispered softly, "Our lives were never the same again."

I set the watering can down. Coffee probably wouldn't have been any worse for the rubber tree than the chocolate milk in the cat's dish had been for the cat's digestion last week—leading to a couple of messes to clean up but perfectly survivable—but I wasn't about to find out.

I took Dad by the arm and led him up the stairs.

"The battle for Marstown," he said. "You should have been there. You were in the Academy still, of course. All those low flying warblers coming in at low-altitude, flaring their deep bombs and scaring the greenies . . ."

It sounded like gibberish. It probably was gibberish. The doctors to whom I'd started taking Dad about six months ago said that he had some form of dementia. I wasn't so sure. It was more as if he'd sulked permanently away from reality and into a more exciting world of his own creation—an amalgam of all the pulp science fiction tales he'd read in his youth.

I led Dad slowly up the stairs to the second floor of his house, his feet shuffling on the steps with hesitant, slow, small movements, as if the control of his legs were completely divorced from his brain and carried on with no more intent than an automatic process. I'd take a step up the stairs and wait until he sort of shuffled up, then take another.

And all the while, his voice went on, with all the liveliness missing from his brown-suede-slippered feet. "I thought it was going to be a total massacre. Particularly if they hit the underground habitat and it—"

I coaxed him up the final step and he followed, onto the long narrow hallway of the Victorian he and Mother had bought half a century ago. It had been old then. Now it was organic, a house that was part of people, and whose meandering rooms filled with the knickknacks and remnants of their life together resembled a living organism more than anything else.

Then down the hallway, shuffling step by shuffling step, while he shouted and commanded and instructed about greenies, warblers, glimmerers, zoomers and who knew what else. He was describing some sort of battle set, as far as I could tell, on Mars, and he seemed to be under the impression that he was some great hero, some commander, someone that future generations would care about.

"Historians will say that my decision to mine the deep-under habitat caused the loss of invaluable hydroponic cultures that could have prevented the near-famine of ninety-nine," he said, in a reasonable tone. "But you'll find that without it, we'd have lost humans, and humans must always be the measure of the universe."

While his voice carried on in this way, his body shuffled along in the hesitant steps a toddler might take along the hallway to the door to his room—next to my own childhood room. Which was good because that meant I could hear him when he decided to get up and do chores in the middle of the night, or—even worse—to go walking through the darkened streets while his unmoored mind flitted around some other universe.

He'd been like this since Mother died six months ago. Though, to be honest, it might have happened before, and Mother might simply never have said anything about it. In fact, she might not have noticed. She'd always considered Dad as somewhat of a child and a danger to himself, so taking sharp objects away from him and making sure

he didn't leave the house alone might have crept into
their routine so gradually that she'd never noticed.

But when I'd come for my mother's funeral, I'd found
Dad like this. And I hadn't been able to leave since.

I led him to his bed, turned back the roiled covers and
coaxed him into lying down, then covered him up. I
closed the curtain he had opened. Outside, the snow fell,
ever faster and thicker over the neighborhood of tall, narrow gingerbreads in which I'd grown up.

Looking out, I almost understood my dad, too. Where
were our flying cars, our rolling sidewalks, our space-
ships, our moon colonies? Here we were in the twenty-
first century, and it looked dismally like the nineteenth.

"Euridyce?" Dad said, from the bed.

He sounded so much like his old self, like the man
who held my hand and explained it all to me while the
moon rockets flew in our black-and-white TV, that I
turned around. "Yes?"

"Shouldn't you be going back to Colorado?" he asked.
"Don't you have a job to return to? You know you can't
take this long off just to nurse me."

Surprised by his sanity, I blinked. My job in Colorado, the accounting job that my boss said he'd hold for
me, might very well vanish in another month. I thought
of how much I loved the mountains, the sense of self-
sufficiency and freedom of the west. And I thought of
Glen, and my heart seized.

Glen was a redheaded giant computer programmer, the
companion of my hikes through the wild country. We'd
been going out together for a year, slowly ambling toward feelings that surpassed friendship.

I'd thought we were coming to an understanding, but
he hadn't called for the last month, and could I blame

him? I had disappeared into Rocktown in the wilds of Connecticut and never returned. I answered his calls but never called first.

He couldn't know that days spent chasing after Dad and keeping him away from sharp objects and from watering plants with rubbing alcohol or giving his life savings to the UPS delivery man left me too exhausted to think of anything else.

But now, for the first time in six months, my dad was speaking softly, and it wasn't about some space war. "I know you're worried about me, honey," he said. "But you have a . . . duty, you know?"

I got near the bed and put my hand on his hand, which rested on the covers. His hand was still as large and bluntly square-fingered as it had been in my childhood, but it felt papery and brittle like parchment against my own skin. The suggestion of strength had been replaced with something else—a dryness, as if he were fading from the inside out and becoming a shadow of himself.

"It's okay," I said. Perhaps he'd only gone distracted over Mom's death. They'd never been what you'd call a classically happy couple, but you could never judge these things from the outside. Perhaps he'd gone a little crazy and would be all right now. "Now that you're getting better I'll just stay a little longer. It won't hurt anything."

But he shook his head, a flurry of anxiety against the pillow, white hair flying this way and that. "It can hurt a lot, Euridyce. Think about it. If you're not there and I'm not there and they attack the moon colonies, they could have a complete victory. And find Earth defenseless. The troops won't know what to do without a Mayhem in command. "

"What—"

He pulled his hand out from under mine and patted my hand reassuringly. "Get you to Colorado and take the jumper to Tycho as soon as possible. Don't you worry about me. I've been laser-burned in battle before, and it will all come out all right. The Space Command will take good care of me."

I pulled my hand away, turned off his light and closed the door softly.

"Goodnight, Dad," I said, just as the phone started ringing down in the living room.

The only phone in the house was in the living room and sturdily wired to the wall. For reasons known only to her, mother disapproved of wireless phones, cable TV, and microwaves. And I'd thought I'd only stay on a little while after her death. I hadn't bothered bringing the conveniences of life with me. Nor had I had much time for shopping.

However, running and slipping along the wooden living room floor, trying to reach the phone before the person on the other side gave up, I promised myself I was going to buy a wireless phone if it was the last thing I did. Or remember to charge my cell phone, no matter how many times my dad watered the cat or fed kibble to the rubber plant tomorrow.

I grabbed the phone mid plaintive ring and panted "Hello," into the receiver.

For a moment there was no answer, and I thought I'd got it too late; then Glen's voice said, "Dicey?"

"Yes." It was probably a revolting nickname, but it was okay because *he* called me that. "Yes."

He hesitated and cleared his throat, and my heart thumped so loud and fast I thought I wouldn't be able to hear anything, anyway. He was going to tell me he was seeing someone else. He was going to tell me I'd stayed away too long—

"Er," he said. "Dicey . . ."

"Yes," I said again. I thought I heard a door close upstairs, but though I strained to hear anything else, nothing came. I was just imagining my dad was leaving his room. I was hoping my dad would stage one of his aimless escapes so that I didn't have to stand here and hear the bad news.

"I've been thinking," he said.

"Yes?" Was that a step on the stairs?

"Will you . . . I mean . . . I know you're looking after your father, but maybe if we can put him in a home near us. I mean, there's some good—"

Near us? What did he mean?

"Dicey, what I want to ask is, would you consider coming back and marrying me?"

"I . . ." I said and thought that I couldn't. I couldn't leave Dad alone for long enough to even arrange a wedding. And a home . . . what if we put Dad in a home and it turned out to be one of those nightmare places where they abused old people? I could never live with myself.

The truth was, I'd be worrying about Dad all the time. My marriage would wilt before it even began.

Still . . . being married to Glen. Just the thought of being with him all the time, of being loved and cherished, of not being alone with my fears for my dad and an insane load of work.

I wanted to accept. But it was impossible. We should wait until my father was a little more stable. We should . . .

The metal on metal noise of the back-door latch being

opened, then the sound of the screen door slamming echoed in the silent house. A rush of cold, cold air streamed from the door between the kitchen and the living room.

"Oh, Lord," I said.

"Dicey?"

"Dad has gone out," I said. "I have to go." Slamming the phone down, I ran through the kitchen, past the dinner dishes stacked on the counter. I opened the screen door and ran out, hearing it swing closed behind me.

Outside, the snow was coming down fast and blinding and the cold stung through my flannel shirt and my jeans. The indoor moccasins on my feet were, fortunately, fur lined.

I listened for the sound of Dad's shuffling steps, but all I could hear was the dead silence of a snow storm—the snow absorbing all sounds and giving back only the loudest.

"Dad?" I called, half hoping he would answer me. Not sure why, because he never had before. When he was on one of his walks around the neighborhood, he was more lost than ever in the world of the mind. "Dad?"

Nothing. From a few streets away came the muffled sound of a car horn.

I looked down and thought I saw, on the glimmering fresh snow, the faint track of shuffling feet fast being erased by the piling on of new flakes. I started following it, hesitantly.

The cold stung on my ears. I folded my arms on my chest and tucked my vulnerable hands under my arms. My nose dripped with cold. "Dad?"

Nothing. The traces on the snow were very faint indeed, and they could easily be the track of some animal that had passed through here hours ago.

I strained to hear, but there was nothing. The snow clung to my long chestnut-brown hair, soaking through it to wet my scalp.

The door. I'd left the door open and only the screen door on. The neighborhood was safe, but still . . . The cold would stress the heating system. I might end up with frozen pipes.

I should go back. I should go back and call nine one one and let someone else find Dad in this white, blinding maze.

But if I did, the traces of his shuffling—if they were that—would surely be gone. And then what? Dad could freeze to death out here, alone, in the cold, and no one would know.

He hadn't been the best of fathers. Too restless to hold any real job after he'd left the Air Force, too much of a dreamer for any of his investment schemes to pay off. And I often thought he and Mother had been too involved with each other to even notice I existed.

But Dad had been the one who read books to me, and talked to me about the bright future of flying cars and moving sidewalks and interstellar colonies that awaited my generation.

He'd taught me to believe in a better future, and even if his dreams hadn't come to pass, I couldn't quite forget them.

"Dad?" A shuffling sound, just ahead. "Dad?" I stretched my hand.

There was a flare ahead, a multicolored flare—bright red and green light fading away to tones of violet and glaring yellow. A hand grabbed my hand. Not Dad's hand. A strong, young hand with supple skin.

It enveloped mine, and another hand reached for my arm, and then it pulled me, and I fell to the soft snow with a heavy, warm male body on top of me.

"Keep down, keep down, keep down," he shouted and, all the while, his body covered mine. "They're warbling Rocktown. The command shields are flaring, but zoomers still might get through."

The voice was familiar—Glen's voice?—and the hands were strong, and around us lights were changing color and there was a soft, never ending pop pop pop pop, and things—like little pebbles—zoomed by my face, leaving a trail of incandescent heat.

Then it all stopped, and it was just white snow falling, and silence all around, and I was being hauled to my feet like an ill-stuffed potato sack, and Glen's voice was saying, "Lady, don't you know a hush-down alert when you hear one? What did you think the white-out was for? What are you doing out of the shelter?"

And then he looked at me—in the insufficient light at the heart of the snow storm—and his green eyes widened further, and his mouth opened a little and he said, "Dicey! I thought you were in Tycho."

My heart was beating near my mouth, the proximity of him, the scent of him—sweat and soap and cologne— felt like coming home after the six months apart. I'd never thought we'd meet again and I'd thought—

I reached for him and touched his sleeve, which felt odd and oddly warm, as if his bright blue cling-on shirt were made of living tissue. And then I realized he was wearing very odd clothes indeed—a bright blue shirt and bright blue pants, all of it clinging to his body and mold-

WAIT UNTIL THE WAR IS OVER

ing every muscle from his broad shoulders to his narrow hips, and the long legs beneath. A sort of collar around his neck held what could only be described as a military insignia—if military insignias were little rockets topped with a row of stars.

Still, he looked exactly like himself with that ruddy tan that pale people acquire when they're outdoors a lot, and the square chin and the too-open-to-be-handsome bright green eyes.

He looked like the Colorado boy he'd been in his childhood, like the mountain town man he'd grown up into.

All of it at odds with the science fiction-movie getup.

I opened my mouth to ask about the costume and why he hadn't told me, on the phone, that he was in the neighborhood, but he grabbed me and enveloped me, totally, in his muscular arms. "Dicey, damn it, Dicey, I thought you were in Tycho. I thought you were dead."

"Tycho?" I asked, blinking puzzledly at him, and thinking that Dad had said something about Tycho.

"Tycho Under. It was warbled by the greenies. An hour ago? Don't you know? Weren't you plugged in?"

He looked at me and ran his hands over my head, as if expecting to feel something. "Where's your halo?" he asked. "And why are you out of uniform? Were you on injured leave? Why didn't you tell me?"

I shook my head. Something was wrong with me. I had started sharing Dad's illusions. "I . . ." I said. "I was looking after Dad. I was—"

Glen nodded. "Commander Absalom Mayhem. None of this would have happened if he'd been at Tycho." He nodded. "If we'd had a Mayhem in command . . ."

His voice trailed off. He shook his head. "No matter.

You couldn't have known. At least you came out at the hush-down call." He grinned, his mischievous grin. "Even if without your uniform or halo. Still, I'm glad you're ready to resume duty. Let's galoomph."

I looked blankly up at him. He stared down at me and nodded, as if understanding my expression. "No galoomph boots? No prob. I've got the belt."

And before I knew what he was doing, he put the belt around my waist and attached it to his and then started . . . jumping. Only jumping seemed like a strange word to describe taking block-long leaps and falling gently onto the snow. But now, it couldn't be snow, could it?

I had stopped feeling cold after Glen showed up. And the stuff falling around us had a dry, papery texture, like shredded Styrofoam. It crunched underfoot like crushed walnuts each time we landed. And during the jump itself, there was a Gaaaaa-loooooom-phhhhh sound.

"I hate galoomphing in white-out," Glen said. "Fortunately, I have the halo guide on."

I had absolutely no idea what he was talking about and wished he'd go back to greenies. At least I could understand that.

As it was, I could do no more than allow myself to go along, limply, as he—ah—galoomphed for what seemed like half a mile.

It was a dream. It had to be a dream. But my dreams had never been this vivid. I could smell Glen and feel his muscles against mine, as the belt pulled us together.

He was here. Or I was here. I'd swear to it.

Real.

And then we emerged from the white-out. The fake snow receded. And there was . . .

My mouth dropped open and I swallowed, convulsively. That was it. Dad's hallucinations were definitely catching, and I'd caught them.

Ahead of me was the future. At least the future as it was going to be circa nineteen-thirty—brightly colored domes and towers erected cheek to jowl and seemingly with no pattern. Around them wound even brighter colored . . . they looked like plastic car tracks, of the sort that bent into improbable configurations. Along the tracks, people slid. Or rather people stood on the tracks and seemed to slid along. The people closer to us, those I could see well enough, wore clothing that looked much like Glen's but which ran to stranger colors, like bright purple and glaring pink. And there was a shine around their heads and, as I looked at Glen, I saw the same shine around his. Was that the halo he'd talked about? And what did it do?

"Well get you into Command," he said. "And get you haloed in. That white-out there was the first attack on Earth in fifty years. I think the shields held. At least the halo says so. But you know the next hit will be harder. I'm just glad both you and your father are here."

He undid the belt around my middle. We were standing at a door—a round door—to a building. It irised open as we walked forward. There were a lot of people dressed like Glen, though some wore red uniforms and some had silver emblems on their collars.

Inside the building, it looked as though the walls had been poured of glass—all gleaming fluid curves in colors as vivid as the clothes—pink, purple, yellow, lime green and electric blue.

They saluted each other according to some protocol I couldn't fathom. And they all saluted me. We floated up a central open space that Glen called an antigrav well, up to a third floor railing, where he reached and hauled himself into a platform. I followed.

We were in some sort of command center, and Dad stood there—in a red uniform with a collar bearing a spaceship and ten stars—on a little platform, talking to people. Haranguing them.

I understood very little of what he was saying. Something about Tycho Under being gone and no defenses remaining between the greenies and Earth. How it was up to us to keep the home of humanity safe. How it was time to show the greenies they couldn't wipe humanity out. We weren't ready to go. We'd never be ready to go.

It had the sound of a brave speech and a desperate speech. But the thing is, Dad sounded as he would have at his most persuasive. He was the commander, and with him in command, things just might be all right.

Father had found the vocation that had eluded him in the life I remembered. He was respected and obeyed.

He paused in his speech and looked at me, "Ah, Euridyce. Glad you joined us. And Captain Glen Braxladen, of course. The greenies will return. They'll be better armed, ready to penetrate our shields. This time people must defend the world. I'm glad we have our best fighters here. We need all of them."

I wanted to say I had no idea what they were talking about, but somehow I couldn't. The room was packed with uniformed men and women and they were all looking at Dad and then at me, as if they believed him some sort of Messiah and had almost equal faith in my abilities.

Glen led me to a room where the door irised open and he said, "Get suited up and haloed in. I don't think we have much time and I'd like to . . . Remember what I asked last time I haloed you in Tycho? I'd like to do it now, if you don't mind. I'll mention it to your father. Just get suited up, and let's see if we have time before we take off."

I wanted to ask enough time for what, but his eyes had gone all serious. He leaned in and kissed me. "Just in case, you know . . ." he said.

His lips were warm against mine, his mouth hungry, his tongue probing.

I nodded, dazed by his kiss and not sure what he meant. Inside the room, which was small and oval, the white walls gave the impression of having been poured out of some glassy material. There was a red suit hanging.

I put it on. It fit perfectly. On the hook, where the suit had been, there was what looked like a very fine, metallic circle. Something that might have been made of piano wire. The halo. Obviously.

I set it on my head, wondering if there was something else I should be doing.

There was warmth. I could tell it was glowing.

And then . . . Oh, it wasn't that I remembered. I mean, this world still didn't make any sense to me. I still didn't know how I'd got here and thought it all too likely that Dad had some sort of contagious madness.

But with the halo on, I found facts being fed to my puzzlement, my questions being answered before they were asked.

It was all still madness. I was still sure I was hallucinating. But this hallucination had footnotes.

Greenies were insect-like aliens. They'd come just after we'd got to the moon. At first, they'd almost exterminated us. But we'd got their technology and reverse-engineered it.

We had moon colonies and rolling sidewalks and ships and. . . .

And Dad's heart murmur, which had precluded his ever joining the space program in the world I remembered all too clearly, had been fixed here. The aliens had brought in biotechnology that helped the regeneration of defective organs.

The price of all that advancement had been a war of extermination waged on us.

Dad had been one of the first astronauts. He'd become the chief commander of the troops when the aliens had attacked Marstown, our first Martian colony. He had achieved a resounding victory against superior numbers and become a legend in his own time.

I walked out of the dressing room, in a daze. A beautiful redheaded woman smiled at me, didn't salute. She too wore a red uniform.

The halo told me she was commander Hazel Stone. She'd been my roommate in the Space Academy, where I'd learned to pilot flitters and command flitter detachments.

Her husband was . . . Robert? I could not remember. I remembered they had twin sons, though, and I smiled at her, in as friendly a way as I could manage, considering I had no real memory of our friendship.

"Don't worry," she said. "My wedding was a five-month nightmare of preparation followed by a hellish three-day whirlwind. This will be quick and easy. You'll survive." Her face clouded momentarily. "At least, I hope you will. The greenies are returning in force, they say. We don't have much time for personal business before they get here."

The halo informed me that the greeny battle squadrons had encircled Earth, that they'd destroyed the other solar system colonies, that the grimmest phase of the war was about to begin.

Meanwhile, Hazel escorted me into a small room that had . . . Dad, standing at the front and on either side, forming an isle down the center, a group of people—men and women—in uniforms that my halo identified as friends, acquaintances and my subordinates.

Glen was up front, looking nervous. He turned as I came in, with Hazel by my side and gave me a wan smile.

This looked like a wedding. Were we—?

As I got up front, Glen took my hands. "Thank you for agreeing to do this. I know we'd agreed to wait until the war was over, but what if it never is?"

The ceremony was brief and utilitarian. Halfway through it, my halo started screaming, "Greeny ships flying toward Peace City. White-out called in New York. White-out Denver Outbound Spaceport. White-out Cape Canaveral. White-out in Rio. White-out Milan. White-out Paris. White-out Venice. White-out—"

Through it, I heard Dad's words, "Take this man to be your lawfully wedded husband, to love and honor and—"

When he stopped talking I said, "I do."

Glen took me in his arms. The halo was going crazy, its voice-thought overrunning my own thoughts.

And over it all Dad said, "To those who say it is foolhardy of them to marry just before the great battles, I say we all get married before the great battles. If humanity waited until the war was over there would be no humanity. Go forth and multiply and—" his voice subsided for a moment under the halo's mind screams that New York was being warbled and came back again, full force, "wipe the bastards from the galaxy."

And then we were running, Glen and I side by side, and the halo let me know which ship to take, and I jumped in.

Suddenly there were memories. Or at least, not memories, but the ship felt familiar. The vaguely ozony smell inside it, the fit of the seat, like a living thing wrapping around me. The ship felt like something I'd known and loved a long time.

It was a one-person ship, shaped roughly like a kidney bean and bright yellow.

It closed around me. The seat . . . hugged me in a tight, cushiony embrace.

Before I could even look for a button or lever, it took off. Very fast. Other ships zoomed around me. My stomach flew to my mouth.

I swallowed.

My eyes closed in an involuntary flinch.

When they opened again, I was in space or at least somewhere dark and deep like rich black velvet pinpointed with flickering fireflies.

Around me, here and there, like colored marbles scattered on a black pavement, other ships ranged. I wished I knew which one was Father's, which was Glen's.

The halo started to transmit something about Glen's ship, but suddenly the enemy showed up.

Their ships were gray, circular, and flat, like coins or saw blades.

They didn't so much look evil as inhuman. Something about them proclaimed that no ape hands had fashioned it, no humanoid brain had designed it.

This was why the greenies wanted us gone. We were just as alien to them—as filled with otherness. As evil.

One of the ships made straight for me and flared. I saw a ray of light fly toward me.

I couldn't find any controls, and the halo started saying it was all mentally controlled, through the halo, which was connected to a series of computers, which controlled all of—

I wished myself sideways. The ship flipped.

Light flew by.

Another enemy ship approached, flaring at me.

And another.

I thought up, down, sideways, tilt and jump.

My ship danced and skipped like a skittish gymnast.

Around me, vaguely glimpsed other ships flared and fired laser beams. Our ships or theirs. I couldn't tell.

I hoped Glen was all right and heard his voice in my head, "Fire at them, Dicey. You can't just wait till they're all around you. Fire now. Don't try to be a hero."

I wasn't trying to be a hero. I didn't know how to fire.

But if I didn't, they'd mass around me. And if they massed around me, they'd go past to bomb Rocktown.

If they bombed Rocktown, they'd get the Space Command.

Earth's defenses would be headless.

Saw-blade ships surrounded me on all sides, and I skipped and jumped and—

I had to *kill*. Now, now, now.

I heard a hiss, and then a brightly burning laser shot out from the front of my ship. It exploded in all directions, slicing the gray disks in two.

And then they exploded, in a dazzle of blue.

And I felt cold.

* * *

"Losing her——" a stranger's voice.

"Quick graft, quick——"

"The bio regen——"

"Why didn't she shield?" Glen's voice, with a hint of desperation. His hand in mine. "So many ships. She had to know that the radiation——"

"She didn't have time to think," Dad's voice said. "In the excitement of battle it is possible——"

The sounds were fading, fading, going away.

And I was cold.

I was in the middle of the snow, and there was a shuffling of feet ahead, and Dad's voice saying, "We stopped the greenies. They didn't even warble New York. Euridyce is a hero. She'll survive. She'll be all right."

My dream? His dream? Or some reality beyond dreams?

"Dad," I yelled and ran to him and put my arms around him, tightly. He was cold, but warmer than the snow.

I grabbed his arm and started leading him back, while he told me about the successful battle, and in my mind there was a feeling of being elsewhere, of being at the same time in the other world, with the warblers and the zoomers, the sliding sidewalks and the attacking greenies.

If the price for the future was a vicious enemy trying to exterminate mankind, perhaps it was best we'd stopped going to the moon. Perhaps it was best the twenty-first century looked like the nineteenth.

But part of me didn't really believe it. Part of me thought it was more likely this world was an illusion, and the world out there, with the greenies, was the real one.

Perhaps the greenies were spinning these lies into our brain.

Or perhaps both worlds were real, and Father's mind had become unmoored and perceived the wrong one at the wrong time.

I got Dad into the house, anyway. I took him up to his room, covered him up.

In both worlds, Father and I were fighting a war. Even the bright, glimmering future that had been the past's dream had its price, and the price might be the end of mankind.

In this world . . .

I needed to go back to the living room and call Glen back and accept his proposal before he thought better of it. Yes, Dad still needed my care. We'd need to put Dad in a home. Money would be tight. I'd worry.

But if humanity waited till the war was over, there would be no humanity.

On the bed, Dad was speaking to himself. He was issuing orders for a counterattack.

I paused at the door to his room. "Give them hell, Dad," I said.

For a brief moment, he looked at me, and his face was the face of the man in my—dream? Hallucination?

He smiled. "Oh, I will."

I turned off the light.

THE DOORWAY IN STEPHENSONS STORE

Peter Crowther

Author, poet, editor, critic/essayist and now, with the multiple award-winning PS imprint, publisher, Peter Crowther has produced 19 anthologies, more than 100 short stories and novellas (many of which have been collected into five volumes: The Longest Single Note, Lonesome Roads, Cold Comforts, Songs of Leaving *and* Dark Times*), plus* Escardy Gap, *a novel written in collaboration with James Lovegrove. Two of his stories have been adapted for British TV. He is currently working on the second volume of his SF/Horror novella cycle* Forever Twilight, *plus a mainstream novel, a collaborative short novel (with Tim Lebbon), a couple of anthologies and another TV project plus more short stories.*

One

In his mirror, Jeff Mennark watched the plume of dust travel out behind the Oldsmobile and swirl across the deserted blacktop.

"Can't we stop yet?" Lorraine moaned from the back seat, the sound of the flat of her hand slapping the window serving as an exclamation mark after the question.

"Soon." When he spoke—which was infrequently these days, here in the arid desert of the dog days in the couple's eighteenth year of marriage—his voice was matter-of-fact and bereft of emotion. The consummate news anchor passing on details of multiple vehicle smashes on an iced-up Interstate.

Lorraine shifted around on the seat and started messing with the ashtray in the central panel.

"D'you have a good sleep?"

"I haven't *been* asleep," Lorraine snapped.

"Oh."

"What does that mean? *'Oh'?*"

"Oh'? It means 'Oh.' It means, 'I didn't realize you had not been asleep.'"

"And why is that? Why would you not realize that?"

"Your breathing."

Lorraine flounced into an upright position on the back seat and straightened her hair. "That's a problem to you? The fact that I'm breathing? Like, I don't breathe when I'm asleep? Jesus Chri—"

"Not 'you *are* breathing' but '*your* breathing'—the breathing that is yours."

"What about it?"

"It was noisy."

"Noisy? What the hell does 'noisy' mean?"

"Loud. Make that loud. Not noisy. Never noisy."

There was silence for a few seconds, and then Lorraine said, in a quiet voice, "I was thinking."

"Pardon me?"

"I was *thinking*," she repeated with a snap, adding "asshole" more softly.

Jeff let out a sharp snort. "Well, we'll all sleep a little easier *this* night," he said. "Lorraine has been thinking. Chee!"

Lorraine shook her head and looked out of the window. Outside, more fields went by.

"I take it you do have an idea," Lorraine said, adding, after a brief pause, "You know . . . an idea *where* we're going. Don't you?"

Jeff sighed. "Well, according to the map book the last time I looked, we're heading for Forest Plains."

"You read the map book while you were driving?"

"I glanced at it when we hit a traffic signal a few miles back. It's on the seat here, right alongside me."

"And where and what the hell is Forest Plains?"

She saw Jeff's shoulders shrug once and then he said, "It's bigger than a bend in the road and smaller than a town. We'll get gas there, something to eat maybe, take a look around. Stretch our legs."

Lorraine grunted. "I need a restroom."

"We can do that, too."

Lorraine couldn't resist sneering. "And all in the busy metropolis of Forest Plains?"

Jeff nodded.

"Why Forest goddam Plains?"

He shrugged and shuffled back in his seat. "I like the name."

"As good a reason as any, I guess," Lorraine said tiredly.

"Better than most," Jeff said.

Two

They had been staying in a motel in a little coastal Maine town called Wells, a good hour's drive from Boston where, fresh from Manhattan (if anyone ever was fresh from Manhattan), they had spent a few days sightseeing and trying to forget things back home . . . which was just another way of looking anyplace but at each other and of indulging in vitriolic and sometimes hysterical exchanges of blame and recrimination.

The fact was that things back home were not so good for the Mennarks, hadn't been good for them for days and weeks and months and years. In fact, if you asked either one of them, they would say that things hadn't ever been good, and they'd say that with a snort and a scowl and maybe an icy look in the direction of the other one. But the truth was a little different from the headlines in the paper, as the truth usually is.

Things *had* been good at the start, which was in the summer of '81 when Jeff, fresh-faced from business school in New York City and looking for a career, had instead found Lorraine Larruto, a dark-haired beauty who reminded him of Lori Lemaris, the comic book mermaid who occasionally vied with Lois Lane and Lana Lang for the affections of Superman. Lorraine had been sitting in the park eating a pastrami sandwich and throwing pieces of bread to the birds and the squirrels. Her bench was a little oasis of peace and tranquility, while all around them the great city of Manhattan shifted and scratched itself, never truly comfortable and always on the move. When he saw her, it was like magic—in fact, it really *was* like magic. He had been walking along, lost in a comicbook, when he thought he had heard thunder . . . and when he looked up to see what the noise was, he had seen Lorraine. Even better for Jeff was the fact that, when he stopped to talk with her—

did you hear that?

Yeah . . . sounded like thunder

yeah

sky's clear though

yeah . . .

—he discovered that Lorraine had the double-L handle, which he took to be a divine sign sent to him from Comic book Valhalla. But that was Jeff all over—comic books and, to an extent, old magazines and paperback books. But it was the comics that took pride of place.

Comic books were Jeff's life, his reason for getting out of bed in the morning and—increasingly, this past few years—a reason to get back into it at night, when he would curl up and read and reread the adventures of his favorite characters, particularly the stories from the so-called Golden and Silver Ages, when reality had not yet come to play such a large role in the funny pages. After all, who needed reality in a comic book! Jeff could get all the reality he needed out on the street, dodging the muggers and the addicts, and the wide-eyed whackos who shouted profanities in the park and the subway stations, and the cab drivers and the reality TV shows and even the fiction shows of hospital emergency rooms and precinct houses, which seemed to delight in cutaway shots of festering wounds, profound pain and brutalized dead bodies.

Life sucked, and Jeff set out right at the start to give it

as wide a berth as possible. It was probably for this very reason that he avoided regular work—no nine-to-six job for Jeff, no suit and shirt and tie, no neat hairstyle, no having to be polite. In short, no joining the rat race. No *conforming*.

Thus a series of part-time jobs had ensued, all of them simply a means for Jeff to pull in enough money for his rent—the middle floor of an old brownstone on the perimeter of the Village—his smokes, the occasional Michelob or Bud, a once-in-a-blue-moon record album, a few books and, most of all, the four-color fixes he received from reading the funny pages. Sometimes ones he had bought for himself and sometimes for reselling.

It was Lorraine who came up with the idea for Jeff's business, when another job bit the dust and he was faced with scrimping and scraping to make ends meet until something else came along. He was sitting at the old table in the apartment's small kitchenette, with Lorraine cooking pasta and watching a *Twilight Zone* rerun on their small TV set, poring over a catalog listing and shaking his head. It was then that Lorraine turned—with the old *TZ* theme in the background—and suggested he should turn his love of the comic books and magazines and those gaudy good-girl-art Dell mapbacks and Pocket Books into a business.

Well, after a shaky start that saw Jeff borrow money from the bank to set himself up, things went well for a while—Jeff producing fliers and asking for want lists and then filling out the lists by shopping around, buying wisely and ensuring that his mark-ups were always reasonable.

But then came the dawn of the Internet, the ghost in the ether, and, following hot on the heels of that, the

Comic Book Grading Certification scheme and abe-books.com. Suddenly everyone knew where to pick up that elusive Gold Medal paperback original in whatever condition they fancied, and they knew sure as shooting how much the comics were worth . . . resulting in the Overstreet guide—tried and trusted for fifteen years—going out of the window, with key books in nice condition changing hands at high multiples of guide. Soon after that, it was not-so-key books. And then—looking back, it seemed like it happened overnight—the bottom fell right out of the whole thing, with the value of restored books taking a nose-dive. And as it turned out, Jeff had just paid a little over twenty-eight thousand dollars—another loan—for a collection of key DC books from the 1950s that turned out to be restored items when the CGC crew sent the books back in their protective plastic slabs. The estimated retail value fell like a stone, far below what Jeff had paid for them. And even at cut-down prices, he couldn't shift the books. He was considering breaking the slabs open and trying to sell them as though they had not been graded when the letter from the IRS appeared in the mailbox.

"Well, we know where at least one fucking weapon of mass destruction is," Jeff whined loudly, waving the letter in front of Lorraine. "It's goddam right fucking here."

The gist of the terse note was that the IRS was hitting on him for an inspection—"some anomaly Mister Mennark, that's all I can tell you at this stage," was all a hard-voiced woman by the name of Muzz (that was the way she announced herself) Batdorf was prepared to tell Jeff when he called them for clarification. *Yeah, eat shit and die*, Jeff thought. And even as he was thinking it, replacing the receiver, the phone rang, and, just for a second, he wondered if it would be Muzz Batdorf calling back to tell him all IRS personnel could read minds as well . . . and would he mind coming in for a meeting right away. But it was only—"only" . . . hah!—Jackie from the repair shop over on Bleecker calling to say there was a major problem with the Olds. Shortly after that, with Jeff still dazed, Lorraine came in in tears because some guy had lifted her purse out on the street. She didn't have much money in there—twenty-five, maybe thirty dollars and change—but it was just a bridge too far for Jeff.

"Didn't you try stop him?" Jeff asked.

"He told me not to be a fucking hero," Lorraine gasped breathlessly. " 'It's only fuckin' money, lady!' " she added, affecting the gruff patois of the street.

Jeff stared at Lorraine wide-eyed. "I have got to get the fuck away from all this," he announced to her, in a soft and calm voice that made her more apprehensive than if he had screamed it out while opening the window to take a dive out onto the street.

She nodded. "Where to?" she said.

Jeff glanced around the apartment for inspiration, scanning the walls and the chair arms and the table littered with papers and little piles of comicbooks. At one side, sporting a Waldenbooks bookmark, was Stephen King's *The Girl Who Loved Tom Gordon*, which Lorraine was in the middle of reading. "New England," he said

"New England?"

Jeff shrugged. "Maine, I think."

"Anywhere in particular?"

"Some little town off the beaten map, one of those Rockwell *Saturday Evening Post*-cover, picket fence communities where the whole town sings hymns on a Sunday and the kids spend their summer vacations fish-ing for catfish or swinging from tires fastened to old oak trees with ancient rope."

"And sit outside on porch chairs listening the radio and watching the shooting stars," Lorraine said.

"All of that."

"Are you okay?" Lorraine asked.

And Jeff smiled at her, a real tired smile . . . the first sign of softness that had passed between them for many years. "Not really."

And so, on an overcast August morning that was more fall than summer, they set off from Manhattan in the Olds—whose return to the fold had hit Jeff's MasterCard with seven hundred dollars and change—heading north-ward, away from the city and the bills and the car-horns . . . the idea being to soak up some rays, eat some burgers, read some books and hit the surf. But then Jeff told Lorraine she should keep an eye on him out there be-cause, ". . . the way I feel right now, I just may keep on swimming until I get too tired."

Not quite the saddest thing about that statement was that Jeff wasn't entirely joking. The actual saddest thing was that, so long as she knew where the keys to the Olds were, Lorraine couldn't give a damn what the hell Jeff did.

Three

Nobody ever really knows when a relationship begins to fail.

It's not like, one minute it's okay and the next minute it's gone. It's a gradual thing, like a tree growing from an acorn or a mountain getting whittled down by the wind and the rain, or the formation of stalactites and stalagmites. A relationship going bad is like that—it happens so slowly that the two parties don't see it souring. But sour it does.

And sour Jeff's and Lorraine's relationship had done. In spades.

So the storm clouds gathering around them during the summer break (it was hardly a vacation, a time of relaxation and catching breath) had not only been in the sky above the Atlantic coast . . . just as the icy chill that lay between Jeff and Lorraine was not merely the consequence of meteorological developments. Indeed, in the Olds, heading out of Wells into the Maine hinterland, the heater did little to lift the temperature.

In the few days leading up to their hitting the road, Jeff had visited every old bookstore in the area and failed to pick up much of anything except for a few old *Posts*—two with Rockwell covers and in pretty nice shape—and a handful of Ace Doubles, including Dick's *The Man Who Japed*, in near mint condition. But even those, at reasonable prices (seeing as how they had cost Jeff only a few bucks apiece), would take an age to get rid of. The problem was that collectors and enthusiasts could get pretty much everything they needed on the net, and then there was eBay—in Jeff's opinion, a glorified yard sale visited by people wanting to pick up top quality items for nothing.

One more morning of getting out of bed to face the slate-gray sky and an increasingly similar-colored face on her husband had been too much for Lorraine.

"I've had it with freezing my buns off on the beach and then spending hours searching goddamn bookshelves before we sit down at a Jolly Whaler or a KFC for dinner," she announced over cartoons and breakfast cereal. "How's about we go for a drive?"

"Where to?" asked Jeff.

Lorraine shrugged. "Just someplace *different*." She imbued the word "different" with a sense of magic, and, just for a second, Jeff looked at her as though he were almost making out something or someone other than his wife . . . but then the moment disappeared.

"Sounds okay with me," Jeff said. One glance out of the window had pretty much made up his mind for him, and, of course, there was always the possibility of happening on a good-stuff bookstore in this different and magical someplace.

And so it was that, a little before 9:30 on an overcast and drizzly Thursday morning, the sky above them a deep battleship gray, the pair set out from the Wells motel and headed inland and upstate.

Looking for someplace different.

Looking for magic.

Four

It seemed as though hours had gone by since they had started out—so long, in fact, that Lorraine had had Jeff pull over so she could stretch out in the back seat, catch a bit of shuteye.

Neither of them was sleeping well at night, falling off fine-and-dandy at about eleven or eleven-thirty and then waking up at two or three am, padding to the bathroom for a pee before returning to the bed and listening to the other's fitful breathing.

In addition to pulling over to allow Lorraine's seat change, Jeff had already stopped twice: once for gas and rest rooms, and once again for coffee and donuts from a roadside stand that boasted a smoking chimney.

The land outside the car seemed to have graduated back from the barren wildernesses they had been passing to something approaching civilization. Houses—more resembling shacks—were now going by on either side of the two-lane blacktop, along with occasional cemeteries, roadside stands selling vegetables and flowers, with sheets of see-through tarpaulin pulled across them to protect the produce, and restaurants and fast food outlets by the dozen, pretty much all of them seeming to specialize in crab and mako shark . . . each sign emblazoned with the word "fresh," so they were clearly still in reasonable proximity to the sea. But no bookstores.

Every now and again a tow-headed kid or two—boys usually—stopped on their bikes and watched the car speed by, one foot on the ground, grubby hands wrapped around rubber grips, their heads following the car. Way behind them, sometimes plopped in the middle of manicured lawns and sometimes set back a way and surrounded by trees and bushes, wood-framed houses stood silent in the midmorning rain.

"Jeez," Lorraine, now fully awake, said as they passed by three such kids on bikes, her voice soft, as if she didn't want anyone to hear, neither the tow-headed boys nor the silent houses, "it's like a well-moneyed Mississippi. The only thing that's different is the kids are white, the house paint isn't peeling off, and there are no old Dodges blocked up in the front yards."

Jeff glanced up at the mirror and watched the boys watching the car—watching *him*. "Yeah, it's like we're intruding on their world," he said. "Like they never seen a car before, driving by like this."

"Maybe they just know all the usual cars," Lorraine said. "Can't be many folks heading out from the coast to Forest goddam Plains."

"Hey," Jeff said perkily, pointing at the windshield. "We got a result!"

The sign by the side of the road read:

FOREST PLAINS
11 MILES
DRIVE SAFELY

"Be still my heart," Lorraine grunted.

The car engine gave a little cough as though to agree.

Jeff glanced in the mirror. "Okay back there?" he said, raising his voice.

Lorraine said, "Yeah."

There was another cough and then a dull clunking sound from the engine.

"Jesus Christ," Jeff said. "What the hell was that?"

Now a thudding noise sounded out from the engine compartment and Jeff could feel power fading from the gas pedal. The car started juddering forward in short bursts.

"That doesn't sound good does it?"

"Fucking mechanics," was all Jeff could say.

He turned to Lorraine and said, "You bring your cell phone?"

Lorraine shook her head. "But you got yours in the side pocket there. I saw it just—"

"It's dead. I meant to take it into the motel to charge it up but I forgot."

Lorraine faced forward and stared out onto the blacktop and the steady rain that bounced down. There were no buildings to be seen anywhere.

Jeff checked the dials—plenty of gas, temperature okay . . . so what the hell was wrong with the damn car. He visualised himself marching into the Bleecker repair shop carrying a wrench, saw Jackie look up from some Chevy's hood, black grease all over his hands and painted in stripes on his face like an Indian . . . saw him start to back away as Jeff swung the—

The car clunked once and then again, this time making a sound as though something were trapped in there, being caught up in the fan belt or something, getting twisted and turned around, batting itself against the underside of the hood.

"That does not sound good," Lorraine said in a low voice.

"You said that already."

"So? I'm just confirming my initial diagnosis."

"Thank you."

A handwritten sign appeared just over the top of a slight hill.

Stephensons General Store
Stop in and see us
for all your needs, yesterday and today

"I cannot believe your luck," Lorraine said without humor.

Jeff looked in the mirror and his eyes met Lorraine's. For a second he wanted to snap something right back at her, some smartass remark—

well, even my luck couldn't be so bad forever

—but, seeing Lorraine's tuft of hair stuck up like a

feather from the way she had been sleeping, he didn't want to do that. He looked away without saying anything, his eyes catching just a flicker of a frown from hers. As though she knew what he'd been thinking and was wondering why she had been so spared.

"Don't you just hate that?" Jeff said.

"What?"

"No apostrophe."

"No apostrophe?" Lorraine looked puzzled at him.

"Stephensons. No apostrophe."

"Oh. Yeah. My day is ruined."

Jeff looked out of the side window as they turned off the road and, in spite of his melancholy mood, let out a little laugh. "Boy, that's quite a sight."

And it was.

Stephensons-without-an-apostrophe General Store stood back from the road about a hundred yards on the left. It looked like something out of the old *Waltons* TV show—a couple of buildings, wooden-built with a pitched roof of slates, and complete with hitching rail and walking boards set up a couple steps from a dusty parking area. Around the side of the main store was what appeared to be a high-boarded storage area stretching over toward the trees.

Glancing down at the dashboard, Jeff saw the counter on the temp gauge sliding slowly upward. "This isn't a moment too soon," he said as he turned into the parking area, the car shuddering as if it were about to fall over and die.

Jeff had barely engaged park when steam started issuing from under the hood. He turned off the ignition and watched as the temperature gauge needle stopped rising and then, very slowly, began to drop again.

"Think they'll be able to fix it?"

Jeff looked at the storefront and shook his head slowly. "Looks a bit 'dueling banjos' to me. But they'll have a phone." There was something in the way he said that that suggested he wasn't completely sure.

"And what the hell does that mean?" Jeff said. " 'For all your needs, yesterday and today'?"

Lorraine shrugged. "A clever marketing campaign aimed at trying to make folks think they needed to move fast and buy buy buy. You know . . . like yesterday?"

Jeff flipped the hood release and stepped out of the car. He breathed in the cool wet air and stretched, glancing across at the still steaming hood.

"Not gonna catch fire is it?" Lorraine asked as she pulled herself upright from the back seat.

Jeff eased the hood catch and lifted it clear. The steam disappeared almost immediately, its soft hiss replaced by occasional spits and crackles as raindrops fell onto the engine block.

"No, I don't think so," Jeff said, scanning the various pipes and hoses, mountings and wires as though he knew what he was looking at. But he didn't. Asking Jeff to fix a car engine would be like asking Fred Flintstone to perform open-heart surgery on Wilma or Barney. Not that he cared so much for the Olds, of course.

"Not much of a General Store," was all Lorraine could think of to say as she stared into the greasy double-fronted windows.

Jeff left the hood up and started over to her. "I guess there isn't much need out here." He looked over at the road, stretching his neck first to the left and the right. "Not a house to be seen," he said.

"No, but look," Lorraine said, waving a hand at the window.

Jeff looked.

Behind the dirty and grease-stained glass, it looked as though someone had maybe had an idea of making some kind of display. A large hand-printed card, set upon a nest of tousled sacking and propped against the window-back, boldly stated:

**EVERYTHING YOU NEED
FOR YOUR HOME—
FROM YESTERDAY
TO TODAY**

But apart from that, the window was empty.

Lorraine moved across and looked in the second window. "It's the same here," she said. "Same kooky sign, same sparse display.

"Seems to me they've forgotten something," Jeff said.

"And what the hell does that mean? 'From yesterday to today'?" She turned around and looked back at the sign they'd passed on the way in, but she could only see the back of it. "The sign coming in said 'yesterday *and* today.' Now it says 'yesterday *to* today.'"

Jeff shrugged and looked back at the road again. For some reason, he had a sudden inclination to slam the hood on the Olds and try limping on the few extra miles to Forest Plains. Surely there would be a repair shop there. He looked back at Stephensons General Store and gave an involuntary shudder.

"Hey, Jeff," Lorraine hissed. "You gonna go inside? I need to use the bathroom."

"Just go in!" Jeff snapped at her without moving from in front of the window, "For crissakes," He added.

For a second, Jeff thought she was going to say something back to him, and he kind of cherished the prospect . . . an opportunity to go into his—

. . . *to the moon, Alice!*

—Ralph Kramden repertoire, but she didn't speak. Instead of smartassing something back at him, Lorraine just shuffled her feet and looked first at the door to Stephensons General Store and then across at him. There was something about that look—something little-girlish and vulnerable—that, just for a second, froze Jeff right in his stride.

Jeff marched over, building up his steam to ignore Lorraine on the way, and stepped onto the boards. The sound of his boot heels clattering on them and the smooth polished surface of the hitching rail made him feel like Gary Cooper in *High Noon*. True to form, the porch door screeched loudly. Jeff pushed the inside door open and stepped inside.

Inside the store it was like a ghost town.

Two counters—sitting at ninety degrees to each other—filled an otherwise empty space. There were rails and cupboards, shelves and stands . . . but no produce and no goods.

"This is a weird general store," Jeff said, his voice low.

"I don't like it," Lorraine said from close behind him. "It feels like we're in a cheesy horror movie except we're too old to be axe-bait." She grabbed a hold of Jeff's sleeve and pulled. "Let's go."

"I thought you wanted to use the bathroom?"

"I'll do it by the side of the road or in my pants," Lorraine hissed. "Hell, I'll hang my fanny out the car win-

dow and spray the crops if you want, but I want to leave
here and I want to leave here *now*."

"Hello?" Jeff yelled.

"Jesus Chri—"

"Anybody here?"

No answer. Lorraine backed out onto the boards again,
let the porch door swing closed.

Jeff banged one of the counters with the flat of his
hand, sending up a cloud of dust.

"Hel-*lo*!?"

Nothing. Except for a shout from Lorraine.

Jeff walked out onto the boards and looked around before stepping down onto the dusty driving area. Leaning
forward, he saw again the boarded area attached to the
back of the store and stretching over to the trees.

"Jeff, I *wanna* go," Lorraine said.

"The car?" Jeff said. "You forget about that?"

"It's what . . . two, three miles into Forest Bend and—"

"*Plains*. It's Forest *Plains*."

"Whatever. It's two damn miles. The car will make
two damn miles."

"And if it doesn't? Then what?"

He walked over to the boarded area and walked alongside it, trailing his hand across it. He slapped the fencing
boards a couple of times before he found a knothole. He
bent down and looked through.

On the other side of the boards it was desolate. Like a
corral but without any horses. There was nothing—no
pump, no washing line to hang clothes, no rain barrel up
against the back of the store, no toys scattered around the
yard . . . not even any windows in the store, just a flat
wall. And no basketball hoop bolted up on the wall. Just
a single door and that was it.

"Looks deserted," Jeff said. Then, "Hallo back there—anyone home?"

"I'm getting soaked here," Lorraine observed.

"I don't get it," Jeff said, standing up from the knot-hole.

"I said, I'm getting soa—"

Jeff spun around. "I know what you said, Lorraine. Jesus!" He marched around to the front of the store again. Lorraine was starting to feel a little less threatened now, and, with nothing more than a roll of her eyes, she followed after him.

As Jeff walked up the two steps up to the decking, the screen door pushed outward and a tall man stepped out. The man was followed by a woman, a girl of maybe fifteen, sixteen and a young boy—Jeff figured maybe eleven or twelve. The boy was carrying a comic book. Jeff blinked. Stared. Blinked again.

"Howdy," the man said, a big smile spreading slowly across his face.

Howdy? Who the hell said 'Howdy' these days?

"Hey," Jeff said. "Sorry to bother you but—"

"No bother," the man said. "Is it, Susan?"

"No bother," the woman agreed. "We was just leaving."

"Leaving?" Jeff looked around for a car or truck but couldn't see anything. "Vacation?"

The man nodded, smiling. "You might say that," he said.

The kids watched. The little boy, catching Jeff's wide-eyed glance at his comic book, shifted it around behind him.

"This is my wife," Jeff said, ushering Lorraine up alongside him.

"Lorraine," Lorraine said, smiling woodenly. The man and woman nodded, returning the smile.

Jeff said, "We called out for you but . . ."

"Oh, we were out back," the man said.

Jeff frowned. "Out back behind the store? We checked there: looked through a knothole . . . shouted. It was deserted."

The man smiled, tousling the boy's head. "Oh, we were *way* back."

"Getting set to leave," the woman said.

Jeff nodded, his eyes flicking from the man to the woman and then to the little girl and finally to the boy. The boy with the comic book. *Had he been imagining it, that com—*

"Name's Stephenson," the man announced, holding out his hand. "Paul Stephenson. And this here's my wife, Susan." They all shook hands. "And Molly and Josh," he said, rubbing his son's head and his daughter's shoulder in turn.

"So, you need something to eat? Freshen up maybe?" the man said.

"There's a small town three, four miles down the road," Susan Stephenson said.

"Forest Plains," Josh said.

"I could use a bathroom if—" Lorraine was about to say if you have one but just managed to stop herself at the last minute. Who the hell didn't have a bathroom.

Susan Stephenson took Lorraine by the arm, her grip firm but easy and her smile genuine friendly—Lorraine always said she could tell real hospitality and this was as real as she had ever seen—and ushered her into the empty store. The girl—Molly—followed, while Josh hung back and stood behind his father's legs.

"Not too many folks stop by here," Paul Stephenson said evenly, squinting into Jeff's eyes. "Lessen they needs to," he added as he glanced across at the Olds. "Want me to take a look?"

Lessen they needs to? Jesus Christ, this guy talked like he was rehearsing for the remake of Sergeant York. "You know anything about cars?" Jeff said, skillfully avoiding referring to his Olds as a newfangled contraption that'd never replace the horse and buggy.

"Some." The man didn't shake his head, didn't nod. He just stepped down off the decking and strolled over to the car. He seemed to be oblivious to the rain, though it had eased a little since Jeff and Lorraine arrived.

"Whyn't you go on inside," he called over his shoulder. "Got a Mister Coffee in the kitchen and cookies in the jar. Josh, you take the gentleman inside and see after him."

"Yessir," Josh said. Then, taking hold of Jeff's hand, "Come on, mister."

Jeff allowed himself to be led.

As they went inside, he said, "You like comic books?"

"Yessir," Josh Stephenson said.

"Me too," Jeff said.

The sound of their shoes clattered on the bare boards as the boy led Jeff through a door at the back of the store and along a little corridor that opened up into a kitchen area. The smell of coffee filled Jeff with a sudden rush of optimism and cheer.

Lorraine appeared from a side door to the sound of a toilet flushing. "Well," she said, wringing her hands the way she always did when she'd just washed them, "that feels so much better."

"Can't think on a full bladder," Susan Stephenson said

sagely from the counter over by the sink, "and drinking coffee on one is just out of the question."

Molly sat at the table, her head perched on her hands and her legs swinging in perfect unison, and watched Jeff. She caught his eyes looking over at Josh, who had slumped into a big chair over in the corner.

"Look out, Jay, he's after your comic," the girl said.

"Molly!" Susan snapped as she carried two full-to-brimming mugs across to the table and set them down. "You mind your manners."

"That's okay," Jeff said.

Lorraine took a sip of coffee and remarked how good it tasted, but Jeff couldn't even think about taking a drink. Instead, he said, "I must say that I do still enjoy reading them, now and again." He walked over to the boy as casually as he could and bent over so that he could see what Josh was reading. "Boy, that looks like a good one," he said.

"You wanna look at it?" The boy held it out and Jeff nodded, hardly able to speak. He grunted and took the comic, holding it in his hands as if it were the most fragile china pottery.

The comic was more than a 'good one': It was one of Jeff's favorite editions of DC's long-running SF title, *Strange Adventures*—number 110, November 1959 . . . the cover showed a giant hand appearing behind a speeding car. But best of all was that it looked to be in absolute mint condition . . . a $100 comic book, and that was just according to the Overstreet guide, and not something one would usually entrust to a ten-year-old. The pages were white—pure white, not 'off white' or 'cream to white': it was as if the comic were brand new.

Jeff had seen books from Edgar Church's so-called

"Mile High" collection, and they were pretty good . . . streets ahead, in purely quality terms, of either the Mohawk Valley or Bethlehem collections, which, although they retained their cover gloss, were let down by tanning or browning interior pages. But this book . . . Jeff felt like he was going to drool. If this went to the CGC folks, it would come back at eight to twelve times guide: in other words, a one-thousand-dollar comic book being read by a teenage boy in a lonely—

empty—let's not forget goddamn empty

—general store outside a godforsaken one-mule New England town called Forest Plains.

Susan Stephenson must have seen something in Jeff's face—possibly the fact that his jaw had dropped down onto the floor between his bent knees—because she said, "You know about comics?"

He snapped his head around, mouth still open, and, just for a second, thought about bullshitting. But the woman's face was all-knowing.

"I run a small business buying and selling antique books and magazines, and—" He handed the comic back to Josh. "—comic books. That just happens to be one of my all-time favorites. It's the story that introduced me to adrenaline. It's the best story I ever read," Jeff said wistfully. "Next to the reworking of The Flash in *Showcase* 4 of course. It's commonly regarded as the first Silver Age comic book—some say that honor belongs to *Detective* 225 from the previous year—1955, the first appearance of John Jones, Manhunter from Mars—but I say phooey to that. My, but I'd give anything to have a mint copy of *Showcase* 4."

Susan frowned and placed a pot of sugar, a couple of small spoons and a glass jar filled with cookies on the table. "Sugar?" she said. "Cookies?" And then, "So it's valuable, this *Showcase* comic?"

Jeff nodded enthusiastically. "It would sure solve a lot of our problems," he said, glancing across at Lorraine and immediately wondering just how many of their problems it *wouldn't* solve. "Is the book yours? Or your husband's? It's certainly in nice shape for a forty-five year old comic book," he added as he looked enviously across at the boy.

She let out a short snigger and shook her head. "It's certainly not mine, I don't read much of anything and never comics. And Paul, well . . . he just likes to curl up with a mystery novel."

"So it's . . . it's your *son's*? It's not *Showcase,* 4 but it's a very expensive book."

She moved her head from side to side and said, "It's *kind* of his . . . for a while anyways. He brought it back."

"Brought it back?" Jeff hardly wanted to continue with the question. "Brought it back from where?"

The woman seemed to chew on something for a few seconds and then looked across at her daughter.

Molly Stephenson nodded, her eyes smiling, and said, "Makes no nevermind, ma. Go ahead and tell him."

She pointed to a curtain hanging on a section of the wall at the back of the room. "From out there," she said.

Lorraine looked over at the curtain.

Jeff looked over at the curtain.

Young Josh lifted his head from reading "The Hand From Beyond," with all of its glorious Carmine Infantino artwork, and looked first at one of them and then the other, before returning his attention to more interesting fare.

Jeff grunted and walked across to the curtain, half expecting to be stopped in his tracks. But nobody moved.

That is, nobody moved physically; there was a frisson of some kind of energy—electrical energy, Jeff would have guessed—that seemed to pass from them and then among the whole group.

Turning to watch them as they watched him, Jeff set the mug of steaming coffee on the table and reached out to touch the curtain.

Still nobody moved.

The curtain felt just like . . . well, just like curtain. Like any other kind of material he had ever felt. Like, maybe, his mother's skirt fabric or the cotton weave of his father's work overalls; the thick grain of his first baseball uniform or the cool blackness of his Batman cape from childhood. He tried to think of other things—contemporary things—but couldn't. All of the things the curtain reminded him of were in the past.

"Jeff—"

Jeff glanced across at Lorraine and gave her a very slight shake of the head. He had no idea why. He had no idea as to why he might need to be quiet, but, deep down, he realized that it wasn't because of danger or the fear of being discovered . . . but rather of reverence.

He pulled the curtain aside to expose a door.

A simple and straightforward door, complete with handle and cross-nailed struts securing a series of vertical planks interspersed with three horizontal ones. As doors went, it was not the finest construction Jeff had ever seen. But then he didn't know diddly about doors.

The slightest of flutters came from the curtain, which wafted briefly and then settled. Jeff felt the breath stop in his throat, but the loud banging of the screen door behind him caused it to blow out in a single gust.

"She ain't going nowhere right now," Paul Stephenson

announced in a sing-song voice, clapping his hands together by way of punctuation. "Doubt you're gonna be able to do much with her. You can maybe have another look, but you'd best wait until she cools down a mite," he added.

"What is it, honey?" Susan Stephenson asked.

"Hose," came the reply. "Just a hose. But it's causing a whole heap of trouble, I can tell you. Gonna need a replacement."

"Honey," Susan Stephenson said. "I told them about the doorway."

He nodded. "Kind of figured that out, him standing there right in front of it," he said.

"Well, actually, you *haven't* told me about the doorway," Jeff corrected her, his hands were trembling. "You've kind of *hinted* at something about the doorway but—"

"The door's a gateway," the man said. He lifted his own mug to his mouth and took a big sip. "Leads to different times."

"A gateway?" Jeff said.

"*I* found it," the girl said.

"No you did not!" Josh snapped.

"I did, too. I found—"

"Doesn't matter who found it," Stephenson said and there was just enough of a hint of annoyance in his voice to make both the kids clam up.

"We were passing through," Stephenson continued, "about eight, nine months back, on our way from one bad decision to what was then already shaping up to be another. Came up from Oklahoma to see Susan's cousin about a job offer—"

"And with hardly two dimes to rub together," Susan Stephenson said softly.

The man nodded thoughtfully. "We hitched a ride that dropped us about six, seven miles back, place called Bellingham. We walked the rest of the way through a storm right out of the Bible and—" He shrugged and nodded at the surroundings. "—we found this place to shelter in."

"It was deserted at the time," his wife said. "Nothing in here but a pile of clothes."

"Clothes?" Lorraine said from over by the table. "What kind of clothes?"

Stephenson thumbed over his shoulder at an open door leading into a back room. "They're still back there. Pants and jacket, a shirt, necktie, and smalls, and a woman's skirt, jacket and blouse, more smalls. Nothing special," he said. "We didn't figure the significance until a little while later."

"Significance?"

"Until *I* found the doorway," Molly said. And she stepped forward to take center stage, under a withering glare from her younger brother.

Jeff turned to the door. Reached out a hand for the handle.

"Couple things you need to remember before you do that," Stephenson said, his voice soft. Jeff held his arm rigid and waited.

"First off, don't forget it's a different time and place for each person goes through there," the man said, matter of factly. "And you hafta hold onto each other or you'll wind up in separate places."

"And times."

"And times," he added, nodding to his wife. "If you

hold onto each other, you'll go back to the place and time that the first one picks."

"What, you just wish for someplace?" Lorraine asked.

"Seems to be that way, yes indeed. You don't need to wish right out loud," he went on. "In fact, seems like you don't actually need to think anything. The door just seems to know." His eyes took on a wistful glaze as he looked across at the door. "It just takes you where your heart wants to go," he said, softly, as if he were saying it just to himself.

It turned out that, depending on who was in front at the time, the Stephensons had been to the Metropolitan Stadium, home of the Minnesota Twins, on August 25, 1970. Paul had gone up there with his father to see the Twins play the Boston Red Sox and had never forgotten it because there was a bomb scare, and the 18,000 fans just had to sit it out while the police checked the outfield and the parking lot. Keeping the 16-year-old Paul calm, Dick Stephenson—then, unknown to everyone, busy building a tumor in his gut that would take his life before Thanksgiving—told him about when he went with *his* father to watch the first ever game in San Francisco . . . at the Seals Stadium in the spring of 1958.

"Wheels within wheels," Stephenson said wistfully. "Seeing my daddy again after all those years . . . well—" He shook his head and looked down at the floor.

In addition there had been an unspecified Christmas morning on a Kansas City street circa 1955 (Susan had been born after her parents had left their hometown, but she had listened to her mom's account of their walking to church so many times that she just wanted to see for herself); the early morning of December 7, 1941, Pearl Harbor, a silence broken only by the sound of approaching airplanes; a 1912 pre-election address in Milwaukee given by a wounded Teddy Roosevelt (only an overcoat, a glasses case and a folded copy of the speech he was about to give saved Roosevelt's life); the massacre of some 150 Minneconjou Sioux at Wounded Knee Creek on a freezing late December day in 1890 (a trip that had Susan in tears for almost two days after they got back); and the killing (Susan couldn't bring herself to use the word "massacre" a second time) of four students on the Kent State campus in 1970; Jimi Hendrix's remarkable interpretation of The Star Spangled Banner at Yasgur's farm during the Woodstock music festival in August 1969 (after that one, Paul had sat for long hours looking out of the greasy windows of the derelict store wondering where the innocence had gone); and a rope swing hanging over the stream out back of the Stephensons' home in Chickasha, the occasion being Josh's finally being able to make it right across to the far bank . . . and actually let go. "And all the time he told me he never went near that creek," Susan explained to the transfixed Jeff and Lorraine.

But there were many other times as well, some from their own experience and others pulled from some subconscious wishlist of places and times they suddenly decided they'd like to visit.

The silence that followed what amounted to a virtual presentation seemed to Jeff to be louder than the actual recollections themselves.

The Stephensons, having interrupted and cajoled and reminded each other throughout a full fifteen or twenty minutes, seemed out of breath. So it fell to Jeff to break the spell.

"I don't know whether to believe you," was how he did that.

Stephenson shrugged. "One way to prove it or disprove it," he said.

"Jeff!" Lorraine snapped.

Jeff ignored her and turned to face the door.

He didn't know whether to turn the handle or back right out of Stephensons General Store and just thumb a ride into town, pick the car up later, maybe tomorrow. Next week even. But, the more he looked at it . . .

"When we found it, we figured right away we could start up a business or something. Bring things back from then into now and sell them to folks—old toys, clothes, you know . . . stuff. But it didn't work out that way. Seems things don't want or aren't able to stay in our time. Eventually, two or maybe three days after, you turn around and poof!—" he clapped his hands. "—there it is, whatever you brought back . . . gone."

"Jeff," Lorraine said from across the kitchen. "Let's go."

"Go? Leave?"

She moved silently across the kitchen and took hold of her husband's jacket. "I don't like it."

Jeff looked first at her and then at Stephenson. Then he looked at Stephenson's wife, the little girl and . . . Josh. And the November 1959 copy of *Strange Adventures*. "I have to go," he said, saying the words right into Lorraine's face. He looked over at Stephenson as Lorraine stepped even closer to him.

"How do you get back?"

Stephenson shrugged. "Same way you arrived. It'll be a door or an opening of some kind—differs from place to place."

Jeff nodded, took a deep breath as he turned around, and turned the handle. Then, just before he stepped out of Stephensons General Store, Lorraine took hold of his jacket.

Five

Sounds and smells.

"Where are we?" Lorraine whispered, still hanging on to Jeff's jacket.

Jeff breathed in and sniffed.

"All I can tell you is we're on a street," he said, looking around. "And, at a guess, I'd guess it's late summer 1956."

People walked by them, looking in windows, talking, paying them no real attention . . . though Lorraine's jeans and covering skirt combination caused one or two second glances.

"That's pretty accurate for a guess," she said as she searched for clues.

Jeff took hold of her wrist and freed her clenched hand from his jacket. "Come on," he said. "We need to find somewhere."

And they set off along the street.

A couple of stores along, Jeff said, "It's Providence. I remember it."

"Providence in 1956? You been keeping something from me?"

Jeff held back on the chuckle as he watched cars go by—with their wonderful fins—and registered that almost every man over the age of twenty was wearing a hat.

"I spent an entire summer here living with my Aunt

Deborah on Poplar Street. I used to come down here two, maybe three times a week buying comic books."

"Now why doesn't that surprise me," Lorraine muttered.

"And, if I remember correctly, there's a little soda shop right along here and they—" He pointed. "It's there!"

And it was.

Over on the corner of the street. McDougall's was the name on the awning, and Jeff repeated it aloud as though it were a magical mantra . . . a kind of open sesame.

"You remember it?"

Jeff nodded and then shook his head. "The store, yes. But not the name. I guess I wasn't interested in the name." He checked the street for traffic and pulled Lorraine after him.

"So, where did you ask for . . . you know, in your heart?"

"I didn't ask for any specific *place*," Jeff said as they reached the sidewalk on the other side of the street. "It was a specific *time* I was after."

"And that time was *summer* 1956? Are you out of your mind here?"

"Here we go," Jeff said as he pushed the door open and dragged Lorraine into McDougall's Soda Shoppe . . . or so it said on the banner behind the counter.

The store was an L-shape, with the soda bar and counter over to the right of them and the rest of the store occupying the left and the full area of the turn all the way up to a pharmacy counter at the far end. In between— sandwiched in a dead area at the end of two rows of wooden shelving units—were three tall metal stands, each with four faces and each face chock-full of comic books, stacked maybe twenty or thirty books deep.

When they had come into the store, the guy behind the counter had been preparing a three-scoop (chocolate, vanilla and either raspberry or strawberry—Jeff couldn't decide which) sundae for a youngster sitting on one of the stools. Now, as he served the tall glass and took the boy's nickel—

Jesus Christ . . . a nickel? Susan thought

—he looked up at them, gave a small smile and a nod. "Help you folks?" he asked.

He was youngish, maybe late twenties or early thirties, and sporting a lime-bordered apron emblazoned with the word McDougal's in orange, and one of those little caps that the air force fly-boys always wore on the movies.

For a second, Lorraine didn't want to speak . . . was sure that, if she did, the young man would stagger backwards in horror and—

they're from the future!

—point at them, and then the whole town would start chasing them down the street like in that *Body Snatchers* movie about the pod people. She tugged at Jeff's sleeve.

"No, we're fine," Jeff said. "In here to pick up some comic books."

"Pardon me?"

"Comic books," Jeff said, and he pointed at the metal racks. "Comics."

"Oh," the man nodded. "Sure, go ahead."

Jeff thanked him, and he and Lorraine walked around towards the pharmacy section and the swirling racks of four-color-wonder.

"I don't believe you brought us here to look at a bunch

of goddamn comics," she snarled as quietly as she was able.

"They're not just *any* bunch of goddamn comics," Jeff hissed back as he reached out for the first rack. "Oh my God," he said. And for a moment, Lorraine thought he was going to cry.

Jeff pulled out one comic after another, speaking their titles, the lead stories and occasionally some of the dialogue balloons on the covers.

"*Adventures Into The Unknown*," he said. "*Rex The Wonder Dog . . . Superman*—will you look at that cover! And here's *Batman, Detective, Marvel, Spellbound, Uncanny Tales, Blackhawk, Strange Adventures . . .* and they're all 1956 issues." He flicked the tops as carefully as he could, ensuring that he didn't cause even a slight crease at the top of the spines. "They return all the out-of-date ones . . . or sometimes just scrap them." He shook his head and lifted out a copy of *Mr. District Attorney* with the cover showing the DA with a dog as his star witness (the dog moving letters around on a blackboard beside him) and just let it lie on his outstretched hands.

"It's like it's brand new," he said. "It's actually pristine."

"I just put a whole load of new ones in, mister," a bespectacled man in a white coat said as he stepped out from behind the counter with a thick batch of comics. "You know which ones you're looking for, do ya?"

"I, er . . . I think—" Jeff stumbled over what he wanted to say. And then, "Hey, tell me . . . he's asking about some new character they're trying out this month."

"Yeah?" The man paused and rested his pile of comics on the counter edge. "You know what he's called, this character?"

Jeff nodded, swallowed and said, "The Flash I think he said."

"The Flash? Heh, *he* ain't new, mister. He's old as the hills. Wears a tin hat and—"

"No, no, they're redoing him. In *Showcase*—new costume and everything. Sounds good, he says. My son. *Our* son," Jeff added as he glanced at Lorraine.

The druggist started flicking. "Okay, then, let's see if we can—Oh, here it is. *The Flash*. Hey, you're right . . . new uniform. Heh, looks good enough to read myself," he added with a whisper. He pulled out a copy and handed it to Jeff, who took it and, open-mouthed, held it out in front of him.

"You okay, mister?"

"Huh? Oh, yeah, sure . . . I'm fine. I'm just, you know, pleased I was able to get it for him."

The druggist nodded. "Any others he needs before I put them out?"

"Yeah, some more," Jeff said mechanically. "Say, I just thought . . . you got any more copies of that Flash one? Our son, his friends'll want the same comic as him. You know what they're like. Kids."

The man shuffled back into the pile as Jeff sidled around to get a good look, and suddenly, he lifted the top of the pile clear and produced another four or five copies of the *Showcase* issue featuring The Flash. "Here you go. How many you need?"

Jeff reached a quivering hand into his pocket. "You mind if I take them all? He's a popular boy, our . . . Tommy." Jeff turned to Lorraine and said, "Isn't he, honey?"

"I guess he's more popular than he knows."

"You can take the whole pile for all I care, mister. Save me putting 'em all out. You need any others?"

"I'll come back," Jeff said. He waved the batch of six identical comics at the druggist. "This is the main one." And as he waved them, one copy slipped out of the middle and—

"Look out!" Jeff shrieked.

—fell to the floor, bouncing off of the counter, into the wire racking and finally sliding, spread-open, beneath the racking.

Jeff looked up from the comic book and looked at the druggist.

The druggist stared at him.

Lorraine was staring at him.

Jeff gave a weak smile and reached down to retrieve the book.

"It's just a comic, mister," the druggist said. "If your boy's fussy then just make sure that one goes to one of his friends."

Jeff nodded. "Okay, what do I owe you?"

"Well, you got—" He flicked through the comic-books. "—six copies . . . let's call it fifty cents even." He handed the books back to Jeff. "You need a bag or anything?"

Jeff shook his head and pulled a handful of change from his pocket. He found two quarters and dropped them in the druggist's open palm.

"Well, you come back now once you know what else he wants."

Jeff looked across at the metal racks, at the thick bunches of comics in each slot, eight slots per face of the rack, four faces per rack, three racks . . . and, for a few seconds, he felt physically sick.

The latest Overstreet guide had *Showcase* 4 at around $30,000 in near mint condition but he knew that if he were to send these books—the six he now held in his hand, for which he'd just paid one half of one dollar—to the CGC people, they'd come back graded 9.4, 9.6 or maybe even 9.8. And that could mean multiples of guide were highly probable.

"You know," Jeff said, lifting the comics and taking another look inside, "one day, these things are gonna be worth a fortune."

The druggist looked questioningly at him. "Yeah?"

"Yeah. Absolutely."

"Like what?"

"Oh—" Jeff stopped and looked at the druggist's face. And then he looked across the store, past the boy and woman eating nickel sundaes, around the man in a snap-brim Fedora hat browsing yet another spinning metal rack filled with Pocket Books, Perma Books, Ace Doubles, Dell mapbacks and the like . . . all the way out onto the 1956 Mainstreet, Anytown, USA resplendent in tail-finned cars, everyone smoking—

what was it Peter Finch said in Paddy Chayefsky's Network about nobody getting cancer at Archie Bunker's place? Well, surely the same held doubly true for Ozzie and Harriet, James Dean, Andy Griffiths . . .

—and he stopped himself and then looked closer into the druggist's eyes.

Telling this man that, in fifty years, a mint copy of *Action* Number 1 would probably be worth a half-million dollars or that the half-dozen books the man had just parted with in return for fifty cents would almost certainly be worth a quarter-million dollars . . . well, there was something about it that was wrong.

Why had he bought the damn things anyway? He couldn't take them back with him—well, he *could* . . . but then, according to Stephenson, they'd just disappear one day, back to where they came from.

Jeff felt a sharp pain in his chest, and he threw out his left hand. Lorraine took hold of it.

"Jeff?"

"You sure you're okay, mister?"

"I want to—" Jeff began but his mouth was dry. He glanced down at the six copies of *Showcase* 4 and strengthened his grip. Then he looked at Lorraine's face and he saw . . . he saw concern.

"I'm okay. Really," he added when Lorraine didn't look too sure.

Then Jeff handed the six books back to the druggist. "Put these back in the rack," he said, a slight smile tugging at the corners of his mouth. "I'll only lose them. I'll call in tomorrow when I have my briefcase with me."

The man accepted them, frowning. "You want me to hang onto them for you . . . you know, put them on one side for you?"

Jeff shook his head. "No, I might forget or we could find out that he—our son—has already picked up what he wants someplace else."

The man shrugged and produced a handful of change from his pants pocket.

"Hey, no . . . don't bother with a ref—"

"You don't pay for things you don't buy, mister," the man said. He counted out five dimes into Jeff's hand and then slipped the quarter-million dollars into the metal racking, tamping the tops of the books into the already tight space allowed by the other titles.

With Lorraine's help, Jeff walked unsteadily out of the

store, his vision slightly blurred. Outside, Lorraine asked him if he was really okay.

"I'm fine. Truly. I think . . . hell, I don't know what I think." He looked around and breathed in some more nineteen-fifty-six. "Part of it was why buy the books when I know I can't keep them—though, my God . . . how that would have saved our lives." Jeff smiled at her and, even though part of him said not to do it, he reached out and squeezed his wife's shoulder.

"But the real thing was that the guy was selling me those books as though they were just *comics*."

"They *were* just comics."

"No. They weren't just comics to me . . . not when I'd paid for them and was holding them. They were an investment . . . a means to get out of our problem. Here in 1956 they'll be bought by kids . . . kids who are simply buying comics, and buying them to read. Sure, they'll get folded up, slipped into the back pockets of denims, get creased, scuffed, stained—but they'll be read. And enjoyed."

He stopped and took hold of Lorraine's arm.

Together they walked back down the alleyway and, after Jeff took one last long look around a fifty-year-old Providence street, they opened the door and stepped back into an empty Stephensons General Store.

Six

"Where is everybody?" was the first thing that Lorraine could think of to say.

Jeff shouted, "We're back—hello?"

But the store was silent. No, it was more than silent: it was . . . deserted. Empty. Devoid of life. There was not only nobody here, Jeff knew, deep in his heart, but nobody was coming back.

Outside, thunder rolled and a flash of lightning lit up the now dismal interior. That was when Jeff noticed the heap of clothes scattered in the middle of the floor: dress, workpants, couple pairs of blue jeans—kids' sizes—four pairs of shoes, various smalls.

Neither of them said anything.

Jeff went to the window just in time to see a fork of lightning straddle the ground on the other side of the road. The roll of thunder that followed almost immediately rattled the floor where they were standing.

"Maybe they went outside," he said.

Lorraine nodded. "Yeah, took off all their clothes and went dancing out into the monsoon. That makes a whole lot of sense."

Jeff felt a deep sense of loss—no, not loss . . . of being wrong. Of being wrong for too long.

"I think we both know where they've gone," was all Lorraine could think of to say. "Well, not exactly where they've ended up," she added, looking around at the door, which was now closed. "And they definitely won't be coming back."

"How's come?"

"It's what he said when we arrived. They were planning on going." She pointed to the clothes on the floor. "And they said that things they brought back from the past disappeared after a couple days. Maybe it's the same the other way around . . . which means they were away from here a couple days before the clothes came right back of their own accord."

"But to the very instant they left," Jeff ventured.

Lorraine breathed in a deep sigh and looked over at the door.

"I wonder where *my* place—*my* time—would be," she said, sidling up to the door and placing a hand on it . . . as though she were looking for a heartbeat.

Jeff looked back at the window. "Well, I think we should go try the car again. Maybe it'll be okay now."

As he leaned against the window, with the thunder rolling above the store, he neither saw nor heard Lorraine open the door.

The sight beyond took her breath away. "Oh, Jeff . . ."

He turned and saw.

Then he looked back at the window, with the rain running down it in torrents, splashing the yard beyond and coating the land across the highway with what appeared to be a gray mist.

And then he looked back at Lorraine and the open door.

And the lush greenness of summertime Central Park, and the sunshine, and the distant sound of car horns. And of 1981.

He walked over to her. "That's your time? Your special time?"

She shrugged. "Looks that way."

"I can't remember exactly where you were sitting."

She pointed to where one of the winding lanes ran round a group of young oaks. Next to the trees was a bench. Sitting on the bench, her back to them, was a young woman. She was eating a sandwich.

"But where are you?" she said, scanning the surrounding area.

"I came into the park from Columbus Circle," Jeff

said. "So I guess I would be coming-" He stopped and looked. "Oh, God . . . there I am."

And he was. Walking along the lane, his head buried in a comic book out of a bag he'd just bought at the drug store on Central park West.

"It was . . ." Jeff frowned as he tried to remember. "It was an old *Conan* I think. Yeah, one of the Moorcock ones—"

The lightning lit the inside of the store like a strobe, and the boards shook beneath their feet. A single piece of wood detached itself from the door-frame and hung down, momentarily swinging before it landed with a thud on the floor. Without thinking, Jeff placed an arm around Lorraine as the doorway shifted to one side.

"Jeff!"

Jeff saw even before she pointed. Over on the lane, the young Jeff had looked up—

did you hear that?

yeah . . . sounded like thunder

yeah

sky's clear though

yeah . . .

—and was saying something to the young Lorraine.

Behind them, a piece of wooden rafter fell into the middle of the store, quickly followed by a tumble of planks.

Jeff pulled Lorraine toward him and watched the rain darken the floorboards in a big circle. Up above, he could see the black sky.

"We have to get out," he said.

Lorraine said something that was lost beneath the thunder. But Jeff knew pretty well what it was: or we could go back.

He looked back at the doorway and saw it was now

slewed drunkenly to one side. He turned her around so she could see, and together they watched summertime Central Park crackle and blur, like a badly tuned TV set, until all there was was rain and wind, and an empty boarded-up area leading to some trees.

"It's gone," he heard Lorraine say, and he felt her shoulders slump.

"No, it's still there," he said. "And we're still there."

She looked around at him and then at the side of the store, a whole section of panelling was now looking set to fall out into the storm. "We have to go," she said, "don't we?"

He nodded. "We can sit in the car."

"Okay." She stood clear of him and reached out for his hand. Jeff took it.

"Be a shame to let them go through all that for nothing," he said, nodding his head at the now wrecked back door.

Lorraine smiled. "Time to get on with our lives," she said. "And we'll face whatever comes up together."

And together, they ran out of the store.

Seven

The pickup appeared when they were halfway across to the car. Jeff waved at it but it was already pulling in.

An old man—maybe seventy, seventy-five years old—rolled down the passenger window when he was alongside them and, leaning across the seats, stared first at Lorraine and then at Jeff.

"Need a ride?" was his opening gambit. And then, as Jeff opened the door and pushed Lorraine inside, he said, "Been out here three times this past couple weeks. Every day it rained," he added.

Jeff slid alongside Lorraine and caught his breath. "You're either real unlucky," he said, "or you just *like* rain."

The man shook his head. "Neither." He held out a hand and said, "Been a long time. Name's Josh Stephenson."

A cluster of boards flew across in front of them before Jeff could think of what to say. The General Store was falling down.

"I'll take you back into Forest Plains," the old man said as he swung the pick-up back onto the road the way he'd come. "You can find a place to freshen up, stay the night. Maybe get someone to pick up your car tomorrow."

Neither Jeff nor Lorraine knew what to say, so the old man did the talking.

It turned out that after Jeff and Lorraine had gone through the door, Josh's father had gathered the family together and they'd gone through themselves. They had landed in Cedar Rapids, 1946—for no particular reason as far as any of them could make out. But they felt right at home almost immediately. And so they stayed.

Josh's mom and dad had passed on a good few years back, but, he told Lorraine and Jeff, they'd both sent their best wishes. Molly was still around—a little cranky now she had eighty in her sights—and living in Florida, where the weather suited her arthritis. But she'd told Josh to say Hi.

"They all knew you would come out to see us?" Jeff said as they pulled into town.

The old man nodded. "Oh, sure. I always said I would. But I couldn't figure out which day it was, so I been out here a good few times this past month or so . . . whenever it looked like rain." He paused and looked straight ahead, and Jeff knew the man wasn't seeing the Main Street of Forest Plains.

"I saw us all," he said, his voice cracking. "I thought about pulling in and saying hello, giving them both a hug . . . you know. But I just couldn't face it." He looked around at Jeff. "They all looked just the same."

Lorraine squeezed the old man's shoulder.

He straightened up and gave a little cough. "Anyway, here's where we part company. You go along there—" He pointed down the street to an intersection. "—and make a right. Couple of blocks down, there's a little guest house. Tell Mary I sent you."

Jeff shook his hand and said thanks, and Lorraine did the same. There was nothing else either of them could do. Then they slid out of the pickup onto the sidewalk, pleased that it had stopped raining.

Just as Jeff was about to close the door, the old man suddenly waved him back. He rummaged in the glove compartment where Jeff had been sitting and produced a packet, about A4 size. "Almost forgot this," he said, "been looking after it so damn long."

Jeff took the packet and weighed it in his hands. It felt solid but light.

"What is it?" Jeff asked as he pushed the door closed.

"A present," the old man said. "*Three* presents in fact. Been looking after them since the fall of fifty-six." As he shifted into gear, he added. "You owe me thirty cents."

And he pulled away from the sidewalk.

"What is it?" Lorraine asked.

Jeff opened the packet and removed a Scotch-taped hard-plastic container. He flipped open the container to find three mint copies of Showcase 4.

"Ohmygod!"

"I-I don't *believe* it! That's—That's—" He flicked through each comic very carefully. "The condition is absolutely superb. Completely white pages, full gloss, no visible defects at all."

"Are they worth a lot, honey?"

Jeff turned to her and kissed her on the lips, watching her eyes widen.

"Money-wise, they're going to get us out of a hole." He looked at her then, maybe for the first time in many years, and with a heart that had been lightened and freed of pressure. It was as though he were seeing her completely new, a time machine of his very own. And yet, his wife had always been there . . . if only he had stopped to look. "But I already had everything I *really* needed," he said at last. And a big smile lit up his face.

"Me too," Lorraine said.

The storm had passed. The sky above Forest Plains had cleared, and the sidewalk was already showing signs of drying out. Jeff took a deep breath and, with the comics safely back in their case, he took hold of Lorraine and the two of them started walking. They weren't sure where their steps would take them, but they didn't care: arriving at a destination after a long journey is rarely as exciting or as mysterious as the journey itself.

The main thing was they were together again. Nothing else really mattered.

"All my possessions for a moment of time."
        Allegedly the last words spoken by
        Queen Elizabeth I (1533-1601)

For Julius Schwartz, without whom—of course—this story could not have been written.

WORLDS ENOUGH . . .
AND TIME

Kristine Kathryn Rusch

Kristine Kathryn Rusch is an award-winning mystery, romance, science fiction, and fantasy writer. She has written many novels under various names, including Kristine Grayson for romance and Kris Nelscott for mystery. Her novels have made the bestseller lists—even in London—and have been published in fourteen countries and thirteen different languages. Her awards range from the Ellery Queen Readers Choice Award to the John W. Campbell Award. She is the only person in the history of the science fiction field to have won both a Hugo award for editing and a Hugo award for fiction. Her short work has been reprinted in seven Year's Best collections.

"Watch," Marissa says.

She brings her small hand to her temple, then extends her arm. She tilts her head sideways, black curls falling against her neck, and stares at something I can't see. Finally, she twists her fingers ever so slightly, and a window opens in the sky.

It's a tiny window, the size of a hand mirror, and it looks like a photograph floating on the summer breeze. The window blots out part of a birch tree, but not the lake beyond.

A floating miracle, adrift in a sea of air.

I crouch to Marissa height, barely over three feet, and stare into the window. All I can see are waves, like heat waves that appear on a highway on a sunny day.

Marissa giggles, clenches her fist, and the window disappears. All that remains are the birch trees, the dandelion fluff decorating the air, and the chill breeze off the lake.

The emptiness startles me.

My heart is pounding and my own fingers clench. I want to grab her, shake her, demand that she do it again.

Instead, I close my eyes, trying to control my own trembling. Marissa laughs, the sound farther away. She's probably running off, but I don't care.

Her father will find her. Bastard. He said nothing of this. He should have known how interested I'd be.

A son owes his mother. He always owes his mother.

And he should never forget that.

I was Marissa's age when I first had the feeling, the sensation of worlds dividing, multiplying, changing around me. I had snuck into the attic. The air smelled of dust and mildew, the floor simple pine boards, the boxes slowly rotting in the summer damp.

My mother's wedding dress hung in a metal wardrobe, the latch rusted open. I pulled the door, saw the white

dress yellowing with age and inattention, the black cocktail gown beside it, and a blue silk evening gown with a
plunging neckline and room for a bustle.

Only I didn't know what a bustle was or a cocktail
dress or an evening gown. I brushed against the blue silk,
part of it trailing to the dirty metal floor of the wardrobe,
and saw the dress as it had once been: hanging off a
voluptuous woman, accenting her narrow waist, her high
breasts, and adding to her already ample behind. The diamonds around her neck winked in the gaslight, and she
smiled, her skin unlined and pale against the blackness of
her hair. In the background, music played—a waltz—
and couples twirled on a polished dance floor, none of the
women as beautiful as the one before me, the one in the
dress, the one who made the dress live.

She turned, saw me, eyes widening, and shrieked that
my filthy hand was ruining her dress. Her skin, warm and
soft, brushed mine, and dislodged my fingers.

Then she faded as if she had never been.

The dress hung in the wardrobe, forgotten against the
black and the rusting wall.

My hand had fallen to my side, the skin still tingling
from her touch.

I told my mother and she had laughed. "Miracles in the
attic," she said with enough contempt that even I, child
that I was, realized she thought I had made the entire
thing up.

Darren slams open my kitchen door. He drags Marissa
by the hand, pulls her inside, and takes her upstairs. I sip
my coffee, warming my hands against the mug, and lean
against the kitchen counter.

Outside, the breeze has become a gale. The birch trees

sway and bend as if they are dancing to a music only they can hear. The sky has grown dark with an on-coming storm.

"Jesus, Mom," Darren says from behind me. "She fell into the lake. She could've drowned."

"She can swim." I don't turn around. I know Marissa can swim because I'm the one who took her to swimming lessons before she could walk. She would giggle and paddle toward me, dipping her head in the water like a baby seal.

"And if she'd been knocked unconscious? What then?"

Then she would have drowned. But I don't say that.

"You were supposed to be watching her." He steps into my line of sight, his face mottled with anger just like his father's used to do.

"I did watch her." My voice is amazingly level, considering how odd I feel. "I watched her create a hole in the sky."

At four, you're too young for theories. You simply know that things are not exactly what they seem.

I could never get the lady with the dress to come back. I visited the attic day after day, touched dress after dress and saw nothing except dust motes and the occasional moth.

But the air was alive up there, and I had a sensation that if I touched the right thing at the right moment, I could see worlds I hadn't even imagined. Not just visages of the past, but possibilities of the future, permutations of the present, times that exist outside of ours.

In some of those places, my mother believed me, nurtured my talent, told me of hers. In most of those places,

I believed the world was a much better, much friendlier place.

Darren takes Marissa home. The supervised visit is over. I am told I should not see her again.

I am left in my small house eighty miles from nowhere, one of Minnesota's ten thousand lakes only yards from my front door. Nowadays, motor boats and airplanes break the stillness with startling regularity, but when I moved here more than thirty years ago, silence was the norm.

I needed silence to concentrate, the glitter of the sun on the lake water to focus, the sparkle of deep winter snow to catch and hold my eye.

Sometimes I could slip—find an already existing window and start to step through it, as I first did in my mother's attic—but I could never create my own.

I learned that in 1970, when Darren's father left me.

By then, the theory I couldn't form at four had become a full-blown dissertation, complete with footnotes and bibliography. I saw each conversation as my orals—a chance to convince the people around me that we were in one timeline out of millions, each linked by events, separated by choices in response to those events, and tied to each other by a single touchable moment.

My theory had pieces of *Alice's Adventures Through the Looking Glass* mixed with some C.S. Lewis and twisted by a touch of Ray Bradbury.

Years later, I would add more pages—chaos theory, string theory, the theory of everything—as well as musings on time by scientists from Dirac to Einstein.

But those scientific principles were in the future. In

1970, I was exploring inner space, trying to expand my mind, thinking the adventure came from within, not from without. My guru was Timothy Leary, my expansion of choice LSD, my trips cosmic, significant, and oh so wrong.

It was a sign of the time that Darrell—Darren's father—who couldn't take my constant drug use, my discussions of the limitlessness of the universe, my willingness to sit at the feet of anyone who believed in the existence of alternate worlds, left me alone, pregnant, and broke—and no one blamed him for what happened next.

They blamed me.

The shrink has her own theory. She still tells me about it, even though I heard it in court when Darren got the judgment against me, forbidding me to see my own granddaughter for more than two hours, and never, ever unsupervised.

The shrink thinks I make up alternate worlds because I do not like this one.

No matter how many books I bring her, no matter how much my aunt testifies to the Talents within our family, the shrink persists in her belief.

"Roxanne," she says to me when I complain about Darren's hasty departure, "you have to face what you do. You cannot constantly escape to other worlds."

What the shrink does not understand is that I did not escape that afternoon by the lake. I wanted to, but I couldn't reach the window. I couldn't even see what was inside.

I was there the entire time.

I was there, just as I was supposed to be.

*   *   *

There will be a new hearing. Some legal assistant arrives at my house with court papers. My son has decided to exclude me from my granddaughter's life forever.

I hesitate before I call my attorney. I cannot sound hysterical. I cannot let him know what I will lose.

I walk through my small house, touch the antiques that have once opened the past for me but no longer do. The desk I found at a flea market outside of Boston, which took me to a dark gray afternoon with a filthy harbor out the window, and a man writing a letter with a quill pen. The letter began *Dearest, She has learned of us. I must end—*

Then he saw me, started, and the pen scrawled awkwardly along the page. He shouted, pushed, and I fell backwards, out of wonderland, and back to the flea market where a dozen people stared at me as if I had lost my mind.

By then, I knew: Only two trips are allowed through a window into another time—a trip there and a trip back. After that, the window closes.

Still, I buy the objects that open worlds for me: the desk; a book of poems written in Latin (once held by a sobbing priest who screamed when he saw me); a glass serving bowl that in a not-too-distant past had held salad and matching glass tongs (lost to time). The woman who had been mixing the salad in the bowl had seen me and smiled, thinking I was one of her guests, until she saw my attire—blue jeans, a Cal Tech sweatshirt, bare feet. Then she frowned and spoke to me in a language I did not understand. Someone nearby grabbed my arm and shoved me backwards—and that window closed, like all the others before them.

I can find windows—existing windows—but I cannot create them.

Not like Marissa.

Marissa, who holds universes in one tiny little hand.

Perhaps doctors are right. Perhaps newborns should not ingest mind-altering chemicals in their mother's milk.

Over the phone, my mother called Darren's screams colic, but when those screams didn't end, the neighbors called the police. They took him away from me, claiming he was malnourished, claiming he was addicted, claiming he would be brain-damaged forever.

He programs computers now, graduated at the top of his class at Harvard, lives a mundane life with a wife who refuses to meet me and the most beautiful child in the world.

The doctors were wrong: He is not damaged. At least not visibly. But he has a paranoia I recognize from my hippie days, a tendency to believe the worst of everyone around him; a rebellion against authority must have come through the milk as well.

That the authority he rebels against is me is something I have trouble dealing with. I freely admit that, even though the shrink believes I do not—I cannot—understand.

I remember the first time we met. He was eighteen. He had used his powerful mind to track me down.

I believe he remembered me from those first few months—inside that complex mind of his were images of me—and I had a hunch that he too had peered into alternate worlds and saw how happy we would have been if only I had done things right.

We had eight years. I was clean and pretending to be unimaginative. My visits to antique stores were infrequent, and I tried to stay away from estate sales, garage sales, and public auctions so that I couldn't touch the past.

I tried very hard to be normal, to hide my secret life.

We would talk about everything from politics to aliens, from the things we could touch to the things we could only imagine, to the importance of belief and the willingness all humans have to understand something beyond themselves.

We would talk, then.

And he would listen.

Finally, I call the lawyer.

He is my age, expensive, and world-weary, with a high tolerance for alternate lifestyles, even though he hasn't lived one himself in nearly thirty-five years.

He takes my call. He has gotten the papers; he expected to hear from me.

I am slightly annoyed that he did not call first.

I sit on my screened-in porch and stare at the lake as we speak. Sunlight glitters on the water, making diamonds, making tiny untouchable windows that might—if we're lucky—open alternate worlds.

Sometimes I am distracted, but my lawyer is used to that.

Today it seems to irritate him.

"I asked, Roxanne, if you were supposed to be keeping an eye on her," he snaps, his voice metallic through the phone.

"The visits are supervised. I'm never the only one

watching her." I rock back in my chair, looking at the lake from a different angle.

The prisms of light flicker, but do not move.

"Don't you remember the fight we had to get Marissa out to the lake house in the first place?" he asks. "Don't you remember the discussion with the judge, your promise—in writing, Roxanne—that you would never take your eyes off her?"

"I blinked," I say. A blink of an eye: The lid closes, then opens. It takes only a moment, or perhaps an entire night. The amount of time passing depends on your definition of time. If a moment is a blink of an eye, and a blink is the closing of the lids, followed by the opening of the lids, then I looked away for only a moment.

"It says here you left her." I can hear papers rattling through the earpiece. "It says you went inside and made coffee."

"Darren was already going to her. I knew she'd be fine." Then I whisper: "She swims, you know."

"I know." He sounds so exasperated.

The swim classes convinced the first judge that I cared. I was the one who drove Marissa there, the one who held her in the water, the one who listened to her coach, swam with her, helped her learn to use those tiny limbs.

I was the only one thinking ahead—knowing, fearing, if she fell through a window into another world, there was no guarantee she would land on ground. She might find herself a pond or a pool or a too-full tub. She might need to know how to hold her breath before she move backwards, into the world she had just left.

Of course, I never explained it quite that way. Lawyers, judges, logical minds—they never entirely understand. So I said simply, convincingly, apparently, that swimming is a survival skill as important as walking and it's always better for children to learn early, particularly if they're going to be around lakes.

Back then, that had been a point for me.

"But that's not the point now," my lawyer says. "The point is that you should have gone after her. You should have saved her, not Darren. He sees it as one more sign of your growing irresponsibility."

"I'm not irresponsible," I say.

"Your granddaughter nearly drowns and you make coffee?"

"She didn't nearly drown." I have to struggle to keep my voice level. "She can swim."

"I'm going to be honest with you, Roxanne," he says to me, and I hate the tone. It is the same tone Darren uses with me now—an I-will-speak-slowly-because-you-will-never-understand-tone. "You've blown this. Even if we do go back to court, the best you can hope for is supervised visits in a neutral place—like Social Services. You'll never get to see her at your house, and certainly not at Darren's. Maybe it's best if you let Marissa go. Your record with children is poor. Wait until she's an adult, like you did with Darren. Wait until the two of you can talk."

I did not wait until Darren was an adult. He was taken from me, and no one would tell me where he went. He found me.

And for a brief time, I was his alternate world.

"No," I say. "I have to see her."

"Why, Roxanne?" he asks. "And don't give me the grandmother-granddaughter crap. I don't buy it. Other people aren't real to you."

"There are things in life that only I can teach her, only I can show her."

"Yeah," my lawyer says. "Which is precisely what your son is afraid of."

He was too old when he came to me, my son, my Darren. His mind had already formed around precepts someone else had taught him—that solid objects existed only in one space-time, that this world was the only one (except for Heaven and Hell—which Darren himself called mythical concepts—he had taken his disbelief one step further than even the world around him had taught him).

Although I tried to tell him about our family's talents—my aunt's ability to know what had happened in someone else's past, my mother's sudden inklings of what was to come, my own ability to reach into already existing windows—he did not believe me. He laughed, calling our talents superstitious nonsense that could be explained logically, he was sure.

Later, he called my beliefs fantasies, and even later, drug-induced hallucinations.

By then, he had married.

By then, his mind had been poisoned, by his wife.

Since that day near the lake, I have thought a lot about Marissa and how she fits into this world. She is one of the window-creators. If she touches an object, she doesn't find the window, as I do. She makes it.

Like the woman in the dress (a great-grandmother, I later learned), like the man at the desk, like the priest with his poetry, my granddaughter has the ability to open moments in time.

I suspect she also has the ability to close them.

I have searched for this my entire life—something I cannot explain to my lawyer, who sees my actions as negligence—and something my shrink willfully misunderstands. My granddaughter is special, but only people who understand her special ability will help her develop it.

She needs me, even more than I need her.

It takes planning, of course. And silence. I speak to no one, confide in no one, write to no one.

I act alone.

I let my lawyer pursue our defense in court, even though his heart is not in it. Neither is mine. Supervised visits in Social Services will do neither me nor Marissa any good.

I let my shrink enroll me in more rehabilitation programs, even though I am still clean, and have been for nearly twelve years now.

Of course, I do not tell her that I plan to be gone before the first program starts.

Darren's house is in a modern neighborhood with large lots and houses that the media calls McMansions. His is a 6,000-square-foot monstrosity with an indoor and an outdoor pool, a four-car garage, a guesthouse, and a state-of-the-art security system.

The system funnels into the guesthouse and the garage as well as the house.

People forget that I was once a beloved member of the family—or at least a tolerated one. I have keys. I have codes.

I can—and have—slipped in and out unnoticed.

Marissa's bedroom is in the south wing, on the second floor. She has a suite with a playroom, a bedroom, and a second bedroom for guests or the nanny that Darren keeps threatening to hire. The south wing has a door at its far end that leads into the apartment above the garage.

It is so simple to enter the garage by the side door, shut off the alarm before it even blares, climb the stairs to the apartment, and then cross into the house. So simple that I worry I will get caught whenever I do it.

This night it is even simpler. I wait until everyone is asleep. I have a flashlight which I only use in the non-windowed parts of the hallway, but I really don't need it.

I know this place as well as I know my own—the worlds we travel between, the lives that get lived within these little boxes, in this quiet walls.

Marissa's suite is filled with nightlights. I close and lock the main door, then slip into her bedroom. She is asleep on her side, her hands tucked under her head as if she were praying. Her curls float behind her.

My hand hovers near her temple, wishing I could pull the window from it with a touch of my fingers. But I dare not try.

Instead, I cradle her against me, coax her awake. She blinks sleepily at me and smiles—to his credit, Darren has never said anything negative about me to her—and settles into the crook of my arm.

"Remember?" I whisper. "Remember showing me how you can make pictures in the sky?"

She nods.

"Can you do it now?" I ask.

She nods again.

"Watch," she whispers.

She brings her small hand to her temple, then extends her arm. She tilts her head sideways, black curls falling against her neck, and stares at something I can't see. Finally she twists her fingers ever so slightly, and a window opens right in front of us, a window filled with light.

I look through it, but I cannot see clearly, just like before.

I reach out my hand, but Marissa shakes her head. "Papa says not to touch."

Damn him. Darren knows—and believes—his daughter, but denies the talent to me.

Damn him.

Still, I smile at her. "Grownups can touch," I say.

I touch the edge, and the window widens. I still cannot see through the light.

Marissa puts her thumb in her mouth, a little girl now, in a world she does not understand.

I would comfort her, but I do not. She needs to remember this. She needs to remember it as I remember the attic, as the defining moment, the beginning of her understanding of the nature of the universe.

She will explore, on her own, her abilities, if she only remembers how I behave.

I am nervous, but I can't let her see that.

My heart pounds. I ease my body away from hers, then kiss her forehead. She looks at me with wide, frightened eyes.

I place both hands into the light. It is warm there, and I catch the scent of daffodils.

"Remember," I say, and tumble through.

She reaches out a hand to stop me—and instead, closes the window.

Just as I expected.

A blink of an eye—

—and suddenly, I am sitting beside a row of daffodils,

planted against a headstone. The cemetery is carefully mowed, the trees are large—birches—and beyond, you can catch a glimpse of one of Minnesota's ten thousand lakes.

Sunlight glimmers off the water, creating prisms of light, little windows into yet even more worlds.

I am not willing to travel beyond this spot. I am comfortable here. It is quiet, and I always do best in the quiet.

The air is alive, filled with visages of the past, possibilities of the future, and permutations of the present.

I know this world is a much better, much friendlier place.

CJ Cherryh
Classic Series in New Omnibus Editions

THE DREAMING TREE
Contains the complete duology *The Dreamstone* and
The Tree of Swords and Jewels.   0-88677-782-8

THE FADED SUN TRILOGY
Contains the complete novels *Kesrith*, *Shon'jir*, and
Kutath.   0-88677-836-0

THE MORGAINE SAGA
Contains the complete novels *Gate of Ivrel*, *Well of
Shiuan*, and *Fires of Azeroth*.   0-88677-877-8

THE CHANUR SAGA
Contains the complete novels *The Pride of Chanur*,
Chanur's Venture and *The Kif Strike Back*.
                                              0-88677-930-8

ALTERNATE REALITIES
Contains the complete novels *Port Eterntiy*, *Voyager in
Night*, and *Wave Without a Shore*   0-88677-946-4

AT THE EDGE OF SPACE
Contains the complete novels *Brothers of Earth* and
Hunter of Worlds.   0-7564-0160-7

To Order Call: 1-800-788-6262